A Groom for the Taking

ALLY BLAKE
REBECCA WINTERS
MELISSA McCLONE

MILLS & BOON

First Published in Great Britain 2016
By Mills & Boon, an imprint of HarperCollins*Publishers*
1 London Bridge Street, London, SE1 9GF

A GROOM FOR THE TAKING © 2016 Harlequin Books S. A.

The Wedding Date, *To Catch A Groom* and *Wedding Date With The Best Man* were first published in Great Britain by Harlequin (UK) Limited.

The Wedding Date © 2011 Ally Blake.
To Catch A Groom © 2004 Rebecca Winters.
Wedding Date With The Best Man © 2010 Melissa Martinez McClone.

ISBN: 978-0-263-92058-1

05-0316

Our policy is to use papers that are natural, renewable and recyclable products and made from wood grown in sustainable forests.The logging and manufacturing processes conform to the legal environmental regulations of the country of origin.

Printed and bound in Spain
by CPI, Barcelona

THE WEDDING DATE

BY
ALLY BLAKE

When **Ally Blake** was a little girl she made a wish that when she turned twenty-six she would marry an Italian two years older than her. After it actually came true she realised she was onto something with these wish things. So, next she wished that she could make a living spending her days in her pyjamas, eating M&Ms and drinking scads of coffee while turning her formative experiences of wallowing in teenage crushes and romantic movies into creating love stories of her own. The fact that she is now able to spend her spare time searching the internet for pictures of handsome guys for research purposes is merely a bonus!

Come along and visit her website at www.allyblake.com.

This one's for white chocolate raspberry muffins
and macadamia choc chip cookies.
Or, more specifically, the fab staff at my fave local cafés
who let me write this book in their welcoming warmth
and know my order by heart.

CHAPTER ONE

'YOU'RE him! Aren't you?'

The gorgeous specimen of manhood in the dark sunglasses, at the pointy end of a squat pale pink fingernail, sat stock still. To the eclectic, late-afternoon Brunswick Street crowd rushing past the sidewalk café he would have appeared simply cool. Collected. Quietly attentive behind a half-smile so effortlessly sexy it could stop traffic. Literally.

Hannah knew better.

Hannah, who worked harder and with longer hours than anyone else she knew, would have bet her precious life savings on the fact that, behind those ubiquitous dark sunglasses he was hoping, almost desperately, that the older woman on the other end of the finger might quickly realise she had mistaken him for someone else.

No such luck.

'You are!' the woman continued, flat feet planted determinedly on the uneven cobbled ground. 'I know you are! You're the guy who makes that *Voyagers* TV show. I've seen you in magazines. And on the telly. My daughter just *loooves* you. She even considered going into training once, so she could be one of those regular-type people you send off into the wild and up mountains with nothing but a toothbrush and a packet of Tim-Tams. Or however it goes. And that's saying something! It's all but impossible to get that girl off the couch.

You know what? I should give you her number. She's quite pretty in her way, and unquestionably single...'

Sitting—with apparently Ninja-like invisibility—on the other side of the rickety table that served as Knight Productions' office those times when the boss felt the need to get out of the confines of their manic headquarters, Hannah had to cover her mouth to smother the laugh threatening to bubble to the surface.

Any other time of day or night her boss was like the mountains he had so famously conquered before turning his attentions to encouraging others to do the same on TV. He was colossal, tough, unyielding, indomitable, enigmatic. Which was why seeing him wriggle and squirm and practically lose the power of speech under the attentions of an overtly loving fan was always a moment to relish.

It had taken Hannah less than half a day of the year she'd worked for Bradley Knight to realise that overt adoration was her boss's Achilles' heel. Awards, industry accolades, gushing peers, bowing and scraping minions—all turned him to stone.

And then there were the fans. The many, many, *many* fans who knew a good thing when they saw it. And there was no denying that Bradley Knight was six feet four inches of very good thing.

Just like that, the laughter tickling Hannah's throat turned into a small, uncomfortable lump.

She frowned deeply, cleared her throat, and shifted on her wrought-iron seat, redistributing the balance of her buttocks. And more importantly her train of thought.

The very last thing her boss needed was even the smallest clue that in moments of overworked, overtired weakness he'd even given *her* the occasional tummy-flutter. And sweaty palms. And hot flushes. And raging fantasies the likes of which she wouldn't dare share with even her best friend, whose good-natured ribbing about Hannah's constant proximity to their gorgeous boss had come all too close to hitting the mark on a number of occasions.

The beep of a car horn split the air, and Hannah flinched out of her heady daydream to find herself breathing a little too heavily and staring moonily at her boss.

Hannah frowned so hard she pulled a muscle in her neck.

She'd worked her backside off to get there, to take any job she could get in order to gain experience before finally finding the one she loved. The one she was really good at. The one she was meant to do. And she wasn't going to do anything to risk that career path now.

Even if that wasn't reason enough, pining after the guy was a complete a waste of time. He was a rock. He'd never let her in. He never let *anyone* in. And when it came to relationships Hannah wasn't prepared to accept anything less than *wonderful*.

Don't. Ever. Forget it.

She glanced at her watch. It was nearly four. Phew. The long weekend looming ahead of her—four days away from her all-consuming job and her all-consuming boss—clearly could not have come at a better time.

Still on the clock, she turned her concentration back to the woman who might as well have had her boss at knife-point he was sitting so eerily still.

She scraped her chair back and intervened, before Bradley managed to perform the first ever case of human osmosis and disappeared through the holes in his wrought-iron chair.

The woman only noticed her existence when Hannah slung an arm around her shoulders and none too gently eased her to the kerb.

'Do you know him?' the woman asked, breathless.

Glancing back at Bradley, Hannah felt her inner imp take over. Leaning in, she murmured, 'I've seen the inside of his fridge. It's frighteningly clean.'

The woman's still glittering eyes widened, and she finally focussed fully on Hannah. She was very thorough in her perusal of the kinks that always managed to appear in Hannah's straightened hair by that time of the afternoon. The countless creases in her designer dress. The chunky man's diving watch hanging loosely around her thin wrist. The cowboy boots poking out from beneath it all.

Then the woman smiled.

With a none too comfortable flash of realisation it hit Hannah that she was being compared unfavourably to the daughter who never got off the couch. Her inner imp limped back into hiding.

Eight hours earlier she'd looked the epitome of personal assistant to Australia's most successful television producer—even despite the little odes to her tomboy roots. You could take the girl out of small-town Tasmania, but...

But she didn't say any of that. With a shrug she admitted, 'I'm Mr Knight's personal assistant.'

'Oh.' The woman nodded, as if that made so much more sense than a man like him *choosing* to spend time with her—because when he said jump, she knew how high without even having to ask.

After a little more chat, Hannah turned the woman in the opposite direction, gave her a little push and waved goodbye as, like a zombie, she trudged away down the street.

She brushed off her hands. Another job well done. Then she turned, hands on hips, to find Bradley running long fingers beneath his eyes, sliding his sunglasses almost high enough to offer a teasing glimpse of the arresting silvery-grey eyes beneath. But not quite.

Then slowly, achingly slowly, his rigid body began to unclench. Muscle by hard-earned muscle, limb by long, strong limb, down his considerable length until his legs slid under the table and his large shoes poked lazily out at the other side.

The apparent languor was all an act. The effort of a private man to restrain whatever it was that drew people to him like moths to a flame. Unfortunately for him it only made the restrained power seething inside him more obvious. More compelling. A familiar sweep of sensation skipped blithely across her skin again—a soft, melty, pulsing feeling.

Even the fact that she knew *she* was about to bear the brunt of the dark mood he'd be in after the one-way love-in didn't make her immune.

At least it hadn't yet.

Time was what she needed. Time and space, so that the boundaries of her life weren't defined by the monstrous number of hours she spent deep inside Bradley's overwhelming creative vision. Thanks heavens for the long weekend!

Actually, time, space *and* meeting a guy would do it for sure. A guy who might actually stand a chance in hell of feeling that way about her.

He was out there. Somewhere. She was sure of it. He had to be. Because she absolutely wasn't going to settle for anything less than everything. She'd seen first-hand what 'settling' looked like in the first of the three marriages her mother had leapt into after her father passed away. It wasn't pretty. In fact it was downright sordid. That wasn't going to be her life.

She blinked as her boss's beautifully chiselled face came into such sharp focus her breath caught in her throat. He was something. But any woman who hoped in Bradley Knight's direction was asking for heartache. Many had tried. Many more yet would. But nobody on earth would topple that mountain.

She grabbed the wayward swathe of hair flickering across her face and tucked it behind her ear, plastered a smile across her face, and bounded back to the table. Bradley didn't look up. Didn't even flicker a lash. He probably hadn't even realised she'd left.

'Wasn't she a lovely lady?' Hannah sing-songed. 'We're sending her daughter a signed copy of last season's *Voyagers*.'

'Why me?' Bradley asked, still looking into the distance.

She knew he wasn't talking about posting a DVD. 'You were just born lucky,' she said wryly.

'You think I'm lucky?' he asked.

'Ooh, yeah. Fairies sprinkled fortune dust on your cradle as you slept. Why else do you think you've been so ridiculously successful at everything you've ever set your heart on?'

His head swung her way. Even with the dark sunglasses between them, the force of his undivided attention was like a thunderclap. Her heart-rate quadrupled in response.

His voice was a touch deeper when he said, 'So, in your eyes, my life has nothing to do with hard work, persistence, and knowing just enough about man's primal need to prove himself as a man?'

Hannah tapped a finger on her chin and took a few seconds to damp down her own latent needs as she looked up at the cloudy blue sky. Then she said, 'Nah.'

The appreciative rumble of his laughter danced across her nerves, creating a whole new wave of warmth cascading through her. Enjoying him from the other side of the mile-high walls he wore like a second skin was imprudent enough. Enduring the bombardment of his personal attention was a whole other battle.

'If you really want to know why you are so lucky, give that lady's daughter a call. Take her to dinner. Ask her yourself.' She waved the piece of paper with the woman's address and phone number on it. 'Talk about a PR windfall. "Bradley Knight dates fan. Falls in love. Moves to suburbs. Coaches little league team. Learns to cook lamb roast."'

She could sense his eyes narrowing behind his sunglasses. He then took his sweet time sitting upright. He managed to make the move appear leisurely—inconsequential, even—but the constrained power pulsing through every limb, every digit, every hair was patently clear to anyone with half an instinct. She could feel the blood pumping through her veins.

'At this moment,' he said, his voice a deep, dark warning, 'I am so very, very glad you are my assistant and *not* in charge of PR.'

Hannah slid the paper into her overstuffed leather diary and said, 'Yeah, me too. I'm not sure there's enough money in the world that could tempt me to take on a job whereby I'd have to spend my days trying to convince the world how wonderful you are. I mean, I work hard now—but come on...'

Frown lines appeared above his glasses as he leaned across the table till his forearms covered half the thing. He was so big he blocked out the sun—a massive shadow of a man, with a golden halo outlining his bulk.

Hannah's fingertips were within touching distance of his. She could feel every single hair on her arms stand to attention one by delicious one. Her feet were tucked so far under her chair—so as to not accidentally scrape against his—she was getting a cramp.

'Aren't we in a strange mood today?' he asked.

His voice was quiet, dropping so very low, and so very much only for her ears she felt it hum in the backs of her knees.

He tilted his chin in her direction. 'What gives?'

And then he slid his sunglasses from his eyes. Smoky grey they were—or quicksilver—entirely depending on his mood. In that moment they were so dark the colour was impenetrable.

The man was such a workaholic he never looked to her without a dozen instructions ready to be barked. But in that moment he just looked at her. And waited. Hannah's throat turned to ash.

'What gives,' another voice shot back, 'is that our Hannah's mind is already turned to a weekend of debauchery and certain nookie.'

Hannah flinched so hard at the sudden intrusion she bit her lip.

Yet through the stinging pain, for a split second, she was almost sure she saw a flicker of something that looked a heck of a lot like disappointment flash across Bradley's face. Then his eyes lowered to her swollen lip, which she was lapping at with her tongue.

Then, as though she had been imagining the whole thing, he glanced away, leaned back, and turned to the owner of that last gem of a comment.

'Sonja,' he drawled. 'Nice of you to show up.'

'Pleasure,' Sonja said.

'Perfect timing,' Hannah added, her voice breathier than she would have hoped. 'Bradley was just about to offer me your job.'

Sonja didn't even flinch, but the flicker of amusement in Bradley's cheek made her feel warm all over. She shut down her smile before it took hold. Not only was Sonja Bradley's PR guru, she was also Hannah's flatmate. And the only reason she knew how to use a blowdryer and had access to the kind of non-jeans-and-T-shirt-type clothes that filled her closet.

Sonja perched her curvaceous self upon a chair and crossed her legs, her eyes never once leaving her iPhone as one black-taloned finger skipped ridiculously fast over the screen.

In fact her stillness gave Hannah a sudden chill. She clapped a hand over her friend's phone, and Sonja blinked as though coming round from a trance.

Hannah said, 'If you are even *thinking* of Tweeting any-thing about my upcoming weekend off and debauchery and nookie, or anything along those lines—even if I am named "anonymous Knight Productions staffer"—I will order a beet-root burger and drop it straight on this dress.'

Sonja's dark gaze narrowed and focussed on the cream wool of the dress Hannah had borrowed from her wardrobe. Slowly she slid her phone into a tiny crocodile skin purse.

'Why do I feel even more like I'm on the other side of the looking glass from you two than usual?'

Hannah and Sonja both turned to Bradley.

He looked ever so slightly pained as he said, 'I'm feeling like it's going to give me indigestion to even bring this up, but I can't *not* ask. Debauchery? Nookie?'

At the word 'debauchery' his eyes slid to Hannah—dark, smoke-grey, inscrutable—before sliding back to Sonja. It was only a fraction of a second. But a fraction was plenty long enough to take her breath clean away.

Boy, did she need a holiday. And *now!*

Sonja motioned for an espresso as she said, 'For an ostensibly smart man, if it doesn't involve you or your mountains, you have the memory of a sieve. This is the weekend our Hannah is heading back home to the delightful southern island of Tasmania, to play bridesmaid at her sister Elyse's wedding—which she organised.'

His eyes slid back to Hannah, and this time they stayed. 'That's *this* weekend?'

Hannah blinked at him. Slowly. She'd told him as much at least a dozen times in the past fortnight, yet it had clearly not sunk in. It was just what she needed in order to finally become completely unscrambled.

Sonja had been spot-on. Bradley had a one-track mind. And if something didn't serve him it didn't exist.

'I have the New Zealand trip this weekend,' he said.

'Yes, you do.' Hannah glanced at her watch. 'And I'm off the clock in ten minutes. Sonja? What are *your* plans?'

Sonja grinned from ear to ear at the sarcasm dripping from Hannah's words. 'I'll be sitting all alone in our little apartment, feeling supremely jealous. For this weekend you will have your absolute pick.'

'My pick of what?' Hannah asked.

Sonja leaned forward and looked her right in the eye. 'Oodles of gussied-up, aftershave-drenched men, bombarded by more concentrated romance than they can handle. They'll be walking around that wedding like wolves in heat. It's the most primal event you'll see in civilised society.'

With that, Sonja leant back, wiping an imaginary bead of sweat from her brow, before returning to texting up a storm.

Hannah sat stock still, feeling a mite warmer in the chilly Melbourne afternoon. Having insisted on planning her little sister's wedding in the spare minutes she had left each day, in a fit of guilt at being maid of honour from several hundred kilometres' distance, she'd been so absolutely swamped that the idea of a holiday fling had not once entered her mind.

Maybe a random red-hot weekend was exactly what she needed—to unwind, de-knot, take stock, recharge, and remember there was a whole wide world outside of Bradley Knight's orbit.

'The groomsmen will be top of the list, of course,' Sonja continued. 'But they'll be so ready for action it'll be embarrassing. Best you avoid them. My advice is to look out for another interstate guest—more mystery, and less likely to be a close relative. Or a fisherman.'

Hannah scoffed, and shut her eyes tight against Sonja's small-town-life bashing.

'You're on the pill, right?'

'Sonja!'

Really, that was a step too far. But she was. Not that she'd found cause to need it much of late. Her hours were prohibitive, and her work so consuming she was simply too exhausted to even remember why she'd gone on the pill in the first place.

But now she had four whole days in a beautiful resort, in the middle of a winter wonderland wilderness, surrounded by dozens of single guys. A small fire lit inside her stomach for the first time in the months since she'd known she was going home.

She was about to get herself a whole load of time, space, *and* the chance she might meet an actual guy. Heck, what were the chances she'd find The One back on the island from which she'd fled all those years ago?

When she opened an eye it was to find Bradley frowning. Though if it was about anything to do with her she'd eat her shoes.

She shoved the last of her papers into a large, heavy leather satchel. Her voice was firm as she said, 'I'm heading to the office now, to make sure Spencer has everything he needs in order to be me this weekend.'

'That's your replacement for a major location scout?' Bradley asked. 'The intern with the crush?'

Her hand turned into a fist inside the bag, and she glanced up at her boss. 'Spencer doesn't have a *crush* on me. He just wants to *be* me when he grows up.'

One dark eyebrow kicked north. 'The kid practically salivates every time you walk in the room.'

That he notices…?

'Then lucky for you. With me gone, you'll have a salivation-free weekend.'

'That's the positive?'

Hannah shrugged. 'Told you—I suck at PR. Lucky for me I'm so good at my actual job you are clearly pining in advance. In fact, it's so clear how much you'll miss me I'm thinking the time's ripe to ask for a promotion.'

It was a throwaway comment, but it seemed to hang there between them as if it had been shouted. His eyebrows flattened and his grey eyes clouded. Behind them was a coming storm. He reached distractedly across the table and stole the small sugar biscuit from the edge of Sonja's saucer.

Blithely changing the subject, he said, 'Four days.'

'Four days and enough pre-wedding functions you'd think they were royalty.' But, no, the bride was simply her mother's daughter. 'The wedding's on Sunday. I'll be back Tuesday morning.'

'Covered in hickies, no doubt,' Sonja threw in, most

helpfully. 'Her mother *was* Miss Tasmania, after all. Down there she's considered good breeding stock.'

Thank goodness at that moment Sonja spied someone with whom to schmooze. With a waving hand and a loud *'daaaarling'* she was gone, leaving Bradley and Hannah alone again.

Bradley was watching her quietly, and thanks to Sonja—who'd clearly been born without a discreet bone in her body—the swirl of sexual innuendo was ringing in her ears. Hannah felt as if all the air had been sapped from the sky.

'So you're heading home?' Bradley asked, voice low.

'Tomorrow morning. Even though last night I dreamt the *Spirit of Tasmania* was stolen by pirates.'

'You're going by *boat*?'

She shuffled in her seat. 'I thought you of all people would appreciate the adventure of my going by open sea.'

A muscle flickered in Bradley's cheek. Fair enough. A reclining seat on a luxury ferry wasn't exactly his brand of adventure. Sweat, pain, hard slog, the ultimate test of will and courage and fortitude, man proving himself worthy against unbeatable odds—that was his thing. She was secretly packing seasickness tablets.

Every time she'd been on a boat with him she picked the most central spot in which to sit, and tended to stare at the horizon a good deal of the time. Trying to keep her failing hidden in order to appear the perfect employee. Irreplaceable.

She was hardly going to tell him that the real reason she'd booked the day-long trip rather than a one-hour flight was that, while she was very much looking forward to the break, she was dreading going home. A twelve-hour boat trip was heaven-sent! She'd been back to Tassie once in the seven years since she'd left home. For her mother's fiftieth birthday extravaganza. Or so she'd been told. It had, in fact, been her mother's third wedding—to some schmuck who'd made a fortune in garden tools. She'd felt blindsided. Her mother hadn't understood why. Poor Elyse, then sixteen, had been caught in the middle. It had been an unmitigated disaster.

So, if she had to endure twelve hours of eating nothing but dry crackers and pinching the soft spot between her thumb and forefinger to fight off motion sickness, it would be worth it.

'Ever been to Tasmania?' she asked, glad to change the subject.

He shook his head. 'Can't say I have.'

Hannah sat forward on her seat, mouth agape. '*No*? That's a travesty! It's just over the pond, for goodness' sake! And it's gorgeous. Much of it is rugged and untouched. Just your cup of tea. The jagged cliffs of Queenstown, where it appears as though copper has been torn from the land by a giant's claws. Ocean Beach off Strahan, where the winds from the Roaring Forties tear across of the most unforgiving coastline. And then there's Cradle Mountain. That's where the wedding's being held. Cold and craggy and simply stunning, resting gorgeously and menacingly on the edge of the most beautiful crystal-clear lake. And that's just a tiny part of the west coast. The whole island is magical. So lush and raw and diverse and pretty and challenging...'

She stopped to take a breath, and glanced from the spot in mid-air she'd been staring through to find Bradley watching her. His deep grey eyes pinned her to her seat as he listened. *Really* listened. As though her opinion mattered *that* much.

Her heart began to pound like crazy. It was a heady thought. But dangerous all the same. The fact that he was unreachable, an island unto himself, was half the appeal of indulging in an impossible crush. It didn't cost her anything but the occasional sleepless night.

She stood quickly and slung her heavy leather satchel over her shoulder. 'And on that note...'

Bradley stood as well. A move born of instinct. It still felt nice.

Well, there were millions of men who would stand when she stood. Thousands at the very least. There was a chance one or two of them would even be at her sister's bigger-than-*Ben Hur* wedding. Maybe looking for a little romance. A little fun. Looking for someone with whom to unwind.

Maybe more...

She took two steps back. 'I hope New Zealand knocks your socks off.'

'Have a good weekend, Hannah. Don't do anything I wouldn't do.'

She shot him a quick smile. 'Have no fear. I have no intention of dropping off or picking up any dry-cleaning this weekend.'

He laughed, the unusually relaxed sound rumbling through her. She vibrated. Inside and out.

As Bradley curled back into his chair Hannah tugged her hair out from under the strap of her bag, slipped on her over-sized sunglasses, took a deep breath of the crisp winter air, and headed for the tram stop that would take her to her tiny Fitzroy apartment.

And that was how Hannah's first holiday in nearly a year began. Her first trip home in three years. The first time she'd seen her mother face to face since she'd married. *Again*.

Let the panic begin...

CHAPTER TWO

HANNAH was in the bathroom, washing sleep out of her eyes, when her apartment doorbell rang just before six the next morning. It couldn't be the cab taking her to the dock; it wasn't due for another hour.

'Can you get that?' she called out, but no sound or movement came from Sonja's room.

Hannah ran her fingers through her still messy bed hair and rushed to the door.

She opened it to find herself looking at the very last view she would ever have expected. Bradley, in her favourite of his leather jackets—chocolate-brown and wool-lined—and dark jeans straining under the pressure of all that hard-earned muscle. Tall, gorgeous and wide awake, standing incongruously in the hallway outside her tiny apartment. It was so ridiculous she literally rubbed her eyes.

When she opened them he was still there, in all his glory—only now his eyes were roving slowly over her flannelette pyjama pants, her dad's over-sized, faded, thirty-year-old Melbourne University jumper, her tatty old Ugg boots.

Even while she fought the urge to hide behind the door, the feel of those dark eyes slowly grazing her body was beautifully illicit.

'Can I come in?' he asked, eyes sliding back to hers.

No *good morning*. No *sorry to bother you*. No *I've obviously arrived at a bad time*. Just right to the point.

'Now?' She glanced over her shoulder, glad Sonja's make-shift clothesline, usually laden with silky nothings and hanging from windowframe to windowframe, had been mysteriously taken down during the night.

'I have a proposal.'

He had a proposal? At six in the morning? That couldn't wait? What could she do but wave a welcoming arm?

He took two steps inside, and instantly the place felt smaller than it actually was. And it was already pretty small. Kitchenette, lounge, two beds, one bath. Small windows looking out over nothing much. Plenty for two working women who just needed a place to crash.

She closed the apartment door and leant against it as she waited for him to complete his recce.

Compared with his monstrous pad, with its multiple rooms and split-levels and city views, it must seem like a broom closet.

When he turned back to her, those grey eyes gleaming like molten silver in the early-morning light, the pads of her fingers pressed so hard into the panelled wood at her back her knuckles ached.

But he was all business. 'I hope you're almost ready. Flight's in two hours.'

She blinked. Suddenly as wide awake as if she was three coffees down rather than none. Had he forgotten? Again? She pushed away from the door and her hands flew to her hips. 'Are you kidding me?'

His cheek twitched. 'You can get that look off your face. I'm not here to throw you over my shoulder and whisk you off to New Zealand.'

She swallowed—half-glad, half-disappointed. 'You're not?'

'The ferry would take a full day to get to Launceston. I looked it up. It seems a ridiculous waste of time when I have a plane that could get you there in an hour. As such, I'm flying you to Tasmania.'

'What about New Zealand? It took me a month to organise the whole team to fly in from—'

'We're making a detour. Now, hurry up and get ready.'

'But—'

'You can thank me later.'

Thank him? The guy had just gone and nixed her brilliant plan to take a full twelve hours in which to rev herself up to facing her mother, while at the same time putting lots of lovely miles between herself and him. And he was doing so in what appeared to be an effort at being *nice*. If things continued along in the same vein as her day had so far, Sonja would walk out of her room and announce she was joining a nunnery.

'It's decided.' He took a step her way.

She held her hands out in front of her, keeping him at bay and keeping herself from jumping over the coffee table and throttling him. 'Not by me it's not.'

He was stubborn. But then so was she. Her dad had been a total sweetheart—a push-over even when it came to those he'd loved. Her occasional mulishness was the one trait she couldn't deny she'd inherited from her mum.

'I know how hard you work. And compared with most people I've come across in this industry, you do so with great grace and particularity. I appreciate it. So, please, hitch a ride on me.'

The guy was trying so hard to say thank-you, in his own roundabout way, he looked as if a blood vessel was about to burst in his forehead.

Hannah threw her hands in the air and growled at the gods before saying, 'Fine. Proposal accepted.'

He breathed out hard, and the tension eased from him until his natural energy level eased from eleven back to its usual nine and a half.

He nodded, then looked over his shoulder, decided only the couch would take his bulk, and moved past her to sit down. There he picked up a random magazine from the coffee table and pretended to be interested in the '101 Summer Hair Tips' it promised to reveal inside its pages.

'We leave in forty-five minutes.'

Well, it seemed happy, lovely, thank-you time was over. Back to business as usual.

Hannah glanced at her dad's old diving watch, which was so overly big for her she had to twist it to read it. Forty-five minutes? She'd be ready in forty.

Without another word she spun and raced into her room. She grabbed the comfy, Tasmania-in-winter-appropriate travel outfit she'd thrown over the tub chair in the corner the night before, and rushed into the bathroom.

Sonja was there, in a bottle-green Japanese silk kimono, plucking her eyebrows.

Hannah's boots screeched to a halt on the tiled floor. 'Sonja! Jeez, you scared me half to death. I didn't even know you were home.'

Sonja smiled into the mirror. 'Just giving you and the boss man some privacy.'

The smile was far too Cheshire-cat-like for comfort. Hannah suddenly remembered the unnaturally underwear-free window. 'You *knew* he was coming!'

Sonja threw her tweezers onto the sink and turned to Hannah. 'All I know is that from the moment we got back to the office yesterday arvo he was all about "Tasmania this, Tasmania that." Everything else was designated secondary priority.'

Hannah opened her mouth, but nothing came out.

Sonja pouted. 'He never offered to fly *me* home for the holidays, and I've been working for him for twice as long as you.'

'Your parents live a fifteen-minute tram-ride away.' Hannah

shoved her friend out, slamming the door with as much gusto as she could muster.

With time rushing through the hourglass, she whipped off her pyjamas and threw them into a pile on the closed lid of the toilet, then scrunched her hair into a knot atop her head as she didn't have time to do anything fancy with it, before standing naked beneath the cold morning spray of the tiny shower. Sucking in her stomach, she turned up the heat and waited till the temperature was just a little too hot for comfort before grabbing a cake of oatmeal soap and scrubbing away the languor of the night.

A plane ride, she thought. *Surrounded by camera guys, lighting guys, and Bradley's drier than toast accountant.* Then at the airport they'd go their separate ways, and she could get on with her holiday and remember what it felt like to live a life without Bradley Knight in the centre of it.

A little voice twittered in the back of her head. *If you'd taken either of the perfectly good jobs you've been offered in the past few months you'd know what that felt like on a permanent basis.*

Swearing with rather unladylike gusto, Hannah turned her back to the shower, letting the hot spray pelt her skin as she soaped random circles over her stomach. She let her forehead drop to thump against the cold glass.

Both jobs had sounded fine. Great, even. Leaps along the career path she sought. But working on studio-based programming just didn't hold the same excitement as travelling to places for which she needed a half-dozen shots. Trudging up mud slopes and down glaciers, canoeing rivers filled with crocodiles, even if she had to count back from a hundred so as not to heave over the side.

At some stage in the past year, small-town Hannah had become a big-time danger junkie. Professionally and personally. And it had everything to do with the man whose impossible work ethic had her feeling as if she was teetering between immense success and colossal failure in every given task.

It was crazy-making. *He* was crazy-making. He was a self-contained, hard to know, ball-breaker. But, oh, the thrill that came when together they got it right.

She shivered. Deliciously. From top to toe.

She just wasn't ready to let that go.

Suddenly she realised she had the shower up so high she was actually beginning to sweat. She could feel it tingling across her scalp, in the prickling of her palms. She licked her lips to find they tasted of salt.

She turned to lean her back against the cool of the door, only to find the water wasn't so hot after all. And she was still sliding the slick soap over her shoulders, down her arms, around her torso, in a slow, rhythmic movement as her head was filled with impenetrable smoky grey eyes, dark wavy hair, a roguish five o'clock shadow, shoulders broad enough to carry the weight of the world...

Heat pulsed in her centre, radiating outwards until she had to breathe through her mouth to gather enough oxygen to remain upright. She wrapped her arms tight around her.

Brilliant, beautiful, intense—and literally on the other side of the door. With no sound in the apartment bar the sound of the running shower. And the door was unlocked. Heck, the walls were so old and warped she had a floor mat shoved at the base of the door to keep it closed. With his bulk, if he walked too hard on the creaky floorboards the thing might spring open.

What if that happened and he looked up to find her naked, wet, slippery? Alone. Skin pink from the steaming hot spray. More so from thoughts of him.

What would he do? Would it finally occur to him that she was actually a woman, not just a walking appointment book?

No, it wouldn't. And thank God for that. For if he ever

looked at her in *that* way she wouldn't even know what to do. They worked together like a dream, but as for the paths they'd taken to stumble into one another? The man was so far removed from her reality he was practically a different species.

'Perfect, safe, fantasy material for a girl too busy to get her kicks any other way,' she told the wall.

But somehow it had sounded far more sophisticated in her head than it did out loud. Out loud it sounded as though the time was nigh for her to get a life.

She determinedly put the lathered soap on the tray and turned off the taps.

She then reached for her towel—only to find in her rush she'd left it hanging on a hook on the back of her bedroom door.

She glanced at the musty PJs piled on the lid of the toilet, and then at the minuscule handtowel hanging within reach. She let her head thunk back against the shower wall.

The pipes in the pre-war building creaked as the shower was turned off in Hannah's bathroom.

Finally. Bradley had told her they only had forty-five minutes, and the damn woman had been in the shower for what felt like for ever.

Bradley loosened his grip on the magazine he'd been clutching the entire time the shower had run—to find his fingers had begun to cramp.

'Coffee?' Sonja said, swanning out from nowhere.

He'd been so sure they were alone—just him in the lounge, Hannah in the shower, nothing but twelve feet of open space and a thin wooden door between them—he jumped halfway out of his skin.

'Where the hell did you spring from?' he growled.

'Around,' Sonja said, waving a hand over her shoulder as she swept towards a gleaming espresso machine that took up half the tiny kitchen bench. It was the only thing that looked as if it had had any real money spent on it in the whole place.

The rest was fluffy faded rugs, pink floral wallpaper, and tasselled lampshades so ancient-looking every time his eyes landed on one he felt he needed to sneeze. He felt as if he was sitting in the foyer of an old-time Western brothel, waiting for the madam to put in an appearance.

Not what he would have expected of Hannah's pad—if he'd ever thought of it at all.

She was hard-working. Meticulous. With a reserve of stamina hidden somewhere in her small frame that meant she was able to keep up with his frenetic pace where others had fallen away long before.

What she *wasn't* was abandoned, pink...frou-frou.

Or so he'd thought.

'I'm making one for myself so it's no bother.'

Bradley blinked to find he was staring so hard at Hannah's bathroom door it might have appeared as though he was hoping for a moment of X-ray vision. He threw the magazine on the table with enough effort to send it sliding onto the floor, then turned bodily away from the door to glance at Sonja.

'Coffee?' Sonja repeated, dangling a gaudy pink and gold espresso mug from the tip of her pink-taloned pinky.

It hit him belatedly that the apartment was pure Sonja. Of *course*. He vaguely remembered her telling him Hannah had at some stage that year moved in with her.

For some reason it eased his mind. The trust he had in Hannah's common sense hadn't been misplaced.

He glanced at his watch and frowned. Though if she didn't get a hurry on he was ready to revise that thought.

'A quick one,' he said.

Coffees made, Sonja perched on the edge of the pink-striped dining chair that sat where a lounge chair ought. 'So, you're schlepping our girl to the wilds of Tasmania?'

'On my way to the New Zealand recce.'

'Several hundred miles out of your way.'

'What's your point?'

'It's not my job to have a point. You pay me to build mystery and excitement,' she said, grinning. 'And what's more exciting and mystifying than you and Hannah heading off to have a wild time in the wild?'

'A wild—?' This time his frown was for real. He sat up as best he could in the over-soft old chair, and pointed two fingers in the direction of Sonja's nose. 'She works damned hard. I'm saying thanks. So don't you start cooking up any mad stories in that head of yours. You know how I don't like drama.'

Sonja stared right back, and then, obviously realising he was deadly serious, nodded and said, 'Whatever you say, boss.'

And with that she got up and strode back towards what must have been her bedroom.

'So long as you promise I'm the first one you'll tell when you have something else to say. About New Zealand,' she added, as an apparent afterthought.

And with a dramatic swish of silk she was gone.

Bradley sank slowly back into the soft couch and downed the hot espresso in one hit, letting it scorch the back of his throat.

If the woman wasn't so good at her job...

But he hadn't been kidding. He abhorred gratuitous drama. He'd gone miles out of his way to avoid it his whole life. Up remote mountains, down far-flung rivers in the middle of nowhere, deep into uninhabited jungles. Dedicating his life to concrete pleasures. Real challenges he could see and touch. Facing the raw and unbroken parts of the world in order to discover what kind of man he *really* was, rather than the kind life had labelled him the moment he was born.

Far, far away from the histrionics he'd endured as a kid, both before and after his hypersensitive mother had decided that being *his* mother was simply too hard. Leaving him to the mercy of whichever relative had had the grace to take him that month and increasing the drama tenfold. Every one of them had expected him to be volubly and effusively grateful they'd taken on such an encumbrance as he. The telling of it had become a daily litany. But that had been nothing compared with the horrendously uncomfortable drama that rocked each household the moment the inhabitants realised that they were not, in fact, as altruistic as they'd imagined they were.

Then they'd each and every one whispered behind half-closed doors, perhaps it wasn't *their* fault. His own mother had given him away after all…

A flash of something appeared out of the corner of Bradley's eye, slapping him back to the absolute present. He sat forward, leant his elbows on his knees, and ran his hands hard and fast over his face in an effort to rub the prickly remnants of memory away.

Then all thought fled his mind as he realised what the flash had been. Hannah. Dashing from the bathroom into her bedroom. Naked.

He slowly turned his head to look at the empty spot where the vision had appeared. Piece by piece it slipped into his mind.

A wet female back, a pair of lean wet legs, and a small white handtowel covering nought but what must have been wet naked buttocks.

Hannah. *Naked.* And right at that moment behind that door, towelling down with something about the size of a postage stamp.

From nowhere a swift, steady heat began to surface inside him. An unmistakable heat. The kind he'd usually invite with open arms.

He dragged his eyes back to the front and stared hard at a pink quilted lamp covered in so many tassels it made his eyes hurt. Better that than focus on the image seemingly burned into the backs of his eyes.

Hannah was hard-working, meticulous, with a reserve of stamina... He stopped when he realised he was repeating himself *to* himself.

A loud bang came from Hannah's room, after which rang out a badly muffled oath and what sounded like hopping.

He found himself coughing out a laugh. Relief flooded through him, and the unfortunate heat brimming inside him dissipated, somewhat. *That* was the Hannah he knew. Hard-working, meticulous, and singularly likely to snap him out of the labyrinth of his mind right when he needed it most.

At that moment Hannah came bounding out of her room. Fully dressed. In fact she appeared to be wearing a grey blanket as she dragged a big black suitcase behind her.

He managed to pull himself from the clutches of the soft couch to stand, just as she plonked her suitcase by the door and turned to face him. Lips parted, breathless. From the suitcase? The hopping? The exertion of running to her room wet and naked?

He gave himself a mental slap.

'You made yourself coffee?' she said, staring at the coffee table.

'Sonja.'

'Oh. *Oh!*' Her eyes opened unnaturally wide, then flicked to the room into which Sonja had disappeared. 'Did she...? Did you...?'

He raised an eyebrow.

But she just shook her head, a new pinkness staining her cheeks and a telling kind of darkness in her eyes. It was the kind of look that told a specific story without need for words. It was the kind of look, when added to the image of naked female flesh, that could turn a man's blood to hot oil.

Though it was far more likely he simply hadn't fully moved on from the 'flash' after all.

You're a man, he growled to himself, *not a rock. Don't be so hard on yourself.*

Suddenly Hannah held up a finger and headed over to the small round table behind the couch, flicked through a bunch of papers. Ignoring him completely. He gave his head a short, sharp shake.

As she moved, Hannah's voluminous blanket—which turned out to be some kind of poncho—shifted, revealing that in lieu of her usual filmy, elegant work number she wore dark skinny jeans tucked into cowboy boots, and a fitted black and red striped, long-sleeved top. Truly fitted. Giving him glimpses of the kind of gentle curves that her filmy, floaty, elegant work numbers had clearly never made the most of.

Curves he'd glimpsed naked, with no embellishment. Curves he could almost feel beneath his hands.

Gritting his teeth, Bradley leant his backside against the edge of the couch and waited. And watched. With the early-morning sun streaming through the old window behind her she looked so young, so fresh. Her nose was pink in the morning cold, her cheeks even pinker. Her lips were naturally the colour of a dark rose. She had a smattering of freckles across her nose he'd never before noticed. And her usually neat, professional hair was kinky and shaggy, as if she'd come from a day at the beach. As if she'd just rolled out of bed.

She glanced up to find him staring. After a beat she smiled in apology. 'Two seconds. I promise.'

He cleared his throat. 'If I didn't know better I'd think you were purposely delaying getting moving.'

She blinked at him, several times, super-fast. Then shook her head so quickly he wondered if his sorry excuse for a joke had actually hit its mark. But he knew so little about her outside of how well she did her job he couldn't be sure.

'Sonja is clueless about paying bills,' she went on. 'It's too cold a winter for me to risk her getting the heating cut off—

even though I can think of a dozen reasons why she might deserve it.'

He found himself stepping over a line he didn't usually breach as he asked, 'Why do I get the feeling there's some other reason you're avoiding heading out that door?'

'I—' She swallowed. Then looked him dead in the eye for several long seconds before offering a slight shrug and saying, 'It's not that I don't want to go back home. I love that island more than anything. I'm just bracing myself for what I am about to encounter when I step across the Gatehouse threshold.'

'The Gatehouse?'

'The hotel.'

'Regretting your choice?'

That earned him a glance from pale green eyes that could cut glass. 'You truly think I would organise for my only sister to get married in some *dive*?'

'I guess it depends if you like your only sister. How long did you say it's been since you've seen her?'

Her cheeks turned pinker still: a bright, warm, enchanting pink as blood rushed to her face. But she chose to ignore his insinuation. 'The Gatehouse, I'll have you know, is a slice of pure heaven. Like a Swiss chalet, tucked into a forest of snow-dappled gumtrees. A mere short hike to the stunning Cradle Mountain. A hundred beautiful rooms, six gloriously decadent restaurants, a fabulous nightclub, a cinema, a state-of-the-art gym. And don't even get me started on the suites.'

Her eyes drifted shut and she shuddered. No, it was more like a tremble. It started at her shoulders and shimmied down her form, finishing up at her boot-clad feet, one of which had lifted to tuck in tight behind her opposite calf.

Sensation prickled down his arms, across his abdomen, between his thighs. He could do nothing but stand there, grit his teeth, and hope to high heaven she'd soon be done and he could get away from this crazy pink boudoir before it fried any more of his brain cells.

Hell. Who was this woman, and where had she put his trusty assistant?

If it were not for those wide, wide, frank pale green eyes that looked right into his, not the tiniest bit intimidated by his infamy, bull-headedness or insularity, he'd be wondering if he was in the right apartment.

That would teach him to try and do something nice for somebody else. Another lesson learnt.

Her foot slid down her calf, and as though nothing had happened she went back to the pile of papers.

'Okay,' she said. 'I think we can safely assume Sonja will survive till Tuesday.' She ruffled a hand through her hair, and it ended up looking even more loose and carefree and sexy as hell. 'I'm ready.'

She ruffled a hand through her hair, and it ended up looking even more loose and carefree, and sexy as hell.

His hands grew restless, as if he wasn't quite sure where to put them. As if they wanted to go somewhere his brain knew they ought not.

So he gave them a job and grabbed the handle of her suitcase. One yank and his stomach muscles clenched. 'What did you pack in here? Bricks?'

A hand slunk to her hip, buried somewhere deep beneath acres of grey wool, temptingly hiding more than they revealed.

'Yes,' she said. 'I have filled the bag with bricks—not, as one might assume, a long weekend's worth of clothes, shoes and underthings that will take me from day to night, PJs to wedding formal. Have you never been to a wedding before?'

'Never.'

'Wow. I'm not sure if you've missed out or if you're truly the luckiest man alive. While you're trekking through some of the most beautiful scenery in the world—bar Tasmania's, of course—I'll be changing outfits more times than a pop singer in a film clip.'

Bradley closed his eyes to stop the vision *that* throwaway comment brought forth before it could fully manifest itself inside his head.

'Car's downstairs,' he growled, hefting the bag out through her front door. 'Be there in five minutes or your—'

Underthings that will take you from day to night.

'Your gear and I will be gone without you.'

'Okey-dokey.'

With a dismissive wave over her shoulder she went looking for Sonja to say her goodbyes.

Feeling oddly as if a small pair of hands had just unclenched themselves from the front of his shirt, Bradley was out of that door and away from all that soft velvet, stifling frills and frou-frou pink that had clearly been chosen specifically in order to scramble a man's brains.

To the airport, up in the plane, drop her off, thanks gifted—and then to New Zealand he and his research crew would go. He, his research crew, and a juvenile intern who could spend half the day discussing 'underthings' and not affect his blood pressure in the slightest.

CHAPTER THREE

HANNAH stood in the doorway of the Gulfstream jet.

Place? Launceston, Tasmania.

Time of arrival? Mid-morning.

Temperature? Freezing.

She breathed in the crisp wintry air though her nose. Boy, did it smell amazing. Soft, green, untainted. She could actually hear birds singing. And the sky was so clear and blue it hurt her eyes. A small smile crept into the corners of her mouth.

She hadn't been sure how she'd feel, stepping foot back on Tassie soil after such a long time in Melbourne. How parochial the place would feel in comparison with her bustling cosmopolitan base.

It felt like home.

A deep voice behind her said, 'What? No "welcome home" banner? No marching band?'

'Oh, Lord,' she said as she jumped. Then, 'I'm going, I'm going! You can get on your way. Go back inside. It's freezing.'

'I'm a big boy. I can handle the cold.' Bradley threw the last of a bag of macadamia nuts into his mouth as he looked over her shoulder. 'So this is Tasmania.'

She looked out over Launceston International Airport. One simple flat-roofed building sat on the edge of acres of pocked grey Tarmac. A light drizzle thickened the cold air. Patches of old snow lay scattered in pockets of shade, while the rest of the ground was covered in little melted puddles.

As far as first impressions went it was hardly going to ring Bradley's adventure-savvy bell.

'No,' she said, 'this is an airport. Tasmania is the hidden wonder beyond.'

'Get a move on, then. I don't have all day.'

She shook her head. 'Sorry. Of course. Thanks. For the lift. But, please, I don't need one back. I'll see you Tuesday.'

With that she gave him a short wave, before jogging down the stairs—only to see the pilot had her bags plonked on the Tarmac next to another set of luggage that looked distinctly like Bradley's.

'What's he doing?' she asked. Then turned to find Bradley was right behind her.

Instinct had her slamming her hands against his chest so as not to topple onto her backside. Her hips against his thighs. Her right knee wedged hard between his.

Hard muscles clenched instantly beneath her touch. Hot, hard, Bradley-shaped muscles.

All she could think was that, God, he felt good. Big. Strong. Solid. Warm. All too real. She blinked up into his eyes to find glinting circles of deepest grey staring down at her.

'You're shaking,' he said, glowering as though she had somehow offended his sensibilities.

She curled her fingers into her palms and hid them beneath her poncho as she took a distinct step back, her body arching towards him even while she dragged herself away. 'Of course I'm shaking. It's barely above zero.'

He looked out across the Tarmac, as though for a moment he'd forgotten where they were. Then his hand hovered to where her hands had been against his chest. He scratched the spot absent-mindedly. 'Really?' he rumbled. 'I hadn't noticed.'

Truth was, neither had she. For, while the wind-chill factor had probably taken the temperature *below* zero, she was still feeling a tad feverish after being bodily against a human furnace.

Hannah took another step back. 'Why has James deposited your luggage beside mine?'

'I'm researching.'

'What? The difference between Tarmac in Tasmanian and New Zealand airports?'

Humour flickered behind his eyes. It made her senses skedaddle and a purely feminine heat began to pulse. Then he slid his sunglasses into their usual hiding place and she had no chance of reading him.

'Less specific,' he said dryly. 'Try Tasmania.' Then he sauntered on past.

'Wait!' she called. 'Hang on just a minute. What am I missing here?'

'You sell yourself short on your PR abilities. You sold me.'

'Sold you what?'

'Tracts of wild, rugged, untouched beauty. Jagged cliffs. Lush forests. Roaring waterfalls. Lakes so still you don't know which way is the sky. Sound familiar?'

Sure did. One of her many effusive speeches about her gorgeous home.

He continued, 'It got me to thinking. So it's decided. The team know what to do in New Zealand. They'll go that way, while I do a solo recce of this area this weekend.'

So that was what they'd been cooking up in the back of the jet. She'd been busy playing holiday, so as not to get caught up in office stuff—sipping on a cocktail, reading a trashy magazine and listening to the music blaring from her iPod— and she'd blissfully let it all go by.

She must have been gaping like a beached fish, because he added, 'Don't panic. I have no intention of invading your holiday. Spencer's hired me a car and planned me a course.'

Hannah snapped her mouth shut. The fact that he was staying was still beyond her comprehension. But mostly she was struggling with the intense sense of envy that the one time she'd cut herself off was the one time she could have proved her producer potential. Sure, Spencer was great with an online map, but *nobody* in Bradley's circle knew the island, the detail, the most TV-worthy spots of her home island more than her.

Her timing couldn't have sucked more.

An insistent voice knocked hard on the back of her brain. *Let it go. Give yourself a muuuuuch needed break. And come Tuesday sit him down and tell him exactly why he needs to put you in charge of the project.*

'Okay,' she said, overly bright. 'Well, that's just…excellent. Truly. You won't regret it.'

With that she turned away and headed towards her luggage. And that was when she heard it. A penetrating feminine voice shrilled thinly in the far distance.

'Yoo-hoo! Hannah! Over *heeeeere*!'

Her conflicted emotions fled in an instant at the sound of that voice. And, boy, did she not blame them?

Why? How?

The text! She'd sent Elyse a quick message saying she'd be getting in early, and how. Dammit!

'Hannah!'

She frantically searched the small crowd awaiting the arrival of loved ones from behind a chicken wire fence. With their matching long, thick and straight dark brown hair, pale skin, shiny baubles, and head to toe pink get-ups, Hannah's mother and sister stood out from the small, chilly, rugged-up crowd like flamingos in a flock of pigeons.

As though the years hadn't passed—as though she didn't have an amazing job and a great apartment, cool friends and real confidence in where she'd landed—Hannah's hand went straight to her hair. Only to remember she'd done nothing with it that morning and now, as she stood on the windy Tarmac, it was making a fly for freedom in just about every direction possible.

In about five seconds flat she went from respected ace assistant to a TV wunderkind to skinny tomboy shuffling a soccer ball around the backyard while her glamorous mother and sister shopped and groomed and giggled about boys.

Her mother pushed through the crowd, opened a gate that probably meant she was breaking about half a dozen aviation safety laws, and headed her way. Hannah knew the grown-up thing to do was walk towards her, waving happily, but she was so deep into meltdown mode she began to physically back away.

And that was when she felt an arm slide beneath her poncho to settle gently but firmly in the curve of her back. The wall of warmth that came with it stopped her in her retreat as nothing else could have.

She must have been putting out such a silent distress call even her famously self-contained boss had felt it. Had come to her defence. Gallantry was becoming a bit of a pattern, in fact. If only the feel of him so close didn't also make her knees forget how to keep her legs straight.

And she needed every ounce of strength she had for what was about to happen. For coming up against her mother unprepared and un-liquored-up. And for subjecting her fuss-phobic boss to the living soap opera that was her family.

Bradley and her mother. Oh, no.

Brain suddenly working as if she had a sixth-sense, Hannah leaned in closer and said, 'Take a sharp left now, head into those bushes to the east and you'll hit the main road in about three minutes. Hail a cab from there. *Go!*'

His eyebrows came together and he laughed softly. 'Why on earth would I want to do that?'

'See that vision in pink hurtling our way? That's my mother.

And if you don't run now you'll feel like you've been hit by a hurricane.'

But it was too late.

She felt Bradley stiffen behind her. His fingers dug into her skin. If her brain hadn't been working overtime on how to keep her boss from going into a meltdown right alongside her she might just have groaned with the intense pleasure of it.

Virginia's eyes had zeroed in on Bradley with a vengeance. No wonder. A six-feet-four hunk standing in the shadow of his own private jet wasn't something any woman could easily ignore. Especially a strikingly beautiful woman currently between rich husbands.

Elyse, ever the mini-Mum, tottered in her wake.

Hannah felt Bradley grow an inch behind her as he breathed in deep. Then he broke the tense silence with, 'So, to downgrade the hurricane to mild sun shower, what do I need to know?'

Just like that, the Tarmac beneath her feet felt like familiar ground. At Knight Productions they never went into any meeting without being completely prepared for any outcome. Without knowing they'd never accept no for an answer. And Bradley always got his own way.

'Number one: call her Virginia,' Hannah punched out. 'Not *Mrs* anything. She's never liked to be thought of as a wife or mother. If people think she is either, it's proof she's of a certain age. Do that and you're ahead of the curve.'

Bradley's eyebrows all but disappeared into his hairline, but at least his death grip relaxed. 'Who does she think people think *you* were? Her fan club?'

Hannah laughed. Unexpectedly. She turned to find he was looking far more relaxed and less rock-like than she could ever have hoped. And as she turned his hand slipped further around her waist. Her breath went AWOL.

'Relax,' he murmured, leaning closer. 'You are so wound

up you're actually beginning to scare me just a little. Don't panic. Mothers love me.'

She shot him a look of despair. '*That's* not the problem. I mean, look at you. I have no doubt my mother will adore you.'

A muscle twitched beneath his eye and his mouth lifted into a sexy half-smile. 'You think I'm adorable?'

'To the tips of your designer socks,' she said, her voice as blank as she could manage. 'And, just for the record, along with *tall* men who *own* private jets my mother also adores rhinestones, tight pink cardigans and fruity cocktails with little umbrellas in them.'

The second the words were out of her mouth she regretted them. But it wasn't as though she never ribbed the guy. Working sixty-hour weeks a girl had to have a sense of humour. And he was oak-like enough to take it.

But comparing him with rhinestones…?

Maybe it was the comfy outfit. Maybe it was giving her brain cells a day off from the blow-dryer. Or maybe her body had gone into some kind of holiday-mode shutdown. Either way, her tongue had come dangerously loose.

So dangerously Bradley's hand slid even further—till it rested possessively on her hip, till his little finger slid between T-shirt and jeans and found skin. A silent signal that if she went one step too far she was at his mercy. As a comeback it was effective. Debilitatingly so.

Hannah was so tense she was practically vibrating.

She didn't have time to think before Virginia was upon them, long hair swinging like a shampoo commercial, high heels clacking loudly on the asphalt.

Then her mother's eyes zeroed in on the lack of sunlight between the two of them. Hannah wished she was wearing work stilettos so she could have kicked her boss in the shin.

'Hannah! Darling!' Virginia's eyes were gleaming, her arms outstretched, and she was looking Bradley up and down as though he was a two-hundred-dollar Hobart Bay lobster even while she reached out for the daughter she hadn't seen for three years.

Virginia's arm wrapped around her none too gently just as Bradley's hand slipped away. She gave in to one while missing the other.

'Virginia,' Hannah said. 'It's so nice of you to meet me, but you really shouldn't have. This weekend of all weekends.'

Over her mother's shoulder Hannah saw Elyse hovering. Her chest pinched at the happy tears in her little sister's bright green eyes.

She mouthed, *Hi*. Elyse did the same.

And then, in her ear, Hannah heard, 'He's very hand-some.'

Not even a whisper. An out-and-out declaration. Heck, even James the pilot, who was now taxiing Bradley's jet down a nearby runway, had probably heard.

'He's my boss,' Hannah blurted, just as loud. 'Thus out of bounds. So leave him alone.'

Elyse hid a shocked laugh behind a fake sneeze.

Her mum pulled back and looked deep into her eyes with what looked like a flicker of respect. Wow. That was a first. Hannah's chest squeezed as she waited for...more. Sadness, poignancy, guilt, regret...

Until Virginia took a step back, flounced a hand up and down Hannah's form and said, 'Jeans, Hannah? Must you always look like a bag lady?'

And there you have it, folks. My mother.

'My work means I fly a lot. All over the world, in fact. I've learnt it pays to be comfortable.' She mentally blew a raspberry, not much caring that it made her feel five years old.

Having said all she apparently felt the need to say, Virginia slid her eyes back to Bradley. In his jeans and fitted shirt, and the soft old leather jacket, he looked extremely comfortable. He also looked good enough to eat.

The scent of macadamia emanating from his direction only made that thought solidify. And expand. Hannah had to swallow down the sensation that rocked through her, finishing in a slow burn shaped very much like a large hand-print upon her back.

'It seems my daughter hasn't the manners to introduce us...'

'Forgive me,' Hannah leapt in. 'Virginia, this is Bradley Knight—my boss. Bradley, this is Virginia Millar Gillespie McClure. My mother.'

Virginia's smile was saccharine-sweet, her eyes cool as she said, 'Darling, you forgot the Smythe. Though Derek *was* rather forgettable, I'm afraid.'

Bradley took off his sunglasses and hooked them over the neckline of his T-shirt before grasping the manicured hand coming at him at pace. Hannah held her breath. Rock was about to meet hurricane. She squinted in preparation for being in the line of fire of flying debris.

'A pleasure to meet you, Virginia,' Bradley said, his deep, sexy voice as smooth as silk. 'And, considering the fact that I've never seen anyone with quite the same stunning colour eyes as Hannah's, this must be Elyse.'

Virginia blinked her own dark brown eyes slowly as she uncurled her hand away from Bradley's and made room for him to pass her by in favour of her daughter. Not used to being upstaged, she stood there a moment in silence, regathering herself.

Hannah placed a hand over her mouth to cover her grin. If she hadn't had a soft spot for her boss before, she had one now.

Elyse's pale green eyes—eyes so much like their dad's—all but popped out of her head as she gravitated towards Bradley. 'Boy, it's an honour to meet you, Mr Knight. I love your shows.

So much. Adore them. Not just because Hannah works on them. They're actually really good too!'

Bradley laughed. 'Thank you. I think.'

Hannah slid the thumb of her right hand between her teeth and nibbled. Amazing. For a guy who usually turned to stone at the first sign of such dramatic declarations of adoration he was handling himself mighty well. She watched him carefully for signs that he was about to cut and run. But his smile seemed genuine.

Bradley's smiling gaze slowly swung to Hannah. His eyes widened just a fraction, enough to let her know that he was well aware he'd stepped into a little bit of crazy but was content to stay a while.

And the only reason she could think of for him to do such a thing was because of her. He'd known her trip home was short, and important, so he'd stepped up to the mark and helped her get there sooner. He'd realised that reuniting with her mother was not quite so looked forward to. So he'd moved in to protect her.

The ground at her feet suddenly felt less like Tarmac and more like jelly.

And then she realised that Elyse was still talking.

'Hannah never mentioned she was bringing a plus one, but of course we'll make room—right, Virginia? Hannah's so secretive about her life in Melbourne—the yummy celebrities she meets at all those TV parties and the guys she's dating. We can get all the goss from you instead!'

'No, no, *no*,' Hannah leapt in. 'Elyse, Bradley's not here to—'

'You *are* coming to the wedding,' Virginia insisted, stepping smack-bang between Hannah and her boss. 'The accommodation is six-star. The food to die for. Cradle Mountain is the most beautiful spot on the entire planet. Bar none. You simply cannot come to Tasmania without experiencing her raw beauty for yourself. In fact it's just the kind of place you should set one of your little shows.'

Hannah shook her head so hard she whipped herself in the eye with a hunk of hair. She slid into the fray and grabbed Bradley by the elbow, practically heaving him out of the clutches of her wily relations. 'Bradley's not here for the wedding. He's here on business. He doesn't even have a minute to spare and stand around here nattering. Do you, Bradley?'

'I couldn't possibly impose so last-minute,' was his response.

She glared up into his eyes to find he was refusing to look at her. Then he shifted his stance, so that her hand slid into the all too comfortable crook of his elbow. Heat slid slyly down her arm.

She tried to pull away. He only clamped down tighter. Then he smiled at her, a quicksilver gleam in his deep, smoky grey eyes.

Her heart tumbled in her chest and she slipped her hand free. Oh, God. Oh, no.

She should *never* have compared him with rhinestones, or tight pink cardigans, or fruity cocktails with little umbrellas in them. He wasn't protecting her. He was punishing her!

'Don't be ridiculous,' Virginia said, linking her hand through his spare elbow. 'Great-Aunt Maude left word last night to say she's entirely sure she's come down with consumption.'

Elyse rolled her eyes. 'For the engagement party it was malaria. Apart from the hypochondria she's the perfect great-aunt. She sends gifts ahead of time!'

Virginia turned towards the terminal and tugged Bradley in her wake. Hannah, as always, had no choice but to follow.

Virginia was saying, 'So there's a spare meal already paid for.'

Elyse, who had taken Bradley's now free other elbow, said, 'And the gift's taken care of too! We'll just pencil your name alongside Great-Aunt Maude's on the card. She'll never know. You won't be sitting with Hannah, as she'll be with Roger all night. But you seem like a man who can take care of himself.'

Hannah rolled her eyes. When they settled back into their normal position she realised Bradley was frowning at her.

'Roger?' he asked, his tone strangely accusing.

'The best man,' Elyse explained. 'He's a fitness guru. As maid of honour she'll be stuck to the guy like glue for the duration. But we'll find you a fun table, I promise.'

'Besides,' Virginia said, 'you're the reason our girl hasn't been able to drag herself away till now. You owe us, so we won't take no for an answer. Now, I'll go find some people to do something about your luggage and get you a hire car. Ours is filled to the brim with things for the wedding, otherwise I'd happily ride shotgun while you took my wheel.' She patted him on the cheek before bustling ahead, with Elyse at her heels.

Bradley slowed up till Hannah was beside him.

'I told you to run,' she said.

'Yes, you did.' He shook his head in wonder, then his cheek kicked into a half-smile that had her heart galloping all over again.

'You can't come,' Hannah said.

He was silent for a beat. Two. She was sure he was about to agree wholeheartedly—until he looked down at her and said, 'And why not?'

With his eyes on her, she said, 'Because you'd cramp my style.'

The sun was behind him, so she couldn't see his eyes, but the rumble in his voice more than made up for it. 'Would I, now?'

She felt a smile creep across her face, and her impish streak flashed back to life as her mother disappeared from view. 'You'll never know.'

His, 'Mmmm...' was far too non-committal for comfort. 'So, how does your father cope around all that frenetic feminine energy?'

Hannah's smile faded. She fiddled with her father's old watch. 'He died when I was fourteen.'

And from the moment it had happened she'd felt like Cinderella, left all alone with the step-family—only the family she'd been left with was her own.

She felt Bradley's eyes on her as she explained. 'He adored Virginia to bits. Elyse and I actually thought it rather disgusting how often we caught them kissing at the kitchen sink. Then he died. And she remarried within six months. Things have been particularly cool between us ever since.'

Several moments passed before Bradley said, 'I'm sorry to hear that.'

'Thanks.'

In the quiet of the great open space, Hannah wondered if the time was right, for the first time, to ask about *his* family. She had no idea if his parents were alive or dead. Missionaries or UFO-chasers. Or the King and Queen of some small European country populated by only the most beautiful people. Or if he spent Sunday lunch with them every weekend.

But at the last second she baulked, unsure how far to press the quiet moment. Instead she just said, 'Mum's been married again. Twice to date.'

Promising to love and honour each of them with as much supposed vim as she had their lovely father. Each and every time clearly nothing more than a pretty lie. It was why Hannah would never make another person such a promise unless she really meant it. Unless she knew she would be assured of the same level of commitment right back. The idea of doing anything else made her feel physically ill.

She looked to where her mother was now drumming up help in the shape of goodness knew who.

She felt Bradley turn away to watch Virginia. Moth to a flame. Then he said, 'Your mother...'

Hannah stiffened, preparing for the thing she'd heard a million times before. *Your mum's so glamorous. And Elyse is like a little doll. While you are...different.*

'She's...' Bradley paused again. 'I do believe that dress of hers is the place ruffles come to die.'

Hannah laughed so unexpectedly, so effusively, so delightedly, it fast turned into a cough.

Bradley gave her a thump on the back. It only made her cough all the harder. And feel *absolutely* certain that her earlier fantasies of Bradley doing anything out of a deeply buried sense of human-being-like protection were just that. Fantasies. The likes of which she needed this long weekend without him in order to stamp out.

Once she'd caught her breath, she said, 'Virginia does like her ruffles. As well as her pink fluffy cardigans and cocktails with umbrellas in them.'

The rhinestones went without saying, but the crease in his cheek told her he'd heard her all the same.

She smiled. She couldn't help herself.

Then, as though he too felt the strange familiarity building between then, he frowned and looked away, up at the clear crisp sky. He sniffed in a trail of ice-cold air and thrust his hands into his pockets. Shutting her out.

And there she was, feeling like a satellite to his moon. If that wasn't reason enough to put an end to her impossible crush, she didn't know what was.

'The day is moving on and we're standing still. Time to get a move on. I'll drop you at your resort and then be on my way.'

'Resort?' Hannah could all but hear her exclamation bouncing off the band of clouds hovering above the hills in the distance.

Bradley didn't even flinch. 'Spencer's itinerary has me

starting at Cradle Mountain. I studied his route, and it actually makes good sense. As does giving you a lift, since you clearly need one.'

Hannah snapped her mouth shut. If she'd been in charge of setting his itinerary she would have said the same. But she was on holiday. Out of the loop. And, yes, she *was* in need of a ride.

She threw her hands in the air and headed for the terminal.

He followed, his long legs catching up with her in two short strides.

She swallowed down the lick of envy at the happy tone in his voice. 'This car that Spencer hired had better be something big and solid. The roads on this island can get mighty windy.'

'It's a black roadster. Soft-top.' His large hands waved slowly through the air, as though he was tracing its curves in his mind.

Never before had Hannah felt so jealous of a machine.

'Are you kidding me? Seems to me he's passed on his drooling habits.'

A gentle kind of laughter tickled her ears.

She walked faster. But with his long, strong legs the blackguard kept up without any effort at all.

CHAPTER FOUR

'ARE we there yet?' Hannah muttered, stretching as much of herself as she could in the confined space of the ridiculous sports car Spencer had blithely allowed their valuable boss to zoom around in. She'd be having a talk with him when they got home!

'Turn left in eight hundred metres,' said the deep Australian drawl of the GPS.

'Ken,' she said, 'you are, as ever, my hero.'

'Who on earth is Ken?' Bradley asked, uttering his first words in nearly two hours. His mind was undoubtedly focussed on the embarrassment of gorgeous scenery they'd passed from Launceston to the mountain.

'Ken's the GPS guy.'

'You've *named* him?' he asked.

'His mother named him. I just chose his voice when you were busy pretending to check the car for prior damage while actually drooling over the chassis. I'm certain you would have preferred Swedish Una, or British Catherine, but it seemed only fair that, since you and my mother have railroaded me over and over again today, I got my way about one tiny part of my holiday.'

'Your way is *Ken*?'

'Don't you use that tone when you talk about Ken. I'll have you know I have him to thank for getting me out of many an oncoming tram disaster when I first moved to Melbourne.'

He glanced her way, giving her nothing more than a glimpse of her reflection in his sunglasses. 'So your idea of the perfect man is one with a good sense of direction?'

'I have no idea what my idea of the perfect man is. I've yet to meet one who even came close.'

She watched Bradley from the corner of her eye, waiting for his reaction to her jibe. He just lifted his hand from the windowsill and ran it across his mouth.

She fluffed her poncho till it settled like a blanket across her knees and said, 'Though Ken *is* reliable. And smart. And always available. And he cares about what I want.'

'Turn left. Then you have reached your destination,' Ken said, proving himself yet again.

Before she even felt the words coming Hannah added, 'And, boy, does he have the sexiest voice on the planet.'

Bradley's hand stopped short. Mid-chin-stroke. It slowly lowered to the steering wheel. 'And there I was thinking he sounds a bit like me.'

He moved the car down a gear. Slowed. Then turned from the road onto a long, gumtree-lined drive. Hannah stared demurely ahead and said, 'Nah.'

But the truth was that Ken's deep, sexy Australian drawl reminded her so much of Bradley's she'd often found herself turning her GPS on even when driving home on the rainy days she drove her little car to work rather than take a tram. She'd told herself it was the comfort of feeling as if there was someone else in the car when driving dark streets at night.

She'd lied.

And then, appearing from between a mass of grey-green flora sprinkled in glittering melting white snow, there was the Gatehouse. A grand façade dotted with hundreds of windows, dozens of chimneys and fantasy turrets. It was like something out of a fairytale, rising magnificent and fantastical out of the Australian scrub.

'If this is the Gatehouse,' Bradley said, slowing to a stop

so that the sports car rumbled throatily beneath them, 'what's behind the gate?'

Hannah placed a hand on his arm, doing her best to ignore the frisson scooting through her at even the simplest of contacts, and pointed to their left. Between two turrets there was a glimpse of the reason a chalet-style hotel could exist in such a remote place.

The stunning, stark, ragged peaks of Cradle Mountain.

Bradley slid his glasses from his face, eyebrows practically disappearing beneath his hairline. 'God must be a cinematographer at heart to dream up this place.'

'I know!' Hannah said, practically bouncing on her seat. When she realised she was tugging at his sleeve, she let go and sat back and contained herself.

Bradley's eyes slid to the building towering over them. 'How many rooms?'

'Enough for cast and crew.'

He finally dragged his eyes from the picture-perfect view to look at her. They were gleaming with the thrill of the find. The buzz of adventure. It was the closest he ever came to revealing anything akin to real human emotion. Moments like those were the reason her impossible crush sometimes felt like it was veering towards something just a little bit more.

Her hand shook ever so slightly as she tucked her hair behind her ear. 'It's perfect, right? Rugged and yet accessible. And wait till you get a load of the mountain up close. You'll *never* want to leave. For me that moment will no doubt come the minute I step foot in the corner spa in my room.'

A crease, then three, dug grooves into his forehead.

Okay, so maybe she was laying it on too thick. But if he understood her enthusiasm for the place, for the project, then come Tuesday she might be in with a chance for the promotion to actual producer she'd so blithely flung out there the day before.

He put the car back into gear and curved it around the

circular drive until they pulled to a stop in front of a sweep of wide wooden stairs. Finally her holiday—read 'Bradley-free time'—could begin in earnest.

When he got out of the car at the same time as her, she gave him a double-take. It turned into a triple when she realised he wasn't dragging her luggage from the boot. He was eyeing the hotel's front doors.

Her stomach sank. She waved a frantic hand at the hotel. 'No, no, *no*! First you show up at my apartment and practically drag me here on your plane. Then you force me into that excuse for a tourist car. And now this?'

He turned to her, his eyes unreadable. 'And there I was thinking I had been *generous* in supplying a private jet and a free hire car as a way of thanking you for all your hard work.'

For half a second she felt a stab of guilt. Then she remembered that Bradley never did anything that didn't somehow serve *him*.

'Fine,' she shot back. 'Play it your way. But I can tell you now you won't get a room.'

For the first time that day she saw a flicker of doubt. So she rubbed it in good. 'Winter is peak season in this corner of the world, so the Gatehouse has been booked out for months. And, apart from the other big party here—a high-school reunion— this wedding of ours is *huge*. My mother knows everybody, Elyse is too sweet not to invite everyone she's ever met, and Tim's mother is Italian. Half the territory will be here. If they have a broom closet they'll be making a hundred bucks a night on it.'

He looked at the hotel, and at the glimpse of ragged peaks beyond. Then his jaw stiffened in the way that she knew meant he was not backing down.

His voice was smooth as honey as he said, 'You clearly have a relationship with the management. Use your magic and get me somewhere to sleep. One night to see this mountain you have raved so much about. And then you won't see me for dust.'

The temptation to wield her organisational magic in order to have him on his way the next day was mighty powerful. But after the day she'd had she didn't trust him as far as she could throw him.

'I'm. On. Holiday. You want a room? *You* go in there and make it happen.'

'Are you intimating I can't even book a hotel room without you holding my hand?'

Hannah tried hard to get the image of holding Bradley's anything out of her mind.

'I'm not intimating anything. I'm telling you outright.' She rubbed her arms and shivered theatrically. 'It gets dark quick around here this time of year. Cold too. And you're still a good two hours to Queenstown. Old copper mine. A couple of old motor inns there. You might just luck out.'

She heaved open the boot and dragged her luggage free. By the time it plopped at her feet she realised Bradley had eaten up the distance between them till they stood toe to toe.

She crossed her arms. 'You won't get a room.'

'Want to bet?'

Hannah wasn't a gambler by nature. She had an aversion to nasty surprises. But the odds were so completely in her favour. When Elyse had told her about Great-Aunt Maude's absence she'd called the hotel, and they'd all but cried with relief at being able to give her room to someone on the list of people desperate for it. Bradley would be driving on within the hour.

'Sure,' she said, a sly smile stretching across her face. 'I'm game.'

'Excellent. Now, we need to talk terms of the bet. What's in play? Ladies first.'

She thought about asking for an extra week off, at his expense. Now she was here, now she'd survived seeing her mum, it seemed like something she might be able to handle. It seemed like something she might need.

But it was unlikely she was ever going to get a chance as good as this to beat him at something. She had to make the most of it. 'I get co-producer credit if you make a show here.'

Bradley's forehead creases were back with a vengeance. Everything suddenly felt all too quiet. She could hear her own breaths gaining speed. Her heart-rate was rocketing all over the place. She wondered if she'd just screwed everything up royally.

Then she thought again. She *deserved* a producer credit, considering the amount of input she'd had in his productions to date. And if this was what it took for him to realise she meant more to his organisation than a way with middle management...

'Deal,' he said.

'Really?' she squeaked, jumping up and down on the spot as if firecrackers were exploding beneath her feet. She swished a hand across the sky as if she was looking at a podium at an awards ceremony. 'I can see it now: *co-produced by Hannah Gillespie*. "And the award goes to Hannah Gillespie and Bradley Knight."'

'Don't you mean Bradley Knight and Hannah Gillespie?'

'These things are always alphabetical.'

'Mmm.' He raised an eyebrow. 'And if I *do* get a room?'

'You won't.'

He grabbed his leather bag and her heavy suitcase and walked towards the hotel as though he was carrying a bag of feathers. She hurried after him.

'Bradley? The terms?'

'What does it matter? You're so sure I'm not going to win.'

He shot her a grin. An all too rare teeth and crinkly eyes

grin. Butterflies fluttered in her stomach. Big, broad-winged, jungle butterflies.

He wouldn't win. There was just no way. But this was Bradley Knight. So long as she'd known him—whether it was getting the green light on every show he pitched, getting any time slot he wanted, or keeping his private life private—he *always* got his way.

She jogged up the steps, puffing. He took them two at a time as if it was nothing. At the top he slowed, opened the door, and waved her through. She shot him a sarcastic smile and, head held high, walked inside.

Two steps in, they came to a halt as one. Hannah breathed out hard as she realised with immense relief that the Gatehouse was as beautiful as she'd hoped it would be. All marble floors and exposed beams and fireplaces the size of an elephant. It was fit for kings. But not Knights. No Knights.

'Stunning,' he said.

'And fully booked,' Hannah added.

Bradley laughed, the deep sound reverberating in the large open space. 'You are one stubborn creature, Miss Gillespie. I do believe it would behove me to remember that.'

She couldn't help but smile back.

Until he said, 'I'm coming to your sister's wedding.'

'I'm sorry? What?'

'If I get a room tonight it would be a waste not to thoroughly check out this part of the world. And if I'm here it would be the height of rudeness not to take up your sister's invitation.'

'And the hits just keep on coming!'

His eyes gleamed with the last vestiges of a smile. 'Are we on?'

The jungle butterflies in her stomach were wiped out by a rush of liquid heat that invaded her whole system. Red flags sprang up in its wake, but the prize was simply too big to back down now.

'We're on.'

He narrowed determined eyes, looked around, then took her by the shoulders and aimed her at the bar. 'Give me five minutes.'

'What the heck? I'll give you twenty.'

As she headed to the bar his laughter followed like a wave of warmth that sent goosebumps trailing up and down her spine.

She plonked onto a barstool in the gorgeous, sparsely populated lounge bar. In twenty minutes' time she'd know if she'd bet her way into a promotion, or if her impossible boss was coming to her little sister's wedding.

Either way she needed a drink.

Hannah let the maraschino cherry from the garnish of her soul-warming Boston Sour slide around inside her mouth a while before biting blissfully down. A pianist in the far corner was tinkling out a little Bee Gees, and the view from the twelve-foot windows was picture-postcard-perfect.

She sighed as the whisky worked its magic. And finally, for the first time since she'd headed off that morning, she began to unwind enough to feel as if she was really on holiday.

'Hannah Banana!'

She spun, to find Elyse barrelling her way. Her eyes instantly searched over her sister's shoulder, but thankfully Elyse was alone.

Elyse threw herself into Hannah's arms and hugged tight. 'Isn't this place gorgeous? You were *soooo* right in suggesting it. Tim and I owe you big-time!'

Hannah hugged back, at first in surprise. But soon she found it felt familiar, and really nice. She closed her eyes and a million small memories came flooding back to the surface. Sharing bedrooms. Sharing dolls. Sharing a secretly pilfered tube of their mum's lipstick to paint their dolls' faces. Memories she'd purposely tucked far away in order to make the move from Tasmania to Melbourne a completely fresh start.

'It's the least I could do,' Hannah said, eventually patting Elyse on the back and pulling away before it began to feel too nice. 'Considering I couldn't do much proper bridesmaid stuff from the other side of the pond.'

'You did just grand. Best maid of honour ever.' Elyse's eyes were already sweeping the big empty room. 'So where's your gorgeous man?'

'Off to chat up the management,' Hannah said, without thinking. She felt herself pinking and glanced into her drink. 'But he's not my *man*. He's my boss. And he's here to work.'

Elyse's perfectly plucked eyebrows disappeared under her perfectly straight fringe. 'So it's pure coincidence that you came on the exact same plane? And that of all the places in all the world he *had* to be today it was Cradle Mountain? The man has ulterior motive written all over him!'

Hannah coughed out a laugh. Her little sister might still look as if butter wouldn't melt in her mouth, but the girl was all grown up. 'Believe me, there is less than nothing going on between me and Bradley Knight.'

Elyse leaned her elbows on the bar and tapped the floor in front with a pointed toe—an old habit from long-ago ballet training. 'So he's not here because he's secretly in love with you and is afraid you're going to run away with the best man and leave him broken-hearted?'

This time Hannah's laughter was uproarious. 'I'm sorry to break your romantic little heart, but Bradley would be more likely to fear a sudden departure on my end would leave him with no dry-cleaning.'

She glanced out through the arched doorway to see the man in question still leaning on the reception counter. His dark wavy hair curled slightly over the back of the wool collar of his leather jacket. His jeans accentuated every nature-hewn muscle. Even from that distance the man was so beautiful he almost shimmered—like a mirage.

She glanced at the guy behind the reception counter and smiled to herself. If he'd managed to land a woman she might have begun to worry her bet was on shaky ground.

'So he's not coming to the wedding, then?'

Hannah dragged her eyes back to Elyse, smile still well in place. 'I'm afraid not. It was sweet of you to ask. But he really does have to work. He's a workaholic. Big-time. Should have the word tattooed on his forehead. If they made marrying one's job legal, he'd beat you to the altar.'

When she realised she was rambling, she put down her drink and with one finger pushed it out of reach.

A glutton for punishment, she looked back towards Reception in time to find Bradley's eyes scanning the massive foyer. They angled towards the bar and stopped.

He was too far away for her to be sure, but she knew he had her in his sights. She could feel it as if a laser had pierced her stomach, burning her up from the inside out. The piano music and the chatter of newly arrived guests spilling into the bar became a blur of white noise behind the thump, thump, thump of her heart.

Bradley gave her a slight nod. All she could do was swallow. There was so much blood rushing to her face it felt numb.

'Anyhoo,' Elyse said, 'everything's going like clockwork. So tonight no organising from you. Just party! Okay?'

Hannah frowned at her toes a moment, before lifting her head with a bright smile. 'Party sounds great.'

'Now, my love bunny and I haven't seen one another all day, and the poor pet will be fretting. I'd best head up to our room and ease his mind.'

With a wink that told of salacious goings on, Elyse flounced off.

Elyse—all grown-up and irreverent with it. Her mother—not unhappy to see her. A pleasant kind of warmth that had nothing to do with flickering fires or Boston Sours or even Bradley Knight began to spread through her.

Until a hotel room key slid in front of Hannah's face, with Bradley's long, tanned fingers on the other end.

'What is *that*?' she asked, her drink threatening to come back out the way it had gone in.

'Do you really need to ask?' Bradley drawled as he slid around behind her, the lapels of his jacket brushing against her back, causing her spine to roll in delicious anguish, before he straddled the bar stool beside her.

She spun on her seat to glare at him. Her knees knocked his before he shifted, placing a hand on her knee and allowing it to tuck neatly between his. Even then he didn't let go—just rested a hand there as if it was nothing.

As cool as she could manage, Hannah said, 'If you promised the man your firstborn son you've lost all my respect.'

The smile in his eyes gave her hot chills. As if she was sitting on the edge of a volcano. The kind from which you knew you ought to flee if only you could just let go of the primal urge to jump right in.

'I didn't do anything drastic,' he said. 'Or illegal. I simply negotiated. The only way I could get a room was to get us a suite.'

'I'm sorry, did you say *us*?'

Bradley glanced at the bartender, who poured a fresh packet of peanuts into a small glass bowl. 'Separate rooms off a shared lounge. Better even than the honeymoon suite, or so I've been told.'

While he was crowing, she was fast turning to a wobbly mess. But what could she say? They'd shared suites on numerous occasions before—at TV trade fairs or in pre-production on new shows—using the joint lounge as a makeshift office. Of course they'd been constantly surrounded by the half-dozen odd staff who travelled everywhere with him. Who were right now in New Zealand.

Her unimpressed air must have been crystal-clear, because he added, 'From what I heard they only let the Platinum Suite to their most favoured VIPs.' She narrowed her eyes. 'That's my mother's suite. I had to schmooze like crazy to make sure she got that room in the first place.'

Something that seemed a heck of a lot like a blush washed across Bradley's face. But Hannah was too infuriated to take any heed.

'I bumped into Virginia at the desk. She overheard my predicament and offered to swap rooms. She now has your single, and we have her suite.'

Hannah had her face in her hands and was rocking on her chair by that stage.

Bradley's thumb curving over her knee brought her out of her trance. She ran her hands down her face and did her best to act as though it was irrelevant that he was touching her at all.

She turned to glare at him, only to find glints throwing out specks of silver in his dark grey eyes. He said, 'Turns out that despite Virginia's predilection for…what was it?'

'Pink cardigans and cocktails with umbrellas in them,' she muttered.

'That's right. I couldn't remember beyond rhinestones. It turns out that she's an entirely sensible woman.'

Sensible? *Sensible?*

'Oh, no, no, *no*,' Hannah said, waggling a furious finger in front of his face. 'Don't *you* go falling for her act. Virginia is the very opposite of sensible. She's a narcissistic, selfish, hurtful creature who *always* has an agenda. And it always revolves around how any situation can benefit *her*.'

Her harsh words seemed to echo in the large space, coming back at her and back at her, like some kind of horrible Groundhog Day moment.

Bradley's hand slipped away from her knee and she felt

the cool slap of his silence. She hunched her shoulders in mortification and stared unseeingly at a patch of carpet.

'Evidently,' he drawled into the painful silence, 'until this moment I wasn't aware just how deeply the issues run between your mother and you.'

She ran her fingers through her hair, needing to shake off the crazies. 'Well, now you are.'

Suddenly Hannah felt very, very tired. As if her years in the city, working her backside off, building an impeccable professional reputation, creating a life for herself from nothing, doing her best to forget the period of her life at home after her dad died, were catching up with her in one fell swoop.

With a groan, she let her head fall to the bar with a thunk.

Out of the corner of her eye she saw Bradley's fingers fiddling with the room key. Maybe one good thing had come from her pyscho rant. Maybe he was realising the level of drama he'd be subjecting himself to by standing anywhere near a Gillespie girl in full flight. Maybe he was thinking of leaving her and her mad family in peace.

She lifted her head and swept her hair from her eyes. He was looking into the middle distance, the expression in his eyes pure steel. Whatever he was thinking there would be no talking him out of it.

She breathed in deep and waited.

Finally he turned to face her, and said, 'I'm coming to your sister's wedding.'

She moved to let her head thunk against the bar again— only this time he saw it coming. He took her by the shoulders, holding her upright. She wobbled like a marionette.

She must have looked as pathetic and wretched as she felt because his hands slid to cradle her neck, to slip beneath her hair, his thumbs touching the soft spots just below her ears. He had to be able to feel her pulse thundering in her neck at his gentle but insistent touch, but he didn't show it.

He just looked her right in the eye—serious, determined, beautiful. 'By the sound of things you're walking into a lions' den this weekend, with no back-up. It wouldn't be showing you any kind of thanks for having my back all these months if I just walked away and let that happen. Especially after exacerbating the problem. I'll be your wing man.'

His hands dropped to her shoulders, and then away.

Hannah wondered if a person could get jet lag from a one-hour flight. Because, blinking slowly at Bradley's mouth, that was just how she felt—woozy, off-kilter, slipping in and out of a parallel universe. Surely the fact that Bradley Knight had just offered to be her *wing man* was a hallucination.

She glanced at her drink. It was still three-quarters full.

'Hannah—'

She closed her tired eyes and held up a hand. 'I'm thinking.'

'About?'

About the fact that she couldn't twist his offer to mean anything other than what it meant. There was no punishment for rhinestone comparisons at play. By offering to throw himself in the path of the drama tornado, for *her*, he was being nice. Thoughtful. Selfless. Things she'd taken pains to remind herself he was not.

She took a deep breath and said, 'It's a really nice offer, Bradley. Truly. But this holiday is not all about my family. It's about taking a break from work...and those I work with.'

She glanced up at him with one eye open.

Taciturn, stoic, unreadable as ever, he said, 'Meaning me?'

She opened the other eye and nodded. 'You. And Sonja. And dealing with prima donnas all day. And Spencer following me around like a lovesick puppy while I'm trying to work. And sixty-hour weeks. And no sleeping-in—'

'Okay. I get it. I hadn't realised you found your job such a hardship.'

Grrr! That one man could be so smart one minute and so dumb the next…

Hannah shuffled on her stool. 'Don't be daft. I love my job. More than anything else in my life. Truly. But in order to do it right I need to recharge. This weekend is my chance.'

Finally, after such a long time she wondered if he'd heard a word of what she'd said, he nodded. 'Fair enough.'

Then, after an even more interminable silence, he said, 'But I know how even the most…thorny of families can have the kind of pull over you nothing else can. And that doesn't mean you have to take their crap. Not alone, anyway. If that's a concern in your case, my offer stands.'

She let out a great fat sigh. And, whether it was from the shock of his little insight, or a masochistic streak she was becoming all too familiar with, she threw her hands in the air and said, 'Fine. Okay.'

'Okay?' He perked up. As if he was finding himself quite enjoying playing the hero.

It was irresistible. *He* was irresistible. And he was going to be her plus one at her sister's wedding.

She was in mounds and mounds of trouble.

He took her hand, slipped it into the crook of his elbow and helped her off the stool.

'Come on, kiddo, let's go see what's so amazing about the suites in this place.'

'Prepare to have your socks literally knocked off.'

Glancing up at him as they walked through Reception, arm in arm, her blood fizzing more and more every time her hip bumped against his, she saw an ever so slight curve to his mouth.

Mounds and mounds and mounds of trouble.

CHAPTER FIVE

THE lift doors opened to reveal a line of people outside the Gatehouse's basement nightclub. The *doof-doof-doof* of the beat echoing from behind the bouncer-manned double doors thundered in Hannah's chest.

It didn't help that she was overly aware of the big warm man standing so close behind her she could feel the brush of his jeans against her backside every time the line moved.

'Stop fidgeting,' Bradley said, his breath brushing her chandelier earring against her bare neck. 'You look fine.'

'Thanks,' she said dryly. But she could hardly tell him the fidgets were all his doing.

The doors opened. Lights flashed over their faces. The line moved forward. Hannah took her chance and arched away from him. The doors closed. *Doof-doof-doof.*

'I was serious when I said you should get a guide to take you out for a night tour of Cradle Mountain rather than coming along to this pre-wedding party thing.'

'I'm fine.'

'Look,' she said, leaning back so she could drop her voice in case any of the bouncy young things in line were from Elyse's wedding party, 'it's just going to be a bunch of locals, all of whom will pinch me on the cheek and remind me they were there the time I took off down Main Street naked. You'll be bored out of your mind.'

When he didn't answer straight away she looked up at him,

surprised to find his jaw was clenched. He asked, 'You took off down Main Street naked?'

The husky timbre of his voice gave her pause before she cleared her throat and explained, 'I was two, and not overly keen on having a bath that evening.'

The slightly haunted look in his eyes disappeared. 'You were a tearaway?'

'Hardly. I was the perfect first child. Studious, polite, a pleaser. I took singing and dancing lessons for four years because Mum wanted me to —even though I'm tone deaf with two left feet. In compensation, when I did have my moments, I made the most of them—usually in front of the entire town.'

'Coming in?' the bouncer asked.

Hannah looked up to find they were at the front of the line. And she was still leaning back against her boss as though they were in the middle of a crushing crowd.

She pulled herself upright, rolled her shoulders and said, 'You betcha.'

The bouncer smiled. 'Knock 'em dead.'

Hannah gave him a bright smile, feeling for the first time that night as if maybe she could. As if she was no longer the naked two-year-old, or the gawky, soccer-playing tomboy kid of the local beauty queen. 'You know what? I'm going to do just that.'

The guy cleared his throat and blushed.

Only when she nodded did he open the door.

Bradley placed his hand against the small of her back and gave her a not too subtle shove. In fact she practically had to trot to stop from falling over.

'Somebody has a fan,' Bradley murmured against her ear once they were inside and the *doof-doof-doof* had become music so loud she could barely hear herself.

'I do not.'

'That big, burly bouncer back there thinks you look more

than fine tonight. He thinks you look downright gorgeous. And you know what?'

Hannah was feeling so dizzy from the effects of that voice skimming her ear she was amazed she had the ability to speak. 'What?'

'He has a point.'

Then the door swung shut behind them, and it was too loud to do anything but shout to be heard.

The club was rocking. Tasmania-style.

There were men with burnt-orange copper mine dust stained into their jeans and the grooves of their hands, mixed with women and men in business suits, twenty-somethings in classic black club attire, and tourists in sensible layers.

And then there was Hannah.

Bradley might not have been to a wedding in his life, but he had seen his fair share of bachelor parties. Leaving studious, polite and pleasing Hannah to her own devices at such a do, looking the way she did, was never going to happen.

Smoky make-up and glossy pink lips. Tousled hair that seemed to shimmer every time she moved. And an outfit that seemed demure at first glance only to cling in all the right places the second she breathed.

Not that his imagination needed help. All that talk of her running naked down Main Street had brought her dash from the bathroom back to the front and centre of his mind. In full 3D. Technicolor. As for her perfume… It had his nostrils flaring like a horse in heat every time she moved.

If she'd come to the wilds of Tasmania looking for a wild fling then she was going the right way about it. Hell, without even turning his head he could see a dozen men checking her out, and the look in their eyes was creating a red mist behind his.

Because *he* had her back. He'd promised he would, and he was a man of his word.

He moved in closer, putting his hands on her shoulders as

she began to snake a path through the club, so he wouldn't lose her in the crowd. Her hair spilled over his fingers, silky soft. His thumbs rested against the back of her warm neck.

The fact that those men with room keys burning holes in their pockets might consider his touch some kind of brand was their problem.

And possibly, he admitted, his.

It would only take one of those goons to show her the time of her life this long weekend and she'd have reason to wonder if sixty-hour weeks working for a stubborn perfectionist was actually a form of sado-masochism.

Resolve turned to steel inside him. Hannah must have felt it in his grip. She glanced back at him, eyebrows raised in question. He tilted his head towards the bar, and lifted a hand off her shoulder to motion that he needed a drink.

She gave him a thumbs-up and a wide, bright smile. Even in the smoky half-darkness the luminosity in those eyes of hers cut through. Showing the lightness of spirit that made her easy to have around.

The goons could go hang. She'd be damned hard to replace.

The crowd bumped and jostled. Then out of nowhere lumbered a guy carrying a tray of beers who looked as if he'd drunk a keg by himself already that night. Instinctively Bradley slid an arm around Hannah's slight waist and lifted her bodily to one side. She squeaked as she avoided having a cup of beer spilled over her in its entirety by about half a hair's breadth.

He found a breathing space in the gap around a massive pillar covered in trails of fake ivy, and let her down slowly until her back was against the protective sconce.

His breaths came heavily. Then again, so did hers. Her chest lifting and falling, her lips slightly parted. Pupils so dark he couldn't find a lick of green.

A wisp of hair was stuck to her cheek. He casually swept

the strand back into place, tucking it behind her ear where he knew she liked it. But there was nothing casual about the sudden burst of energy that coursed through his finger, as if he'd had an electric shock. He folded his fingers into his palm.

'You're making a habit of coming to my rescue this week-end,' she said, shifting until the hand that had remained on her hip nudged at her hipbone. 'A girl could get used to it.'

'Don't,' he growled, shocked at the ferocity of the urge to slide his hand up to her waist to see if it was as soft and warm as the sliver of skin he touched indicated. 'I'm no Galahad. I was thinking of myself the whole time. Of the griping I'd have to put up with if you ended up soaked head to toe in beer.'

He pictured it now. *Her skin glistening. Her white top rendered all but see-through. Her tongue sliding between her lips to clean away the amber fluid shining thereupon.*

He'd never felt himself grow so hard so fast.

But this was Hannah. The woman whose job it was to de-complicate his life. Hannah, whose hair smelt of apples. Whose soft pink lips were parted so temptingly. Who was looking up at him with those wide, bright and clear open eyes of hers. Unblinking. Unflinching. Unshrinking.

He stood his ground for several beats, then slowly, care-fully, removed his hands from her body, sliding one into a safe spot in the back pocket of his jeans and placing the other on the column above her head.

'Now,' he said, his voice as deep as an ocean, 'do you still want that drink?'

She nodded, her hair spilling sexily over her shoulders. It took every ounce of his strength not to wrap his fingers around a lock and tug her the last few inches it would take for those wide, soft pink lips to meet his.

'Boston Sour, right?' he asked.

She nodded again. A waft of that killer perfume slid past

his nose. He gripped the pillar so hard he felt plaster come away on his fingernails.

'I'm guessing beer for you,' Hannah said. 'Imported. Sliver of lime.'

Her words carried a slow smile, and behind that a hesitant note of flirtation he'd never heard from her before. He knew her drink of choice. She knew his. And now they both knew it.

'Stay here,' he demanded. 'Don't move. I didn't save you from that booze-soaked clod so that some other mischief might befall you the second I leave you alone.'

He'd moved to push away, to get her drink and whatever they could pour quickest for himself, when she lifted a hand and flicked an imaginary speck from his shirt. 'Whether you want to admit it or not, beneath the tough guy exterior you are, in fact, an honest-to-goodness nice guy.'

Through the cotton of his shirt her fingernails scraped against the hair on his chest, which sprang to attention at her touch. He clenched his teeth so hard a shot of pain pulsed in his temple.

Nice? Hardly. The truth was her tough relationship with her mother had unexpectedly slid beneath his defences and connected with his own. And in a rare fit of solidarity he'd felt he had no choice but to help.

He wasn't being nice. He was choosing sides in battle. A battle whose lines were fast blurring. Dangerously fast.

It was time to make the boundaries perfectly clear. So that she understood just how close to the fire they were dancing.

'Honey,' he drawled, 'looking out for you this weekend is purely professional insurance. I want you back on dry land this Tuesday, ready to work—not all hung-over and homesick, addled by wedding-induced romantic thoughts. That's it. End of story. You think your mother is egocentric? She has nothing on me.'

He dropped his hand till it rested just above her shoulder.

Edged closer till she had to arch back to look him in the eye. Till his knee brushed against the outside of hers. The rasp of denim on suede shot sparks up his leg which settled with a painful fizz in his groin.

She flinched at the sliding contact. Her cheeks grew red. The crowd jostled, the music blared, and the air around them was so heavy with implication and consequence it vibrated. He was meant to be teaching his protégée a lesson. Instead the effort of keeping himself in check made his muscles burn.

Hannah's hand slowly flattened to rest against his chest. But she didn't push him away. If the thunderous thumping of his heart wasn't enough of a caution to her, he wondered how far he might have to go.

And where the point of no return might be.

It did occur to him—far too late—that he might have walked blithely past it the moment he'd stepped off his plane. The moment he'd made certain they'd be stranded on an island, to all intents and purposes alone.

Suddenly she gave him a hearty shove, then ducked under his arm and took off to the edge of the dance floor. He should have been relieved. But it wasn't often he had a girl literally bolt from his advances—simulated or otherwise.

Feeling suddenly adrift, he made to follow when the strains of a new song blaring over the speakers stopped him short. That particular combination of notes plucked at something inside him. Something that chased all of Hannah's latent heat from his veins and chilled him to the bone.

In his mind's eye he could see a woman standing at a kitchen bench, hand reaching out for an overly full glass of wine, dishtowel thrown over her shoulder, gently swaying from side to side as she quietly sang along with the small radio on the bench at her elbow.

One of his aunts? No. Wrong kitchen.

The woman in his mind turned, but he couldn't see her face. In the end he didn't need to. The moment she saw him her whole body seemed to contract in on itself, and the over-whelming sense of rebuff told him exactly who she was.

It was his mother's kitchen. His mother's disappointment bombarding him. Telling him without words that he was noth-ing to her but a constant reminder that she'd fallen pregnant young and his father had bolted the minute he'd heard. It was *his* fault her life hadn't tuned out as she'd hoped it would.

'No, no, *no!*' a familiar voice shouted at the edge of his consciousness.

He dragged himself back to the present to see Hannah, in her tight capri pants, sexy stilettos, hair tumbling down her back, with hands to her ears, mouth agape, staring into the distance.

At the sight of her—the realness of her, the *now*ness of her—the unbearable memory dissolved like a pinch of salt in a pool of water. It was just what he needed in that moment. *She* was just what he needed.

'Are you okay?' he asked, placing a hand on her arm. Hannah's warmth beneath his fingers further banished the cold memories. Selfishly, he let his hand trail down her arm till it found purchase in the sultry dip of her waist.

At his intimate touch her eyes snapped from the middle distance to glance at him. Cheeks pink. Eyes bright and ques-tioning. Confused.

But mostly curious.

His solar plexus clenched in pure and unadulterated sexual response. It hit so hard, so violently, he just had to stand there and ride it. Either that or haul her over his shoulder like some caveman and drag her back to their room. Their shared room.

The song changed key. Hannah blinked, as if coming round from a trance. Then she waved a frantic arm in the direction of the karaoke stage and yelled to be heard over the speakers buzzing nearby. 'I'm not tall enough to see, but is that my mother?'

Her mother?

'You mean the one singing?'

Hannah nodded frantically.

Bradley searched the hazy room to see Hannah's mother was indeed up on stage, belting out a Cliff Richard classic while swinging her hips and waving at the small crowd who were cheering as if she was a rock star. A man joined her on stage—a man young enough to be Hannah's brother. Though from the way they oozed over the microphone together Bradley assumed the man was *not* blood-related.

'That would be her,' he said, keeping that last part to himself.

The sad, withdrawn, silently accusing woman fading in his mind and Hannah's effervescent mother couldn't have been more diametrically opposite if they'd tried. But neither of them could ever have hoped to be named mother of the year.

Instinct moved him closer to Hannah still. His body protecting hers from the crush. When she didn't pull away he slid his arm further around her waist, drawing her close enough that he collected wafts of that insanely sexy perfume with every breath. Then she leaned into him, the curves of her body slotting so temptingly into the grooves of his, and a slow, steady pulse began to throb in his groin.

Who was playing with fire now?

'Come on, kiddo,' he shouted above the din. 'Let's get those drinks.'

They hadn't taken two steps when they were stopped by a small crowd of people and Hannah was wrenched from Bradley, leaving a chill where her sensual warmth had been.

He shoved his untrustworthy hands back in pockets, and watched as person after person grabbed Hannah in a warm embrace. She was right, her naked run down Main Street *was* well-remembered.

After a minute Hannah sent him a look of apology. He shook

his head once to tell her it was fine. And it was. Watching someone else get mobbed rather than him was something of a novelty.

Attention always made him feel scratchy. He'd never courted it, never coveted it, and certainly hadn't done anything to deserve it. Even if he had, the attention was so foreign he'd never been equipped to know how to deal with it bar turning to stone till the discomfort passed.

Hannah, on the other hand, took attention and affection in her stride. As if it was expected. As if it was her right.

A completely unexpected kick of something that felt a whole lot like envy tightened his throat.

He'd never cared that not one of the folk who'd been forced to take him in had ever come looking for him. Not even since he'd found some notoriety. In fact he'd been relieved. If he couldn't put on an act for complete strangers, there was no way he could have done so for them.

But watching Hannah glow and blush and laugh, revelling in the close company of those who'd been witness to her life, gave him a glimpse at the other side of the looking glass. The sense of belonging he'd never been allowed to have.

This was what she'd walked away from. What she could have again if she ever chose to come home for good.

As if to jab the point home deep, Elyse leapt into the crowd surrounding Hannah, yanking her from the fray and back to his side. She shouted over the crowd noise, 'I want to introduce you to someone!'

With a sweeping motion Elyse invited another man into their circle. Light brown hair, dimples, arms like a wrestler, twenty-five if he was a day. Elyse's fiancé, Bradley assumed. They suited one another. A pair of happy-go-lucky puppies.

'This is Hannah,' Elyse said, wrapping her arm about Hannah's shoulder, her gleaming eyes glancing hungrily between Hannah and... Not Tim, Bradley realised all too late, when he saw the predatory gleam in the other man's eyes.

'I'm Roger,' said Dimples. 'The best man. Elyse, you were being miserly when you described how pretty she was.' Behind his hand he stage-whispered, 'Your sister's a knockout.'

Elyse laughed uproariously and pinched Hannah on the arm. Hannah did her best to pretend she hadn't noticed. Bradley felt a distinctly non-puppy-like growl building inside him.

'Pleased to meet you, Roger,' Hannah said, holding out a hand.

Dimples took it—and kissed it.

Elyse clapped.

Hannah smiled politely.

Bradley stood to his full height and thought weightlifting-type thoughts.

Elyse must have noticed him filling every inch of available space, and gave a perfunctory wave in his direction. 'Roger, this is Bradley Knight—Hannah's boss. He's filling in for Great-Aunt Maude.'

Bradley deflated, not sure he'd ever been given a more underwhelming introduction.

The two men shook hands. Dimples held on a little too tight. *Punk.* Bradley gave the kid one last ominous squeeze before letting go. He couldn't hide his smile when the guy winced.

Lightweight.

'I hear you're an aerobics instructor?' Bradley said.

'Personal trainer,' Roger shot back, seemingly oblivious to the intended put-down.

Hannah, on the other hand, noticed very much. In fact she gave a little cough at the exact time she stamped on Bradley's foot with one of those damned stiletto heels. He shook out his pulsating foot, then shoved his shoe neatly between hers. Her heels slid apart on the parquetry floor, and a hard breath puffed through her lips.

As Elyse waxed lyrical about the hotel, Hannah's hand

drifted behind her to rest against his thigh. He clenched everywhere while he waited to see what she might do in retribution. As it turned out the gentle rise and fall of her pinky finger against his leg as she breathed was punishment enough.

'And, boy, can your mum sing! Am I right?' Roger said, giving Hannah a chummy punch on her arm.

Hannah blinked as though she'd forgotten he was even there. 'Pardon? Oh, yeah. That she can!'

'She was singing in a nightclub when our parents first met,' Elyse piped up. 'She was practising for her Miss Tasmania pageant number. He requested "The Way You Look Tonight", which is her favourite song ever. It was love at first sight.'

'Sounds like your father was a smart man,' Roger said, sidling closer to Hannah.

Bradley had to stop himself from hauling her out of the guy's way. A hard stare had to suffice.

Though Roger, it seemed, wasn't as much of a meat-head as he'd first appeared. He shot Bradley a grin. A take-me-on-if-you-dare-Grandpa kind of grin.

'Do you too have the voice of a nightingale?' Roger asked, shining his dimples Hannah's way.

Hannah waved her hands frantically in front of her face. 'No. Nope. God, no. Uh-uh. No way. Tone deaf. Allergic to microphones. Rabid stage-fright.'

'So that's a no, then?'

Hannah laughed. 'That would be a gigantic no.'

Roger grinned.

Elyse did a little happy jig.

Before he even knew what he was about to do, Bradley reached out and tucked his fingers around the belt of Hannah's pants. His nails grazed the curve at the top of her buttocks. She all but leapt from her tottering shoes before she pressed her hand over his.

He fully expected her to slap his hand away. Or to do worse damage with her lethal shoes. He wouldn't have blamed her.

His move had been so far over the line of propriety it was nothing short of reckless.

But after a moment, two, her hand still remained locked over his. If anything she'd melted closer. Until he was near enough to see her neck was turning pink. To feel the heavy rise and fall of her breaths. To be gripped by the scent of her perfume.

As far as adventure thrills went, that moment was right up there. It was indecent. Torturously tempting. And, with no exit strategy in sight, completely against his own best interests.

He wondered quite how far he could go in the flickering semi-darkness, with her sister and Dimples and half her home town watching on. And how far this vamp version of Hannah would let him. His throbbing pulse ramped up into such a frenzy he could barely see straight.

'Speak of the devil,' Elyse said, and the unexpected angst in the girl's voice was so potent it hauled him back to the present with a snap.

As one they turned to face the distant karaoke stage where the strains of 'The Way You Look Tonight' rang out in Virginia's distinctively husky tones.

With his hand still tucked decadently into her pants, Bradley felt Hannah stiffen. The deliciously dark overtones to their play chilled. No guesses as to why. Virginia was singing the forties torch song her daughters associated with their deceased father. And she was singing it with yet another man.

From out of nowhere fury enveloped him. Fury he could barely control.

He moved himself in closer to Hannah, feeling a need to say…he knew not what, exactly. That he understood her disappointment? That he'd felt it too? That the only way to survive it was to turn your insides to rock so hard no amount of chipping made a dent?

No, he wouldn't say any of that. Couldn't. Not even while she practically crumbled before his eyes.

Besieged by a swirl of raw emotion, this was usually the point where he'd begin to feel icicles forming in his blood.

But then Hannah murmured, quietly enough he was sure only he heard, 'Please, God, somebody remind her that this is her daughter's wedding—not the place to pick up her next ex-husband.'

And he felt as if a pair of huge cold hands was squeezing his chest.

The adventure of the moment had been overtaken by too much stark reality for his liking.

He slid his hand from Hannah's back and moved out of the circle. He clapped his hands loud enough that the small group turned his way. 'Who wants a drink? My shout.'

'There's a bar tab, silly,' Elyse said.

'Even better. So, for the bride?'

'Black Russian.'

'Excellent. Beer for me. Boston Sour for Hannah.'

'Hey, that was Dad's favourite drink,' Elyse said.

Bradley glanced at Hannah. With a deep breath she turned away from the stage and into the conversation. 'The man had great taste—with only the occasional slip.'

Her eyes slid to his, a warm flicker coming back to life within. He couldn't drag his eyes away even as he said, 'Roger? Your favourite drink is…?'

'I'd kill for a tequila slammer,' Roger piped up.

The warmth in Hannah's eyes sparked into a flickering fire, and her mouth turned up at the corners as she stifled a laugh. She had a great smile. Infectious as all get out. Bradley felt his own cheeks lifting in response.

'Now, Roger, while you await your tequila slammer you should ask Hannah about her naked run down Main Street. It's a classic.'

Hannah's smile disappeared as she gawped at him—all hot pink cheeks and pursed red lips, bright eyes and huffing chest. Then she slowly shook her head. A warning of reprisals to come.

It was with that image in mind—that dark promise—that he turned and headed for the bar.

What a difference a day makes.

It had been less than a day since thought of Hannah jetting off for a wild weekend and a family wedding on an island she clearly adored had finally spooked him enough to abandon a long-planned New Zealand research trip on a plane.

Checking out Tasmania was a smart business move, but there was no avoiding the fact that the timing purely came down to his need to keep an eye on her. For losing her from the team at that point in time was exactly the kind of drama he did not need.

What with the Argentina show all but ready to fly, and New Zealand well and truly in the works. And now the germ of a new idea about Tasmania. He didn't have the time to break in someone new.

He found a spot at the bar where he was a head taller than every other patron. Three rows back, he still caught the eye of a bored-looking barmaid. She perked up, fixed her hair, smiled, and ignored the throng between them.

He boomed out his order and mimed his room number for the bill. She pretended to write it on her hand. Or maybe she wasn't pretending. She was cute. Willing. Lived miles away. But no part of him was stirred. Literally. Odd…

Drinks ordered, his thoughts readily skidded back to where he'd left them.

Breaking in a new employee was always frustrating. Not Hannah. She'd been a breeze from day one. With the stamina to keep up with him, the temperament to handle him, and a light-hearted nature that made her popular with staff, crew and station management alike. She could have said *Yes, Bradley, you're right, Bradley,* a tad more for his liking—rather than contradicting him so readily. But all in all Team Bradley was the better for having her.

He was smart enough to know it wouldn't last. Nothing ever did. One day she'd move on. It was the natural order of things. Every man for himself. No exceptions. Not for promises. Not even for blood.

It appeared as though she was sticking around for the immediate future. Hell would freeze over before she'd realise how much she missed living near her mum. As for the lightweight best man? Nothing to fear there.

A woman's voice called out his room number. He reached over and collected the drinks. The barmaid batted her lashes and gave him an eyeful of cleavage. He gave her an appreciative smile, but nothing more. No need to raise the girl's obvious hopes.

He was a busy man. On a mission to keep his assistant on the straight and narrow and out of the way of any who sought to knock her from her current path.

Hannah's familiar laughter tinkled through the air. He turned to catch the sound. She was regaling the group with some story or another, and they were laughing their heads off. This was the Hannah he wasn't ready to see go. Easy. Uncomplicated. Straight up.

She tossed her head and smiled widely at someone to her left, giving him a view of her profile. She waved and laughed. Bright and vivacious. Confident and extraordinarily sexy.

Several parts of him were stirred in an instant. Dramatically.

The fact that *he* seemed to be one of those with a craving to knock her from the straight and narrow was a whole other kettle of fish.

CHAPTER SIX

HANNAH nibbled at her little fingernail until there was nothing more to nibble without taking the top off her finger.

For a weekend that was meant to be about relaxing and recharging, sorting out her head, she felt as if she'd been walking a tightrope blindfolded.

What with Elyse being so unexpectedly fabulous. Her mother driving her even crazier than she'd expected. And poor Roger flirting up a storm every chance he had while she thought him about as interesting as a potted plant.

But they were mere wallpaper compared with the most glaring factor in the story of her lack of a pinky fingernail.

What had got into Bradley?

Even thinking her boss's name had her teeth aiming for a new nail.

No matter how she played out that first half an hour inside the bar, she kept coming back to the indisputable fact that Bradley had been hitting on her. The dark glances, the whispering in her ear, the unexpected touches…

She bit down so hard on her fingernail it stung.

Wincing, she snuck a glance across the table to where the man himself sat, all six feet four inches of him, sprawled out in his chair, long fingers clasped around a glass of beer, smiling contentedly as he watched Elyse and Tim belt out 'Islands in the Stream' on the karaoke stage.

'I'm sorry?'

She blinked, realising he was leaning towards her, one eyebrow cocked, the edge of his mouth lifted in the remnants of a smile. How did the man manage to make even the word *sorry* sound so sexy?

'Did you say something?' he asked, almost shouting to be heard over the music.

'Nope. Nothing going on over here. All quiet my end.'

He looked at her a beat longer. His deep grey eyes burning into her. Heat she'd never sensed from him before was now arcing across the table and turning her knees to butter. When he finally looked away she let out a long, slow breath.

Something had shifted back there. But how much? How far? She was confused and jumpy and prickling with anticipation all at once.

Then she asked the question she'd been finding any way to avoid. Was she looking at the early stages of a fling? She gave in to a delicious shiver that tumbled through her from top to toe.

But no. No way. Anything but that. Not with the boss. She'd worked too hard to prove herself indispensable—irreplaceable, even—to turn into a cliché now.

She leant her chin on her palm and bobbed her head in time with the music, all the while watching him from the corner of her eye.

She'd have to see something way beyond fling on the horizon to even *consider* that kind of risk. Whereas Bradley... She knew first-hand that the women who dated Bradley were lucky if they stayed on his mobile phone longer than a month.

Her enigmatic, heartlessly delicious, emotionally stunted boss suddenly picked up his chair and plonked it down beside hers.

She leaned away. 'If you can't see from there I'll happily switch places.'

'Stay.' He placed a hand over hers, cupping it on the table. 'I don't plan on shouting to be heard all evening.'

She slid her hand away and used it to scratch her non-itchy head.

'Elyse is a pretty fair singer too, you know,' he drawled. 'How *did* you miss that gene?'

Hannah shook the cotton wool from her head. *'That's* what you came over here to say? Not *Are you're having a good time, Hannah?* Or *Can I get you another drink, Hannah?* But what's with the talent deficiency? You *are* a charmer.'

He laughed softly—a low rumble that whispered to all the deep, dark feminine places inside her. Serious face on, he was heart-stoppingly gorgeous. Smiling, he was devastating. Laughing, he was…a dream.

This man had been hitting on her? *Her?* Sensible, back-chatting, small-town Hannah Gillespie? She felt it, but couldn't quite believe it.

Needing to know for sure, to see if her radar was so rusty it was no longer even functional, she turned in her chair, giving him her most flirtatious smile.

'Okay,' she said, 'just so we can put this topic to bed once and for all—'

He raised an eyebrow. Her heart rate quickened. And all the places his large warm hands had glanced that night pulsed.

Hannah met his raised eyebrow and raised him another. 'I'm talking, of course, about my lack of singing and dancing skills.'

'Riiight.'

'I don't want you sitting there feeling all sorry for me because I can't do a series of triple-spins while belting out "I Dreamed a Dream".'

When he opened his mouth, she held up a hand. 'Before you ask, all I'll admit is that routine had fake peacock feathers and sequinned masquerade masks.'

'I was going to say that I don't feel the least bit sorry for you. A woman doesn't have to be able to sing and dance to have it going on.'

He lifted his beer and finished it in one slow swallow. All she could do was stare.

Oh, yeah. Bradley was flirting, all right. Batting her about like a lion with a moth. She wondered what she might do if he decided to stop playing and get serious. The very idea petrified her to the spot.

Even in the low light of the club she could see the gleam in his eyes. The thrill of the chase.

Utterly out of her depth, she reached for her drink.

Bradley got there first, snatching it out of her way. But not before her fingers had brushed across his. Pure and unadulterated sexual attraction wrapped itself around her like a wet rope, slippery and unyielding. And even in the darkness she was sure his pupils had grown so large the colour of his eyes was completely obscured.

From an accidental touch of fingers. Oh, God...

Bradley swirled the ice around in her drink. Once. Twice. Each time ice hit glass her nerves twanged sharply—like an out-of-tune guitar.

She sat on her hands and bit her lip. *He's your boss. You love your job. He's not looking for for ever. And you are. Just allowing this flirtation to continue is going to change everything.*

He lifted her drink to his mouth and took a sip. The press of his lips where her lips had just been made her tingle in the most aching anticipation.

Then his face screwed up as if he'd just sucked on a lemon. 'Holy heck—that's atrocious! How can you drink this slop?'

'It's not slop!'

'What on earth's in it?'

'Whisky, lemon juice, sugar, and a dash of egg white.'

'Are you *serious*?'

He picked up his empty beer glass and practically ran his

tongue around the rim in search of leftover foam. Hannah's limbs went limp so quickly she had to look away.

'It was my father's favourite drink. So clearly it's meant for a palate far more discerning than yours.'

To prove it, she put the glass to her mouth and took a giant swig—only instead of tasting the sharp mix of ingredients that had always felt nothing but warm and comforting, she was certain she could taste a whisper of beer as left by Bradley's lips.

She slammed the glass to the table, then pushed back her chair. 'I need to...do some urgent maid of honour things.'

He crossed his arms and looked at her a long time. 'Right now?'

'You know I don't like leaving things till the last minute. *Boss.*'

There. Put things back in perspective. Remind him who you are. Who he is. How things are meant to work between you.

'Need company?' A slow smile slid across his face, proving he was apparently happy to forget.

As he began to uncurl his large lanky self from the chair she backed up so fast she bumped into some poor woman who spilt her drink. Hannah pulled her emergency ten dollars from her cleavage and shoved it in the girl's hand.

Bradley sank back into the chair, his eyes glued to her décolletage as though he was wondering what other secrets she held down there. *None to write home about!* she wanted to shout.

Instead she demanded, 'Sit. Drink. Grab a lighter and sway. Whatever gets you through the night. I'll come find you later.'

And with that she spun and, head down, feet going a mile a minute, took off through any gap she could find.

Until that moment she'd enjoyed her crush on him *because* it had never had a chance of going anywhere. Bradley was impossible. Untouchable. Out of her league. In fact he'd been a convenient excuse not to get close to anyone else while she concentrated on consolidating her career.

And now?

Someone clearly cleverer than she had once said, 'Be careful what you wish for or you just might get it.'

She wished they were there right now, so she could shake their hand. Or ask if they'd mind slapping her across the back of the head as many times as it took to make sure she made it back to her bedroom that night.

Alone.

Bradley glanced at his watch to find Hannah had been AWOL for over an hour. That was as long as he'd decided to give her. Because if she was *actually* off doing maid of honour business he'd shave his head.

After five solid minutes of frustrated searching, he found her. Back against the wall in a quiet cocktail lounge at the far end of the bar. Stuck between Roger and her mother.

Even in the half-light he could see that she was struggling. Both hands were clasped tight around a tall glass of iced water as her eyes skimmed brightly from one hostage-taker to the other.

Something must have alerted her to his presence as he excused himself and made his way through the chatty crowd towards her, because her eyes shifted to lock instantly with his.

That very moment she went from dazed to delighted. Her whole face lit up as if the sun had risen inside her. It felt... nice.

'Hi,' she said on an outward breath.

He nodded.

Virginia and Roger turned in surprise, and expressed understandably different levels of excitement to see him. He gave Virginia a kiss on the cheek, and patted poor Roger on the shoulder. Poor Roger's eye began to twitch. But Bradley had more important things to worry about.

'I've been searching for you for some time,' he said.

Hannah's eyes widened in a plea for help. 'I've been right *here* for quite some time.'

Guilt clenched at him. While he'd been stewing about the way she'd walked away, right when things seemed to have been going so fine, he'd greedily forgotten why he was really there. He'd promised to watch her back. He'd already let her down. Some white knight he was.

'We've monopolised her terribly,' Virginia said, blinking at him coquettishly over a glass of champagne—clearly not her first.

Through clenched teeth Hannah said, 'Virginia's been telling Roger all about my lack of flair for any of the Young Tasmanian pageant sections she aced as a kid.'

'Has she, now?' Bradley asked, frowning at Virginia. It didn't make a dent.

It seemed it would take more than his presence to give Hannah the upper hand. All he could think of for her to do was the same thing he'd done in order to shake off the shackles of his own mother's disappointment. Prove to her, himself and the world that it didn't matter.

'On that note,' he said, 'did you forget we're up next?'

'Up?'

'Karaoke.'

'But I thought you couldn't sing,' Roger said.

'I can't,' Hannah said, hand to her heart, eyes all but popping from her head.

'She's not kidding. She really can't.' That was Virginia.

Having seen enough, he reached in, took Hannah by the hand and dragged her from the local axis of evil. He shot them a little over-the-shoulder wave before he took their plaything away.

He skirted his way through the crowd in silence. Hannah

kept close, tucking in behind him when things became overly cramped. Her small hand in his felt good. Really good.

'Maid of honour business all finished?' he asked, his voice gruff.

'It is, thank you,' she said stiffly. 'Now where are you taking me?'

'I said we were going to sing, so now we have to sing.'

Suddenly his arm was almost yanked from its socket. He spun to find she'd dug in her heels and was refusing to budge.

He glanced towards the cocktail lounge. 'It we don't they'll just think it was a dodgy excuse for you to ditch them.'

'Wasn't it?'

'Only if you're happy with them thinking so.'

Two little frown lines appeared above her nose, and she nibbled at her full lower lip. He found himself staring. Imagining. Planning.

Finally she shook her head. 'But I really can't sing.'

'Can *they*?' He motioned to the wannabe boy band who could barely slur out a sentence yet still had a rapt and voluble audience. 'Now, pick a song. Something you can recite in your sleep.'

'Oh, God. This is really happening, isn't it? Umm… In my dreams when I audition for random TV talent shows I'm always singing something from *Grease*.'

He felt a grin coming at the thought of such innocent dreams, and struggled to bite it back.

Apparently not well enough. Her face fell. 'You don't know *Grease*, do you? Well, I am *not* going up there on my own.'

'You're safe. I had the biggest crush on Olivia Newton-John when I was a kid.'

The manic tugging relaxed instantly as she gawped at him. He used her moment of distraction to drag her to the edge of the stage.

'I love it!' she said, grinning from ear to ear. 'You used to sing her songs into your mum's hairbrush, didn't you? You can tell me. I promise I won't tell a soul. Well, bar Sonja, of course—and you know how discreet *she* is.'

She shook her head, her thick dark hair curling over her shoulders—sexy, unbridled, exposing a curve of soft golden skin just below her right ear that was crying out for a set of teeth to sink into it.

He stared at the spot, finding himself wholly distracted by the imagined taste of her spilling into his mouth. Better that than to brood over the fact that somehow he'd promised to leap onto a spotlit stage and in the act of performing beg a crowd of strangers for their superficial devotion.

He took solace in Hannah's luscious creamy shoulder as he pulled her closer—close enough to lose himself in the last subtle trails of her scent as he whispered in her ear, 'What the lady wants, the lady gets. *Grease* it is.'

Then he turned her in his arms and pointed to the stage, looming dark and high in front of them.

Her smile disappeared and she swallowed hard. 'So we're really doing this?'

'One song. Show them that even though you have no flair for pageantry you have pluck to spare.'

'You think I have pluck?'

He turned away from the stage at the softness in her voice, only to find himself drowning in the heat of her eyes. 'To spare.'

She blinked at him. Long dark lashes stroked her cheek, creating flutters as he imagined their light graze caressing his skin as she kissed her way up his—

She breathed deep and shook out her hands. 'Let's do it. Now. Quick. Before I change my mind.'

He went to move away and she grabbed his hand again. Hers was warm, soft, small—and shaking. Trusting.

Holding on tight, he had a quick word in the ear of the guy in charge of the karaoke line-up, and slipped him a twenty so that they could get this over and done with as soon as humanly possible.

'Okay,' she said, bouncing from foot to foot, tipping her head from side to side to ease her neck. Warming up as if she was about to do a triple-jump, not a little show tune. 'We've established that I'm doing this because I'm a cowardly pleaser. But why are *you*?'

'When in Rome...'

She shook her head. 'I've worked right by your side for nearly a year now, Bradley. I know you. Putting yourself up there like some piece of meat to be picked over must be akin to torture.'

She was so close to the truth—a truth he had no intention of sharing with her or anyone—he shut his mouth and avoided those big, clear, candid eyes.

'Fine,' she said. 'Don't tell me. I'll figure it out eventually.'

And then she smiled. The smile of a woman who knew him. Who cared enough to *try* to know him. A woman who didn't care if he knew it too.

Dammit. He was in the middle of a bar without a drink, and if he'd ever needed Dutch courage the time was now.

Lucky for her the thing propelling him forward was his inability to stand by and allow her to be so summarily dismissed. He'd rewritten his story. He wasn't merely a little orphan boy any more. He was a man who conquered mountains and showed others how to do the same.

What Hannah had yet to realise was that in going up on that stage it wouldn't matter if she proved her mother right by not holding a tune. What would matter was that her story would no longer be about being her mother's great disappointment. Her story would be the time she summoned the kind of guts she never knew she had in order to belt out a song at her sister's fabulous pre-wedding party.

And, in the spirit of watching her back, if he had to endure a little excruciating drama to give that to her, then so be it.

The current song had stopped. The guys were ushered off-stage to a round of bawdy cheers.

Bradley took Hannah's hand and dragged her limp body on-stage. Once there, he gave her a little push till she was beneath the glare of the spotlight. And, just as he'd hoped, the second they saw who was on stage the crowd cheered like nobody's business.

She laughed softly. And blushed. Then curtsied. The crowd went wild.

Her face glistened with perspiration. Her eyes were wild and glittering. But her chin jutted forward, as if she was daring *anyone* to tell her this was something she couldn't do. The strength of her inner steel surprised him. It even seemed to steady him until he stared, undaunted, out through the bright lights to the braying faceless crowd beyond.

The strains of 'You're the One That I Want' blared from the speakers, and the entire club got to its feet and cheered as one.

Hannah came to, as if from a trance, lowered her micro-phone, and looked up into his eyes. 'Can *you* sing?'

He put the mike back to her lips and said, 'We're certainly about to find out.'

Hannah's high heels dangled from one hand as she padded across the marble floor towards the bank of lifts leading to the Gatehouse's extensive rooms.

Her ears rang from the after-effects of hours of overly loud music, while her limbs felt loose and languid. The rest of her buzzed from a mix of cocktails and exhaustion and coming down from the high of her karaoke duet with Bradley which had brought the house down.

She turned to walk backwards, smiling at her partner in crime who strolled along behind her. 'Of all the crazy moments of this bizarre night, the biggest shock has to be the fact that you can really sing!'

'So you've mentioned once or twice,' he drawled, his eyes following her closely as she swayed.

'I suck. I mean, I *really* suck. But you were right—it didn't matter. I felt like a rock star. And, no matter how strong and silent you are being about the issue, I know that somehow you knew I would.'

'Lucky guess,' he said, quietly eating up the distance between them.

She grimaced at her bare feet, indecision warring with the most intense sexual attraction she'd ever felt. Judging by the tumble of sensations bombarding her every sense as her eyes met his, it was clear which was winning.

Needing some physical distance from all that manly heat, she skipped over to the lift and pressed the 'up' button. In the quiet, deserted foyer it made such a loud noise she giggled. 'Shhh!'

'Shhh, yourself.'

'Nah,' she said, nice and loud. 'No shushing me tonight. I have sung in front of strangers and friends alike, I have sung badly, and yet I have survived. That calls for a lack of shushing. It calls for dancing.'

So she danced. Her bare feet sticking to the floor, her hips swaying, her arms flying out sideways, she started spinning and spinning and spinning. She'd been so scared of being judged and found wanting for so long she'd only done things she knew she was great at. And she'd done them as well as she humanly could.

Now, having thrown herself at something that had always been tied up in her mind with a deep-down bruising kind of hurt, she realised it wasn't so scary after all. She felt as if she could do anything. Fly. Play the ukulele. Bradley…

When his strong, solid arm slid around her waist—when he pulled her close and began to sway to the beat of the tune inside his head—she wondered if her desire had been so immense she'd summoned him to her against his will.

Then again, there was nothing forced about the way his body pressed against hers, the way his chin rested atop her head, the way his hand cradled her waist. Nothing mistakable about the hard jut she felt pressed into her belly.

He spun her out and tugged her back in. Giddy laughter shot from her lungs as she tried to regain her footing. When he tucked her tight into the warm cocoon of his embrace he was humming. Something slow and soft and sweet and poignant, melodic and unrecognisable. And quieting.

She leant her droopy head on his shoulder—or as close as she could get since it was so very, very high off the ground and she was barefoot on tippy-toes. In fact she was closer to his heart. She could feel the steady beat against her cheek. It was the very same beat that throbbed within her.

He did better. He lifted her till her feet were on top of his.

What could she do but throw her shoes over her shoulder and thread her hands around his neck, slide her fingers through the springy thick hair at the back of his neck? How long had it been since she'd first ached to do just that?

And now she was slow-dancing.

With Bradley.

With her boss.

Somewhere deep down inside her a little voice tried reminding her why that was a bad idea. She shook her head to shut it up. Didn't it realise that she couldn't remember ever, in her whole life, feeling this way? As if she was made of melted marshmallow, all hot and soft and sweet and yummy.

She breathed in deep and was soon drowning in the heavenly scent of hot, clean, male skin. No man in the world had ever smelled so good. So sexy. So edible.

The lift doors opened with a loud 'bing'. Neither of them paid it any heed.

Hannah pulled her head away from its heavenly pillow and looked up into the most beautiful mercury-grey eyes on the planet.

She threaded her fingers deeper into Bradley's hair, her thumb caressing the soft spot beneath his ear. His eyes grew dark, like the sky before a winter storm.

The swaying stopped. He pulled her tighter still, and the air escaped her lungs as her head rocked back on her all but useless neck. Moonlight slanted across his strong, angular profile as though all it wanted was to touch him too.

So big, she thought, *so tall. So private. So exceptional. So, so beautiful.*

Bradley lifted her off his feet and placed her gently on the floor. The marble beneath her bare feet was ice-cold, but the rest of her was filled with a licking flame so hot it barely registered.

Neither did the lift doors as they slowly slid closed.

And then, as though it was the most natural thing in the world, Bradley bent his head and kissed her.

Hannah's eyes fluttered closed as fireworks exploded behind her eyes, and then down and down and down her body, until she felt as if her blood was made of popping bubbles.

He pulled back, his lips hovering millimetres from hers. Giving her the chance to stop things before they went any further. But it was way too late. The kiss was out there. For eternity. There was no going back now.

Whether it was because of the press of her hips to his, or the miserable groan that rumbled through her, he held back no more.

He slid his hand deep into her hair and his mouth plundered hers until she could barely breathe for the intensity of feeling cascading through her.

When his tongue slid knowingly across hers that was the absolute end of her. She was gone—lost in a swirl of sensation and heat and need. She lifted up onto her toes and wrapped her arms around his neck, pressing as close as she could. Needing to feel his warmth, his skin, his realness. Aflame with the impossible desire to crawl inside him.

But in her bare feet he was too tall, too big, too far away, and she wanted to be closer. She wanted to be a part of him.

Buoyed by frustration and desire for the liberating sense of release she leapt into his arms, wrapping her legs about his hips.

His hands cupped her, holding her as if she weighed nothing. But his kiss deepened, heated, ratcheted up a dozen levels—as if she meant anything *but* nothing to him. As if his own long-held frustration had broken through a dam and now nothing was going to stop it.

And then his lips were on her neck, her collarbone, her bare shoulder. His teeth sank into the tendon below her neck and she cried out in pleasure, her hands gripping the back of his head. The most delicious heat she had ever known pooled deep inside her.

She sighed and murmured, 'If I'd had a clue this would feel *this* good I'd never have been able to hold back all these months.'

Hannah felt Bradley stiffen in her arms. Then the lift went *bing*. Or maybe it happened the other way around.

Either way, the sound of the lift opening registered somewhere in the fuzz that was Hannah's brain at about the same time she felt Bradley's arms unwinding from around her.

She looked into his eyes, confusion taking hold of her still liquefied system. But she didn't have time to decipher a thing as a pile of Elyse's friends spilled out of the lift, laughing, screaming, half way to being drunk.

She scrambled to fix her hair. Her lipstick. Her crumpled clothes. Then saw her discarded shoes were in their stumbling path. She leapt away from Bradley, grabbed the shoes out of their way before somebody impaled themselves on a stiletto.

'Hannah Banana!' one of Elyse's oldest friends called out, grabbing her and trying to pull her in their wake. She managed to extricate herself and tell them to have fun. And then, as suddenly as they'd appeared, there was nothing left of them but their echoing laughter.

The quiet foyer was filled with nothing but the sound of her puffing breaths. Adrenalin poured through her like a flood, till her body shook from the shock. Her body—which was still throbbing from head to toe as it baked in the intensity of Bradley's kiss.

Bradley.

Shoes gripped in her tight fist, she glanced up to find him watching her. A huge dark shadow of a figure in the pale moonlight. Hands in pockets. Still as a mountain.

The lift 'binged' again. This time instinct had her stepping inside. The doors started to close until she reached out and held them at bay.

'Coming up?' she asked, shoes swinging against her leg.

A muscle worked in his jaw as he flicked a glance up in the direction of their suite. Then he took a step back. 'You go. I'm going to track down a nightcap.'

The fact that they had a crazily well-stocked bar in their über-suite seemed to have eluded him. Or perhaps not. Hannah felt a wretched little cramp in her stomach. She wished Elyse's friends would return, so she could throttle them one by one.

'Okay,' she sing-songed, as though she didn't realise she'd just been wholeheartedly rejected. Then, falling back into ever helpful assistant mode, she said, 'I'm pretty sure the foyer bar is open all night.'

He nodded. Yet didn't move.

The cramp in her stomach gave way to hope. Maybe he was being a gentleman, waiting for a sign from her. Though she wasn't sure she knew a bigger sign than throwing herself into a guy's arms and wrapping her thighs around him.

The lift 'binged' several times, ready to get a move on. She clenched her teeth and jabbed at the 'open door' button till it shut the hell up. Didn't it realise what a delicate moment this was?

Maybe that was the problem. Maybe subtlety didn't work on mountains. Maybe the guy needed not a sign but a sledgehammer.

'Bradley, would you like to—?'

'Get some sleep.' He cut her off. 'It's been a big day.'

Her stomach sank like a stone dropped into the lake behind their hotel. She desperately tried to locate some dormant thread of sophistication somewhere inside her but just ended up babbling. 'Right. Sleep. What a great idea. Just what I need.'

Clearly to him what had just happened was just a kiss. And a little necking. And, okay, some extremely dextrous fondling. Maybe it was an everyday occurrence for him and it had simply been her turn. Maybe she'd come on too strong and he already regretted it. Maybe. But then again he'd absolutely come on to her first.

As her head began to spin, the only thing Hannah knew was that she should take his advice and get the hell out of there before she said or did something really stupid.

She looked away to jab hard and fast at the number for their floor. 'Goodnight, Bradley.'

He nodded. 'I'll see you in the morning.'

Slowly, slowly the lift door closed. When her own reflection stared back at her and the lift began to rumble she could still see his face clear as day. Dark. Stormy. Stoic.

Somehow, some way, whatever forces had come together to create that moment back there had disappeared as if in a puff of smoke. If only she knew why.

CHAPTER SEVEN

BRADLEY cradled the now lukewarm cup of coffee in his palms as he sat in the big, empty foyer bar.

Unfortunately the mind-numbing normality of a late-night coffee hadn't done a damn thing to numb one bit of him.

He wasn't a reckless man. Even as he'd lowered his head to kiss Hannah's soft, pink smiling lips he'd known there would be consequences. He'd weighed them, measured them, and decided that after negotiating such a riotous night with commendable finesse a celebratory kiss was a pretty fine idea.

What he hadn't expected was for the effortless sensuality she wore so lightly to explode into a raging furnace the second his lips had touched hers. Though that he could handle.

What had him sitting alone in a bar at three in the morning was, *'If I'd had a clue this would feel this good I'd never have been able to hold back all those months.'*

Her words hadn't stopped ringing inside his head since he'd sat down.

It appeared as though Hannah had feelings for him. Perhaps only nascent ones, but that was still too much. He'd never let himself become involved with any woman who didn't view relationships with the same lack of gravity he did. Doing so would be nothing short of hypocritical. He knew all too well how it felt to have the world you thought you knew cut out from under you.

So why did the same mouth that back-chatted constantly,

barked remonstrations whenever he ran late, and grinned delightedly any time he was pushed outside of his comfort zone have to be an instant gateway to paradise?

Dammit. He pushed the porcelain cup aside in frustration.

'Another, Mr Knight?' the barman asked.

'No thanks, mate,' he said, his voice ragged. 'I think I've done enough damage for the night.'

'Very good, sir.'

Bradley hauled his heavy self from the bar stool and walked slowly to the lift. Standing on the very spot where for the sake of that mouth he'd ignored the signs and kissed her anyway.

The lift door opened and he stepped inside. He looked at his feet rather than his reflection in the mirrored doors, not wanting to look himself in the eye as he considered things again.

Hannah liked him. He'd never use that to his advantage. If he did he'd be no better than those who'd hurt him in the pursuit of making their own lives a tad more comfortable.

Even though she kissed like a siren. As if there was a fountain of untapped heat bubbling beneath her small frame. As if she wanted nothing more than for *him* to be the one to release it.

All he could hope was that by the time he got back to their shared suite Hannah's room would be dark and quiet. Then he could retire to his own room, strip down, open his bedroom window as wide as it would go and let lashings of bitterly ice-cold air do what will-power and boiling hot coffee could not.

Bradley shut the suite door behind him as quietly as humanly possible. Ears pricked, he couldn't hear anything beyond the faint swoosh of winter wind gently buffeting the unadorned windows that stretched the entire length of the shared living space.

He shucked off his shoes and lifted a foot to sneak to his room. Then he heard a noise. His whole body clenched and adrenalin kicked his senses into overdrive.

He heard it again. It sounded like the clink of glass on wood. Probably a tree branch scraping against the window. Only one way to be sure.

He padded down the wide steps into the lounge, to find all the lights were off bar a lamp at one end of the modern cream leather four-seater couch. Beneath the lamp a magazine was open and turned face-down. In the far corner of the room embers burned red in the fireplace. It seemed Hannah hadn't been able to instantly fall into the sleep of the innocent either.

The clink pinged in his ears again and he turned towards the sound. It was coming from the corner of the room in which the spa pool sat, tucked into an alcove with a window over-looking the forest. It was hidden discreetly from view behind a half-wall.

Blood pumping in his ears, Bradley took two more steps. The deep dark blue of a large square dipping pool came slowly into view...

And there she was.

Hannah. Awake. Sitting on the edge of the pool. Top half covered in a loose pale grey sweater. Naked legs dangling into the lapping water. A half-glass of red wine at her fingers. A hot pink cowboy hat sitting incongruously atop her head.

The groan he swallowed down was deep and painful. For she couldn't have looked any sexier if she'd tried.

He could walk away right now and pretend he'd never seen her. *Pretend to who?* a strangled voice shouted inside his head. *Because sure as you're a grown man you ain't ever going to forget it!*

Her fingers reached out and played with the stem of the glass, twirling it back and forth. The edge of her top slipped, revealing the creamy skin of one beautiful bare shoulder.

Skin he'd tasted less than an hour before. Skin that tasted of honey and heat and such sweetness he couldn't get it out of his head.

He took a step closer.

She turned her head. He stopped, the toes of his right foot clamping together as he held himself statue-still. But she only looked as far as her glass, her long hair shielding half her face like a curtain of brown silk. She dipped a finger into the glass and brought it to her lips, slowly sucking the red droplet into her mouth.

Something finally alerted her to his presence—probably the fact that his blood was pumping so hard and fast through his body people could hear it three floors down—and she turned with a fright, her hand to her chest.

'Where did you spring from?' she asked, breathless.

'The bar,' he said, sounding as if he'd swallowed a ream of sandpaper. 'Had a coffee. They do pretty good coffee. Now I'm back.'

Bradley Knight, the great communicator.

'What's the time?' She glanced at her huge watch, her eyes opening wide as she saw how long had passed since they'd parted.

'It's late,' he agreed. But he didn't give a hoot. It might as well have been ten in the morning. He felt so alert. So conscious of every sound, every movement, every shift and sway of her nubile half-naked form. 'What's with the hat?'

'The—? Oh.' Her eyes practically crossed as she looked up. 'You wanted to know what was in my suitcase? This. And feather boas. A hot pink veil. Dozens of packets of condoms. A box of dried rose petals. A veritable traveling maid-of-honour's just-in-case bag of tricks.'

She took off the hat, strands of her dark hair catching in the weave. She ran her fingers through the waves till they fell in messy kinks across her shoulders.

His feet moved as though driven by a deeper force.

'Couldn't sleep?' he asked.

She twirled the hat around one finger and caught it before it tipped into the pool. 'Wasn't entirely sure I wanted to.'

She shot him a quick glance. Far too quick for him to be able to read it fully. But the fact that she was up, waiting… It would be rude not to join her.

'Perhaps that's because we never did get to finish that dance,' he rumbled, hating himself even as he said it. If he was Catholic he'd be spinning Hail Marys in his head. As it was he was pretty sure he was going straight to hell.

'Mmm,' she said. 'We were rudely interrupted before the big finale.'

'It did feel like we were building up to…something.'

She raised an eyebrow. 'I was all prepared for a grand Hollywood dip. You?'

Despite the tension swirling about the room, Bradley laughed.

She laughed too, her cheeks pinkening charmingly. She pulled her knees up to her chin. Water glistened down her lean pale gold legs. Toenails painted every colour of the rainbow twinkled in the misty light reflecting back off the water. She had been busy while he was away. And he didn't blame her. If she felt anything like he did she'd have to climb a mountain to have any chance at burning off the adrenalin rocketing through her system.

Damn, but she was something. Sexy, playful, smart, and completely unpretentious. And in his world—a world peopled by pretenders—that was a truly unique quality. All this from a woman who, somewhere in her room, had dozens of packets of just-in-case condoms. Just sitting there. Going to waste.

She watched out of the corner of her eye as he slowly rolled up the legs of his jeans. She rubbed her chin on her shoulder, her eyes straying over the flecks of hair covering his moun-taineer's calves.

In two steps he was beside her, sinking down onto the cool

tiles, his bare feet all but sighing in pleasure as they dipped into the glistening hot water. The temperature came close to matching the heat his body was already radiating now he was sitting within touching distance of that shoulder, that hair, those legs. That mouth.

It was all there for the taking. If only her expectations weren't too high. Or his too low. If only they could meet somewhere…

'I have a proposal,' Bradley said, before he even felt the words coming.

She blinked at him. 'Do you, now?'

'I do. And here it is. You're here another three days. I have nowhere else to be. And this suite is built for all the decadence and debauchery a wild weekend can muster.'

Her chest rose and fell as she breathed deep. But she didn't for a moment look away.

'I propose we don't waste another minute. But here's the clincher. Come Tuesday…whatever happens in Tasmania stays in Tasmania.'

Her hands curled over the tiled edge of the spa pool until the knuckles turned white. His did the same. He moved his finger half an inch and it connected with hers. Her head dropped back and a tremble shook through her.

And in the end that was all it took. An arrangement they could both live with and the touch of a finger.

With a moan that was half-anguish and half-relief Hannah straddled him in one deft move. Her hands were deep in his hair, her mouth on his, and she was kissing him as though her life depended on it.

That mouth. It was nothing short of divine. Bradley wrapped his arms about her oh-so-slight form, closed his eyes, and let that gorgeous mouth take him to heaven and back. Deal or no deal, that mouth was as close to heaven as he was ever likely to get.

Eons later the kisses slowed. Softened. Sweetened. His

hormones continued to rage through him, looking for release. Gentle discovery was such gorgeous agony.

Hands on his shoulders, she kissed his temple. His cheek. The very corner of his mouth. He turned to take sanctuary there again, but she moved on to nibble at his earlobe.

'Devil,' he groaned.

Her laughter whispered across his ear, soft and sexy. Just like her.

He slid his hands straight to her backside and pulled her close, dragging the curve between her thighs across the hard peak of his denim-clad erection. She gasped and clung to him, her teasing laughter nothing but a memory.

He registered a pair of underpants before his hands slipped beneath her top. His thumbs ran over her hipbones, his fingers delving into the soft, feminine flesh at her waist. His exploration continued and he found nothing but skin. Scorching hot, velvet-soft naked skin.

When his thumbs brushed the underside of her bare breasts she bucked in pleasure. His stomach clenched tight to keep himself upright. To keep him from knocking himself out on the tiles or falling into the spa.

Though the thought of Hannah slippery and wet was almost enough to blow his mind, the thought of being stuck in wet jeans and unable to shuck his way out of the blasted things kept him rooted to the spot.

He cupped her breast to find a perfect handful. Beautiful. Every inch of her was staggeringly beautiful. The way she reacted at his slightest touch overwhelmed him again and again. He knew he had skills. But Hannah made him feel like a Grand Master. It only made him want to prove her right. To prove to them both their pact would be worth it.

But before he even had the chance she'd whipped her top over her head. Then, with a twinkle in her eye, she was gone. The warm body writhing so deliciously in his arms was now nothing but a cool empty space.

It took him a moment to realise Hannah had slipped into the spa. Then she reappeared, water streaming over her face, glistening from her long dark hair. Hot, wet, slippery. And then a tiny pair of black underpants appeared on a twirling finger before she flipped them onto the tiles.

Bradley was on his feet, stripping down before he even realised what was happening. Jacket. Top. Singlet. Jeans.

Dammit. Button fly!

His fingers felt fat and numb as he struggled with what felt like a thousand buttons.

He slipped into the water, searching for her. The damn pool wasn't any more than two metres by two metres, but the floor was a mottled midnight-blue, and lit only by the filmiest of winter moonlight.

Then he felt the slightest pressure on his inner thigh. His hipbone. His belly button. It was her lips as she kissed her way up his body.

She emerged from the water like some kind of siren. Dark slick hair, skin like cream, mouth creating the most delicious havoc with his senses.

He leaned his elbows on the tiles, relishing the cold hardness, hoping it might keep him from teetering over the edge into oblivion. It did. Barely.

She slid a slow hand up his chest. Her tongue followed, creating a burning hot path across his ribs, around his left nipple. Her soft naked flesh slid sensually against his.

And then, as her teeth sank hard into the sensitive tendon across the top of his shoulder, her other hand wrapped around his erection. One finger at a time. Till she had him in her complete thrall.

The primal growl building up inside him finally found release. It echoed against the black windows. It reverberated across the top of the water. And Hannah's grip, both up top and below, faltered.

At the first sign of a pause in her utterly sensual seduction of him he wrested back control.

He lifted her out of the pool, spun her about, and sat her unceremoniously on the tiles.

She squeaked in shock, her limbs flailing as she tried to get purchase on the slippery floor. She sat before him completely naked, nowhere to hide.

She looked down at him. Wide pale eyes rimmed by smudged eyeliner. Pink-peaked breasts turning to dark nubs in the cooler air.

Vulnerable. Completely at his mercy. He realised with a jolt what kind of responsibility that engendered. Just what kind of line he was treading.

Then her naked foot slid up his side. He jerked beneath the heated caress. Shuddered. Then focussed. She was a grown woman. A woman who knew the boundaries. A woman who wanted this as much as he did.

Bradley placed his hands on her knees. She flinched. *Good*, he thought. He wanted her completely aware of what was about to happen to her.

She never looked away. When he began to press them apart slowly, oh-so-achingly slowly, she let him.

Her eyes grew dark—so unexpectedly dark, so beautifully dark. Her lips parted. Her skin grew pink. All over. How had he never noticed the sensuality that oozed from her pores?

Fine. He'd noticed. He'd just worked the both of them to the point of exhaustion every time his body reacted to her, in an effort to keep his life uncomplicated.

Fool.

He yanked her closer, her backside sliding along the tiles till her legs dangled in the water. A surprised sigh rushed from her lungs. Then he lifted her legs slowly, one by one, and draped them over his shoulders. Her heels bounced against his back, creating hot swirls of need that coiled tightly in his gut. And while a thousand conflicting emotions flittered across her face she gave in to him without a murmur. Loose as a rag doll, she slowly lay back on the tiles, her head coming to rest on his rolled-up jacket.

Trusting him completely.

Again realisation jarred him. How could she? Why would she? He'd never done anything to engender such faith from her. He was pretty hard guy most of the time, and she didn't seem to care. She needed to toughen up. Big-time. And fast.

He'd tell her so. Later. Much later. For right then all his brain function went into demanding that his hand run down her front, graze her breasts, take its time over the sexy little rise at her belly. Her torso lifted and curled to follow the trail of his touch, as if not being touched by him was simply too much to bear.

Desire the likes of which he'd never felt roared unimpeded through him, lit by a need to please her. To show her that her trust wasn't unfounded. And to drive every thought she'd ever had completely out of her mind.

Then he lowered his mouth to her inner thigh, the scent of her making his nostrils flare in anticipation. Her hands slammed out sideways, grabbing onto his shirt, his jeans, whatever purchase she could find.

He ran his tongue along the muscle quivering in her thigh. God, she was temptation incarnate. So responsive, so lush. How he managed to keep from hauling her back into the water and having his way with her he had no idea.

He pressed her legs further apart again. Her heels dug into his back, tugging him closer. Her desire for him was so bold he ached. A gorgeous, pleading little whimper escaped that beautiful mouth, and he lowered his own mouth to the warm waiting juncture.

He took her to the very edge of madness, and himself right along with her. She endured and endured and endured the pleasure with rabid delight—until she finally hit a height of pleasure even she could no longer maintain and completely fell apart.

He kept his hands on her, feeding off her luxuriation as a series of aftershocks trembled through her. The way she responded was so gratifying he could have done the same again and again. All night long if she'd let him.

When the trembles abated, he slid his thumbs up her thighs till her hands clamped down on his.

It seemed she had other ideas.

She pulled herself upright, clearly having been sapped of a good deal of her strength. *He'd* done that. It gave him a hell of a buzz to know he'd turned her to jelly.

She slid slowly back into the water. He held her by the waist and helped her. As her feet touched the bottom, she held his face in both hands and looked deep into his eyes. All he could do was breathe and look right back.

No fear. No reticence. No holding back. No regret.

Rules or no rules, boundaries or no boundaries, somewhere inside him a portal opened, so that he felt her serenity, her surety, her blissed-out satisfaction infiltrating him. It was as if he was physically experiencing her afterglow.

Then she smiled. A smile fuelled by pure sin.

Wham! All sense of serenity fled as he was slapped across the face with the triple threat of that inner light. That natural impudence. That glorious mouth.

The portal snapped shut. His erection ached.

His turn had come.

The condoms.

Hell. Hadn't she said they were in her suitcase?

Bradley was so far gone he couldn't even remember which direction her room was. The idea of a mad dash to her room and back was about as appealing as eating fried worms.

But she was on the pill. That little pearl had come up in conversation at some point. Could he let that be enough? God, he wished he could let that be enough—

Hannah reached over, and from next to her discarded wine glass appeared a square foil packet. She *had* been waiting for him. With intent. His divine little siren. He wondered how many of the dozens of packets she'd strewn around the suit, *just in case*. Then again he didn't give a damn. Right now he only needed one.

She peeled the packet from around the latex disk with her teeth. Then slid slowly back into the water, dark, dark eyes looking right into his. She moved up to him, rolled the sheath into place, slowly wrapped her legs around his hips, and lowered herself onto him. He pressed deep, perfectly deep, into her ready flesh, as though he'd been waiting his whole life for that moment.

Twenty-four hours, a small voice reminded him. *Somewhere between twenty-four hours and twelve months.* And he had no more than three days in which to fully satisfy himself.

With that divine mouth gently tugging at his, that heavenly tongue sliding along his, those clever teeth creating havoc with his earlobes, she rode him.

Slowly. Achingly slowly. Then faster. And harder.

He took over, losing himself inside her until the pressure became too much. Too wild. Too heavy. Too powerful. And he came as he'd never come before.

He could feel her playing with the back of his hair. Her chin rested lightly on his shoulder, her outward breaths puffed against his earlobe.

All that heat and release and temptation and response, from the light, lean creature bobbing in his arms.

Compared with the intensity of what they'd just experienced she felt so slight. So small. So breakable. He felt an immense urge to hold her close. To keep her safe from all harm.

It was a crazy thought. Random. And impossible. Especially considering *he* was the biggest threat she had in her line of sight right then.

He slowly uncurled her from around him, hoping physical

distance might make the floor of the spa not feel as if it was about to give way at any moment.

Only the second she lifted her head and smiled up at him, all lethargy and loose limbs, his gaze went straight to her mouth. To her moist pink lips. Between one breath and the next his body revved up like a hot-rod car, waiting for the green light. And all he could think was, *More*.

Apprehension flashed inside his head. If *that* hadn't sated him, at least for the moment, what on earth would it take? Well, whatever it took, it had to be done by the end of the long weekend.

It was already after four in the morning on day two. They had hours of daylight in which to sleep. It certainly wouldn't hurt him taking until sunrise to find out *just* what it might take to get Hannah Gillespie out of his system for good.

With a caveman grunt, he hauled her over his shoulder and walked them out of the pool.

'Where do you think you're taking me?' she yelled, laughing, pounding useless hands on his back.

'Bed.'

She lifted her head and tried to angle it around to see his face. Her backside wriggled against his cheek. He literally began to shake with arousal. Sunrise was an arbitrary end point, surely?

'Bed?' she cried. 'But we're sopping wet!'

'That's why I'm going to yours,' he added.

She laughed. Easy, free, gorgeous. Ready for more. Ready for anything.

He kicked open her bedroom door. This was going to be some night.

Waves of gold and pink blurred across the backs of Hannah's eyelids. Keeping her eyes closed, she stretched, her naked limbs sliding unhindered across her massive bed.

She creaked her eyes open to find sunlight pouring through

the windows. It was morning. Make that late morning. And muscles she hadn't even known existed twinged in protest.

Then, in a rush of bright and beautiful heat, it all came back to her.

Bradley. The slow dance. The kiss. The rebuff. The resolution not to take it lying down, so to speak. The spa. Oh, my—the spa! And lastly, but certainly not least of all, hours and hours of the most intense feats of sexual prowess in the bed in which she now lay.

Taking a sheet with her, she curled luxuriously onto her side. And grinned.

'Wow,' she whispered, her voice rough and husky.

Wow, indeed. If anyone had asked how she'd hoped the first day of her long-awaited holiday might turn out, she'd never, even in her wildest dreams, have imagined she'd end up in bed with the boss.

A whisper of cool air tickled at her feet. And at her conscience. She curled up tighter and rubbed them together.

Everything was fine. Gorgeous, even. Had been from the moment Bradley had opened his beautiful mouth and said the magic words, *'Whatever happens in Tasmania stays in Tasmania.'*

The second he'd uttered those words the fantasies that had niggled at the corner of her mind since she'd known him had been given free rein. Within limits. Limits that meant she had no choice but to put a stop to any hope this might become more. Limits that gave her the comfort that in the aftermath Bradley wanted things to go back to normal too.

And once they got back to town—to real life, to work— they could both count on the fact that everything that had happened that weekend would be over. Niggling desires satisfied. Blissfully, beautifully, erotically satisfied.

Bradley could go back to being aloof and cool and stubborn and untouchable.

And she could happily continue…

What? Not dating? Ignoring the sensual side of herself so as to concentrate on her serious side? While hoping to one day magically find herself a man who could give her the love and loyalty and romance and openness that she refused to settle without? A man who would somehow manage to live up to what had happened to her last night. Who could make her feel wanton and cherished and beautiful and sexual, as she did when Bradley's lips were on hers. When his teeth scraped over her hipbone. When his tongue slid around her breast. So far, in the first twenty-five years of her life, she'd never even come close to feeling that way with any other man.

Hell.

The crackle of oil popping on a frying pan sizzled through the ajar door. Breakfast! The desire to stick her head under the pillow and stay there for ever had to wait. It turned out she was beyond hungry. Stomach-rumblingly, mind-numbingly famished. And the man of the moment had ordered Room Service.

She wrapped a massive king-sized sheet around herself, and made a quick stop to check herself in the bathroom mirror.

'Wow,' she said again.

Her eyes were huge wells of liquid green, surrounded by smudges of leftover make-up. Her lips were puffy. Her cheeks pink and warm. She looked ruffled, tousled, and well-ravaged.

She glanced towards the door. Well, he was the one who'd done that too her. And brilliantly too. What was the point of pretending nothing had happened when it most certainly had? Without fixing a hair on her head, she swept up her makeshift toga and headed towards the delicious smell.

Halfway to the über-modern, stainless steel and Caesar stone kitchenette, Hannah pulled up short.

Bradley was cooking. And he was cooking what looked and smelled a heck of a lot like eggs Benedict with extra bacon.

Her favourite meal on the entire planet. She was ninety-nine percent sure she'd told him as much. A few dozen times.

He'd remembered. Just as he'd remembered her favourite drink. While seeming intent on nothing more than working her to the bone, he'd paid attention. Her stomach felt as if it had been inhabited by a chorus line doing fan kicks.

He looked up, his quicksilver eyes grazing her naked shoulders before moving down the massive expanse of white sheet trailing behind her. It felt as if his hands had followed the same path.

'Good morning,' he said.

'Oh, so it *is* still morning?'

'Just.'

'How long have you been up?'

'A while.' He glanced at the empty coffee cup and open newspaper on the glass-topped breakfast table.

With a yawn, and an inelegant hitch of her sheet, she said, 'You should have woken me.'

His mouth hooked into the kind of half-smile that made the chorus line in her stomach start bumping into one another in blissful confusion.

'I could have,' he said. 'But I thought you might need the rest.' He didn't need to add, *After last night's marathon efforts*.

'I'm fine,' she said. Unfortunately another yawn cut off her declaration halfway through.

Bradley laughed softly, then turned away as a pair of English muffin-halves popped up from a toaster.

Hannah and her sheet managed to curl up on a gilded, beautifully adorned, wrought-iron dining chair. 'This place does have Room Service, you know.'

'Where do you think I got the eggs and muffins?'

'Good point. So, it appears as if the man can cook.' *And sing. And dance. And create amazing television that changes people's lives. And make love like no man I've ever known.*

A warm glow began to fill her. A glow the likes of which she'd never felt before, but her deepest feminine instincts understood all too well. She pulled her sheet tighter in an effort to suffocate it, to forcibly remind herself: *what happens in Tassie stays in Tassie.*

That's your only lifeline here, hon. Hang on tight!

Bradley said, 'A person can't survive on café food and Chinese takeaway alone.'

Hannah flicked the newspaper before closing it. She could beg to differ.

'I am a single man,' Bradley continued, 'living alone. It was learn to cook or starve. You don't cook?'

She shook her head.

'So Sonja cooks?'

Hannah laughed so hard she all but pulled a muscle.

'What do you live on?' he asked.

'Fresh air, hard work, and as many eggs Benedict with extra bacon as I can stomach.'

He laughed again—only this time a small frown creased his forehead. As if he was trying to figure her out. Really trying. She couldn't remember her boss ever doing anything but taking her at face value. The glow inside her began to pulse.

It didn't help that every few seconds images kept springing unbidden into her head. The sensation of hot water lapping against her thrumming naked body as she watched Bradley strip. His mouth becoming more intimate with parts of her than she had herself. The feel of all that hot muscle bunching under her fingernails as she bucked beneath him...

'So, what's the plan for today?'

Bradley's voice cut into her daydreams. She glanced at her wrist, and then rubbed at the naked spot. She must have put her dad's watch somewhere during the night.

'Today's grand plan? Well, I'm sorry to say we missed the practice releasing of the doves. But no matter. Just after lunch there's a sewing class for the girls. And burping contests for the boys.'

She contemplated adding something that involved the entire wedding party getting together to decorate the chapel. But he *was* making her breakfast.

'You *are* kidding?' he said.

'Am I?'

She looked up to find Bradley's eyes had finally contacted fully with hers. Deep, dark, smoky, beautiful grey. Perhaps more distant than they had been hours earlier. But that was forgivable. She was feeling a little tender and unsure herself.

'God, you're easy,' she said. 'There's a day-long movie marathon in the ballroom. Beanbags and blankets to snuggle into as you watch Tim and Elyse's favourite romantic films, one after the other. And this time I'm not kidding.'

His eye twitched at the thought.

'Relax,' she said. 'Since you've been so nice as to make me breakfast, I'm letting you off the hook.'

'Whatever will we do instead?' He licked a blob of hollandaise sauce from his finger, switched off the stove, and moved around the counter. Her body responded like a heat lamp on a chilled lizard—it stretched and unfurled and curved towards the source of heat.

She held on tight to her sheet and put her bare feet flat on the ground. She realised she needed a little time to fully come to terms with what had happened. What was still happening. What Bradley was imagining would happen. At least till Tuesday. And jumping back into bed with Bradley was not going to help.

She held up a hand. 'I have a proposal.'

The last time those words had been spoken between them it had directly led to her pouncing on him. Clearly he remembered it too.

'Do tell.'

She waggled a finger. He stilled. *Good boy.*

'There is a beautiful mountain right on our doorstep. It's a foothill compared with what you're used to, but it's still something really special. There are twenty-odd walking trails, plant and animal varieties found nowhere else on earth, horseback rides, mountain-biking, fly-fishing. Let me show you a sneak peek. If you don't get to see any more of this island than the inside of this hotel, I'll never forgive myself.'

His dark eyes flickered to life, and his mouth curved into the kind of smile that told her that getting to know every inch of the inside of this suite was fine by him.

Her blissfully aching inner thighs tingled in anticipation. But they needed a break. They needed time to recuperate. What better way than an arduous walk around a mountain on a freezing cold morning?

She was going to be the best, most professional tour guide ever.

'Indulge me?' she begged.

'Fine,' he said, finally turning back to the bench where he finished plating up. 'Breakfast first. I need to regain my strength. Then you can be my tour guide. Prove to me why this place makes you go all sentimental and glistening and get that crazy schmaltzy look in your eye.'

Hannah shook her head. 'I'm not sentimental, or a glistener, or in any way schmaltzy. I am a sharp, cool-headed professional.'

He slung a plate in front of her. It smelled insanely good. Soft gooey egg, perfectly toasted muffin, gorgeously rich sauce. She felt herself curling towards it, her nostrils flaring, a hum of appreciation buzzing in her chest. She might even have licked her lips.

'Sharp, cool-headed professional?' he said, grinning at her. 'Want to know the three words *I'd* use to describe you right now?'

She sat up straight. 'No. I really don't.'

Bradley did as he was told and said not another word as he dug into his food.

She did the same. And it tasted as good as it looked. Better, even. Way better. As the egg yolk popped in her mouth and the strong tang of the sauce curled around her tongue she knew it was the best eggs Benedict she'd ever eaten or would likely eat again.

CHAPTER EIGHT

BRADLEY followed the puffs of white from his breath up the steep walking track that took Hannah and himself around the edge of Dove Lake and up into the craggy edges of Cradle Mountain's beautifully eerie crater.

Ice-fresh air burned at his lungs, a clear pale blue sky hovered above, tough and challenging terrain disappeared beneath his feet, and all around was the kind of pristine, unblemished, singular view that climbers and TV audiences alike would go ga-ga over.

This gem of a place had been on the periphery of his life all this time and he'd never even known it was there. Forever in pursuit of the next extreme challenge, he'd never cared to look right under his nose.

Half the thrill had been the fact that he was miles from where he'd come from.

But this felt just as good. It seemed that at some point it had become about new experiences, and not about the exorcism of old ones.

Speaking of new experiences… He felt a tug on the back of his jacket. He turned to find Hannah puffing laboriously behind him.

'Slow…down…please,' she begged, between heaving breaths.

He did as she asked. Her face—or the small part of it he could see in between her beanie hat and the furry neck of the massive parka she'd borrowed from the hotel—was bright pink.

So caught up in his need to burn off some of the adrenalin that still infused him, even after the marathon efforts of that morning, though more likely because of them, he'd forgotten she wasn't an experienced climber herself.

She didn't cook. And by the looks of her she didn't exercise. Two things he'd never known. That, and the fact that she had an adorable strawberry-shaped birthmark in the very centre of her right butt cheek. He wondered what other gems he'd discover about his able assistant this long weekend.

'How much further?' she asked, hands on her knees.

'I thought you were meant to be my tour guide?'

She looked up at him, green eyes sharp. Then she waved a hand around. 'This is Cradle Mountain. That's Dove Lake. Gorgeous, huh? Now can I go back to the hotel?'

He laughed. She glared at him for even being *able* to laugh. It didn't help that she was trying to look angry while dressed in enough clothing for three people. If it wasn't so cold that he couldn't feel his nose, he would have believed she'd gone out of her way *not* to look sexy.

Little did she know he'd spent half the walk intent on getting their little field trip over and done with just so that they could get back to the hotel, where he planned on stripping off those layers one by one.

He glanced ahead. 'Come on. I see somewhere we can stop.'

'Oh, thank God.'

He laughed again. Then moved around behind her to give her a push up the track.

'Now, why didn't I think to wear rollerskates?' she threw over her shoulder. 'You could have done this the whole way.'

'Downhill too?'

'Right. Good point.'

They stepped over the safety fence and took a seat side by side on a large, flat outcrop. Bradley went straight for his water bottle, and jiggled his feet so his muscles wouldn't cramp up. Hannah flopped onto her back and didn't move.

From their position they had a perfect unheeded view over the curving lake and the ragged peaks of once sub-volcanic rock covered in winter green. Spirals of chimney smoke gave away the location of the Gatehouse, otherwise hidden discreetly in the alpine forest.

And if this was a glimpse of what the island had to offer then he was certainly willing to discover more—and soon. Lucky for him he had a human guidebook on the island on his team. One who had indicated an interest in taking a leap forward into producing. He'd half thought she was teasing. Maybe not. The creative wheels in his head began to crank up for the first time in a whole day.

'Having fun?' Hannah asked from her prone position.

'Loads. You?'

'Mmm. Would it be a complete *faux pas* to ask why on earth mountains float your boat?'

The wheels ground to a halt. The wide-open feeling he'd been experiencing closed down as tight as a submarine preparing to submerge.

'Why not mountains?' he shot back, giving her the same line he'd given a thousand times over, in press interviews and private conversations alike.

Her stare was blank. 'That's all I'm going to get?'

After last night, was left unsaid.

Bradley shuffled his backside on the hard ground.

Hannah rolled her eyes, not even pretending she was happy to await an answer with unlimited feminine patience. 'Fine,' she said. 'Go into shutdown mode. Just remember you're the one who said what happens here stays here. I took that to mean my attempt at Karaoke last night and my mother's undie-flashing high-kick extravaganza, as well as any other private revelations we might encounter.'

He looked down at her prostrate form. She was right. He'd been privy to parts of her life she'd *clearly* have preferred to keep separate from her Melbourne life. He owed her something of the same. A glimpse, at the very least. Just so that at the end of this strange weekend there would be no debts owed.

He braced his hands against the cold hard ground and looked out at the breathtaking vista. 'Why mountains…?'

He felt her head roll his way.

'It goes something like this. When you climb a mountain solo, the challenge is so great, so seemingly impossible, the pay-off is all the sweeter when you reach the peak. You've conquered the unconquerable. Alone. The glory is yours alone.'

They sat in silence a few moments as his words disappeared in the thin air. Then Hannah said, 'But you also have no one to cheer you on when you succeed. No one to look out for you if you fall.'

He slid a quick glance her way.

She was looking at him, brows furrowed. Interested, but concerned. Those pale green eyes were seeing far too much. Wanting too much from him.

How much would it take to negate Virginia's undie-flashing high-kicks? More than something he'd just as readily reveal to a journo, surely?

He cleared his throat and began slowly, the words unfamiliar and uncomfortable on his tongue. 'I've grown used to not having anyone cheer me on. Or care if I fall. In fact I prefer it that way.'

'I know you do. What I don't understand is why?'

He swallowed hard, his throat parched to the point of pain. He couldn't do this. Shouldn't have to. It was none of her damned business.

She dragged herself to sit and waited till he glanced her way. 'I miss having my dad tell me, "That's my girl," when I do something fantastic. I even miss my mother *tsking* when she had to bandage an unladylike scraped knee. I can live without them, but it's nice to know that if I ever need that kind of support I have friends who care about me, who'll come to my rescue. You do too, you know. You only have to let them.'

Bradley shook his head. 'It's my experience that you can never count on anyone but yourself.'

'What experience?' she pressed.

'Formative experience,' he allowed.

'So try again.'

'I can't.'

'Why not?'

The woman was like a dog with a bone!

He turned on her. 'You really want to know?'

'I really want to know.'

'Fine,' he said, the overly loud word echoing across the cavernous space. Then like shots from a rifle, he hit her with his father's departure before he was born. His mother's continued indifference. The day she'd decided looking after him was simply too hard. The plethora of addresses he'd temporarily inhabited. The way in which he'd seen people turn a helpless kid out of their home simply for the sake of ease.

Then suddenly the instances became more specific. Names, faces, places, dates. One draining disillusionment after another.

It was only after some time that he realised she'd curled a gloved hand through his elbow. Offering the kind of support she'd promised he'd have if he just asked.

'Do you see her much any more? Your mum?'

'I looked for her once,' he said, the words all but pouring from him now. 'When I was in my twenties. I'd made some money. I'd bought some real estate. I'd proved to myself that I was worth something. And the need to let her know it too built and festered inside of me until I had no choice but to track her down.'

Hannah gently leant her head against his bicep. Where others might have shuffled and fidgeted and changed the subject, she just absorbed. Like a sponge. He felt himself siphoning comfort from her, but rather than feeling guilty he sensed that she was utterly willing to give it. He felt no inclination to move away.

'I wrote her a letter. She wrote back. We agreed to meet. I turned up at the rendezvous. I saw her through the window on the street. It had been years, but I knew it was her in a second. She didn't look inside the restaurant. Never saw me sitting there. Never even made it through the front door. She was swallowed up by the sidewalk crowd and that was the last I ever saw of her.'

As he relived the moment inside his head he waited for it to burn, to hurt so deeply that he'd learned to close down his emotions so as never to feel so dependent on someone else's opinion of him ever again. Instead he felt a mild ache, a distant sorrow. Soothed by the cooling balm of Hannah's light touch.

They sat like that for some time. No sound bar the wind whistling through the low scrub at their feet. Watching a lone eagle soar across the bright blue sky in a beautiful dance.

'I know now it wasn't about me,' he said. 'It never had been. Whatever her issues were, no matter how good I was, how successful, how sensible, it would never have been enough.'

Then Hannah said, 'So, no singing into your mother's hairbrush?'

And he laughed. Loud. Hard. Releasing laughter. Whatever remaining tension there was inside him cracked across the valley like a thunderclap.

'No,' he said. 'Not that I can remember.'

Her hand slipped from his arm, and ridiculously—considering how well-dressed he was—he suddenly felt the cold.

She buried her face in her hands. 'God, I feel like such an idiot for whining about Virginia's maternal deficiencies. At least she tried. Not well, mind you, but there *was* effort. Why didn't you just tell me earlier to shut up and stop feeling so sorry for myself?'

Why? Because he'd never told anybody. Because he'd never wanted to reveal that weakness in his genes. Because he thought she had every right to be upset at her mother's behaviour.

She turned to smile at him. Then gave his shoulder a bump with hers as she said, 'Thank you.'

'For what?'

She shrugged. But didn't stop smiling.

That mouth. He couldn't for the life of him remember what had convinced him to yabber on when all he had to do was lose himself in that mouth.

The urge to kiss her then was a primal one. Swelling from deep inside. The urge to pull off her beanie and run his fingers through her hair. To slide his thumbs across those soft pink lips. To follow with his mouth. His tongue. To lie her down gently on the mossy ground and make love to her until night fell…

And they froze to death.

For a man whose best interests were his only compass, he felt as if he was no longer exactly sure which way was north.

As though she sensed he'd hit his limit, Hannah blithely changed the subject. 'I can't believe my little sister is getting married tomorrow.'

'Does it feel strange that she got there first?'

'Strange…? No. God, no. I've seen how it can turn out when it's done with no thought, no plan, no certainty. Case in point: my mother. I'm more cautious, I guess. I don't have Elyse's…blind faith. Besides, I'm a career woman, don't you know?'

He laughed softly. 'Good to know.'

She tipped her beanie.

She leant over and grabbed the toes of her boots. 'So, while we're on the subject, tell me how come some gorgeous, sparkly, doe-eyed young starlet didn't snap you up long ago?'

He shot her a glance, but she was still mighty intrigued with her boots.

'Who says I even *like* gorgeous, sparkly, doe-eyed… Okay. I'm gonna stop there, before I sound like an idiot.'

'Too late,' she grumbled.

But while her voice was light he heard the tremor beneath. Her question hadn't been blasé. She wanted to know. Because she was one of the people around him who cared.

He had to make sure she never made the mistake of caring too much.

'I like women,' he threw back. 'But I like being single more. I've always been perfectly transparent on that score. And I've yet to have any woman cling to my ankles as we parted ways. I like to think I've found my perfect balance.'

Hannah picked up a piece of shale and scraped at a tuft of grass. 'Did it ever occur to you that they leave thinking themselves lucky to have had you at all? Even if just for a moment? And that your "transparency" made it impossible for them to wish for more?'

He glanced at Hannah to find she was still super-interested in her shoes. He could have sworn her cheeks had grown pinker. And she was nibbling at her bottom lip.

Suddenly he could hear his blood pumping fast and furious in his ears.

'So you think I'm a catch?' He'd meant it as a joke, a tension-breaker. But his tone came out deadly serious. He wanted to know her answer. Needed to know. Because if this was already more to her than a weekend fling…

Hannah froze. So small beneath her many layers. She slowly lifted her head to squint at the horizon. 'To be a catch one first has to be caught.'

'Don't hide behind semantics,' he growled, temper rising, cursing her for not following the rules.

She turned on him, eyes gleaming. 'Fine. Then I can see why *some* people might think you're a catch. Rich, famous, okay-looking in the right light.'

'But not you?'

She rolled her eyes at the gods—asking for help, or perhaps for a lightning bolt to strike him where he sat. 'You forget,' she said, 'we've worked together too long. I know you far too well, Bradley—on your good days and your bad—to indulge in such daft fancy.'

His eyes bored into hers. Looking for a twinkle of humour. Or, at the other end of the spectrum, a straight out lie. But for once he could decipher nothing within the pretty green flecks.

He was left feeling finessed. Deflected. It was the strangest, most off-kilter sensation, not being the one holding all the cards. He didn't like it.

'Lucky for you you're too smart for me.'

'Lucky for you too.'

To all intents and purposes things were back on track. Unease settled on his shoulders all the same. He pulled himself to stand and stretched out his back, which was stiff with a tension that had nothing to do with the hike or the cold.

He held out a hand and helped her to stand. She attempted to brush herself down but, considering she was so padded he could probably roll her back down the hill, she couldn't reach half of her back.

He spun her around and briskly brushed the grass from her well-cushioned backside. She stood there and let him. Despite everything he felt himself getting aroused. Hell, three layers of clothes and he could *still* have brushed that backside all day and all night.

He pulled his hand back into the protection of his jacket sleeve and headed back down the trail, towards the lake, towards the Gatehouse, towards their suite.

Friction followed in his wake, and its name was Hannah.

All he knew was the second they got behind closed doors all that tension would translate into passion, and they'd not be able to get their hands on one another soon enough.

He curled his gloved fingers into his palm. He craved her enough to allow her to see into his well-protected past. He craved her so much he'd take her despite his niggling concern about her motivation.

She'd become an addiction. One he'd convinced himself he could go cold turkey on in three days' time. When they'd be back to working side by side, ten hours a day, six days a week. When late at night, after everyone had gone, he'd sit at his desk, looking out over the Melbourne skyline, with the lingering scent of her playing havoc with his senses.

'Speaking of work…' he said.

'I wasn't aware we had been,' she said, closer behind than he'd thought she'd be. Apparently she was in as much of a hurry as he to get back to their suite.

He slowed till they walked side by side. 'I was thinking earlier about taking Spencer on the Argentina trip.'

'Oh. Okay. Great. He'll be so excited—'

'Instead of you.'

A spark of hurt flashed across her eyes. His gut clenched unexpectedly. It only made him more determined. He held his ground. This was important. Important he do this now. Before things got any more complicated than they already were.

'Why?'

Because you care too much, and I clearly count on you too

much, and we're both setting ourselves up for disappointment, he thought.

He said, 'He did everything I asked of him yesterday, and well. I thought I ought to see how he goes with more responsibility.'

'Right. That's fair. But *I* set up that meeting. You wouldn't even be going if I hadn't wooed the Argentinians in the first place. I had to stay by the phone till after midnight every night for two weeks so as to be able to take their calls. I went above and beyond for—' Voice getting breathless, she pulled up short and shook her head. 'Why am I bothering? Do what you want. You always do. You're the boss.'

'Glad you remembered that.'

The look she shot him could have cut glass.

'Because, as your boss, I have a job for *you* to do.'

'Tell someone who's not on holiday,' she threw over her shoulder, and she took off down the path in front of him, her ponytail swinging accusingly at him.

He lifted his voice so as to be heard through the thin air. 'When we get back I want you to concentrate on putting together a full proposal for the Tasmania project. Locations. Treatment. Budget. Marketing. Everything.'

Her feet kicked up dust as she screeched to a halt. A full five seconds later she turned and stared up at him. 'Are you serious?'

'Have you ever known me to kid about work?'

'You? Never. Sonja and I behind your back? Every damn day.' Expression deadly serious, she took three steps up the hill and jabbed a finger into his chest. 'Now, let me get this straight. If I'm creating the project specs from scratch...'

'You'll be producing it.'

She shoved her hands into the pockets of her parka and breathed in, obviously thinking very deeply. The longer the moment passed, the more Bradley began to fidget. He'd expected her to leap into his arms with joy. He hadn't expected her to consider it. Or, worse, ponder why.

She spun on the spot. Jabbed him in the chest again. Then took a step back. Her eyes widened as she seemed to lose purchase on the loose ground. And suddenly she was halfway to head over heels.

Bradley reached out and grabbed her by the parka, his fingers clenching tight around the handful of slippery fabric while she wavered at a terrifying angle.

She glanced behind her and let out a cry. 'Bradley!'

'I know.' He could see the ground dropping away. He didn't even want to know the kind of angle she saw.

His fingers ached. Sweat broke out over his forehead. He dug his heels into the ground and, gritting his teeth, all but broke through the outer lining of her jacket in order to haul her back to safety.

She fell into his arms, breathing like a racehorse and shaking like a leaf.

He growled, 'You scared me half to death.'

'How do you think *I* feel?'

He couldn't help himself. He laughed. The sound ricocheted off the surrounding cliffs. It was either that or hold her so tight she'd begin to get ideas.

'So glad you can take my near death so lightly,' she said. 'I'm sure there are *some* who would miss me if I never made it back to Melbourne.'

He breathed deep through his nose and scraped her away from his front to look down into her face. 'Sonja would miss you once her heat got turned off.'

'True.'

'And Spencer. He'd be devastated.'

'He would. But that's all? That's some epitaph. Hannah Gillespie, twenty-five and single, falls to dramatic death from mountain. Terribly missed by semi-estranged family, chilly roommate, and dorky work-experience kid.'

Laughing, Bradley reached out and stroked the back of a finger across her cheek, sweeping her hair away from her eyes. When a strand remained she blew it out of the way with a shot of air from the side of her mouth.

Her eyes remained locked to his. All but begging for him to put her out of her misery and admit *he'd* miss her.

If she only knew how much. More than was in any way sensible. And it wasn't just about her work ethic. It was so very much about the lightness she lent to the rigours of his days.

'Remind me to chastise you for utter stupidity later. But for now...'

He crushed his mouth to hers and kissed her, and kissed her, and kissed her, until the ferocious force of their chemistry took over and nothing else mattered but how soon they could get back to the hotel.

Hannah got back to the room first, as Bradley had been forced to stay behind and read a half-dozen messages at Reception. She could have waited, but the excuse to take a moment apart was welcome.

She tore off her gloves, beanie, scarf, parka and shoes, and stretched out suddenly far lighter limbs as she padded into the room in jeans and long-sleeved T.

But no stretching could negate the confusion that was rocketing through her. She felt more as if she'd spent the past few hours on a rollercoaster rather than a mountain hike. Her roiling stomach could certainly attest to that.

Bradley sharing things from his past she'd never hoped he might impart. While still keeping his emotional distance any time she tried to close the gap.

Bradley offering her a chance at the Tasmania show. While unceremoniously ditching her from the Argentina pitch.

Bradley looking at her as if he wanted to devour her on the spot. While reminding her in no uncertain terms that the devouring wouldn't go on past that weekend.

Bradley, beautiful and bombastic and in his element.

No wonder the documentary-maker who'd discovered him halfway up K2, camera in hand, strong, beautiful face peering out from beneath a month's worth of dark facial hair, looking like the first real man on earth, had appeared unable to control her salivation when asked in the press about that fateful day. The day that introduced the mountaineer to television and Bradley Knight to an unprepared world.

Up, down. Up, down. Her emotions felt so twisted her heart had yet to stop beating as if she'd run a marathon.

Feeling prickly, and fractious, and uncooperatively turned on, Hannah trudged towards her room, stripping off more layers as she went. She passed near the spa. It twinkled darkly at her. As did her half-drunk glass of wine. And the discarded condom packet she'd torn open with her teeth.

And her father's watch bobbing in the water.

'No, no, *no!*' She ran around the edge of the pool and dropped to her knees, gathering it in her hands.

She'd been wearing it as she'd waited for Bradley to return. Had been wearing it still when she'd slipped into the pool. And now water drops sat suspended beneath the large face on which the hands hadn't moved since a little after three that morning.

'What's wrong?' Bradley's voice boomed from the door-way. Her cry must have been loud enough for him to hear it from the hall.

She shook her head. 'Nothing.'

He was at her back before she could scramble to her feet and walk away. To curl up in a ball and cry. In private.

'Hannah, I'm sorry, but I need to know that you're okay.'

She held up her watch. 'It's ruined.'

He glanced from her face to the watch, to the spa and back again. Then his whole body seemed to relax. 'Thank God. I thought you were hurt.'

Hannah recoiled as though slapped. Her voice rose as she

said, 'Did you not hear me say that my watch is ruined? It's dead.'

'Let me have a look.' He took the watch from her hands and checked it out under the light. 'Mmm… I'm not entirely sure it was built for underwater adventure. If you really need a watch there's a gift shop downstairs.'

She grabbed her watch back and cradled it in her palm. 'I don't want another watch. This was my dad's. It's the only thing of his I took with me when I left.'

Her heart squeezed. The turbulent tension of the afternoon was making it hard for her to see straight.

But it didn't matter. Bradley just stood there and said nothing. Doing his deer-caught-in-the-headlights impression. He might have been there for her on the side of the mountain, but the man clearly had no idea how to function in the face of real emotion.

It usually amused her when he froze up, as emotion was the only thing she'd ever seen him not do brilliantly. Right then it pissed her off royally. And instead of being able to revel in feeling pissed off she'd now found out *why* he was the way he was. His bloody mother had screwed him up for every other woman who came into his life.

Hannah had known he was stubborn. Known he was closed off. But the damage done had clearly affected every part of his life. If he couldn't trust his own mother, who could he trust? He was never going to commit. Not to anyone. Not to her.

In the next half-second everything came to a head. The build-up to her trip, her mother being her mother, having an affair with her boss, the fact that no matter what she did from that point her life in Melbourne would never be the same and, yeah, even the fact that her little sister was getting married before she'd even come close.

She felt angry. And hurt. And exposed. Like a great big throbbing nerve.

'Are you really going to just stand there and say nothing?' she asked. 'Nothing to try and make me feel like my heart *hasn't* just been torn from my chest? Can't you even pretend that you care about anything but yourself? Just for a second? You're killing me here!'

She didn't even realise she was pummelling his chest in a release of the most rabid frustration until he grabbed her by the wrists. Shaking still, she glared up at him, eyes burning so hot she might have been looking directly into the sun.

Slowly he lifted her hands and placed them on his shoulders. He didn't let go until they clamped down hard.

He placed his hands either side of her face, looked down into her eyes, stilling her, quieting her, making sure all she could think of was those eyes. That moment. That man.

His lips brushed hers with less pressure than a whisper. Again, and again, and again. Her bones turned to liquid. Her blood to molasses. She hadn't the energy to do anything but cling to him as he administered the most endearing kiss of her entire life.

Her earlier confusion and pain and frustration subsided as pleasure in its purest form took their place.

When he slid an arm beneath her knees and carried her into her bedroom she leant her head against his chest, taking solace from the heavy, steady beat of his heart.

He laid her gently on the bed. Carefully peeled her clothes from her warm body. And gazed at her for the longest time. She felt as if she was falling. From a great height. Even the touch of his eyes could send her spiralling over a precipice. Only he'd never be there to catch her emotionally. And it wasn't his fault. He simply wasn't equipped to know how.

He knelt over her—big, beautiful, a danger to her heart. He made love to her gently, slowly, with unbridled heat in his beautiful silver eyes. She didn't once care that he hadn't said a word. Hadn't eased her mind. Hadn't made any promises he couldn't keep.

How could she quibble when her body pulsed with a slow burn that steadily built until she felt as if she was made of pure fire?

Hannah woke up hours later, naked in bed, the room pitch-black. No moonlight gave her a sense of time or place. Only the warm thrum of her body reminded her who and where she was.

She carefully slid her foot sideways until it kicked a man's hairy calf. Bradley hadn't gone back to his own room. He'd stayed.

The kick must have unsettled him, for he rolled over, draping an arm across her waist, tucking his knees into the crook of hers.

She tucked her sheets to her chin and stared at the dark ceiling, her heart pounding, wondering how she was going to get through the next two days in one piece.

CHAPTER NINE

THE afternoon of the wedding Hannah stood staring at her reflection in the bathroom mirror.

After hours at the hands of myriad professionals, her hair hung in long lush waves, a portion kept from her face with the use of a delicate black and silver butterfly clip, and great big dark, smoky eyes looked back at her. Cheekbones most women would kill for. Soft, moist, bee-stung lips.

She looked…changed. But it had little to do with the makeover.

There was a relaxation of the constant furrow in her brow. An ease of movement that came with the most languid muscles in the world. All the make-up in the world couldn't do as much for a girl's complexion as a weekend spent in Bradley Knight's arms.

All of which was going to come to a screaming halt after the next day. After wishing this weekend would fly, she now found herself wishing it would stop speeding by so very fast.

She was swiping on one last layer of gloss on her lips when a light knock sounded at her bedroom door.

Bradley. Her heart sang. For a moment she had the strangest thought: *He's not meant to see me before the wedding!* A half-second later, when she remembered rightly that they were just bystanders in today's proceedings, she felt a right fool.

'Come in,' she called, shoving the lipgloss wand back into its tube.

Bradley didn't wait to be asked twice. He swept the door open and she caught a waft of his familiar scent on the rush of air. She breathed it as if it was an elixir.

Feigning fixing her hair, she shot him the quickest glance.

Black dinner suit cut to make the most of his broad angles. Hair slicked back. Freshly shaven.

He looked so unfairly beautiful she had to remind herself to breathe.

You've seen him in a dinner suit before, you goose! Many many times! In tuxes just as many. Heck, you've even tied his bow tie before shoving him into cars and off to attend glamorous awards nights.

Only those times it had been business. This time he was all dolled up to be her date. He'd *shaved* to be her date.

She widened her eyes at her reflection and silently told herself to cool it. He'd probably shaved because the mountain air was making him itch.

'There,' she said. 'Enough preening. That's about as good as it's going to get.'

She turned to face him, fully expecting to find him leaning indolently against the doorjamb, nonchalantly flicking a piece of lint from his jacket.

Instead he stood stock still, his broad body filling the doorway, shoulders stiff, jaw clenched, nostrils flared, hands in trouser pockets. He looked as if he wouldn't have had a clue if his entire suit was covered in lint.

His resolute gaze was locked onto her dress. The long full skirt swished at her toes, but it was the top half that him enthralled. From a twisting halterneck, heavy black fabric cut away at the sides, kissing the edge of her breasts and sweeping low at the back, to come together just above her buttocks, leaving her back completely bare.

She saw the moment it occurred to him that it left no room whatsoever for underwear bar the tiniest hipster G-string. His nostrils flared again, and he dragged his eyes shut. She even thought she heard a groan.

She summoned her inner imp to break the tension turning her insides to knots. She held out her skirt and let it fall in soft folds against her thighs. 'So, what do you think?'

Bradley opened his eyes. They followed the movement, and a muscle clenched in his jaw. 'You don't want to know what I'm thinking.'

'Try me.'

When his eyes finally locked onto her eyes she literally swayed towards him, so hot, so brutal, so intense was his expression.

Then his eyes glinted, and his beautiful mouth curved into a corrupting smile. He took a step her way.

She shuffled back—only to bang into the bench. Her fingers gripped the cold marble so hard they hurt.

And Bradley just kept on coming.

'I'm thinking about poor Roger,' he said.

'What?' Hannah shook her head, but she'd heard him right. 'You're thinking about *Roger*?'

'Poor kid's going to split a seam when he gets a load of you.'

'Oh.'

His covetous eyes caressed her throat, as if he was imagining burying his face right there.

The memory of just how it felt when he trailed deep hot kisses across her neck overcame her. Her head dropped back and she let out a long sigh.

At the sound his gaze locked on her mouth. If possible his eyes turned darker. Hotter. Harder. Completely absorbed. She snapped her mouth shut. All that carefully applied gloss…

All the while he continued edging closer, until he all but

filled the bathroom. His beautiful face gazed hungrily down at her from a half-dozen angled mirrors. There was no escape.

He came as close as he possibly could without actually touching her. She had to tilt her head to look at him. To be bewitched by the multiple shades of hot silver glinting in his eyes.

He rested his hand on the cold marble bench, his fingers mere millimetres from hers. She wasn't sure if it was the taste of her toothpaste or the scent of his that tickled her tongue. Either way, she licked her lips. And this time Bradley didn't even try to hide his groan.

'He has a crush on you, you know,' he said, his voice so raw, so deep, it rumbled through her body, leaving trails of goosebumps in its wake.

She blinked. 'Who?'

'Roger.'

She frowned. Again with Roger! She'd opened her mouth to tell him to forget about Roger, for Pete's sake, when finally she got it.

Bradley was using the guy as some kind of prophylactic in order to get her out of this small room without having her expensive, one-of-a-kind dress torn from her body an hour before her sister's wedding.

It was a heady feeling, knowing she could make a man feel that close to losing his grip. Bring him to the absolute cliff-face of sexual need. One touch and she had no doubt she could send him over the edge. The fact that she was doing all those things to *this* man...

Her body felt so quivery and hot her elbows threatened to give way. The sexual tension swirling about the room was intoxicating. It felt as if there was no more oxygen. As if the only way for her to breathe again was to fulfil the need clawing at her insides.

But, dammit, he was right about the dress! There was no

getting out of it, or around it, or beneath it, without ruining its soft folds.

She bit her lip. *Damn.* She'd have to redo her lip gloss. Then again, there was plenty more where that came from.

Without another thought she lifted up onto her toes and pressed her lips to his.

For a moment he resisted. He stared into her eyes and held firm. All that effort he'd put into keeping his hands off was binding him as tight as a corkscrew.

Fortunately she was a glass of champagne ahead of him, and not feeling nearly so well-behaved. She closed her eyes, tilted her head, and kissed him again. Slowly. Softly. Teasing him with the lightest flick of her tongue where his lips pressed together.

When her tongue met his she flinched, but only for the briefest of seconds. For finally he was kissing her back. His lips sliding against hers. His tongue tasting hers. Curling about it, toying with her, showing just how much control he had left in reserve.

After what felt like eons later he pulled away. Without his kiss holding her upright any more she leant her forehead against his chest.

'Apple-flavoured?' he asked, licking his lips.

She smiled at his tie. 'Tasmania is the Apple Isle.'

He laughed, and her stomach did a neat little backflip.

Then he stepped back. And frowned. 'Something doesn't look right.'

She spun to check her dress wasn't tucked into the back of her G-string. 'What?'

'I'm not sure. But I think something's missing.'

He pulled a bag from the gift shop from behind his back. Her heart skipped and tripped and turned over on itself.

'Cradle Mountain playing cards?' she said, with a nonchalance she was far from feeling. 'Souvenir soap? A really tiny towelling bathrobe? Though why I'd need any of those things at a wedding—'

'Shut up and open the damn thing.' He dangled the pretty green bag from a hooked finger.

Brow furrowed, she pulled out a large hinged box. Clueless as to what it might be, she opened it—and then forgot how to breathe. A hand fluttered to her heart.

'Bradley?' she said, glancing up at him.

He took the box from her hands. 'Here—allow me.'

And then with gentle hands he slid her father's watch over her wrist and clasped it. Only now it worked. And was a perfect fit rather than slipping up her arm every time she moved.

'I had Housekeeping suspend it over their industrial dryer in the hope that drying it out might do the trick. It did. Then I asked if they had a jeweller nearby, and they said there was one staying at the hotel as part of the high school reunion party. He took out a couple of links.'

The massive watch sat heavy and familiar on her arm, but her eyes were all for Bradley.

He laughed softly, then took her hand in his. 'Come on. We'd best be off. Time's marching on.'

She followed him out of the room. Let him hand her the beaded purse from the kitchenette bench and help her on with her flat silver sandals.

Time was marching on all too fast. She could practically hear the seconds booming inside her. Time till the weekend was over. Time till they flew back home in his jet. Till they went their separate ways at the airport. Till she reported for duty first thing Tuesday morning.

And went on as though nothing had happened.

As though they'd never made love.

Never been exposed to so much about one another's most private lives.

A strange kind of pain made itself at home beneath her ribs.

She rubbed at the spot with one hand, while smiling blithely at Bradley as he swept her out through the suite door.

Bradley stood next to Hannah, waiting for the lift to take them downstairs. He felt strangely shaken. And stirred.

Seeing Hannah back there, looking amazing in that knock-out dress, he'd felt such a riddle of emotions he hadn't been able to pin down a one. Till now. Now they joyfully lined up one after the other, mocking him.

He spared her a glance. Her face was tilted as she watched the numbers count down. The only giveaway that she was as tense as he was, was the deep rise and fall of her chest.

He ran a hand across his chin, looking for the familiar painful sharp rasp of day-old hair against his palm to knock him to his senses, and was surprised to find it so smooth.

He let his hand drop and glowered at his wavering reflection. *Why not get the girl a corsage, if you're going to act like a sixteen-year-old punk going to the prom?*

He needed to get some perspective back. And fast.

This was a fling. Nothing more. A bit of holiday fun.

For her it was holiday fun. She was the one on holiday. He was *meant* to be scouting the place for gorgeous, treacherous locations for a future gig. The only gorgeous, treacherous thing he'd had in his sights was five feet six and nibbling at her ridiculously sexy bottom lip.

The lift doors opened to reveal a handful of people already inside. He ushered Hannah inside, careful not to touch her. Hell, if he was really afraid that a touch would only lead to more then he was in more trouble than he'd thought.

She glanced at him, caught his eye and smiled. Her lovely green eyes grew dark and dreamy, her smile all too knowing, and every inch of exposed skin flushed pale pink.

Desire rocketed through him so hard and so fast he reached out to grip the hip-high rail for support.

He should have left the second he'd realised she had a

crush on him. Or at the very least the moment he'd sensed how unusually hard it was going to be to walk away. Enough was enough.

He'd put on a show at the wedding, so as not to embarrass her in front of her family. Then he'd feign urgent work and head off. Cut the weekend short. Organise his jet to pick her up the next night while he scored whatever seat he could get on the next commercial plane off the island.

And then Tuesday morning she'd be back at his side. On her favourite chair in his office, cowboy-boot clad feet on the corner of his desk, eating store-bought Caesar salad with a plastic fork. And all he'd want to do was wipe his desk clean with one sweep of an arm and throw her down on the table and make love to her until the building shook.

What a wretched ruddy mess.

The lift stopped at Elyse's floor. Hannah was off to do her maid of honour duties. She turned to say something, glanced at her watch, then laughed softly. With a quick wave she lifted her skirt and walked from the lift.

Watching her walk away, he felt a strange tug somewhere in the vicinity of his chest. He rubbed the spot, figuring his recent feats of athleticism in the bedroom had pulled something.

Nevertheless, as the lift doors closed, inside Bradley's head he ran a long list of mountains he'd yet to climb, beginning with the tallest, hardest, steepest, and furthest away.

Hannah stared at a crack in the concrete balustrade on the balcony outside the bathroom in which Elyse was 'taking a moment'—which in Gillespie female speak was elegant for 'taking a whizz'.

She sniffed in a lungful of cold mountain air, checked her watch. The watch that had used to be her father's watch. Only now when she looked at it she saw the watch Bradley had rescued.

She saw that it was only five minutes till the wedding was

due to start. She'd reached to knock on the bathroom door when the door opened.

'Your man is a beauty.' Elyse slurred the words ever so slightly as she swanned out, continuing the one-sided conversation she'd been having when she first went in. She screwed up her face and held out her hands as if she was pinching an imaginary pair of cheeks. 'He's so big, and manly, and rugged. Rock-god-sexy, you know?'

Oh, Hannah knew. All too well. She had barely gone a minute that weekend not thinking exactly those thoughts. And more. In intimate remembered detail. But only four and a half minutes before Elyse was due to marry sweet Tim wasn't the time to agree.

When the bride-to-be spun around a turn and a half and began heading back into the bathroom, Hannah took her by the elbow and steered her right.

'Lyssy, hon, how much have you had to drink?'

'Just a glass of champagne. I was feeling so anxious I thought I might throw up. And Mum'd kill me if I got anything on this dress.'

Right. Okay. *This* she could handle. In fact it was the most blissfully perfect time for a mini-crisis. She so needed something to take her mind off Bradley. And the watch. And the way he'd looked at her in the lift. And the inconveniently persistent glow that had refused to abate since she woke up that morning.

Time to get her sister married.

Her brave little sister.

Hannah wanted the real thing one day too. She really did. But she couldn't escape the niggling doubts. What if you stopped loving him? What if he didn't love you enough? What if you loved him more than life itself and he died?

Elyse flumped down onto a concrete bench. Hannah winced. If she didn't get moss stains on the masses of ivory silk it would be a miracle.

'Do you think it's possible to love one man your whole life?' Elyse asked. 'To be happy sleeping with one man for the rest of your days? Or the rest of his? Or...you know what I mean.'

Hannah knew exactly what she meant. *Look at Mum—do you think we have her genes?* She sat down carefully next to her sister and took her by the hand.

'I'm not sure I'm the one to ask. I've never been in love before.'

Elyse's eyes opened wide. 'Never?'

Hannah shook her head.

'Not even with Mr Heaven in Blue Jeans out there? Jeez, you have high standards.'

Did she? Was that the problem? She knew she'd moved on from men because they didn't give her that all-important spark, or make her laugh, or have anything brilliant to say, or their fingernails were a weird shape, or their forearms were too short. She'd always told herself she was simply waiting to find everything she wanted in one man. The truth was she'd already found it. In Bradley. Even thinking his name took the warm glow inside her to an all-time high, and Hannah's cheeks heated so fast she felt slightly dizzy.

Then Elyse's bottom lip began to tremble, and she gratefully switched her focus back to the bride. 'Lyssy? Are you okay?'

'I wish Dad was here.' Two great fat tears fell down her cheeks.

Hannah's lungs clenched so hard it physically hurt. She swallowed down the lump that had formed instantly in her throat. Blinked away her own tears. It had taken two long hours to do her make up and she was not going through that again.

She turned to reach for her bag in search of tissues, but Elyse's loud echoing sniff stopped her. Elyse didn't need tissues. She needed her big sister.

She wiped her sister's tears away with the pad of her finger. 'I miss him too. Every day. But you know what? He would be *so* proud of us today. Looking all glossy and glam. Me the high-flying Melbournian. You marrying the man you adore. His girls have done good.'

'We have, haven't we? One thing I remember is him telling me he wanted nothing more than for us to be happy. And I'm happy. Really happy. You're happy, right?'

Hannah blinked. Was she happy? Much of the time. Could she be happier? You bet.

'Bradley would make you happy,' Elyse said, mirroring her thoughts so closely Hannah wondered if she'd said so out loud. 'At least tell me he's good in bed.'

Good? As words went, it was not even the correct language with which to describe what being with Bradley was like. French could maybe do it. Or Italian. Definitely Italian.

'Those long fingers…' Elyse shivered.

'Elyse!'

But Elyse was looking at her with such hope she couldn't deny her. Not on her wedding day.

'Fine. He's… It's better than I ever imagined it could be.'

'Then marry him!'

Hannah shook her head. Then shrugged. How could she explain to a woman about to marry the love of her life the sad little 'what happens in Tasmania' deal she'd made in order to get whatever scraps she could from the guy? 'I don't matter right now. Your life is yours. Not mine. Not Mum's. So, Miss Bride, are you ready to go become Mrs Tim Teakle?'

'I am,' Elyse answered without hesitation. 'I love him so much it hurts, with the most beautiful kind of ache right in the centre of my heart. It makes me want to laugh and twirl and sing. He makes me glow all over.'

'Then what else is there to do but go out there and marry the guy?'

Elyse threw her arms around her and they hugged. Tight. For an age.

Hannah closed her eyes and tried to block out the realisation that Bradley was the only man she'd ever known who made her want to laugh and twirl and sing. And she was glowing so hard right then she could barely see straight.

Something tumbled inside her, as though she'd accidentally stumbled upon the final part of a combination lock.

Oh, hell no. She *loved* him, didn't she?

She loved how he made her think. How he made her melt. Even how he made her halfway to crazy. He stretched her to her very limits and beyond.

She squeezed her eyes shut tighter as a bittersweet pain sliced through the glow.

The previous night, just before they'd made love, she'd run her hand down his stubbled cheek, looked him in the eye, and said out loud the words she was trying to use to convince herself. 'You're *so* the wrong guy for me.'

Bradley's eyes had darkened. Then he'd all but lit up as he'd smiled and said, 'Don't you ever forget it.'

She loved him. But what did that matter when he was too damaged and too stubborn to love her back? What was she going to do?

What *could* she do but go out there and be the most supportive maid of honour ever? Do everything in her power to avoid Bradley so that he'd never, *ever* have a single clue how she felt. Excellent plan.

Then Hannah saw the time. 'We're late!'

Elyse pulled away and straightened herself up. Then with a grin she settled back on the bench and said, 'I love him to pieces, but it can't hurt to keep him wondering just a little, right?'

Hannah sniffed out a laugh. Elyse clearly missed their dad as much as she did, but by God she was her mother's daughter.

* * *

Bradley lounged in one corner of a pink velvet chaise against a wall of the Gatehouse ballroom.

Above him a pink chandelier jiggled gently in time with the music. Beside him pink peonies floated in a crystal bowl filled with water. He was drinking coffee from pink floral Royal Doulton china. Elyse and Tim's wedding was the place pink had come to die.

The speeches were over. The cake was cut. The guests were a few champagnes down. 'Time Warp' blared from the speakers. The post-wedding party had well and truly begun.

But he didn't much care what the other guests were up to. There was only one he was searching for. One who seemed to have slipped through his grasp a good dozen times that day, with the excuse of having something else maid of honourly to do.

'Time Warp' finished, and the sexy drum beat of 'I Need You Tonight' belted out. The older dancers fled for water and chairs, while the young ones cheered and danced on. Young ones including the bride and, with her, a sleek brunette in a backless black dress.

Elyse might well have inherited her mother's dance floor skills, but Bradley would never know. His eyes remained locked on Hannah.

Or, more specifically, on the sway of her hips that had nothing to do with skill or lessons and everything to do with her innate sensuality. On the creamy flash of leg when the split of her skirt swished just the right way. The way she tossed her long hair with the same complete and utter abandon she showed in bed.

Every sensuous move reminded him of how it felt having her wrapped around him, how her warm skin gave beneath his touch, how right it sounded when she breathed his name as she fell apart in his arms.

She raised her arms in the air. Eyes closed. Completely

unaware of the pack of men dancing as near as they could get to her without alerting their dates.

A swan in a duck pond. She didn't fit in there any more—if she ever had. She had outgrown the people and the place. She'd never stay.

He'd followed her and hijacked her holiday so as to make sure she'd return to Melbourne. He was now sure she would. He'd stayed in order to make sure she had a good time—in order to carry out his thanks for all her hard work. He was more than certain she had. If they were the only reasons he was there, he might as well just leave a message with someone that he'd left, then turn and walk away.

He put his coffee on the table and leant forward, bracing his hands on his knees. Then he sat back in his seat. *Dammit.*

'It's bad form to leave before the bride and groom.'

Bradley turned to find Hannah's mother sinking down onto the other end of the chaise, a vision in apple-green. If she'd intended to stand out against the sea of pink, she'd succeeded.

'You've outdone yourselves today, Virginia. I know a class production when I see one.' He held out a hand to give hers a congratulatory shake. She slid a glass of beer into it instead. She lifted her own in salute, and downed half in one go.

Bradley took a more conservative sip. By the look in the woman's sharp eyes he had a feeling he was going to need to be sober for what was about to come.

'I know your type,' she said.

And we're off.

'What type is that?'

'You're a player. Not a stayer. I know because, bar one, I've been drawn to men just like you my entire life.'

'This concerns you how?'

She stared at him, her eyes a different colour from her daughter's but with the same intensity.

Bradley placed his beer on the table and looked out into the crowd. 'Bad form or not, would you prefer me to leave?'

Virginia laughed. 'Please. Do I look like a bouncer?'

Bradley spared her a glance. She looked like trouble, not the mother of the bride. But she was also Hannah's mother. As such, he had no intention of getting into a sparring match.

'Nevertheless...' he said, rising to leave.

She placed a taloned hand on his knee and pressed down hard. 'I see the way you look at my daughter.'

He didn't dignify what was clearly meant as an accusation with a response. Though his eyes did slide straight to the dance floor. Hannah had disappeared yet again. He swore beneath his breath.

'Elyse is far more like me,' Virginia continued. 'She's a shrewd operator. She swam through sharks to find her sweet minnow. As for Hannah? There's not a cunning bone in that girl's body. She plays fair, tries hard, and assumes that will lead her to green pastures. In life, work and love. So much her father's daughter that one. Sees the good in everyone—even those who don't deserve it.'

Bradley's head suddenly felt tight, as if it was being pressured from a dozen different directions. He looked to Virginia, who was watching him like a hawk. He said, 'If you're about to ask my intentions with regard to Hannah, you're going to be disappointed. I am a private person, and as such my business is not open for discussion.'

'Bradley?'

Bradley looked up to find Hannah standing over them. Tousled, pink-cheeked, gorgeous. His blood warmed ten degrees just looking at her. The woman who'd been avoiding him all day.

Then he saw her brow was furrowed in concern, while her eyes flicked between him and her mother. She must have felt the tension fair across the room.

'Everything okay?' Hannah asked.

'Fabulous. Sit,' Virginia said, patting the space between

them on the chaise. 'Bradley was just telling me this is the best wedding he's ever been to. Weren't you, Bradley?'

Hannah looked at him, eyebrows dipping deeper. 'Did he also mention this is the *first* wedding he's ever been to?'

Virginia laughed as if it was the funniest thing she'd ever heard. 'He did not. In fact he's been quite tight-lipped about a good many things. Such as what the two of you think you're up to.'

'All righty,' Hannah said, her tone impatient. Then she grabbed Bradley by the hand and hauled him to his feet. 'Come on, boss. I feel like dancing.'

'Darling,' Virginia drawled, 'I just want to get to know your friends.'

'Leave it alone, Virginia. I mean it.' Then Hannah's hand wrapped tight around his and she put herself bodily between him and her mother. As if she was saying, *If you want to take a swing at him you'll have to go through me.*

What a woman. Five feet six and fifty kilos dripping wet, protecting *him*, six feet four inches of hard-won muscle on muscle.

No wonder she was so good at absorbing the million little dramas a day that came his way at work. Making his life seem easier just by being around. She'd been doing it her whole life. Only now, rather than seeing it as to his advantage, he wondered how many hits she'd have to take before she stopped feeling them. Stopped feeling anything. Before that beautiful bright Hannah light disappeared for ever.

He held her hand tight and curled it through his arm. Time someone absorbed the drama for her for a change.

'Lovely chatting to you, Virginia,' Bradley said.

She raised her glass in salute. 'Bradley. I hope you'll at least find the time to say a proper goodbye.'

The double meaning hit right where it was meant to. The jab of a mother protecting her kid the only way she seemed to know how.

'I'll do my best.'

Virginia nodded. Then turned and called out to another guest, insisting they join her for a 'drinkie'.

Hannah tugged Bradley's hand and yanked him towards the dance floor as though her life depended on it.

'What the heck was that all about?'

'What?'

Her expression was deadpan, then she just shook her head and let the music take her cares away.

And watching her sway, her tousled hair swinging, sexy muscles playing across her beautiful bare back, hips bopping in time with the music, he wondered what his drink had been spiked with if he'd even thought about cutting this weekend a second shorter than it could be.

He tugged her into his arms, slid a hand down her back, and breathed deep as she trembled at his touch.

One more day.

CHAPTER TEN

A SLOW song began.

Bradley saw Roger nearby, hitching his pants and fixing his bow tie, slicking back his ridiculously preppy blond hair, Hannah firmly in his sights.

He swung Hannah out to the end of his arm and growled, 'This one's mine,' in the kid's ear, before sweeping Hannah back into his arms.

With a sigh she didn't even try to hide, Hannah slid her hands up his chest, over his shoulders and around his neck. He fought the intense shudder her touch created, but there was no stopping it.

'I can't believe it's night already. The wedding's over. Elyse made it up the aisle. Tim didn't faint. Mum has yet to try to take the stage. Things couldn't have gone better. And then, I have to say, *this* is very nice,' she said, her voice husky as hell, her fingers playing gently with the hair at the back of his neck.

He wrapped her tighter. His erection pressed into her stomach. She made no mention of it, even though there was no way she could avoid the heat and hardness of him through the thin fabric of her dress. She just shimmied and swayed and smiled, and waved to familiar faces dancing past.

There was no way he was walking off the dance floor with that kind of action going on in his pants. But unfortunately having this woman sliding her body against his meant it wasn't going anywhere either.

Only when she shook her long hair from her shoulders and glanced up at him, a telling gleam in her eyes, did he realise she knew. And she was revelling in it. Then the minx only moved more softly, more sweetly against him.

He slid one hand into her hair and the other lower, down the gentle curve of her back and to the more daring curve below.

Take that.

Her pupils dilated till her eyes were dark as night. While sexual attraction sparked within them as bright and infinite as stars.

Then she waved to a guy on the other side of the room.

'Who was that?'

She sighed. 'Simon. High school crush.'

He pulled back just enough to see into her eyes. 'Shall I leave the two of you alone?'

'Too late. He's married with four kids.' She leant her head against his chest and hummed blissfully, almost standing on his foot every few steps.

'To think,' he said, pulling her hand into his shoulder, 'that could have been you.'

'Doubtful. He runs his dad's hardware store. He was never going anywhere. After Dad died I just never fit in here.' With a flick of her thumb towards the door she said, 'I was outta here the minute I had enough money saved.'

'Looking for adventure?'

Her fingers slid deeper into his hair and stayed there. Her voice was soft when she said, 'Looking for something.'

Like that, they swayed for a good long while. Lost in their own thoughts while caught up together in a familiar, inescapable swirl of sexual tension that only grew as they pressed closer, found ways to tuck more tightly into one another and caress each other till it ached.

Bradley couldn't take it any longer. 'Can we get the hell out of here?'

She raised her heavy head from his chest, her eyes dark and drowsy, as she said, 'I just have one last maid of honour job to do, then I'm off duty. You know what? It's one that you could help with.'

'Having seen inside your "just in case" suitcase, I'm understandably nervous about saying yes before I know what I'm getting myself into.'

She grinned. 'It involves masses of rose petals, bubble bath, champagne and condoms.'

'Then, hell, yeah.'

Moonlight shone through the unadorned bedroom window, leaving the room bathed in an eerie silver light.

Bradley wasn't sure how long he'd been awake, a pillow cradled behind his head as he watched Hannah sleep. Her skin was baby-soft, her cheeks pink from the heat of the still flickering fire he'd lit after the first time they'd made love. A slight frown puckered her brow, and her hair splayed out over the snow-white pillowcase.

And all he could think was that tomorrow things would be back to the way they'd been.

With one undeniable difference.

She wasn't like other women he'd been with. She wasn't cynical and nonchalant and insanely independent. She was sweet, sincere, loyal, and clearly not the type to indulge in a holiday fling.

He'd known that before he'd started this thing with her. He'd known it before he'd set foot on Tasmanian soil. Hell, he'd known it the minute Sonja had suggested the idea at that café in faraway Melbourne.

Yet he'd still let it happen.

He could blame the ridiculously decadent suite. He could blame the rugged beauty and unbelievably fresh air of Tasmania. Or he could blame Venus and Mars.

He could blame the lightness inside her, the ready laughter

nd easy joy that contrasted so blatantly with the darkness of his own experiences. He could blame the fact that she gave him balance. Balance he'd never before had. Balance he secretly savoured.

But the truth was her mother had been right. He was a player, not a stayer. Worse, he was a rotten no-good bastard who didn't deserve to be defended the way this woman had leapt to his defence.

He had nobody to blame but himself.

She muttered something in her sleep, and then finished off with a husky laugh. He hated himself even as the sound of her laughter made him grow hard for her again.

He slid the back of a finger beneath a swathe of dark hair on her forehead, and then let his finger trail down her cheek, behind her ear, to that sensitive spot in the dent at her shoulder.

She stirred, stretching bent arms over her head, legs to the foot of the bed, collecting the sheet with them and revealing her naked torso. Her gently rounded breasts. Her soft, smooth nipples.

The ache in his gut was so convoluted, so heavy, so deep, he had no desire to spend any time discerning what it meant. Instead he leaned over and took one warm rose-pink peak into his mouth.

She groaned. Awake in an instant. Her hands clamping into his hair.

She tasted like caramel and sunshine. It was nothing less than cruel that a woman could taste so good. He closed his eyes as his tongue continued to circle her nipple until she was all but crying out, while holding his head to the spot as if she never wanted him to stop.

He rolled until he was on top of her, using the strength in his arms to stop himself crushing her, while his tongue delved into the shadow at the base of her other breast, then licked slowly and thoroughly upwards without touching her nipple.

As she writhed beneath him, pressing her warm flesh against him, he felt such an urge to plunge himself into her, again and again, until all rational thought was lost to the red mist of pleasure.

It took every ounce of strength he had to keep himself propped on his shaking arms. He'd done nothing to deserve giving in to his raging desires. He deserved to be punished.

He slid to her side. She groaned in protest, her back arching, a hand sliding down his arm, across his chest, scraping through the arrow of hair leading to his...

He closed his eyes. If this was punishment, send him to hell.

He grabbed her hand and restrained it over her head. Using a heavy leg, he pinned her writhing body to the bed.

Breathing heavily, eyes closed, she stopped moving, clearly doing her best to stay put, as though she knew it would be worth it to do as she was told. She was one clever girl.

The pale skin of her breast was shining from his ministrations, and slowly, achingly slowly, he lowered his head until he took her dry, peaked nipple into his mouth.

He worked his way down the sweetest spots of her body until he couldn't stand it any longer. There was no way he could last another minute without enjoying that mouth.

Look at me, he demanded inside his head. He wanted her to know who was kissing her. He needed her to know. To remember.

She opened slumberous eyes and looked right into the dark depths of his soul. Then, as if she knew just what he needed she pulled his head to hers and kissed him.

The sun was just starting to send its pink glow through the floor-to-ceiling windows when Hannah quietly threw on jeans, T-shirt, poncho and boots, scrunched her hair back in a ponytail and quickly washed her face before tiptoeing out of the suite.

She needed a walk. A walk and a think. And clearly she didn't do her best thinking when Bradley was lying sprawled out naked in her bed.

The *bing* of the lift was overly loud in the pre-dawn quiet. She glanced back at the door leading to their suite, but it stayed closed.

Once downstairs, she padded across the empty reception area and straight out through the front doors. The whip of cold slapped her across the face so sharply she almost stumbled. But that morning it was just what she needed.

Outside the sky was silvery grey, the trees stark and brown, the ground a winter wonderland. The air was still, the birds asleep, the only sound the soft fall of snow from overladen trees.

It was like a dream.

She stood there, trying her very best to compartmentalise the whole weekend that way—to believe it was all a lovely dream and to understand that when she woke up the next morning she would be well and truly back in the real world.

Real life suddenly felt so foreign. So far away. And more than a little scary. All she had to do to fix that was convince Bradley that they should stay. For ever. Eating Room Service, having someone else wash the sheets, making love. Easy!

No. She couldn't tell him. How could she? When he'd made it clear again and again that he was not the settling kind of man? His past might have sown the seeds for that behaviour, but he'd cultivated it heartily ever since.

She couldn't tell him and have it thrown back in her face. There was nothing worse than having love with nowhere to put it. When her dad had died it had hurt like nothing else. Had broken things inside her. She'd wandered like a lost kitten for months. Years, even. Until she'd found her feet, her place, her*self* in Melbourne.

No matter which way she looked, neither of them had the stamina or the history to support anything long-term.

She sighed, and her breath puffed white. She rubbed a finger beneath her cold nose, wrapped her poncho tighter around her, and headed back into the blissful warmth.

Reception was no longer empty. A woman in a tight skirt, patterned tights, high boots and a mulberry wrap and matching beret was standing at the desk. She turned at the sound of the front doors swinging.

'Hannah.'

'Mum.' The endearment popped out before she had time to even think 'Virginia', but her mother seemed not to notice, so she didn't edit herself. Instead she slowly headed over her way.

Virginia glanced at the colossal clock suspended above her. 'What are you doing up so early?'

'Just taking a walk. Needed some fresh air. You?'

'Heading home.'

'Oh. But didn't they tell you that your room's paid up for one more day?'

'They did. But I don't think Elyse needs to come downstairs the morning after her wedding night to find her mother at breakfast, do you?'

'No,' she blurted. 'I don't. That's really thoughtful of you.'

Virginia laughed. 'To make myself scarce? Isn't it?'

A man returned to Reception with some paperwork which he slid to Virginia. She thanked him with a smile that made the guy blush to the roots of his hair.

Filling out her paperwork, Virginia said, 'And where's your plus one?'

Figuring there was no point denying they'd been…whatever they were, she said, 'Asleep.'

Virginia laughed. 'If I were you I'd make it my mission in life to be there when he wakes up.'

Hannah swallowed hard. If the choice was hers alone she'd want nothing more for evermore. She felt an unexpected urge to confide in her mum. But history clamped her mouth shut on the subject.

Instead she assembled a grin and said, 'Never fear, I'm heading back that way now.'

'You always were a smart girl. And as it turns out one heck of a wedding-planner. The weekend was simply divine.'

'Wasn't it?' Hannah said with a smile.

'Sophisticated, fun, and a party that'll go down in local folklore. All thanks to you.'

Hannah blinked, trying to find a path inside her woolly, chilly, early-morning brain that could make sense of receiving such praise from her mother. In the end she simply said, 'Thanks.'

Virginia brushed it off with an elegant shrug. 'I've a half dozen names and numbers of young local brides-to-be and mothers-of already clamouring for your services if you have it in mind to have a sea change. To come home.'

Hannah managed a half-hearted laugh. Until she realised Virginia appeared to be serious. Expectant. Hopeful, even. That she might *stay*?

Stay. Home. Near Elyse. Near where she grew up. Where people cared for her. Where she could work for someone who didn't work her crazy hard, or make her fall madly in love with him.

The temptation was so strong in that moment it was almost overwhelming. But a moment was all it was. If she stayed she'd be running away. Again. But since the first time she'd run and not looked back she'd grown up and made a life for herself. Not a perfect life, but it was all hers.

'Thanks, Mum, but I'm happy where I am.'

Virginia's hopeful smile disappeared, and was replaced by a grin. 'Good for you.' Then, 'I so worried about you when you were a kid. Head in the clouds, nose in a book, trailing around after your dad like a puppy.' She placed the pen on the desk and turned. 'I wanted to see the world so badly when I was young.

To live in the city and work in the arts. To be somebody. Don't get me wrong—I loved your dad, and never regretted a single decision I made when it came to choosing him. But I didn't want you girls to be stuck in a small town without having found the rare reason to stay that I had. All I ever wanted for you was to find that something special that made you stand out from the crowd so you had chances I never took.'

She reached out, her hand stopping an inch from tucking Hannah's hair behind her ear, before turning to the desk, grabbing a pen and signing her name on the hotel bill with a flourish. 'I'm so proud that you made it happen for yourself. That you're happy.'

As she stood there in the big deserted foyer, her mother's niceties spinning in her head, Hannah's limbs felt numb—and it had nothing to do with the cold. It was as though that weekend her whole life had been tipped on its head.

Worried she'd never again know which way was up, or which way right, she knew she had to set things straight. Right then.

'Mum?'

'Yes, darling.'

'Can I ask you something...difficult?'

Virginia turned, a devilish grin in her eyes. 'Have you ever met a more difficult woman than me?'

Well. No.

'Okay. Here goes. When you married those...other guys, was it because you thought you loved them the way you'd loved Dad? Did you only find out later you were wrong?'

'No,' her mother answered without hesitation. 'Not even for a second.'

'Then why?'

Virginia took a breath, tapping a manicured finger against her bottom lip. Then she looked Hannah in the eye. Crow's feet fanned out from her beautiful eyes. Too much make-up covering what was still lovely skin.

'The truth is I miss what it feels like to be that loved. And if I can only get that in fits and spurts for the rest of my life, then that's what I'm willing to accept.'

That was what her beautiful, vibrant mother had to resort to? The scraps of love's leftovers? The very idea was reprehensible.

Hannah reached out and took her mother by the arm. 'You're worth more than that.'

Virginia looked at Hannah's hand.

'I mean it. No more settling. Find someone you love. Someone who loves you. And do whatever it takes not to let him go. Okay?'

Virginia smiled, but made no promises. Instead she leaned in and gave Hannah a kiss on the cheek. And fast on its heels came a hug. An honest to goodness hug.

'See you at the next wedding, kid. Even I half hope it will be yours.'

And then, with a wink, Virginia was gone, flouncing through the revolving doors in a swirl of energy and colour. And the sorrow of missing her first true love.

Hannah's mind fled the foyer. It was inside a hotel suite, where lay a man she loved to desperation.

She had always known she would never settle. Only for the first time she realised what that really meant. She wasn't going to settle for a man she *liked*. A man who ticked the boxes of what a husband *should* be. She wanted a lover, a partner, someone who made her laugh and made her think, a great and loyal friend she trusted with her life.

She wanted Bradley.

Hannah had everything she'd ever hoped and dreamed of right there at her fingertips. Right now. She couldn't let herself worry about the outcome. If she didn't at least try to have it all she'd never forgive herself.

Bradley was in the shower when Hannah got back to the suite. Humming something she couldn't put her finger on. Not a surprise. Her head was so full she could barely remember her own name.

She paced up and down his bedroom, prepping. Trying to figure the best way to tell him how she felt.

Casual? *Dinner? Saturday? My place? I promise not to cook.*

Blasé? *Let's shock the pants off everyone in the office and turn up tomorrow engaged.*

Sexy? *I want your hands inside my pants now, and a year from now. And I'm not taking no for an answer, big boy.*

Full frontal? *You're the one that I want!*

Honest?

Honest… She loved him. It was that simple. And that complicated. And that was what she needed him to know.

The bathroom door opened. She hadn't even heard the shower stop. Bradley stepped out, a large white towel slung low around his hips, feet bare. Water dripping from his dark hair. Wet muscles gleaming bronze in the low morning light.

Her mouth turned as dry as sand.

He started when he saw her standing in his room. Then his face broke into a sexy smile.

Her heart began to pound as it had never pounded before.

Courage failing her at the last, she sank down onto the corner of his bed, her hands gripping tight to the comforter.

'I woke up and you were gone,' he said.

'Had a few goodbyes to say. We go home today, you know.'

'We do. The plane's set to pick us up at four o'clock. I'm thinking we'll head off around midday and get something to eat in Launceston. I can't tell you how much I'm looking forward to getting my hands on that Porsche again.'

He *brrrrrmmmed* like a little boy, grinning from ear to ear.

Hannah felt as if she was about to faint. Her self-protective instinct told her to cut and run. To give him a bright smile and thank him for a lovely weekend. Go back to a life of pretending that she wasn't working side by side with a man who made her melt just by glancing her way.

But then he slipped his arms into a crisp white shirt and she found herself drowning in the subtle scent of soap. His skin was still slightly damp, so the shirt clung to him in places, highlighting the muscle, the might, the perfect smattering of springy dark hair on his chest. Her mouth watered so fast she was afraid to open her mouth for what might come out.

But she'd sung karaoke and survived.

She'd lost the dad she loved and survived.

She'd had enough of just surviving. She was ready to live. And to do that she needed the man who put the Technicolor in her day.

She wasn't going anywhere.

'We need to talk,' she barked.

Bradley turned to her slowly as he did up the last of his buttons. 'About?'

She lifted herself off the bed and walked to him, placing shaking hands on his chest. His warmth buoyed her, giving her wings.

'You're a good man, Bradley Knight. You work hard. And you never expect anything to be handed to you on a plate.'

'Sounds like me.' He smiled, but there was wariness in his eyes.

'But I also know that when it comes to women you've had the attention span of a goldfish.'

He laughed, surprise flaring in his eyes, before he let his towel slip, as if showing her she was spot-on.

But she knew there was more to him than that. She knew he was kind, and thoughtful, and heroic when someone he cared for was in trouble. And her heart wanted what it wanted.

She reached over to the chair and found his jeans, handed

them to him. Waited till he'd slipped them on before she said another word.

And when he stood before her, looking more beautiful than any man deserved to be in the crisp white shirt and dark jeans, and bare feet and liquid grey eyes, she took a deep breath and said, 'I've had a crush on you for the longest time. And I think I let it continue because you were so unavailable. It gave me the perfect excuse not to put myself out there for real. And then you had to go and call my bluff.'

She stopped to take a breath. Her blood pounding in her ears. Waiting for his response. Any response. But the room remained dead quiet.

After what felt like a hundred years had passed he reached past her for the light grey sweater on his bed and tugged it over his head.

She hadn't expected him to leap onto the bed and jump around whooping in excitement, but she hadn't expected this level of cool. Not after what they'd been through together. Not after the way he'd made love to her, the way he'd spooned her as they slept.

So she sucked in a deep breath, collected together every molecule of love she felt for the big lug, and without a lick of body armour stepped onto the battlefield alone.

'Bradley, you'd have to be blind not to realise that I'm in love with you, and have been—well, for ever.'

She held her arms out in supplication, then let them fall to her sides. They tingled, wanting to wrap around him. To pull him close. But he just stood there, looking through her with those impossibly impenetrable grey eyes.

Fear and excitement and anticipation came together in a great ball of emotion and she blurted, 'I just told you I love you, Bradley. I'm in love with you. I don't want to go back to work tomorrow and pretend this never happened. I want to date you, and hold your hand, and have dinner with you, and make love to you, and wake up in your arms and—'

She watched in amazement as right before her eyes he literally took a step backwards. But, worse, she saw him retreat further and further inside himself, exactly the same way he did when some effusive stranger stopped him on the street looking for an autograph.

Even while fear flooded her, she understood why. His childhood had made detachment come as easily to him as breathing. But that was just tough. No matter how deep inside himself he fled, she meant to follow.

'Bradley. Look at me. *Really* look at me. I'm opening myself up to you. Completely. Offering you everything I have to give. Because… Because we're like a pair of gloves: functional alone, but not complete without the other. I'm yours, Bradley. For ever if you'll have me.'

'Nobody can promise for ever.'

She almost wept with relief that finally he'd said something. 'I can. And I am. I know with every fibre of my being that I'm yours. Eternally. I'm not going anywhere.'

Feeling as if she might explode if she didn't touch him, lean on him, feel a response from him whatever it might be, Hannah reached out a shaking hand and laid the back of it on his cheek.

He flinched as though burned.

She recoiled as if she'd been slapped.

Feeling more scared than she had in her entire life, Hannah curled her hand into her chest and her feelings into her heart.

Oh, God. She'd screwed everything up royally. Building castles in the air with no foundation but her own woolly romantic mush for brains. Bradley didn't want her. He would never want her. Just as she'd always tried to convince herself was the case.

'This is all the response I'm to get from you?'

Silence.

A great ball of anger—most of it directed at herself for

being so foolish—built up inside her and she leapt forward and pummelled a fist against the wall.

It hurt.

Puffing, she stopped. Defeated. And furious with it.

She waved a hand across his eyes as though he was comatose—which to all intents and purposes he was. Emotionally catatonic. While she loved him enough for the both of them.

With that most ridiculous of thoughts in mind came one last shot of determination—or hope, or sheer bloody-mindedness. She pressed forward, stood on her tiptoes, slid her hands into his thick dark hair and kissed him.

Eyes closed. Heart racing.

Those lips that had burned hers, become intimate with every inch of her, brought her to the edge of ecstasy and beyond over and over again, acted as if she wasn't even there. Heat emanated from him. Soul-deep heat that told her he was wrong and she was right. Yet he remained unmoved.

Then she hiccuped, and a flood of tears poured down her cheeks. That, and the taste of salt in her mouth, woke her from her trance. *Finally.* She made to pull away.

And that was when she felt it. A softening of his lips. A response so subtle she stopped breathing.

And then he kissed her. So gently she was almost sure she was imagining it. If that was the case, oh, what an imagination she had!

Soft, warm lips brushing against hers. Tasting hers. Taking away her tears. It was a kiss so beautiful she could barely remember why she was crying in the first place.

And then it came to her. She loved him, but he wasn't man enough to even summon up a response.

She pulled away, wiping her hands over her face, across her mouth, trying to erase the sensation that felt so much like love returned when it was nothing more than a learned response.

She stumbled to the other side of the bed and leant her

hands on the bedspread. Needing space to breathe, room to think.

He didn't follow. He didn't come after her. He still didn't say a damn thing.

There was only one thing she could do.

Her voice was raw as she said, 'I can't go back to work tomorrow and pretend nothing happened. And since it's your company, and I can't convince you to be the gentleman and sell up, it looks like this is going to have to fall to me. God, I feel so predictable.'

'You're quitting?'

And that gets a response!

'You've given me no choice.'

He took a step her way and held out a hand. 'I never asked you to quit. That's the last thing I want. In fact, if I'm being honest, I'll admit it's the reason I came down here in the first place.'

He ran a hand up the back of his hair. His face was stormy.

'Things are so busy at work right now I had to be sure there weren't any inducements here that might tempt you to stay.'

'You hijacked my holiday in order to make sure I'd come back to work for you?'

Of course he had! She made his life so easy. He *liked* his life to be easy. As a move, it was so self-centred, *so him*, she couldn't believe it had never occurred to her.

Argh!

'Only now I don't know why I bothered. You're leaving anyway.'

'Excuse me? Oh, you are unbelievable. Anyone else in my position would have left months ago. But I loved the work that much, and respected you that much, I relished the long hours and hard work. While you... You push people to breaking point, then shake your head in surprise and say "I told you so" when they finally snap.'

He came around the bed. 'Hannah…'

She took two steps back, far enough away that she couldn't feel the tug of warmth from his body.

He said, 'If you think I *only* made love to you with a view to forcing you out, then you must really think I'm some kind of bastard.'

She threw out her arms in a wild shrug. 'I'm not sure what to think right now. My judgement is clearly impaired when it comes to you. Now I'm wondering how the whole "you take over the Tasmania idea" thing fits in. What was that? Some kind of payment for services rendered?'

Finally she saw some emotion in his eyes. She'd never seen him look angrier. If he was any other man she would likely have ducked and weaved. Her nerves crackled as if they'd been stripped raw.

His voice was as deep as a valley when he said, 'I only ever offered you the Tasmania proposal because you deserved it. Because I thought the subject matter would suit your style more than it suited me. And because I thought it would make you happy. I'm sorry you thought otherwise.'

He was sorry. Not that he didn't love her. Not that she was standing there feeling as if her heart had been trampled by a herd of elephants in tap shoes. He was sorry she'd *misunderstood* him.

This time even *he* couldn't make the word 'sorry' sound as sexy as he once had. This time it meant goodbye.

She turned her back on him, then realised she had one last thing to say. 'I know you think you've found a way to not let what your mother did to you shape the course of your life. But you seem determined to repeat her greatest mistakes. You shut people out. Always. And once you decide to, that's it. No room for compromise. No room for anyone.'

She didn't wait to see if he'd even heard a word of it. 'I'm going for a walk. I'll be back in two hours. Be gone or I'll have

Security throw you out of my room. I can do it, you know. I have a famously magical way with management.'

Without stopping to grab a coat or her handbag, she walked out of the suite door and took off down the hall towards the lifts.

CHAPTER ELEVEN

DAYS later Bradley sat at the café on Brunswick Street, staring unseeingly at a busker who was playing a song he couldn't put his finger on.

Like a mosquito in his ear Spencer babbled on and on about the Argentina trip. How excited he was. What he was going to pack. The vaccinations his mother had insisted he have before letting him leave the country. The fact that Hannah had organised everything so brilliantly he wasn't sure what he'd be called on to do, but he was willing whatever it might be.

'I'm sorry? What did you say?' Bradley asked, something dragging him back to the present.

'Hannah,' Spencer said, and Bradley felt the name hit him like a bullet to the chest.

Nobody had dared mention her name when he'd stormed into the office Tuesday morning with the news that she no longer worked for Knight Productions and made it clear that was the end of that.

'She did a great job of organising the trip,' Spencer finished.

Then he snapped his mouth shut, as though he'd just realised he'd said something wrong but wasn't sure what it might be.

Spencer's mobile beeped, and he grabbed the thing as if it

was a lifeline. 'It's the airport. I'm going to find somewhere quiet to take this.'

You do that, Bradley thought, his gaze winging back to the busker, only to find he was packing up. His disappointment was tangible.

'She hasn't found another job yet.'

Bradley flinched, his eyes sliding to the annoying sound. Sonja. He'd forgotten she was even at the table.

'Hannah,' Sonja said, in case he hadn't cottoned on. In case Hannah wasn't all he'd been thinking about while listening to the busker play.

Remembering the amazing light in her eyes as together they'd belted out that song.

Reliving the light so bright it had been almost stellar when she'd looked him in the eye and told him that she was in love with him.

Recoiling from the darkness in her eyes as she'd stormed out of their hotel room and told him to be gone by the time she got back.

'She's had offers, of course,' Sonja continued. 'They're pouring in every day. But instead she's remaining locked in her room, doing goodness knows what on her computer.'

He glared at Sonja.

'What happened in Tasmania?' she asked.

He gritted his teeth. What had happened in Tasmania had been meant to stay in Tasmania. Yet he felt as if he was carrying every minute of it on his shoulders like a beast of burden.

'She hasn't said a word,' Sonja said. 'She came home looking like she'd been hit by a bus. In fact she looks about as delighted with life as you do right about now.'

Bradley said nothing. Just stewed as the angry knot inside his gut got bigger and bigger.

'Fine,' Sonja said, throwing her hands in the air. 'You can both be stubborn and refuse to talk to me about it. But since

I'm living with her, and working for you, you *have* to talk
to each other before you both drive me out of my mind with
all your moping. So, whatever it is that you did to made her
leave, go and apologise. *Now.* And save us all from all this
drama.'

He shot her a sharp glance. 'What makes you think her
leaving had anything to do with me?'

Sonja looked at him as if that was the most idiotic thing
she'd ever heard in her entire life.

And the worst of it was she was right. It had everything to
do with him. If he hadn't followed her, seduced her, then cast
her away, she'd have come back from her holiday refreshed
and ready to get back to work.

Why couldn't he have left well enough alone? If he had
she'd be sitting there now, laughing with him, picking holes
in his ideas, giving brightness to a day which now felt dull as
dishwater.

He'd still be suffocating his attraction to her deep down
inside, where it could do no harm. He'd never have known
that there was someone out there who found it possible to love
him. Happy days!

He shoved his dark sunglasses tight onto his nose and
pushed back his chair so hard it scraped painfully on the
concrete. 'I'm going to walk back to the office.' He threw the
company credit card on the table. 'Look after it.'

Sonja nodded, concern etched all over her face.

'Tell Spencer I'll be back…later.'

He shoved his hands in the pockets of his jacket and took
off down the street, heading he knew not where. Not a soul
stopped him along the way for a chat or an autograph. He
must have looked as approachable as a rabid dog.

Away from the glare of his staff, he let his mind go where
it had been wanting to go all day.

Hannah.

Wham. Slam. Bam. He rubbed his fist over the spot on his chest that still ached days since he'd last exerted himself.

Losing her had put the whole office off kilter all week. She was the one who'd kept such a high-pressure environment fun. The one who'd meant staff turnover was at an all time low. The one whose work ethic had given him the room to just create, meaning he'd come up with the best ideas of his life.

Still, he'd run Knight Productions for years before she came along. The business had such momentum it would survive her loss. Intellectually he knew it would work out in the end.

Knowing it didn't stop him from missing her thoroughness. Missing the confidence with which she charmed his colleagues over the phone. The way she always had a coffee at his fingertips right when he needed one. The way she finished his thoughts.

He missed her feet on his office desk. The pen constantly behind her ear or clacking manically against her teeth. Her biting sense of humour. Her laugh. Her smile. Her mouth…

Hell.

He missed her taste. Her skin. Her fingers playing with the back of his hair. The soft flesh at her waist. The way his teeth sank into the delicious slope of her shoulder. Waking up with her warm body tucked so neatly into his.

Dammit. He missed *her*.

And as he walked up the bustling sidewalk the feelings he'd kept buried for so long refused to be smothered any longer. They pummelled at him until he felt every one in every bruised muscle. His feelings for her were so sweet, so foreign, so consuming, so deep, he knew there was only one answer.

He'd fallen in love for the first time in his life.

He loved her. He *loved* Hannah.

Of course he loved her! How could anyone not? He'd have to be pure rock not to love her lightness, her sense of fun, her kindness, her conscientiousness, and especially—most astonishingly, most unfathomably—the way she loved him back.

That was the truth. The candid, straight up, no embellishment truth.

But it didn't matter.

It would never have lasted. It was far kinder—to both of them—to cut it off before it had barely begun.

Who says? an insistent voice barked in his ear. He turned to find the source, only to find nobody was paying him any heed.

It's a fact, he continued to himself. *People are inherently self-serving. Relationships never last. They blaze to life and subsist on drama and eventually fade under their own lack of steam.*

She was right. Your relationships have never lasted because you sabotaged them before they had a chance to prove you right. Or prove you wrong.

Bradley felt his footsteps slowing as the other truths he'd always known to be firm began to wobble and crack. It hurt like hell, but he stood there and let it.

She left, he said to the voice he now knew was in his head.

You pushed her away. But she fought back. As long and hard as she could. Because she believed you were worth it. Your friendship was worth it. Your love was worth it. But any relationship has to go two ways, and you never fought for her. She couldn't leave you. You'd already quit.

His feet came to a halt. The Brunswick Street crowd spilled around him, muttering none too quietly for him to get the hell out of their way. But, considering the dressing down he'd been giving himself, it was water off a duck's back.

He'd quit her. Right when she'd needed him most. Right when she'd gathered up every ounce of strength and come to him, with her heart, her soul, her trust, her love in her hands, he'd decided it was too hard.

Yet being without Hannah was harder. Way harder.

It hit him like a sucker punch. It wasn't drama he'd been avoiding his entire adult life, it was rejection. The infernal emptiness that came of loving someone who didn't love you back. For a man who thrived on pushing himself to his physical limits, who relished any and every challenge life threw his way, when it came to relationships he'd been an absolute coward.

No more. Not this time.

He breathed in a lungful of cold Melbourne air. He could smell car fumes, baklava from a nearby Greek bakery, and best of all the thrilling hint that the greatest challenge of his life was just around the corner.

There was only one way he was ever going to know for sure.

He looked up, figured out where he was, spun on his heel and headed off with a clear destination in mind.

There was a knock at Hannah's door. She opened her mouth to ask Sonja to get it, then remembered it was the middle of the afternoon and Sonja would be at work.

She hitched up her PJ bottoms and rearranged her oversized jumper, and let her Ugg boots lead her to the door. She dragged it open to find—

'Bradley?'

Leather jacket. Jeans. Smelling of soap. And winter air. And that yumminess that was purely *him*. Her heart gave a sorry thump. She forced it to limp back to where it belonged, in a crushed and mangled mess, deep in her chest cavity.

'We need to talk,' he said.

'Do we, now?'

The fact that he'd used the words she feared had been the

beginning of the end a few days before would have been funny
if she could remember how to laugh.

'Send me an e-mail,' she said, swinging the door shut in
his face.

He stopped it with a determined hand. 'I don't know your
new one.'

'Right.' Of course. Her old work email had clearly been
deleted the same time she had. With a half-hearted wave she
said, 'Then you better come in.'

She left the door open and moved to the couch, where she
fell back into the over-soft cushions. She picked up a piece of
cold pizza from a box on the coffee table and bit into it, as if
that was far more interesting than anything he had to say.

While the sad truth was the second she'd seen his face her
whole body had begun to thrum in anticipation.

'How old is that thing?' he asked, sniffing in the direction
of the pizza box.

She shrugged. 'It wasn't in the fridge before I left for
Tasmania, so not that old. What are you doing here, Bradley?
If you're here to ask me to come back to work—'

'I'm not.'

'Oh.' Her stomach landed somewhere in the region of her
knees. Maybe he was here to kick her in the shins a few times,
just in case she didn't feel rotten enough.

He moved to look at a row of knick-knacks on the shelf
over the fake fireplace. 'Unless you'd like to come back?'

'No.' She realised she'd said it overly loud, so softened it
with a 'thank you'.

He nodded. 'You might like to know things are in disarray
without you there.'

'You'll survive.'

'I know.' A pause, then, 'Sonja says you've been keeping
busy. On your computer.'

She had. And she had a sudden need to tell him what she'd
been working on. Maybe as a first step to dragging herself

back into the light from the dark corner in which she'd hidden herself. 'I'm going to start my own production company. I'm thinking small to start with. Home-town documentaries. I think I'd have a flair for getting that kind of thing done, and done well.'

He finally turned to her, and she was dead surprised to see a flicker of something that seemed a heck of a lot like respect gleaming in his dark grey eyes.

It gave her courage. She put down her pizza and sat forward on the chair. 'So, if you're not here to beg me to come back, why *are* you here?'

He looked at the spare chair, then, sensibly deciding he'd likely break the silly little thing Sonja favoured, paced instead. 'I was hoping you might give me a chance to say some things. Things I probably should have said a few days ago.'

Heat began in the region of her toes and flowed clean to her scalp. She stood and paced herself. She didn't want to do this again. Couldn't. She could kick him out. She could…

But she needed closure on this thing if she was really going to be able to move forward. To begin her life anew. 'Fine. Go for your life. Talk.'

He looked at her a few long moments.

She tried to steady her heart again, but found she could not. He'd hurt her, but she loved him. Likely would for a long, long time. Unlikely she'd ever love anyone as deeply.

Then he shook out his hands as if they were filled with pins and needles. He was anxious. Skittish, even. She could only watch in amazement as the great Bradley Knight was reduced to a bundle of nerves in her lounge room.

It was with a strange sense of anticipation that she couldn't comprehend that she crossed her arms and waited for Bradley to say what he'd come to say.

'Okay, so here we go. I've been an independent man for a very long time. I like that I get to choose what I do on a

Sunday morning. I like that I have control over the remote. I like things to go my way.'

Big shock! Hannah thought, but she just sat on the arm of the couch and let him talk. The sooner he said whatever he'd come to say the sooner he'd be gone and she could drown herself in a bottle of wine.

'While you…' he said, waving a hand in the air as though hoping to pluck out the words. 'You're a smartass, and your family is like a walking soap opera. You're a disrupting influence.'

She blinked at him, not at all following where he was going. 'Fair enough. But I'd ask you to be so kind as to not put that on a recommendation letter in the future.'

He glanced at her, a first sign of humour in his eyes. She bit her lip.

'I'm trying to say you've been an unexpected force in my life.'

'I have?'

'From the day you landed in my office till the day we landed in Tasmania I never saw you coming. And it's on that subject that I need to ask you a favour.'

Her voice cracked as she asked, 'Which is?'

'That we leave what happened in Tasmania in Tasmania.'

His words ought to have felt like a slap upon a slap, but the sincerity in his voice, the uncertainty in his eyes, gave her pause.

'I thought that was what you'd already done.'

'I don't mean what happened between us there. I was a fool to think that walking away could ever be that simple.'

She breathed out slowly between pursed lips, willing herself not to get ahead of herself. 'Okay.'

'I mean that last day. The way I acted. The things I said. The things I didn't say. When you told me that you loved me…'

Hannah cringed, wishing he'd used some kind of euphemism. The fact that her love had been unrequited hurt as much now as it had then, even if he *had* come to make some kind of amends.

She stood and paced again.

'Hannah, I was taken by surprise. And not for the reasons I am sure *you* think are true. But because it came from you.'

'Right…' she said, while not having a clue what he meant.

'I know you now, Hannah. I know you've known loss. I know you've also struggled with rejection by someone you care for. I know that while you have a light inside of you the likes of which I've never known you are also serious, and cautious, and thoughtful. The idea that *that* woman was strong enough to put all that aside to love me…' His faraway gaze focussed back on her as he put a hand to his chest. '*Me*. A man who never let anything into his life he couldn't afford to lose. I have never, in my whole entire life, seen anything as courageous.'

Nope. No more pacing. Hannah's knees had just turned to jelly. 'Bradley, I—'

He held up a hand. He needed to finish. And, boy, did Hannah want him to.

'That's why when you told me how you felt I froze. I was so unprepared. I handled it badly. I feel ashamed even thinking about it. The look in your eyes…the hurt. I would make all of it mine if I could.'

'Bradley—' she beseeched, her phoenix of a heart beating its wings in her chest. But he held up his hand again. She bit her lip so hard she tasted blood.

'For all that,' he said, 'I'm so sorry.'

Her heart danced. Unlike the last time that word had passed through his lips, it no longer felt like a goodbye. It felt like a new beginning.

'Bradley—'

He cut her off again, clearly on a roll. She physically put her hand over her mouth.

'I know its taken me a while to be able to say it, but the truth is I now know that being my own man pales in comparison with how it made me feel when you told me I was *your* man. I only hope I'm not too late.'

He took two hesitant steps her way. Finally. Her whole body pulsed towards him like a flower to the sun.

'Hannah,' he said, his voice rough and unsure and utterly adorable.

'Yes, Bradley?'

Then, for the first time since he'd walked through her door, he smiled. A slow, sexy Bradley smile. And with a self-conscious shrug he said, 'I came here to tell you that you're the one that I want.'

The reminder of the song he'd made her sing made her laugh out loud. But her boisterous laughter fast turned to the most exquisite ache in her heart.

That was the moment he'd put himself into a position of extreme discomfort in order to give her the closure she needed on an issue that had hindered her through her entire life. *That* had been an act of love. Pure and simple. And she'd never realised.

She should have known he was a man of action, not of words. How could a man who'd never felt love know how to express it? Well, she'd just have to show him. Again and again and again. Every day for the rest of their lives.

Starting now.

She took the final two steps and took his face in hers.

'Bradley Knight. You, my gorgeous, stubborn man, are the one that *I* want. I should have known that you just needed more time. I've always been quicker to see the potential in things than you.'

At that *he* laughed. Loud, reverberating laughter that

rocked the thin walls of her old apartment. 'You are the most audacious woman I have ever known.'

She shrugged, while letting her fingers wander into the heavenly hair at the back of his neck. 'It is one of my most lovable traits.'

She pulled him to her and kissed him. Wholly, fully, showing him every ounce of love she had. He hooked a hand beneath her knees and carried her to the couch. She sank into it, and then some.

His eyes gleamed as he hovered over her. 'That thing is so soft I fear if I get on there with you I may not be able to get back out again.'

She raised an eyebrow. 'Is that a problem?'

His gaze raked over her before he moved his hand slowly up the inside of her jumper, making her curl into his touch. 'Not in the least.'

Eventually they pulled apart, their bodies a tangle of heat and sweat and the kind of joy they'd only ever seen in one another's eyes.

Bradley kissed the tip of Hannah's nose. 'I never thought I'd say the words, much less feel the feelings, my whole entire life. And then there was you. I love you, Hannah Gillespie.'

Actions could speak louder than words—but, boy, was it ever nice to hear the words anyway!

She wrapped her arms tight around him and in his ear whispered, 'I love you right on back, Bradley Knight.'

'Glad to hear it.'

'Do you want to hear it again?'

He shivered as her breath washed across his neck. 'Later,' he said, before covering her mouth with his.

Much later, as the sun set over Melbourne, they stood at the small window, looking out over an array of squat Fitzroy buildings with a glimpse of city lights twinkling in the near distance.

Hannah's back was tucked into Bradley's front, his arms around her waist, her arms on top of his. His chin leaning gently on her hair. Exactly as she'd seen her parents stand looking out over their suburban backyard a hundred times.

Happy. Nowhere else they'd rather be. In love.

'I meant what I said before,' Bradley said.

'I certainly hope so—or I wouldn't have let you do *any* of what just happened on the couch.'

She felt his laughter rumble through her.

'I was referring to when I told you that you're the one. You're it. There's never been anybody else, and I know there never will be. Fate would never be so kind to a guy like me twice.'

She slapped him on the arm. 'Better not.'

He tucked his arms tighter around her, his fingers sliding beneath her jumper to skid back and forth over her hipbones, creating the most delicious shivers in their wake.

'On that score, I have a proposal.'

At the seriousness in his voice she spun in his arms. 'Is this one I'm going to agree to?'

'I certainly hope so, because I'm fairly sure Australian law prohibits marriage between two people if one of them doesn't say "I do".'

She blinked up at him. 'I'm sorry, did you just say—?'

'You're the one,' he said, looking her right in the eye, giving her all the emotion she'd ever hoped to find in one man and then some. 'And now I've found you I don't see any point in waiting. You may as well marry me.'

Her throat was so blocked with emotion she couldn't even find the words.

'Come on,' he said finally, giving her a little shake. 'Do you honestly think we're ever going to find another living soul who would put up with either of us?'

'My man. The last of the great romantics.'

He grabbed her hand and spun her out. She laughed, and squealed so loud one of the neighbours banged something on the wall. But she barely heard it over the pure joy pumping through her brain.

He spun her back in. Their bodies smacked together, as close as two people could be while still fully clothed. Looking into his sultry dark eyes, she could barely drag breath in deep enough. And Hannah thought that if she loved him even a tenth as much in ten years' time she'd be one lucky woman.

Then, before she even felt it coming, he held her across the back and tipped her into the most fabulous Hollywood dip that had ever been.

'How's that for romantic?' he asked.

'It'll do me just fine.'

'Hannah Gillespie, will you *please* stop dilly-dallying and agree to marry me?'

'You say that while in a position to drop me?'

'Unfortunately it's not to my benefit. You already know I'd never let you fall.' He lifted her slowly back up into his arms. 'When I know what I want I go out and get it. I want you. For ever. If you'll have me.'

What could she say but, 'Yes'?

His nostrils flared as he let out a long slow breath. 'And just like that the world is back on its right axis.'

Then he kissed her slowly, gently, deeply. When she pulled away there were stars in her eyes. And rumbles in her tummy, which had been given little but stale pizza and coffee for several days and now craved a feast.

Only the fact that she knew how many days and nights she had to wrap herself around him in the future made her able to pull away. She moved into the kitchen in search of takeaway menus from the fridge.

She glanced at him, watching her from the other side of

her tiny kitchen bench. Big, bad, beautiful Bradley Knight. No longer her boss. Now he was simply her man.

Her inner imp twirled to life.

She said, 'You do realise that one day a show of yours will take on a show of mine in the ratings, and I'm going to take you down?'

Bradley grabbed the menus from her hand and threw them in the bin. He reached into her fridge for eggs and her cupboard for a frying pan. 'Is that a challenge?'

Hannah raised a saucy eyebrow. 'It's a promise.'

And somehow they never did get around to dinner that night.

TO CATCH A GROOM

BY
REBECCA WINTERS

Rebecca Winters, an American writer and mother of four, is excited to be in this new millennium because it means another new beginning. Having said goodbye to the classroom, where she taught French and Spanish, she is now free to spend more time with her family, to travel and to write the Mills & Boon novels she loves so dearly. Rebecca loves to hear from readers. If you wish to e-mail her, please visit her website at: www.rebeccawinters-author.com.

CHAPTER ONE

April 14, Kingston, New York

GREER DUCHESS could tell by tapping feet and shifting bodies that her sisters were getting antsy. "We're almost through, guys. For November is it agreed we'll go with Ginger Rogers Did Everything Fred Astaire Did, But She Did It Backward And In High Heels?"

"Like I said before, not everyone who buys our calendars knows who Ginger Rogers is," Olivia spoke up.

"It doesn't matter, does it? Piper's drawing is so wonderful they'll still get the point," Greer murmured, making a unilateral decision on the spot. She adored the stylized cartoons of Luigio and Violetta, the two winsome Italian pigeons who were in love with each other.

Though Piper did the actual drawings, and Olivia headed sales, Greer was the instigator and power behind their business enterprise.

"Moving on, here are the choices we narrowed down for December. Behind Every Successful Man Is A Surprised Woman, and, A Man's Got To Do What A Man's Got To Do. A Woman's Got To Do What He Can't."

Piper got up and stretched her softly rounded body. "I liked both those sayings the first time you thought them up."

"I still like them," Olivia asserted. "Your clever mind never ceases to impress me, Greer. You make the decision. We trust your judgment," she said, rising to her feet on long, shapely legs. "Now we've really got to go or we'll

5

be late for the reading of Daddy's will. We're supposed to be there at ten.''

"Okay. Get the car started while I e-mail this to Don. It'll take me two secs.''

Within a minute the sent message appeared on the computer screen. She felt relief that next year's calendar entitled, For Women Only, would be printed and ready for distribution in May which was only a few weeks away.

Don Jardine, one of several guys she and her sisters had been dating, was the owner of the print shop. He did a terrific job for them.

Unfortunately he kept hinting that he wanted her to take him seriously because he'd fallen for her. But she wasn't in love with him. Lately she'd found excuses not to go out with him anymore. If they could just remain business friends…

All things considered, Duchesse Designs—her brain child inspired by their only illustrious female ancestor and heroine—the Duchess of Parma, a woman in advance of her time—was doing much better than her initial conservative estimates indicated.

With orders from all over the country quadrupling since Christmas, she and her sisters were going to make a substantial profit. For the first time in five years they would be able to invest part of their earnings while they put the rest back into their company.

Naturally that was going to mean more money for Don and make him happy, too. Maybe happy enough to forgive her? She had yet to find that out. If he sent a reply e-mail that she'd better take her business to someone else, then she would have her answer.

After turning on the answering machine, she dashed out of the basement apartment to join her sisters.

All the rituals of laying their beloved father to rest had been observed except for this visit to Mr. Carlson's office.

It was a formality. Once it was behind them, they'd be able to channel their sorrow by expanding their growing business.

Twenty minutes later they arrived at the law firm in downtown Kingston, New York. The receptionist showed them into the conference room where a TV and DVD player had been set up.

Soon after they'd sat down, Mr. Carlson walked in with a legal file under one arm. He greeted them, shook hands, then took his place at the end of the rectangular conference table.

"Your father asked me to read you a letter he wrote in his own hand." He opened the file and drew it out. Once his bifocals were in place, he cleared his throat.

"To my darling daughters Greer, Piper and Olivia, whom I've always referred to as my precious pigeons. You came along after I turned fifty and had despaired of ever giving your mother children—

"If Walter Carlson has assembled you for the reading of this will, then it means my troublesome old ticker finally gave out and you've already been informed that our humble home has to be sold to pay all the medical expenses.

"I wish I could have left it to you, but it wasn't meant to be. At least you aren't saddled with debts. Walt will pay the latest bills and is taking care of everything. He's aware you need time to find another place to live. Therefore he will be the one to let you know how soon you must move out.

"My greatest sadness is that none of you has ever shown the slightest inclination to marry. It worried your mother before she died, and it upsets me even more. I remember her last words to you: find a good man to marry right away and settle down to raise a family. My last words echo hers.

"To that end I'm bequeathing $5,000 to each of you.

It's from the Husband Fund your mother and I created before she passed away. You can spend it any way you want so long as it's used in the pursuit of a spouse to help you enjoy this life to the fullest.

"You will receive those checks today. For this day and age it's not much, but it's given with all my love. I know my girls will be fine because you're intelligent, talented, resourceful and have created a solid Internet business since college. However as you will discover when you put this money to the proper use, there's more to life than earning a living.

"To stimulate your thinking, I'm insisting you remain in Walt's office to watch your mother's favorite classic. Humor me and make your old dad happy. I want only the best for my beautiful girls. You and your mother always were my greatest joy.

"Signed, Your loving, concerned father, Matthew Duchess, February 2, Kingston, New York."

When Mr. Carlson finished reading the letter and looked up, Greer turned her blond head to eye her fair-haired sisters seated around the table.

Because their dad's health had been deteriorating long before they'd buried him six weeks ago, they'd already been through the most painful part of their mourning period. Certainly with all the bills owing to the extra health care costs for both their mom and dad, the idea of an inheritance had never crossed their minds.

To find out their parents had left them any money at all came as a total surprise. But the mention of a Husband Fund completely soured the gift for Greer.

Not only that…she balked at the idea of being forced to view the film their funny, dear mom must have seen too many times to count.

It was one of those Hollywood movies about three women who decide to get married and scheme to find a millionaire in the process. However their mother had never been able to get Greer to watch it because Greer found the concept utterly absurd.

If a woman wanted that kind of money, she didn't need a man. All she had to do was become a millionaire herself!

But their mother had been born in a different era with a completely different mind-set about a woman's choices in life.

Being a hopeless romantic, she'd named her nonidentical triplets for her favorite movie stars. In fact she'd raised her daughters on fairy tales.

Greer had never been a great proponent of them.

While Olivia and Piper swooned over the beautiful girl ending up with the handsome prince just because she was beautiful, Greer often upset her sisters by fabricating her own renditions.

She much preferred that the beautiful, innocent, helpless heroine use her brain to figure out a financial scheme to buy the castle and lands from Prince Charming who needed a lot more going for him than charm to attract her and win her hand in marriage.

Greer had shocked their mother when she'd told her it was probably a man who'd thought up all those fractured fairy tales.

It wasn't that Greer had anything against men per se. In fact she loved to date and often tripled dated with her sisters. Don and his friends had been the latest bunch of guys they'd gone out with as a group. But she drew the line at a serious relationship.

There was plenty of time for marriage in the future. Her own parents hadn't married until much later in life when they were finally ready to settle down and have a family. That was good enough for her.

Many times Greer, the oldest of the triplets who'd always espoused the "all for one, one for all" theory, had told her sisters that getting married would spoil the fun of building the business they'd started from scratch to see how far they could take it.

She glanced back at the attorney. "Do we have to stay and watch the film?"

"Only if you want your five thousand dollars. That was your father's stipulation. If you choose not to sit through the viewing, I'm to give the money to the cancer foundation in your mother's memory." His brows lifted. "For what it's worth, I've seen it several times and enjoy it more every time."

Greer rolled her eyes in disbelief, ready to bolt, but her sisters made no move to leave. Deep down she knew why. As much as the three of them hated the idea of being a captive audience to such a ridiculous movie, they were faced with a moral dilemma.

Because of the restrictions about the money, it was no good to them and would never be spent. But they couldn't walk out now. That would be like throwing everything back in their parents' faces. The sobering realization that they'd had the best mother and father in the world kept them nailed to their chairs.

After crossing one long, elegant leg over the other, Greer waited while Mr. Carlson, who had to be in his seventies, moved the TV closer.

Once he started the DVD, she sat back in the leather chair prepared to suffer through another story no doubt written, produced and cast by men, for men.

Not only was the movie much worse than she'd thought, Mr. Carlson was glued to the screen, glassy eyed. Ten minutes into the film and Greer had to bite her lip to keep from bursting into laughter.

Flashing her sisters a covert glance, she sensed they were having the same problem. But out of respect for their father's wishes, they managed to contain themselves.

When the show came to an end, a collective silence filled the room before Mr. Carlson realized it was time to shut off the DVD.

He turned to them. "Would thirty days give you girls enough time to vacate the house?"

"We've already moved to Mrs. Weyland's basement apartment across the street from us," Greer informed him.

The girls nodded. "We left our home spotless."

"The keys are in this envelope along with a paper that lists our cell phone numbers and the address of our new apartment." Greer pushed it toward him before she shot out of her chair, ready to go.

He rose more slowly and handed them their checks. "You're as remarkable and self-sufficient as your father always told me you were. Yet I could hope for your sakes you'll take your parents' advice." He stared pointedly at Greer. "Women weren't meant to be on their own."

The man's sincerity couldn't be doubted. But his comment happened to be one of the twelve comments appearing on the calendar she'd thought up last year featuring Men's Most Notable Quotes About Women. The calendar had been an instant success.

Greer didn't dare look at her sisters or she would have cracked up on the spot. Hilarity had been building inside her. She couldn't stifle it any longer. They had to get out of there quick!

"Thank you for everything, Mr. Carlson."

So saying, Greer made a beeline for the door, clutching the check in hand. Her sisters followed.

They hurried down the hall to the crowded elevator. By some miracle they reached their father's old Pontiac parked around the corner before they exploded with laughter.

Since Olivia had a better sense of direction than the others, she always drove them when they were together.

"After the first close-up of Betty Grable, I thought we were going to have to call emergency for Mr. Carlson!"

"That generation's hopeless."

"The movie was dreadful!"

"But our mother loved it, bless her heart."

"And Daddy loved her!"

"And we loved both of them, so what are we going to do about the—"

"No—" Greer blurted. "Don't say the 'H' word."

For the rest of the drive home they giggled like school-girls instead of twenty-seven-year-old women.

When they pulled to a stop at the curb across the street from their old house, Olivia looked over her shoulder at Greer who was seated in the back. "Let's go get us a new car. This one already has 122,000 miles on it."

That sounded like her impulsive sister. "Right this minute?"

"Why not?"

Before Greer could negate the suggestion, Piper, the romantic, shook her head. "With fifteen thousand dollars to put down, we could buy a new house. What do you think?"

Greer, the pragmatic one, said, "I think I'm too exhausted to think." It came out sounding grumpy because the Husband Fund money was untouchable and they all knew it.

"Mrs. Weyland says we need a vacation," Olivia muttered.

Piper rested her head against the window. "I'd love to visit the Caribbean."

"Who wouldn't, but we can't go."

Both sisters blinked. "Why not?"

Greer leaned forward. "Because it's April. By the time we could get away from the business, it would be June. I think we could run into a hurricane."

"How do you know that?"

"Our northeast distributor, Jan. She scuba dives there in February when the weather is perfect."

"Then how about Hawaii?"

Olivia wrinkled her nose at Piper. "Everybody complains it's too touristy. I'd rather go someplace more exotic, like Tahiti."

"The airfare alone would be exorbitant."

"So what's your suggestion?" Both sisters were waiting for Greer's answer.

"I don't have one, and you guys know why."

Olivia's eyes resembled the blue in a match flame when she felt strongly about something. "Then we'll go through the motions of husband hunting in some wonderful place like Australia where the beaches are reputed to be the most beautiful in the world. Mrs. Weyland's right, you know? We haven't had a break in several years."

By now Piper's irises were glowing an iridescent blue-green. "Daddy didn't say we had to *end up* with a husband."

Greer could acknowledge she had a point. "You're right. All he said was, you can spend the money any way you want so long as it's used in the *pursuit* of a spouse. With $5,000 apiece, we should be able to go someplace exciting for a couple of weeks. I'm all for visiting the Great Barrier Reef."

"Or South America!" Olivia interjected. "Don't forget Rio. Ipanema and Copacabana are supposed to be two of the most fabulous beaches on earth."

"Wait a minute—" Piper spread her hands in front of her. "Wherever we decide to spend our vacation, I've got this delicious idea how we'll provide the bait to bring the men on fast!"

Olivia smiled. "I bet I know what you're thinking."

So did Greer. They'd all watched that idiotic film and

weren't triplets for nothing. "You mean turn things around by pretending *we're* the millionaires?"

"Why not?"

Why not indeed. Greer realized it was a stretch, but if her business projections held true, they'd be doing very well for themselves by the time they were thirty.

"Guys—" Piper broke in with dramatic flourish. "We have a lot more going for us than money. We're *titled!* Ladies and gentlemen, may I present the Duchesses of Kingston!"

Brilliant.

So brilliant in fact, Greer was still staring at her talented sister in wonder when Olivia suddenly blurted, *"The Duchesse pendant!"*

No one's mind could leap faster from A to Z than Olivia's.

"Yes?" Greer prompted. "What about it?"

The pendant was a gold rectangle. It was encrusted with amethysts surrounding a pearl-studded pigeon with a red-orange eye of pyrope garnet.

According to the story their dad told them, a court artisan fashioned the pendant for the Duchess of Parma, otherwise known as Marie-Louise of Austria of the House of Bourbon. On the back of the pendant was a stylized "D" and "P."

When she died, one of her children inherited it, and then it was given to a granddaughter who passed it down through the Duchesse line until it fell into their father's hands.

In anticipation of their sixteenth birthday, Greer's parents had gone to a jeweler who'd had two matching pendants fashioned using the original for a model so each of their daughters could have the same memento.

"For your children to cherish," their parents had said, giving them a loving hug and kiss along with the gift.

Eleven years later and their daughters were still single. Greer assumed that one day they'd all be married and have families. She just didn't know when, and couldn't have cared less.

"Think, my dear duchesses!" Olivia grinned. "Where is there a lovely beach with a whole bunch of gorgeous playboys running around looking to marry a titled woman wearing the family jewels?"

"*The Riviera,* of course."

"Of course!" Greer's sisters cried.

"Except that we came through the illegitimate line of the House of Parma-Bourbon," she reminded them.

"Who cares? We *are* related!"

"Only if the story's true."

"Daddy seemed to think it was," Piper reasoned, "otherwise how would he have ended up with the pendant?"

"Somebody could have made up a tall tale about it that grew legs down through the years," Greer reminded her sisters. "Still, we *do* have it in our possession, and no one's been able to prove we're not related. Anyway, you've given me an idea.

"We know Marie-Louise went by three other titles; Duchess of Colorno, Duchess of Piacenza and Duchess of Guastalla. So what if we each took a title representing our relationship to her? We could outcon all the playboys we want."

At this point her sisters stared in awe at Greer whose eyes reflected the exact color of the Duchess of Parma violet.

The flower had been named for their ancestor who loved violets so much, when she wrote letters she often left the imprint of the flower rather than her signature.

A conspiratorial smile broke out on Olivia's face. "I say we start on the Italian Riviera with one side trip to Parma and Colorno to see the palaces where she lived.

Then work our way along the coast to the French and Spanish Riviera, letting it be known we've been in Italy visiting our...royal relations?''

Brilliant! Sometimes Olivia's innovative ideas reflected pure genius.

Greer's thoughts leaped ahead. "We'll do business while we're there so we can write off our trip as an expense on our taxes. It shouldn't be difficult to find someone to translate our calendars into various languages and distribute them for us. It might be the start of something really big.''

Piper's eyes gleamed. "In time Violetta and Luigio could become household words all over Europe. Just don't forget we'll have to honor Daddy's wishes by trying our hardest to snag a husband at the same time," she reminded them.

"It'll be a piece of cake," Olivia declared. "As soon as we let it be known we're duchesses, our unsuspecting victims will fall all over us.''

"And we know why, don't we," Greer said with a definite smirk. "Because they're nothing but a bunch of impoverished adventurers who prey on wealthy women and prefer to marry a titled one if possible." One delicately arched brow lifted.

"Their black moment will come when we smile sweetly and admit we're the *poor* American duchesses. 'Sorry. No tiara.' So if they want to take back their proposals...''

Piper shook her head at Greer. "You're wicked.''

"Terrible," Olivia concurred.

"Not as terrible as *they* are. Just watch the bodies fall!'' Greer eyed her sisters with unholy glee. "Let's go inside and make our plans while we eat lunch.''

Piper was the first one out of the car. Olivia followed. "If we hurry, we can apply for passports before the place closes today.''

Greer brought up the rear. "Airfares are really cheap to Europe right now, which is good news since we'll need new wardrobes."

"If we're going to do this thing right, maybe we should charter a private yacht."

"I'm way ahead of you but I don't think we could afford it."

"It wouldn't hurt to find out," Olivia said. "Maybe if it were a small one?"

Once inside the apartment Greer hurried over to the computer in the living room, which they'd made into their office. The girls hovered around while she did a dozen searches of yachting services.

"Hmm. I'm afraid they're out of our price range. So far the best we can do is charter a crewed sailboat for twelve people. It's $5,000 a week per person if the boat is full at the time of departure. That's no good."

Piper leaned over Greer's shoulder. "Just for fun, click to the crewed catamaran listings. It's says they're cheaper."

When the information appeared on the screen, they studied the names of the boats with avid interest.

"Look!" Olivia blurted. "There's one called the *Piccione*."

Greer had already spotted the Italian word for pigeon. Their dad had always called his daughters his "pigeons" because of the beautiful white Duchesse pigeon the Italians had named in honor of the Duchess of Parma. Just for fun she clicked to it. After the specifics popped up, she read them aloud.

"This immaculate, white, fifty-one-foot sloop sleeps two to six guests. Crew of three. Full amenities, three meals per day. $3,000 per person. Ten days on the Mediterranean.

"*Ten* guys! Plan your own itinerary. The swift way to

get close to any beach. Contact F. Moretti, Vernazza, Italy.''

Olivia nudged Greer. ''That's what you call exclusive at the right price. It must be destiny! E-mail them and find out if they have any openings left for this summer or early fall.''

''Do we care which month?''

They both shook their heads.

After sending an inquiry, Greer joined them in the kitchen. They hurriedly ate sandwiches before rummaging around for their birth certificates.

Once those were found, they left for the passport office. En route they stopped to get their passport pictures taken, reminding them they all needed a new hairdo to go with their new duchess look.

An hour later they started for home. On the way Piper noticed a travel agency. She told Olivia to stop the car so she could run inside and get some brochures.

On the way back to the apartment, they almost got into an argument because everyone wanted to savor the brochure on Vernazza. Greer had to admit the place sounded like heaven.

One of the most unspoilt areas of the Mediterranean. To visit Vernazza is to visit the Cinque Terre, a kingdom of nature and wild scents; five villages suspended between sea and sky, clinging on to cliffs and surrounded by green hills. Who visits Cinque Terre can choose between a dive in the sea, a hike in the hills, a walk in the narrow "car-ruggi," or a boat trip to a sanctuary or to a seafood lunch.

Piper was the first to reach the computer after they'd entered the apartment.

''We've got an answer to our e-mail!''

Greer and Olivia leaned over her shoulder while she read it to them.

''Thank you for your inquiry. Due to an unexpected

cancellation, the June 18 slot is available. *Woohoo!*'' She jumped up and down in the swivel chair.

"You are very fortunate since the twentieth is the date of the Grand Prix in Monaco where we have docking privileges. If you wish to take advantage, you must advise us immediately.''

Piper swung around in the chair. "Monaco, guys. The playground of the rich and 'wannabe' rich and famous. The Grand Prix! Think, Olivia— Maybe you'll be able to see that dashing French race car driver you talk about all the time. The one that puts Fred's nose out of joint every time you mention him.''

"It's Fred's fault if he introduced me to Formula I racing. Wouldn't it be something to bring home Cesar Villon's autograph?'' Olivia's eyes were shining.

Greer was thinking it would be even more exciting to meet an Italian from their own Duchesse family who could provide the documentation proving their relationship to the Duchess of Parma.

"Piper? Find out if they'll accept another thousand a piece from us so we can have the boat to ourselves.''

"Ooh, I forgot about that, Greer. Good idea. I don't dare tell Tom about this or he'll want to come along.''

"What he doesn't know won't hurt him. It isn't as if you're in love with him.''

"How do you know?''

"Well are you?''

"Maybe.''

"Then ten days away from him will prove it one way or the other. Right?''

"I suppose so.'' Piper finished typing the question and sent an instant message.

While they waited for an answer, Greer studied one of the brochures with a map detailing the Mediterranean coastline bordering Europe.

Another shriek of delight came out of Piper. "They're willing if we pay in full now."

"Before we commit, we've got to find out if we can get plane reservations," Greer cautioned.

"I've already inquired." Olivia put her hand over the mouthpiece. "Everything's booked solid into Milan, Rome and Bologna, but we could still get seats to Genoa for June 16, returning June 29."

Greer looked at the map once more. "That's only fifty or so miles from Vernazza," she estimated aloud. "We could take a train and find a hotel for the 17 and 28. Book those flights for us, Olivia!"

Piper turned to Greer. "How do we want to pay for the boat?"

She pulled the wallet out of her purse. "Here. Use our business credit card to pay the bill in full. Let them know it's the Duchess of Kingston of the House of Parma-Bourbon making a reservation for an exclusive party of three, and you want that information kept confidential."

When the deed was done, their laughter bounced off the living-room walls.

"That was good thinking, Greer. Now it's guaranteed word will leak out," Olivia murmured. "We'll have to arrive at the dock looking sensational."

"Oh—" Piper cried. "You just made me think of something else. Remember that Paris elevator scene in the film about the American girl whose fiancé falls in love with a French girl? Remember the knockout dress she had on?"

Olivia's delicate brows arched. "Who could forget? We ought to be able to find inexpensive outfits and beachwear like the ones she wore. Maybe a hat or two? No one will know we didn't pay a fortune for them."

"Not if we wear our pendants," Piper inserted.

"Exactly. The men we're targeting survive by going after women with jewels. Without a jeweler's loupe, they won't be able to detect the fakes from the original.'' To this day Greer couldn't tell the difference.

"Then it's settled! We'll arrive in Italy wearing our pendants and see what happens! Since we have to stay at a hotel the first night we get there, I say we make a big splash. What's the most exclusive one in Genoa?''

"Just a sec, Olivia.''

Piper got busy on the Internet once more. "Hmm…how about the Splendido in nearby Portofino, first discovered by the Duke of Windsor. 'Preferred by royals overlooking Portofino harbor, gateway to the Riviera.' Twelve hundred Eurodollars a night for the three of us. It's about twenty-five miles from the airport and they have limo service. Do you guys think it's worth it?''

Both Greer and Olivia nodded.

"So do I. Let me check to see if there's a room available for the seventeenth. By the time the twenty-eighth rolls around, we'll have had our fun and can stay in a youth hostel if our funds are running low.''

Greer's eyes narrowed. "A hostel will be the perfect place to invite our 'would be' husbands when we drop our little bombs.''

Olivia started chuckling. "You have no heart.''

"You're scary,'' Piper told Greer.

She gave them her innocent look. "Did Cinderella have a choice when the carriage turned into a pumpkin on the way home, leaving her with one glass slipper?

"Can *we* help it if all we'll have to show for our attendance at the ball is the pendant we were wearing when we arrived?''

CHAPTER TWO

June 17, House of Lords, England

"MY LORDS, we will begin by hearing the opening statement from Signore Maximilliano di Varano of the House of Parma-Bourbon. He is the chief counselor avvocato for the Emilia-Romagna Farmers Consorzio of Italy, of which the Federazione del Prosciutto de Parma, a member, is the appellant in the case brought against the United Kingdom Supermarket Cartel, known as UKSC, represented by Lord Winthrope."

Back in the House of Lords for the second time in a year, Max got to his feet, determined his appeal would force the case to be moved to the European Court of Justice for a definitive decision.

"Thank you, my lords," he began with virtually no trace of accent, thanks to an elite private school education that included four years at Oxford and extensive travel in the U.S. and Canada with his cousins.

"To refresh your memories, Prosciutto de Parma, or Parma ham, has been made in Parma from pigs reared in northern and central Italy since Etruscan times. It is famous throughout the world with a name that is a protected designation of origin.

"The Corona Ducale, a five-pointed coronet symbolizing the ancient Duchy of Parma, is the outward guarantee of authenticity. According to Italian law, it has to appear upon the product in whatever form it is sold to the customer. If he buys a complete ham, or slices cut up at a shop, it has to bear the brand. If he buys prepackaged slices, it must appear stamped on the package.

"The second respondent, Prime Choice Affiliates, is a reputable food processor in Herefordshire that prepares packages of authentic Parma ham slices and pieces to be sold to the first respondent, UKSC, which sells them to the public in its supermarkets. Unfortunately it's done *without* the Corona Ducale on the package.

"The Federazione del Prosciutto de Parma maintains this is an unlawful practice under Italian law, as well as European law, enforceable in the courts of all the member states.

"In the present proceedings, the Federazione claims a continuing injunction against Prime Choice Affiliates and the UKSC, restraining them from marketing the packages as Parma ham until the European Court of Justice can hear the case and make a definitive ruling. I now yield my time back to Lord Winthrope."

When Max sat down, his assistant, Bernaldo, handed him a note.

With one ear taking in the QC's opening remarks, he read the message. But his mind was focused on the case to the degree that it didn't register until he'd read it a second time.

Your secretary in Colorno just received a call from the head of security at Cristoforo Colombo airport in Genoa Sestri. You're to phone Fausto Galli at 555 328 as soon as possible. It's a classified matter of great importance.

Translated, it meant there was no crisis such as his own personal family or extended family being injured in an accident or some such thing. Relieved, he put the message in his suit pocket, making a mental note to call Signore Galli back during the recess.

For ten minutes Max listened while the QC pontificated. Finally the man came to the point.

"In my view there exists a fair argument that the supervisory role of the Parma Federation in ensuring that only the genuine product is sold as Parma ham, has been discharged once it leaves the Parma area. I yield back to Signore di Varano."

Once again Max got up from the chair. "My lords, the issue here is whether the Federazione del Prosciutto de Parma's prohibitions contained in a legislative measure of a member state can achieve community wide effect to the U.K. and elsewhere. Therefore I respectfully appeal this case to the European Court of Justice. Otherwise it will continue to remain at an impasse which achieves nothing for either party."

Following his remarks, presiding judge Lord Marbury announced a fifteen-minute recess. Curious to discover what the call from Genoa was all about, Max pulled the cell phone from his breast pocket and dialed the number written on the paper.

He only had to wait two rings before he heard a male voice say, "*Pronto*. Signore di Varano?"

"*Si?*"

"It is an honor to speak to you. I have some news that I know will be of great interest to your family. Since you handle its legal affairs, I felt it prudent to alert you first."

"Go ahead, signore."

"A half hour ago three American women passed through customs after deboarding their flight from New York. My men detained them using the excuse they were vetting incoming passengers for information due to a suspicious person being aboard the plane. In truth, it was discovered they're each wearing the Duchesse pendant."

"Each?" Max shook his dark head in exasperation. "That's impossible!"

There was only *one* pendant in existence, but it could be anywhere because well over a year ago the Duchess of

Parma jewelry collection on display at the family palace in Colorno had been stolen.

The pendant was the least valuable of the items taken in terms of monetary worth, however its historical and sentimental value was inestimable, especially to Max's family.

"Did you consult an expert?"

"*Si.* During the interrogation, photographs were taken. They were enhanced for our forensics expert who compared them against the photo of the pendant you had distributed to the police after the theft. They were a perfect match."

Max blinked in astonishment.

"That's why I'm calling you, Signore di Varano. Do you wish me to confiscate the pendants so they can be examined? So far the Americans still don't know why they're being detained."

"That's good. Let's leave it that way for now. I appreciate your discretion and quick thinking, Signore Galli. You've handled the situation perfectly."

"However we've had many leads since news of the theft was made public and a reward for its return was offered. So far all the leads have turned out to be false. But I must admit this little joke initiated by some brazen Americans was meant to draw attention for a reason. One can only wonder why."

"My very thought, particularly since the joke gets even stranger."

The odd inflection in the other man's voice intrigued Max. "Explain what you mean."

"They're sisters."

"You mean professed nuns?"

"No, no. They are the same age with the same birthday."

"Triplets?" You didn't see that every day. "How old are they?"

"Ventisette."

Twenty-seven and already leading a life of crime...

"Molto bellissima!"

Beautiful, of course.

"Their paperwork states they are the Duchesses of Kingston from New York."

Duchesses of Kingston?

Max flicked his gaze to Lord Winthrope. *If* such a title existed, the esteemed QC would know who they were in an instant.

"Unfortunately I'm in London and can't return to Genoa before evening to investigate this matter. Did you find out their purpose for being in Italy?"

"They claim to be on vacation with a little business thrown in. We checked the information they gave us. It's been verified they're booked at the Splendido tonight and have chartered a sailboat for tomorrow."

"From Portofino?"

"No. Vernazza."

A frown slowly replaced Max's smile. That little bombshell hit too close to home to be a coincidence.

Two years ago he'd given the *Piccione* to his good friend Fabio and his two younger brothers after their parents had been lost at sea in the family fishing boat. The Morettis now made their living crewing for tourists.

To his friend's credit and business prowess, he'd paid Max back every last Euro, though Max had never asked or expected repayment. For twenty months like clockwork he'd received a good-size installment with a note of heartfelt gratitude from the man he didn't see nearly as often as he would have liked.

Besides watching after his brothers, Fabio now had a wife and they were expecting their second baby. Since they ran the only sailboat charter business in the tiny town which had been Max's backyard growing up, he knew exactly where to find these Americans. That is *if* they intended to stick to their agenda once they were freed to leave the airport.

"You may release them, Signore Galli, but have them followed and closely watched. After my flight touches down I'll make contact with you."

"Bene. Arrivederci."

After hanging up the phone, Max wrote a note on his scratch pad. He asked Bernaldo to hand carry it to Lord Winthrope. "Wait for his answer and bring it back to me."

Bernaldo went off to do Max's bidding. He returned a few minutes later. Max opened the note, eager to read what the other man had to say in response.

Glad to be of help, Max.

   Evelyn Pierrepont succeeded his grandfather as the second duke of Kingston. He was primarily famous for his liaison with Elizabeth Chudleigh, who claimed to be the Duchess of Kingston, but the Kingston titles became extinct on the duke's death around 1733. He had no children. Hope that answers your question.

Indeed it did.

Max lifted his head and smiled at Lord Winthrope who smiled back.

So…these American women weren't only audacious imposters, their impudence showed a certain shrewdness to pick an English title that had become extinct over two hundred years ago and pass it off as their own.

What kind of a game were they playing to come to Italy wearing pendants identical to the stolen one? Where did they get such an idea? Why would they do it?

"Much as I'd love to run to the room and change into my swimming suit, I'm too tired."

"Jet lag's caught up with me, too. Let's go to bed. You coming, Greer?"

"In a minute—"

The magic of the balmy Genoese night held her in its thrall. She'd always dreamed of coming to Italy. Though ninety percent of their ancestry was English and Scotch-Irish, their father had favored their Italian-Austrian roots. As a result he'd infected Greer with that love.

"Okay. Just don't make noise when you let yourself in."

"I promise," she said before their footsteps faded.

After several business meetings which might or might not produce a foothold in Europe, followed by a late dinner, they'd taken a walk to the San Giorgio church and visited the interior.

From there they'd strolled around the tropical gardens on the grounds of the Splendido, a former sixteenth-century monastery. They'd finally ended up at its outdoor pool overlooking Portofino harbor.

In Greer's opinion the view was worth a king's ransom. How their mother would have loved this flower-scented paradise.

There were quite a few guests climbing in and out of the water. Waiters moved around unobtrusively refilling champagne glasses. Every so often Greer caught snatches of conversation and laughter from beautiful men and women enjoying the elegant amenities of the privileged class.

As she stood next to a palm tree wearing her designer sundress in a stunning tangerine color, her attention was caught by a man doing laps with the speed and fluidity of a shark. A great black shark, if there were such a thing she mused fancifully.

Glimpses of a bronzed, well-toned male physique and

jet-black hair kept her gaze riveted. Suddenly he levered himself from the water onto the tiled deck.

The shark had legs.

Strong, powerful legs that propelled his tall, black trunk-clad body past the admiring glances from women and the envious stares of men toward Greer.

His total disregard of the surroundings testified to his inbuilt radar system which had targeted its next victim. How easy her subconscious had made it for him by sending out the message that she wanted to see if all of him lived up to her image of the quintessential playboy.

All of him did...

From an aquiline face, whose Italian bones had been refined and molded down through the centuries, gleamed a pair of black eyes that resembled volcanoes erupting in the night sky. One intimate look from them beneath expressive black brows and she felt as if her body had come too close to the mesmerizing magma.

Burned alive would be the more accurate description.

The pulse in her throat throbbed so violently, she could feel it move the pendant she wore around her neck like a choker.

She watched him watching it. He'd taken the bait.

Piper would be especially pleased to find out her suggestion to wear the family heirloom had proved to be a winner their first night in Italy.

"I saw you walking on the grounds earlier, *signorina*." His heavily accented English delivered in a deep masculine voice, vibrated to her insides. Its cadence sent a delicious tremor through her system even though the night was warm. "I hoped you would come to the pool."

Of course he did.

"I noticed you, too," she responded boldly, for once throwing her innate caution to the wind. "That's why I didn't go upstairs with my sisters."

It was a lie. She hadn't seen him. He was too much of a predator to have given himself away beforehand. Like his species, he'd lurked in the depths until it was time to make his attack.

"Swim with me."

His ardent demand, whispered with a pulsating urgency that said his life wouldn't be worth living if she didn't consent, decided her.

"I'm not wearing a suit."

"Does it matter?" came the breathtaking question.

She could have toyed with him a trifle longer and enjoyed every provocative minute of it. But in the end she decided not to tempt fate.

"No."

The second she said the word, she saw something flare in the dark recesses of his eyes.

Had she surprised him with her answer? To her knowledge sharks didn't have human emotions, only instincts that led them to their nearest prey.

Well, here I am... Let's see how long it takes you to swallow me.

With great daring she slipped off her gold sandals, left her gold watch and gold lame clutch bag on a table near the deep end of the pool, then dove in headfirst.

Having lived along the Hudson River all their lives, their father had taught Greer and her sisters to be strong swimmers. As a result, it was their favorite sport which they enjoyed on a regular basis.

The bottom of this pool was tiled in a fabulous design. She swam lower to get a better look, but was halted in her quest when a strong pair of male hands found her hips and brought her swiftly to the surface.

She emerged with her neck-length hair plastered around her head, no longer the picture of classic royal grace. Unfortunately that wasn't what disturbed her. It was the fact that her dress had ridden up to her waist, which meant nothing was separating his hands from her skin except her underwear.

With his arresting face only centimeters from hers, she would have to put on the performance of her life not to let him know how alarmed she was by this shocking turn of events.

"We haven't been properly introduced. My name is Greer Duchess."

"Greer," he repeated softly. The way he pronounced it made even the hard "G" sound beautiful. His slow white smile dazzled her. "Your name is as unique as you are. What brings a beautiful American woman like you to Italy?"

It was time to try out the story she'd rehearsed. "My sisters and I are here to visit relatives."

"Ah, yes?"

"Yes. My ancestor was the Duchess of Colorno."

His black eyes flared in recognition. "You're referring to Maria-Luigia of Austria of the House of Parma-Bourbon?"

So he knew his Italian history well enough to recognize the Duchesse pendant! This was so easy it was scary!

She couldn't wait to tell Olivia and Piper she'd caught a real playboy on her first night! Now all she had to do was play him for a while before she reeled him in and got him to propose marriage.

When she unmasked herself, he would slip off the hook and swim away. Then she would be able to enjoy the rest of this fabulous vacation knowing she'd followed her father's stipulation about the Husband Fund to the letter.

"Yes. That's right. My sisters and I are the American descendants from her Duchesse line." No need to add "the illegitimate line" at this juncture. "Now that I've told you something about myself, I'd like to know who *you* are,'' she said in the most seductive tone she could produce.

"Why don't you guess my name?" he came back in a deep voice that was equally tantalizing.

As if to emphasize his remark, she felt his thumbs making lazy circles against the nylon, increasing her awareness of him while they tread water. Her insides turned to liquid.

She gazed at his incredible male beauty through veiled eyes and said the first thing that popped into her head. "Luigio?"

His lips twitched, as if what she'd said had truly amused him. "No."

Greer had never been this daring in her life. But something about the man was like an elixir in her veins, increasing her bravado. She flashed him a brilliant smile. "This might take a long time."

He gave an elegant shrug of his broad Italian shoulders before drawing her closer. "I've been in London on business. Now I'm on vacation for the next week and would love nothing better than to spend every second of it with you, *bellissima*."

Every second? That meant day *and* night. She just bet he would!

To her consternation she realized she would love the same thing. A shiver of delight ran through her body.

She'd always heard the expression "carnal thoughts," but she'd never understood their true meaning until now...

Greer could find no fault in this Italian heartthrob who had it all down pat. Most likely he'd just left a woman in London and was now on the lookout for his next conquest.

As long as she was the bait with jewels and a title, why not tease him for a while longer first. She had an idea it would be a new experience for him.

"Unfortunately my sisters and I are leaving for Vernazza in the morning and won't be back."

"I know it well. Since you show no fear of the water, I would be happy to take you to a secret grotto which can only be reached by swimming a short distance beneath the sea."

She flashed him an artless smile. "Like Edmond Dantes who found Abbe Faria's treasure on Monte Cristo, will I discover gold and silver and precious pearls?"

His hard-muscled body stilled before he cocked his dark, handsome head. Even wet, his vibrant hair had a tendency to curl. "Is that what you're looking for?"

Again she had the oddest sensation that she'd said something unexpected, something that puzzled him. "Isn't everyone searching for treasure that will bring them ultimate happiness?"

"Ultimate happiness?" he murmured the words as if to himself, but his gaze was playing over her features, dwelling on each feminine attribute for heart-stopping seconds. "What is that I wonder?"

The philosopher emerging from the adventurer. He was a better actor than she'd first supposed.

"Thanks to Alexandre Dumas, we do know one thing…"

"That's right," he whispered. His lips were so close she could feel the warmth of his breath on hers. In reaction her toes curled against his hair-roughened legs as their limbs tangled beneath the water. "Though the Count of Monte Cristo had his revenge against his enemies, he didn't find happiness after all."

"Except that Dumas's book was a tale of fiction," she countered.

Again his eyes glimmered like black fires burning on a distant hill. "If you wish, I will take you to the island of Monte Cristo. It's not far from Vernazza. Perhaps there you will find what you're looking for."

You mean *you,* of course.

She struggled not to laugh at the pure conceit of the man. "Perhaps."

"Does that mean—"

"It means...perhaps," she interrupted with a flirtatious smile. "Now I'm tired and must say good night."

His hands remained fastened on her hips. "But it's not late, and you're too young to be tired."

"True, but we just flew in today, and were detained by the police while we were going through customs. Three hours to be exact. It was very exhausting."

"I'm sorry such a terrible thing happened to you in my country. Why would the police do this?"

"The head of security said there was a suspicious person on board our jet. He and his men took statements from the passengers who sat near this person."

"Were you able to help?"

"I don't know. We tried to remember the people seated around us, but no one looked suspicious to me. When we were finally let go, all we wanted was to reach our hotel and go to sleep."

"Of course," he whispered with compassion. His eyes wandered over her in intense appraisal before he said, *"Momento—"*

With one hand still possessively molding the curve of her hip, he signaled a waiter, rapping out something in rapid Italian. The other man nodded and disappeared.

Reading the question in her eyes, her captor explained, "I asked him to bring you a robe to wear back to your room. Such a delectable sight should not be for everyone's eyes."

Only *yours,* and you've been drinking your fill with unabashed enjoyment, she thought. He played it just right. The lothario with a streak of chivalry to keep him from being a complete cad.

"Thank you, Signore…Mysterioso," she improvised in her best Italian which, sadly, left a lot to be desired.

A bark of laughter escaped his throat, the first unorchestrated response to come out of him. In that millisecond of time she was allowed a glimpse of what lay beneath the polished veneer and felt an emotional tug totally foreign to her.

Not wishing to delve any deeper into her suddenly confused emotions, she arched backward to escape his grasp and struck out for the shallow end. That way she could use the steps and retain some semblance of dignity.

However he managed to get there first. In a surprisingly protective gesture, he placed the extended white toweling robe around her shoulders. She was quite amazed at the speed with which the waiter had obeyed the stranger's command without question.

She raised violet eyes to meet the smoldering depths of his. "Thank you. I was feeling a little vulnerable."

"Like Venus rising from the sea?" he suggested.

The second the words came out of his mouth, Greer could picture the famous painting of the Roman goddess of beauty awakening from a seashell without any clothes on.

Greer blushed at the shocking analogy and turned her head away. But he made the situation even more explosive and intimate by lifting the pendant and lowering his head to kiss the tiny pulse fluttering madly beneath it.

"One day soon when we have no audience except the sun on our skin and the sand beneath our bodies, I hope to see you exactly as Botticelli created her," he murmured against her scented throat.

Between the sensuality of his remark and the brush of his lips branding her heated flesh, she drew in an audible breath before wheeling away from his grasp.

Trembling, she plucked her watch and purse from the

table where she'd left them. Before she could decide whether to wear or carry her high heels, he'd looped his index finger through the gold straps.

"I'll escort you to your room. Not even the Splendido can guarantee the safety of a woman on her own who looks like you. In your exhausted state you would be no match for someone who would like to spirit you away to some secret lagoon for the night…"

The image he'd created sent another shiver through her body, part ecstasy, part fright.

Before this trip, the playboys Greer had pictured in her mind were likable. Manageable. Easy come, easy go.

Maybe a little miffed to recognize they'd been conned, but gallant enough to salute the girls as worthy adversaries who'd pulled off a well-executed charade. No hard feelings as they made their charming retreat from the playing field.

Up until this moment she'd been enjoying a game that had its nascence back in Kingston two months earlier. But just now when he'd kissed her and whispered his daring remark, she'd sensed a power shift.

Now *he* was the one dangling her as surely as he dangled her shoes from his fingers.

Instinct told her this was a dangerous man, the kind you didn't lure back to a youth hostel to tell him "sorry, wrong duchess." *He* would be the one to decide when he was tired of playing, then he would move in for the kill. Until then he would keep her trapped in his sights, and there'd be no place for her to hide.

A thrill of alarm caused her to walk faster.

When they reached the elevator where other guests were coming and going, she was in a state of panic and used the brief interim to extricate the hotel room key from her purse.

However by the time they'd exited onto the third floor, reason had reasserted itself. She told herself it was lack of sleep that had made her so uneasy. She would be leaving the hotel tomorrow and since she had no intention of ever seeing him again, she was even able to smile up at him with renewed confidence.

After the long transatlantic flight followed by a grueling three hours detainment at the hands of the police, she hadn't been herself at all. Otherwise she wouldn't have given a perfect stranger the green light to pursue her.

For a woman to plunge into the pool with her clothes on in order to sink her hooks into him, what else was a man like him supposed to think?

Tonight had been an experiment. A dry run. Whoops. A wet one, she mused nervously to herself, realizing her emotions bordered on hysteria.

She'd blown it, but she'd learned from it. Tomorrow would be a new day filled with more playboys and fresh possibilities.

The hotel room door was in sight. With one fluid movement she unlocked it, but before she could slip inside, he left a kiss on the side of her neck that set her whole body on fire. "Until tomorrow."

His promise sounded more like an avowal.

"Goodbye," she announced through the crack in the door before shutting it hard and locking it.

Congratulating herself on making it safely to her room, she staggered over to the nearest chair and held on while she attempted to recover from her fright. Her clutch bag fell to the floor with a soft thud.

Too late she remembered he still had her shoes. No matter. She didn't need them. In truth, she never wanted to see them again. She never wanted to see *him* again.

CHAPTER THREE

THE lights went on.

"Greer?" The second her sisters saw the condition she was in, they scrambled out of their beds toward her.

"How come your dress is wet?"

"Where did you get that robe?

"Where are your shoes?"

The questions pelting her one after the other stripped her down to the bare bones. This was no laughing matter. The only reason she'd escaped at all was that *he'd* allowed it.

She could still see the mixture of triumph and mockery glinting from the black depths of his eyes before the door closed, keeping him momentarily at bay.

"Guys?" Never in her life had their faces been more dear to her. "I'm in big trouble. We've got to get out of here now! I'll tell you about it when we're in the taxi." She removed the robe and wet sundress.

"They only have chauffeur driven cars here at the hotel."

"Well *we're* going to call for a taxi. Will one of you do it please?" she begged. "Tell them to be here in fifteen minutes."

"Where are we going in such an all-fired hurry?"

"Across the border to France. We'll drive to the nearest airport and take the first flight leaving for anywhere that puts as much distance as possible between us and hi— Italy," she amended.

"You've got to be kidding."

She shook her damp head at Olivia.

"I've seen that look before. She's not kidding," Piper whispered. They followed her to the bathroom. "Does this have something to do with what happened today when the police kept us so long?"

"No." She removed her watch, then her necklace, her skin still seemed to burn where he'd kissed her.

"I detect the scent of a man."

At Olivia's adroit surmise, a distinct blush covered every particle of Greer's skin. She was thankful for the protection of the elaborate sculptured design on the glass shower door, although it reminded her of the one on the floor of the pool.

The floor she never got to inspect at close range because she was snatched away by a force that still caused her to tremble.

"I didn't think there was a man alive who could make you run."

"If you must know, I tangled with a shark."

"In the pool?" Piper blurted incredulously.

"This one had arms and legs…" And a masculine appeal that ought to be banned from existence Greer groaned inwardly as she washed the suds out of her hair.

"Did he manhandle you?"

She reached for the tap to shut off the water. "Not exactly."

"Then he threatened you."

Greer shivered. "Not in so many words."

"If you expect us to check out of the hotel tonight when we've only had a couple of hours sleep, then you'd better tell us everything first."

Olivia was right.

After they left the bathroom, Greer grabbed two fluffy towels. With one encircling her head, the other fastened around her body, she padded in the other room after them.

Her sisters sat on their own beds cross-legged, waiting

for her. She sank down on the side of hers. "I—I have this horrible feeling I'm not only in over my head, but there could be serious consequences. It's my own fault of course."

She jumped to her feet, unable to relax. "In the beginning, the idea of turning the tables on an honest to goodness European playboy sounded very fun and challenging. That was until—"

"Until you met up with a real one tonight," Piper supplied.

Greer nodded jerkily. "There was this black-haired Adonis in the pool who would put any Olympic swimmer to shame. When he got out—"

Images flashed before Greer's eyes. She couldn't believe such an attractive man existed.

"Since you can't find the words, we get the picture." Olivia steepled her fingers. "Did he throw you in the pool without your permission?"

Her face went scarlet. "No."

Piper leaned forward. "Did you fall in by accident?"

"No! It was nothing like that," she confessed in a quieter tone.

"Then what *was* it like?"

"If you must know, he took one look at the pendant and asked me to swim with him. Everything happened just as we planned it back in Kingston. There was this gorgeous playboy who knew who the Duchess of Colorno was. He came on to me because of the pendant."

"So you just jumped in the pool with him?" By now their eyes had rounded.

"The Duchess girls don't jump, remember?"

Olivia's mouth broke into a grin. "Of course not. Still wearing your clothes, you executed one of your graceful dives to make certain you captured his attention."

"I guess," came her muffled admission.

Laughter filled the room, but Greer didn't join in. It was something they noticed.

"So what happened next?" Piper urged her to keep talking.

Greer kneaded her hands convulsively. "That's when everything went wrong."

"What did he do? Come on," Olivia prodded. "Let's hear it all, no matter how embarrassing it might be. Otherwise we won't know how much trouble you're really in."

"It's bad," she whispered. "Trust me."

That wiped the smiles off their lovely faces. "He didn't—"

"No—" Greer blurted. "But he *could* have done anything. My dress was floating around my waist and he was so powerful and so...so— " Heat suffused her face.

Piper slid off the bed. "And you think that if you'd been alone with him, he would have taken advantage of you whether you told him no or not?"

She drew in a sharp breath. "What I think is, that man goes *where* he wants, *when* he wants, and does *whatever* he wants. Period. The pendant seemed to have particular significance for him."

In the next breath she told them about the conversation in the pool, leaving out the parts about both kisses which were too personal. They'd shaken her so badly she couldn't discuss it, not even with her sisters.

"What's his name?"

"I have no idea."

Olivia rolled her eyes. "Greer—"

"I know," she muttered in self-deprecation, rubbing her arms nervously. "It gets worse. I tried to outbluff him by pretending that I wasn't in the most compromising position of my life. I flirted a little before telling him I wouldn't be in Genoa after tomorrow because we were going to Vernazza.''

"You *told* him we were going there?''

"I'm a fool, Piper, and I know it, b-but that was before I realized how dangerous he was. And after what he said about a secret grotto and the sun and the sand and me rising *au naturel* from a seashell, my gut instinct says he'll follow me there with the excuse he wanted to give me back my shoes.''

After his words to her at the door, Greer just *knew* he was the type of man that would turn up again.

"It sounds thrilling to me,'' Piper murmured.

Olivia nodded. "Me, too.''

"Guys—'' Greer cried in sheer panic, "this man *invented* the double-entendre. He's...dangerous.''

"You're saying that because you've never met anyone so gorgeous in your life, and you don't know how to handle your attraction to him.''

"I'm not attracted, Piper!''

"Yes, you are,'' Olivia contradicted her.

"All right. But even if I am, he's the kind of man who's off-limits!'' her voice shook. "When we decided to spend the Husband Fund, we should have stuck to the movie version we saw in Mr. Carlson's office and targeted sensible men. It would have been a lot safer than making ourselves the targets to wealthy playboys.''

Olivia frowned. "Our plan worked in theory. You're just not used to Italian men. It's perfectly natural for him to have been forward with you. It's the way they're made.''

"Olivia's right,'' Piper backed her sister up. "After all, you are very beautiful, Greer. Don can't ever take his eyes off you, but he's American, and American males aren't as obvious. Look how long it took him to make his first move toward you.''

"Try six months," Olivia drawled. "Greer—maybe this stranger *is* totally unscrupulous. Then again, maybe he isn't. You haven't given him enough of a chance yet to find out."

"You had to be there, Olivia!" Greer snapped.

"Not necessarily. You said he has black hair. With you being so blond, and having the most unusual violet eyes, it's no surprise he was drawn to you. I noticed a ton of men staring at you all day today. He couldn't help himself any more than they could. You *did* say he restrained himself."

Heat crept over Greer's body. "Not completely," she finally admitted. "He kissed me in the pool, a-and at the door."

"I thought so," Olivia murmured.

"Did you kiss him back?" Piper prodded.

"Of course not! H-he didn't kiss my lips."

Her sisters eyed each other before Piper said, "That explains everything."

"What do you mean?" Greer fired back.

"You're a take-charge kind of woman. He knew that and found his way around you. Sounds like you'll be getting a marriage proposal out of him before long."

"I don't want a marriage proposal. I just want to get away from him. Maybe we should just go home."

"We will, *after* our vacation is over," Olivia placated her. "Since we've already paid the money for the boat and can't get it back, I say we put the pendants away, drop the Duchess act and enjoy the rest of our trip like any normal tourists."

"I second the motion," Piper concurred.

"But I already told the stranger I was related to the Duchess of Colorno."

"It's too late to worry about the fact that we made reservations for the boat in the name of the Duchess of

Kingston,'' Olivia advised. "We just won't pull it on anyone else we meet."

"You're overreacting. However if or when Signore Mysterioso does show up," she mimicked Greer's pronunciation, "and you still want protection, he'll have to deal with all three of us."

"That's right," Piper chimed in. "Should he come around, we won't let you out of our sight for a single second. How does that sound?"

"In theory, it sounds fine."

"Good. Now that we've got everything settled, let's go to bed and sleep in until they throw us out. Okay?"

"Okay..." Greer's voice trailed, not nearly as confident.

Within a few minutes the lights had been extinguished and everyone had crawled under their covers. Soon Greer could tell her sisters were dead to the world.

It took a lot longer for her to succumb to the fatigue draining her body. That was because neither Olivia nor Piper had ever been stalked by a shark.

She kept feeling the spots where his mouth had scorched her throat and neck, imagining he'd actually taken little bites out of her.

"Nic? It's Max. I've got Luc on the line with me so we can have a three-way conference call."

"Luc?"

"I'm here, Nic. Good to hear your voice."

"It's like old times."

Max's two cousins, Nic and Luc, the son's of his father's sisters, were as close to him as brothers.

One aunt had married Carlos de Pastrana from Marbella, Spain. The other was married to Jean-Louis de Falcon from Monaco. All three parents were the direct descendants of the House of Parma-Bourbon and had married royalty. Max felt as at home at their residences as they felt at the Varano villa in Colorno.

Being between the ages of thirty-three and thirty-four, the Varano cousins had spent every possible moment together growing up, be it at school or on vacation. But five months ago tragedy struck, killing Nic's fiancée and almost causing Luc to lose his leg.

The accident had robbed both cousins of the joie de vivre Max had thought inherent in their natures. Much as he hated to admit it, he, too, had been in a state of despondency even before the ghastly accident. As far as he was concerned, if the three of them weren't careful, depression would turn them into old men before their time.

He could use their company right now and was glad for any excuse to bring them together.

"Forgive me for calling both of you at one in the morning, but this is important."

"What do you mean forgive?" Nic fired back. "As I recall, I kept you up half the night for weeks after the accident."

"And you spent the other half in my hospital room," Luc reminded him. "Hearing your voice is like a much-longed-for blast of fresh air. Especially when all I do lately is go from bed to work, to physical therapy, and then back to bed again."

"I couldn't agree more with Luc," Nic assured Max. "Thank God you've called. Tell us what you need and you've got it!"

Max was going to hold Nic to that. "Do you two think you could give me about ten days of your time?"

"Starting when?" they both demanded with such telltale eagerness, Max had his answer. Gripping the phone tighter he said, "In about six hours from now. It'll be a reunion *I've* needed."

Hard to believe there was a time when the three of them

had been young, inseparable *and* immortal. They hadn't believed the problems of ordinary men would ever touch their lives.

"You want us to join you in Colorno?"

Encouraged by Nic's question he said, "No. Vernazza, aboard the *Piccione*. I need you to help me crew."

Luc made a gruntlike sound. "With this damn cane, I'm afraid cooking is the only thing I'm good for at the moment."

"You're reading my mind, Luc. Since you're still out of commission, that's the job I'm assigning you. As we've learned from past experience, if preparing meals was left to me or Nic, we'd all starve to death. Nic can play captain."

"How come the *Piccione*?" Nic wanted to know. "You gave your boat to Fabio Moretti a couple of years ago."

"That's true, and it's his by right. I received the last payment on it several months ago."

"Good for him." A pregnant silence ensued. "So, I used to be fairly adept at reading your mind, but this time I have to admit you've got me baffled. What's going on?"

"Where are the Morettis going to be?" Luc asked.

"On an unexpected paid vacation."

"I take it this is some kind of emergency."

An image of the bewitching creature wearing what looked like their family's prized pendant flashed through Max's mind.

Her gorgeous eyes could have been spilled drops from those very amethysts. He pursed lips that could still feel and taste the flawless, perfumed skin where her life's blood throbbed close to the surface.

"I'm not sure what it is, Luc. But I know one thing. We have to strike now."

"Strike? That sounds cryptic."

"We may have our first break in discovering the person,

or persons, behind the theft of the family jewelry collection."

An expletive came out of Luc. "My parents never stop talking about it."

"Nor mine," Nic murmured. "Just before I left Marbella for the bankers' conference in Luxembourg, I heard Mama complaining to Papa because the head of security hasn't come up with a single lead in the case. As far as I'm concerned it's like we all said. Long ago the family jewels were removed from their settings and are sitting in someone's strong box."

Or around the delectable neck of an American vixen without scruples.

"It might interest you to know that yesterday morning Signore Galli, the head of security at Genoa airport, detained three American women on entry because they were each wearing the Duchesse pendant."

After a collective silence, "There's only *one* pendant!" Then they exploded with laughter.

That had been Max's first reaction, too. The jewelry collection was one of Italy's greatest treasures. Whoever stole it from the ducal palace in Colorno was the object of an intensive search.

For over a year now Italy's top investigators in conjunction with the CIA, Scotland Yard and Interpol had been working on the case without success.

"This Signore Galli's eyesight must be impaired."

"I don't know, Nic. The Duchesse pendant I saw a little while ago looked like the genuine article."

Quiet reigned once more.

"You *saw* one of the pendants they were wearing?"

"I did, Luc. Up close and very personal, if you know what I mean."

The inference that Max had been with one of the females wearing it didn't escape his cousins who after another telling silence urged him to explain everything.

"These women, Greer, Piper and Olivia, are extremely beautiful, twenty-seven-year-old blond triplets."

"Triplets?"

"*Si.* Not identical up close. Together they make an amazing sight. Their passports say their last name is Duchess. They live in Kingston, New York.

"I found out they were planning to go sailing from Vernazza later today. According to Fabio's records, the person who chartered the *Piccione* called herself the Duchess of Kingston from the House of Parma-Bourbon."

His cousins' sounds of disbelief rattled the phone line.

"I did a little homework and discovered through an impeccable source there is no such Kingston title in existence today."

"Which sister thought up the idea of capitalizing on such a blatant piece of fiction?" Nic demanded.

"I have no idea," Max muttered. "Greer claimed her ancestor was the Duchess of Colorno."

"Incroyable!" Luc bit out.

"I agree the whole situation sounds unbelievable. I wouldn't have taken any stock in Signore Galli's report if I hadn't followed the three of them from the Splendido to the San Giorgio church and back. They were each wearing a matching pendant. It's anyone's guess why, especially in light of the theft."

"Why would they enter the scene of the crime wearing copies of the genuine article unless they wanted to be caught for some reason?"

"I don't know, Nic. Perhaps it's an elaborate joke perpetrated by the thieves to rub it in the family's face that we'll never find out who was responsible."

"Or, it's possible one of the pendants they're wearing

is the genuine article and they're bargaining for bigger stakes," Luc muttered.

"My sentiments exactly. To make this even more interesting Greer claimed they were in Italy visiting their... relatives."

"Relatives—" Nic blurted. "*We're* the relatives."

"Exactly. Under the circumstances I thought you and Luc would like to help me facilitate a meeting between long lost cousins."

"Go on," Nic urged. At this point Max had garnered his cousins' undivided attention.

"We need to find out who they really are, why they're here. Are they acting alone? If not, who sent them? What is their agenda? The only way to get that kind of information is to use the old-fashioned method of extracting information, if you know what I mean," he drawled. "I trust you two haven't lost your touch."

"I like the idea of six 'kissing cousins' very much," Luc said, easily reading Max's mind. "There's no place cozier than the *Piccione* for what you're suggesting."

"Agreed. While we're crewing, we'll do everything we can to get their undivided attention. Here's my plan. Nic? When Fabio first brings them aboard, I want you to keep them entertained while I go through their luggage and steal the pendants.

"We'll sail for Lerici. After dinner I'll take them on a tour of the castle. That will give you and Luc time to fly to Parma by helicopter, show the pendants to Signore Rossi for examination, and be back on board the *Piccione* before my return with our guests.

"Depending on what we learn about the pendants, we'll know if we need more time to get information out of these women, or call in the police immediately and have them arrested."

Low laughter rumbled out of Nic. It was the first genuine emotion Max had heard from his cousin since the funeral, a sure indication he wasn't completely dead of feeling after all.

For that matter, Luc actually sounded excited about something which was a huge change from his brooding apathy of late. Both cousins' reactions constituted a plus Max hadn't counted on.

"I'll be honest and admit I'm looking forward to spending quality time getting as close as possible to Greer Duchess." In fact Max was living in anticipation. After tasting the satiny skin of her neck and throat, not once but twice, he'd developed an instantaneous addiction for her he needed to satisfy before the day was out.

"I'll meet you at the boat at seven," Luc declared.

"What about you, Nic?" After losing his fiancée, Nic hadn't looked at another woman.

"I'll be there."

Good. Better than good. Nic had been in hibernation long enough. "I've a feeling this is going to be like old times. *Ciao.*"

The brochure described Vernazza as a jewel. But the picture of it hadn't in any way prepared Greer to appreciate its spectacular beauty. The only natural port village of five towns making up Cinque Terre had a cut and polish like no stone she'd ever seen.

As she took in the brilliant facets of tower-shape houses clustered in different levels against the steep cliffs, the stark blue clarity of sea and sky made her eyes water.

She gasped at the range of color pitting forest and emerald-green mountains against the yellow, pink and rose of the more elaborate palaces and castles decorated by portals and porticos.

The delighted sighs coming from her sisters bespoke their mutual entrancement of this Mediterranean masterpiece the Genoese had protected against barbarians and Saracens centuries earlier.

Greer longed to hike the narrow paths climbing dizzily from the small square up the rocky face. But she would have to explore the town and hidden Vernazzola stream at the end of their trip because they were already late to board the sailboat.

Due to the thousands of tourists flocking to the Riviera for the Grand Prix, there was a lineup at the train station for tickets. As a result, Greer and her sisters didn't reach the stone jetty of Vernazza's small harbor until three in the afternoon, three hours past the appointed time.

A dozen or more boats in various colors were moored on the sheltered side of the dancing blue water. But there was only one catamaran. It stood out from the others like white chalk on a new blackboard.

She couldn't wait until they were at sea.

Though the haunting stranger from last night hadn't been waiting outside her hotel room door this morning with her shoes, or accosted her in the lobby when they'd checked out of the Splendido, *or* shown up at the dock, she still didn't feel safe.

Something about him had threatened her peace of mind in more ways than she could explain, even to her sisters. Given the slightest opportunity, she feared he might just devour her whole. Mind, body, soul, psyche—all of her…gone.

It was an absurd notion of course. He couldn't really do that, yet until the boat left the harbor, she wouldn't be able to breathe normally.

"Buon giorno, signorine," a male voice sounded behind them. Greer jumped in reaction, fearing the worst. "I'm Fabio Moretti, the owner of the *Piccione*. Welcome to Vernazza."

She heard her sisters introduce themselves. Piper gave

her a nudge. With her breath still trapped in her lungs, Greer turned around.

Relief swamped her to discover a smiling, dark blond Italian of medium height wearing blue trousers and a darker blue sport shirt. His hazel eyes gave them an admiring glance before he shook hands with them.

"Which one of you is the Duchess of Kingston?"

"We all are," Olivia declared. Greer moaned inwardly.

He tugged on his earlobe. "Ah, because you are—how do you say it? Treeplets. *Capisce!*" His head reared back in understanding.

Piper nodded. "But as we indicated in our e-mail, we'd like that kept confidential."

"Of course. Just so you know, I arranged for a special chef for your trip. He has cooked for several royals of the House of Parma-Bourbon. Right now he's busy in the galley preparing dinner. You are in for a very special treat while you sail on the *Piccione*."

Greer eyed her sisters in consternation before she looked back at him. "You didn't need to go to all that trouble, *signore.*"

"It was my pleasure. Though the people of Vernazza are Ligurians, the Duchy of Parma holds a special place in our hearts, mine in particular. If you'll follow me below, I'll introduce you to the captain who's anxious to get underway.

"Don't worry about your bags. The first mate will bring them to your staterooms. He'll be your steward and go through the boat safety drill with you once you've cast off. Shall we board?"

They stepped off the dock onto the boat and started up the side stairs after him. At this point Greer was feeling horribly guilty over the whole Duchess deception and knew her sisters were, too.

Under other circumstances she would have loved to chat

with Signore Moretti, a local who might be able to shed light on the story about the Duchess and her progeny. But at this juncture Greer realized it wouldn't be prudent for several reasons.

His boat more than lived up to her expectations, diverting her attention for the moment. Not only did it feel like an elegant luxury apartment at sea, but it came loaded with a wind glider, snorkeling gear, fishing gear, water skis, knee boards, sun mattresses... Anything and everything to ensure a dream vacation.

Then Greer caught sight of a striking, thirtyish looking male in sunglasses coming out the crew's quarters at the head.

Because of his well-defined physique visible beneath the indigo T-shirt and white cargo pants he was wearing, he bore a superficial resemblance to the tall stranger from the Splendido.

Her heart rose in her throat. But when he joined them in the main saloon where there was more light, she realized her mistake.

This man's hair was straighter in texture and had brown highlights among the black. His rugged features put her in mind of the group of proud, handsome Castilians who'd flirted with them on the train as it had passed through one tunnel after another.

The owner of the boat said something to him in Italian. When he removed his glasses, she found herself looking into black fringed eyes the color of rich brown loam.

"*Buenas tardes, señoritas.* My name is Nicolas, but please call me Nic. We are always informal on the *Piccione.*"

A gorgeous Spaniard who knew it, and spoke Italian and English, too. Impressive. Greer had been right about his origins.

Everyone said hello.

"It is indeed a pleasure to sail a boat with three such breathtaking sisters who look alike, yet are so different." His gaze traveled over each of them, but seemed to rest on Piper the longest. "Forgive me for staring, *señorita...?*"

"Piper."

"*Piperrre...*" He seemed to relish rolling her name across his tongue. "Your eyes are the same rare hue as the aquamarine waters along the Riviera di Ponente. *Muy muy bella.*"

Piper did have remarkable eyes. The trail of men who'd looked into them and been smitten was miles long. Obviously she didn't have to wear the Duchesse pendant to attract this man's attention.

Not for the first time did Greer regret last night's reckless, impulsive, unquestionably dangerous escapade.

"Thank you."

"We're sorry we're late," Olivia inserted.

"No problem, *señorita...?*"

"My name's Olivia."

He flashed her a seductive smile. It seemed not only Italian men, but all European men in general, had a way of invading a woman's space like nobody else, giving her no breathing room whatsoever.

To Greer's chagrin she discovered their captain, like the dark-haired stranger from last night, had the kind of overwhelming good looks you didn't run into every day, or every year. Or possibly never.

"As I was saying, *señoritas,* do not be concerned about the time. This is the busiest season of the year and delays on land are routine. That is the beauty of traveling by water. When there's no wind to fill the sails, we have engine power to take us where we want to go. I know places where we can be virtually alone."

Greer tensed at the unmistakable innuendo. "All we require is that you follow the itinerary we worked out with Signore Moretti.''

She felt his slight hesitation before he said, "Naturally, *señorita*." The assurance rolled off his liquid tongue, almost as if he'd sensed her misgivings and could read her mind. Almost as if he was mocking her. "But we will make one slight exception."

Greer *knew* it!

"Before we dock at Monterosso tonight, I thought you might enjoy a visit to the port town of Lerici. There's a castle you should see."

When Greer didn't say anything, Piper filled in the uncomfortable silence. "That sounds exciting."

Normally it would have sounded exciting to her, too, but for some reason she couldn't shake, Greer wasn't sure she trusted the captain completely.

"I don't remember hearing your name, *señorita*."

Really. It was on the tip of her tongue to play the same game the stranger had played with her last night and ask the captain to guess, but she restrained herself. "It's Greer."

She saw intelligence reflected in those dark brown eyes studying her with such unusual intensity it made her suspicious. Perhaps it was her imagination, but the captain still reminded her a little of the stranger from last night.

"Greer is an obscure yet charming diminutive of Gregorio, the first Greek pope, yet you all have the gilt-blond hair of the Saxons," he observed. "Why were you not given commensurate names?"

Commensurate? Who *was* this man?

"If our mother were alive, you could ask her." Ignoring her sisters' frowns she said, "If you'll excuse us, we'd like to freshen up."

Signore Moretti who'd been oddly silent throughout their exchange said, "There are three staterooms ready for you with your own queen-size beds and private bathrooms. Before I leave you in Nic's capable hands, allow me to show you.''

Without casting another glance at the captain, Greer took the lead behind the owner of the *Piccione*. Her sisters might be blinded by the captain's charm, but Greer wasn't!

For a seaman, he possessed an amazing grasp of etymology. Too amazing in her opinion. She felt like they'd jumped out of one proverbial frying pan into a fire where things were threatening to get a lot hotter.

As if to add to her concerns, their plan never to be separated was foiled when she realized the light, airy staterooms were located in three different corners of the catamaran.

Each one contained fabulous oversize baskets of flowers, fruit and chocolates, plus a well stocked minifridge with every kind of drink from mineral water to soda and wine.

Everything was lovely. She had no complaints.

But by the time Signore Moretti had wished them a happy trip and disappeared, she had the premonition something was wrong. When she detected vibrations running through her feet, she jumped. They were moving!

It was too late to get off.

CHAPTER FOUR

PIPER SIGHED. "I think Vernazza is more beautiful than Portofino, if that's possible."

Greer's sisters had scrambled on top of the bed and were looking out the porthole at the receding harbor.

"Admit the captain's the most beautiful man you've ever laid eyes on."

Greer knew of one exception to Olivia's observation, but she wisely chose to remain quiet on that subject. "Don't get too excited about him," she cautioned.

They both swung around, darting her a vexed glance. "What's wrong with you?" Piper chided.

Olivia folded her arms. "You were rude to him a few minutes ago, you know."

"That's because something about him doesn't ring true."

"For heaven sake's, Greer. Just because he's attractive doesn't make him a predator."

"I'm not talking about his looks, though they are exceptional. It's his whole demeanor. Your eyes, Señorita *Piperrre*—" She did a faithful representation of the captain. "They are like aquamarine waters. Your name, Señorita Greer, is obscure yet *charming*— My gosh— The man's a menace!"

Piper grinned. "You mean he reminds you of the way the stranger talked to you last night. I thought we decided that European males come on to women much more directly, so we just have to learn to deal with it."

"Piper's right," Olivia argued. "The captain may be Spanish, but they all have Mediterranean blood flowing

57

through their veins. It makes them different from the men we're used to dating.''

''I don't know, guys. I've a feeling our captain plays by a set of rules we've never heard of.''

''That's what you said about Signore Mysterioso.''

''They remind me of each other.''

''Greer—do you have any idea how paranoid you sound?''

''*He's* the one who sounds too educated to be doing work like this. If he were a real sea captain, he would be running a naval vessel or a passenger ship or something.''

Olivia hunched her shoulders. ''Maybe he does this for fun when he's on vacation. What do we care? We came to the Riviera for ten days of fun, plus the hope of meeting some authentic playboys.''

Greer shook her head. ''Technically we came with a definite plan to get them to *propose!*

''Can you honestly picture that three-tongued Don Juan above deck bringing himself to ask for a woman's hand in marriage? Even if he knew the Hope diamond could be his?'' she exploded.

''Probably not,'' Piper admitted. ''But then he's the captain, so he's not in the running.''

''Then somebody needs to tell him that. I saw the way he was devouring you with his eyes, as if you were a feast and he couldn't decide which dish to try first.''

''That stranger last night really freaked you out,'' Olivia said softly.

''The captain freaks me, too. Let's face it, guys. When we thought up our absurd plan, we'd just gotten home from Mr. Carlson's office. It was grief that made us delusional.

''I vote that when we dock at Monterossa tonight, we say 'thanks, but no thanks,' and head straight for the train station. I don't care if we have to stay there all night. Once we're back in Genoa, we'll wait on standby for a flight home."

"Home?" Piper's brows knit together. "No way, Greer. It's too big a waste of Daddy's money."

"We paid a trip cancellation fee," Greer reminded them. "I say we ask for a refund. Of course we won't get all the money back, but it's better than nothing."

"I came to see the Grand Prix."

"I realize that, Olivia, but there'll be another car race next year. You can come again for the right reason, and on your own money. I just think we're in over our heads here."

Olivia eyed her soberly. "You're serious."

Greer nodded. "What kind of a vacation will it be if the whole time we're trying to have fun on this catamaran, we're fighting off a captain who thinks he's God's gift to women and believes we're titled and dripping in money and jewels? If you think Signore Moretti withheld that vital piece of information from his crew, then you'd believe we're sailing on the Caribbean!"

"You don't have to be sarcastic," Piper murmured, sounding hurt.

Olivia trained concerned eyes on her. "With all of us protecting each other, the captain will be helpless to do anything, so I don't see the problem. It'll be three against one. If we stick together, he can't make a move we won't know about."

"Don't be so sure. He's runs this boat. You heard him say he knew of places where we could be virtually alone. He wasn't kidding. We're out of our depth here. They're not ordinary men. They know how to seduce a woman."

"Then we'll have to be on our guard."

"You say that now, Piper, but they have ways of getting you to do things you never planned to do."

Olivia drew closer. "Are you saying something else happened last night we don't know about?"

Greer's heart pounded in her ears. "No," she confessed shakily, "but—"

"But you think you won't be able to hold out against him if you were ever to see him again."

After her experience last night, she knew it would take a strong woman to resist a man like him or the captain and secretly she just didn't know if she could.

"Let's just say I don't want to find out." If she gave the dark stranger one inch, he'd take ten thousand miles. There would be a price to pay for carrying on a passionate ten-day affair with him. After it was over she would return home alone where she would stay in pain for the rest of her life.

No way... She was a Duchess, and a Duchess girl held out for marriage and everything that went with it.

"Guys—we've enjoyed our moment of insanity pretending to be duchesses. Now it's over."

"But not the whole trip." Piper stood firm. "We won't let the captain take advantage of any of us. We'll room together the whole time. One of those sun mattresses will work for an extra bed."

"I was just going to suggest it," Olivia murmured. "Now what do you say we go up on deck in a few minutes and enjoy the view until dinner? I don't know about you but I'm thrilled we have a French chef on board who'll guarantee us a fabulous meal."

To lighten the mood she handed everyone some chocolate and pears, one of their favorite fruits. "I figure we need a snack before the first mate gives us the boat drill."

"I just hope *he* isn't anothe—"

"Give it up, Greer!"

At Piper's admonition, Greer bowed her head, not wanting to entertain the possibility there could be another one like the shark from last night swimming anywhere loose around this boat.

It was such a troubling thought, she sat on the bed covered in a blue print spread and munched away. In a few minutes she got up to dispose of the wrappers and cores.

When she emerged from the spotless white bathroom loaded with all types of soaps, perfumes, lotions and shampoo, she announced, ''I'm going to go to the stateroom on the other side of the boat where I saw my suitcase. I'll be right back with it.''

''Mine's in the other one. I'll go with you,'' Olivia said. Together they slipped into the passageway and parted company by the stairs.

The vibrations had stopped, which meant it was the air in the sails, not the engine, that was propelling them. Greer loved the gentle rocking motion of the boat. Under other circumstances, this would have been the dream trip of a lifetime.

What an imbecile she'd been to touch the money their father had left them. They'd *all* been imbeciles. Look what had happened because they'd gone along with his ridiculous stipulation to try to find a husband!

Furious with herself, she flung open the door to the stateroom, which had been left unlocked. When she entered, she expected to see her suitcase on the floor, but it was nowhere to be found. The first mate must have put it in the closet. She crossed the expanse and opened it.

A surprised cry sprang from her lips to discover her clothes on hangers, her shoes neatly placed in separate compartments.

Her *gold* shoes.

Greer felt the blood drain from her face. There was the faint sound of a click behind her. She didn't have to turn around to know who was standing a few feet away, blocking her only escape route with the greatest of enjoyment.

I know Vernazza well. Since you show no fear of the water, I would be happy to take you to a secret grotto, which can only be reached by swimming a short distance beneath the sea.

Noooooooooo— It couldn't be. She'd known he would show up at some point on their trip, but not as a member of the crew aboard the *Piccione*! This couldn't possibly be happening.

"*Buona sera,* Greer." His haunting voice sounded like the night breeze swishing through the cypress trees, carrying the scent of lemon and jasmine down to the sea.

"I couldn't sleep all night anticipating being with you again. It's the only reason I was able to let you slip away, although I'll admit I came close to carrying you down to the sea for a moonlight swim."

Get a grip, Greer.

You can't let him see what this has done to you. Brazen it out till later. Play it cool.

She could hear her father's encouraging whisper, "Play it like a Duchess."

The thought of her loving parent gave her the courage to turn around and present an imperious smile to the one man who could be her total ruination if she didn't put an ocean between them in the next eighteen hours.

She steeled herself not to react to the devastating sensuality he emitted wearing one of those short-sleeved black crew necks. He'd tucked it inside thigh-molding jeans that rode low on his incredible male body.

Greer flashed him an imperious smile. "*Buona sera, signore.* So the first mate is last night's man of mystery."

"Life plays many tricks, does it not?"

"How did you know I would be aboard the *Piccione*?"

"As soon as you told me you were coming to Vernazza, I asked a close friend of mine to keep an eye out for you. It must be fate that brought us together without my having to lift a finger to find you. Especially when I distinctly heard you tell me goodbye through the hotel room door. That was cruel, *bellissima.*''

Fate my foot!

She raised her chin to combat position. ''You spend a lot of free time at the Splendido?''

''Actually I haven't been there for over a year. If I hadn't noticed you on the grounds, I would have left the premises and we would have been like ships that never passed in the night.''

''What if I hadn't gone to the pool?''

''Then I would have made inquiries until I found you, wherever you were.''

Though she willed it otherwise, her heart ran away with her. ''Are you always this persistent?''

''About something I want? Yes.''

Such an electrifying answer delivered in that deep tone, immobilized her. ''You want me?''

''Si, signorina,'' came his low velvety voice. ''In every conceivable way.''

His stark honesty was so shocking, she couldn't think, let alone breathe normally.

''But then you already know that, Greer, because you feel the same way about me,'' he added.

''You're very sure of yourself, aren't you, *signore.''*

His black gaze studied her features relentlessly. ''You would understand if you could see your eyes.''

''What about them?''

''You've heard the expression 'mirrors of the soul'?''

''So you believe my soul has been speaking to yours?''

''Loud and clear from the moment I saw you watching me do laps in the pool.''

Greer couldn't refute that statement. The second she'd laid eyes on him, she hadn't been able to look away. ''Do you use this same approach with every female stranger who looks at you?''

''I've never said it to another woman in my life.'' His voice throbbed the way it had done at the pool last night when he'd asked her to swim with him.

Greer threw her head back and laughed. ''I bet every American woman you've spoken to like this has believed you.''

''American?''

''Yes. They say the Italian accent to the American ear is the most provocative sound in the world. I have to admit I find it pretty irresistible.''

Lines darkened his handsome face. ''But you don't believe me.''

''There isn't a woman alive who wouldn't want to. After all, you *are* every woman's fantasy come true.''

''Even yours?''

''Especially mine.''

''Why is that?''

''My love affair with Italy began when I first found out I was part Italian.''

''You mean through Maria-Luigia's husband.''

Greer kept her smile in place.

This man had known exactly who the Duchess of Colorno was, which meant he was playing dumb with her now *on purpose*.

Any serious student of European history, of Italian history in particular, knew the Duchess of Colorno had *two* husbands, Napoleon Bonaparte, and Count Von Reipperg.

She'd been on the verge of telling him she was talking about the granddaughter of Maria-Luigia who allegedly had an Italian lover. But she thought the better of it because this man was toying with her for a definite reason.

''What about your ancestry?'' she asked, effectively changing the subject.

He cocked his head. "You didn't answer my question. Tell me more about the Italian side of your family. You have me completely enchanted, Greer. I want to learn everything about you."

Everything?

Beneath the ardency of his words she could tell he was driven by a curiosity separate from his desire for her. Of what real interest could Greer's roots be to him?

She gave him the benefit of a full, unguarded smile. "I'm afraid I left little to the imagination when I joined you in the pool. You've already learned I can be impulsive, and that I love to swim.

"Isn't it nice that in this new century, the working class can enjoy their time off at the Splendido in exactly the same way as the aristocracy?"

She'd posed the question while he pulled a life jacket from the footlocker.

He flashed her a mystifying smile. "That all depends on what you mean by enjoy. The worker is there on borrowed time and limited funds which adds a certain...edge to the experience." He moved toward her.

The first mate exuded an urbane sophistication that sat at odds with the kind of job he did. He seemed too powerful a personality, too shrewd and intelligent to take orders from anyone else.

Though he appeared perfectly at home on the boat, she was convinced he ruled another world apart from this one.

"I wouldn't know."

"Who could blame you. After all, you were born to be the Duchess of Kingston."

Though his silky observation had sounded totally offhand, Greer had the sudden revelation he was after her for whatever he could get out of her. Money...jewels...her virtue.

It shouldn't have shocked her. This was what she and

her sisters had hoped would happen when they came to the Riviera. But now that he was calling her bluff in earnest, the charade no longer felt like a joke.

To hide her dismay, she gave a careless shrug of her feminine shoulders, drawing his attention to the periwinkle silk blouse that crisscrossed the bodice.

His bold gaze dropped from her curves to the wide belt cinching her waist. By the time his eyes took in the line of her matching skirt which flowed from the flare of womanly hips, he'd managed to squeeze every ounce of breath from her lungs.

"It seems criminal to have to cover up what nature has so exquisitely endowed." Without asking her permission, he helped her into the jacket and secured the front straps.

After the way she'd plunged into the water at the hotel, she supposed he had every reason to believe she'd thrown maidenly virtue out the window long ago.

Little did he know her primal instinct was to slap his face. For the moment, all she could do was keep up the pretense until she could get away from him.

Restraining herself she said, "Seeing you busy like this at your job helps me understand why you were solicitous of my needs last night. Even to the point of returning my shoes? Has anyone ever told you *you* would make an excellent personal valet?"

With those words, she thought his patrician jaw hardened just a trifle. "No. You're the first. Are you offering me a full-time job?"

"Would you take it?"

"I would for the right price and benefits."

Her pulses throbbed. "I'll bet you're expensive."

"But that wouldn't be a problem for you."

"You mean because I'm a duchess?"

His lips twisted in a subtle smile. "Some titles have no money or property to back them up. But the pendant you were wearing last night tells me you can afford my exclusive services.''

It all got down to the pendant.

''Ah, but for how long?'' she asked with great daring.

''For as long as we continue to desire each other.''

Her body trembled. ''I'm afraid you misunderstood me. I was talking about valet service only.''

''So was I. Shall we test out one of my duties to see if my work measures up to your expectations?''

In the space of a millisecond he'd tugged on the straps he'd been tying so that she fell against his hard, powerful body. Without the life jacket separating them, her heart would have jammed into his.

His other hand cupped the back of her head where the gossamer strands brushed his fingers. He had the kind of strength that made it impossible for her to evade the insistent pressure of his male mouth. She was prepared to fight him with all her might.

But when that mouth closed inexorably over hers, he didn't swallow her alive in one gulp as she'd feared. Rather he played with her lips, nibbled on them, tasted them slowly, each time coaxing them farther apart, a little more and a little more.

After their exciting verbal skirmish, she felt a seductive rhythm building like the flow of the tide, racing up the beach a little higher, a little stronger. It filled all the aching spaces in her body which yearned toward him of its own volition.

His mouth created such sweet ecstasy, pleasure pains never before awakened came alive, demanding assuagement from the source that created them.

The moans she heard turned out to be her own.

Moans of need, of desire she didn't know she could feel. She felt helpless, beautiful. Alive. She didn't know herself anymore. He was making her feel immor—

"Greer?"

Olivia's voice.

The door flew open. "Quick! We've got some—Greer!"

Piper's shocked cry reverberated in the cabin.

Greer wrenched her lips from the man who'd been kissing her into oblivion and turned around in guilty reaction, but her senses were reeling.

Ironically her captor had to be the one to steady her in his strong arms. It would take time to recover from an experience that had been a breathtaking education in what really went on between a man and woman.

"Buona sera, signorine."

"What's going on?" Olivia demanded in a quiet, yet chilling voice. Piper looked ready to tackle him to the ground. Greer didn't know her siblings could be this fierce.

Of course they wouldn't have had any success if they'd tried to restrain him. The fact that he ignored their edicts and still held her arms firmly in his grasp testified to that truth.

"I-it isn't what you think," Greer stammered. "You've misinterpreted what was happening."

"That's right," he said in a suave tone. "Your sister and I were getting…reacquainted. Last night there was so little time before she ran off to bed, leaving me desolate."

Her chest heaved.

"Olivia? Piper?" Every breath sounded ragged, even to her own ears. "T-this is the man I met at the Splendido last night."

After the way she'd carried on about him earlier, she couldn't believe she was defending him now. However she drew the line at accusing him of a crime her sisters assumed would have taken place if they hadn't barged in.

To her shame, nothing had gone on she hadn't let happen and he knew it!

The truth was, it had given her a perverse thrill to spar with him. She'd loved baiting him. The last thing on her mind had been to scream her head off at the first sight of him so her sisters would come running.

When they recalled this incident later, they would have to admit she hadn't been struggling with him. Au contraire. She'd ended up being an eager participant.

That's what was so mortifying—to realize how completely out of control she'd been the second his mouth had covered hers.

He'd kissed her as if he were starving for her. Admittedly she'd kissed him back with a matching hunger that seemed to have come out of nowhere and sought appeasement only he could give.

Who knew how long their passionate interlude might have gone on if her prolonged absence hadn't prompted her sisters to come in search of her? She had only herself to blame for this latest disaster.

Piper made no move to leave. "Aren't you going to introduce us?"

"I don't believe we caught his name," Olivia murmured.

A betraying blush crept into Greer's cheeks.

"Allow me to do the honors," said the man whose mouth had done things that were still sending out shock waves to the tiniest follicle of her body.

"I'm Max, the first mate on the *Piccione*. I saw the three of you out walking last night. It was a beautiful sight, one I'll never forget."

His hands caressed her arms down to the fingertips, then relinquished them. While Greer continued to tremble in reaction, he'd reached the open doorway in a few athletic strides.

Before disappearing he said, "*Signorine?* Meet me on

deck in five minutes with the life jackets you'll find in the footlockers of your staterooms. I'll show you how to fasten them correctly. Knowing what to do will save your lives if, heaven forbid, there should be an emergency on board.''

CHAPTER FIVE

IN THE wake of his departure, Greer realized an explanation was in order. She blurted, "What you saw was nothing more than the result of my insulting him. Rather than fight him, I decided it might be wiser to let him get it out of his system."

To her surprise, her sisters shut the door, then put a finger to their lips.

"What's wrong?" Greer whispered.

"Just listen," Piper whispered back. "Our pendants are gone." Greer blinked. "We discovered them missing while we were putting everything away in the drawers of our stateroom.

"I only opened my cosmetic bag to get out some sunscreen. That's when I noticed the pendant wasn't there. I asked Olivia to look in her bag thinking maybe I'd put it there by mistake last night, but hers was gone, too."

"Since our bags never left our sight after we packed them this morning, it means the members of the crew have to be jewel thieves who believe they've stolen a small fortune," Olivia surmised. "Do you still have yours?"

Did she?

Galvanized into action, Greer ran to the bathroom where the first mate had put her cosmetic bag. She opened it and found the little case she kept it in. The pendant winked up at her.

"Mine's still here," she said in shaky voice. "He was probably in the process of stealing it when I surprised him by accident."

The three of them stared at each other before Olivia said

to Greer, "We thought you were overreacting earlier, but now we know your premonitions have been right about everything."

Piper had a far away look in her eye. "For the stranger you met last night to show up today claiming to be the first mate, and then for us to discover him kissing you like there's no tomorrow, it's obvious something out of the ordinary is going on here, even if you are fatally attracted to him."

Fatally attracted. That's what it felt like.

A shiver chased across her skin. "I knew it couldn't be a coincidence. Remember my telling you how drawn he was to the pendant?"

"Yes. If all he'd wanted was to get you into bed, he probably could have managed that last night."

"Thanks for the vote of confidence, Olivia," Greer said before averting her eyes.

"We saw you in his arms just now," Piper pointed out. "You were hardly fighting him off. No one's blaming you. Good grief. He looks like a god, and it's perfectly evident he's attracted to you, as well. But he has come on way too strong, too fast! As for the captain, you were right about him. He's— He's—"

Greer groaned. "I know what you're trying to say." She took a deep breath. "Let's face it. Signore Moretti has an interesting little operation going here. It might be legitimate, but he gets lots of perks when idiots like us charter his boat pretending to be something we're not. We don't have anyone else to blame but ourselves for our loss. If the parents knew…"

"We can't think about that right now." Olivia glanced at her watch. "The first mate said five minutes. If you're up not on deck in about twenty seconds, he'll use that excuse to come down and find you. I suggest we hustle topside on the double, pretend nothing's wrong, and talk about what we're going to do later.''

''Agreed.''

In the next breath they hurried to the other stateroom for more life jackets, then emerged into the dazzling late-afternoon sun for which the Riviera was famous.

A mild breeze filled the sails imprinted with a stylized pigeon in flight. It propelled the boat away from the post-card perfect coast receding farther into the distance.

''*Signorine?*''

Every time Greer heard the deep resonance of the first mate's voice, a current of electricity traveled through her body igniting her nervous system. Except that this time she was on to him and the captain. They'd been in the cockpit, talking. Plotting…

Some job those two had.

She wondered how many hundreds of wealthy women over the years, married or not, had been swept away by their amazing looks and overpowering charisma, never to be the same again. Never to recover their jewels again.

Science hadn't invented a vaccine to inoculate the fe-male of the species against the invasion of such spectacular foreign male specimens. There was no known antidote. The best you could do was run for your life in the opposite direction and never look back!

That was exactly what she and her sisters intended to do tonight after they docked. Until then they would have to stick together like Vienna sausages in the can and bluff their way through this last poker game. Greer could only pray they escaped from their doomed adventure relatively unscathed.

As her nemesis approached, the devastating white smile he flashed convinced her he could read her mind. She avoided his gaze while he inspected the way her sisters had fastened their life jackets. Once he'd given them a few pointers, their drill began.

The boat and everything to do with it seemed to be a part of him, which ironically she had to admit was reassuring. In twenty minutes they knew where to find extra life buoys, a two-way radio, flares, fire extinguishers, an ax, sea rations, water, tool and first-aid kits, navigation lights, buckets, oars, the horn and a waterproof sea chart with compass.

"Do the two of you know how to swim as well as your sister?"

They nodded.

"Nevertheless you'll do exactly as I say when you're playing with any of the water gear. Even dive masters like myself or the other crew have to be prepared for the unexpected, so we'll obey the rules to the letter. Do you have any questions?"

Greer had one. "Why are we sailing in the opposite direction from Monterosso where we're docking this evening?"

She'd planned that part of the itinerary herself. Monterosso had the best beach of the Cinque Terre.

If this was going to be their last night in Italy, they would at least be able to tell their friends they'd bathed *once* in the waters of the Mediterranean.

His black eyes impaled her. "You're very astute to realize we've made a minor detour."

"You call 'due east' a minor detour, *signore?*"

His captivating smile might as well have caught hold of her heart and upended it. "Didn't the captain tell you we're making a stop at the port town of Lerici?"

"He mentioned it. What's so important?"

"A sixth century castle which is just magical. You and your sisters can explore to your heart's content."

What a bald lie! This was a setup he and the captain

had obviously worked out over years of enticing rich women. Drop the jewels off at Lerici, then proclaim innocence at a later date when it was discovered the pendants were missing.

The boat proved to be the perfect vehicle. Seduction on the high seas, their vulnerable captives at the mercy of their potent masculine appeal.

They had the moves and the jargon down so perfectly, they could do it in their sleep—read each other's minds without conversing! Greer could read the first mate's since it was as transparent as a bride's veil.

He thought himself as irresistible as Valentino, but he couldn't be more wrong. Though he'd shocked the daylights out of her with kisses that revealed her own sensuality—a sensuality she hadn't realized she possessed, it didn't mean she wanted to repeat the experience.

You only had to be scalded once to know you should stay away from boiling water.

"Since when does a captain take orders from his first mate?" she challenged him. "Surely as long as you're getting paid the going wage, your job has nothing whatsoever to do with the itinerary we decided on weeks ago."

Her attention was caught by his hands which opened, palms upward, in a gesture so typical of Italian men she couldn't look away.

"It was a mere suggestion, *signorina.*"

And I'm the Duchess of Kingston!

"If we'd wanted to go on a tour of the paranormal, we would have started out in Transylvania."

His eyelids lowered to half mast. "It was very wise of you not to travel there. Even I, who do not have a drop of vampire blood in my veins, find it increasingly difficult to resist taking a bite out of you myself."

At the mention of the word "bite," the spot where he'd

kissed her neck beneath the pendant began throbbing again. She fought not to react.

On cue her instinct for self-preservation came to the fore. Her chin jutted. ''You can inform the captain we're not interested. Unless there's something else you needed to tell us that could save our lives, we'll be resting in our cabin until dinner's served.''

After delivering her exit line she started walking toward the stairs, all the while feeling his fiery black eyes on her retreating back.

''It's ready now,'' he called out unexpectedly. ''The chef is waiting.''

The girls followed her to the stateroom. ''Let's eat so they don't suspect anything, then we'll decide what we're going to do about our situation,'' she whispered as they removed their life jackets.

By tacit agreement they moved to the saloon. It was nothing short of amazing to see how it had been transformed. The table with an alençon lace cloth had been set for three.

Greer noted the Waterford crystal, fine Limoges china and a centerpiece of roses in reds, pinks and yellow. Her mouth watered the second she detected the fragrance of a seafood dish escaping the covered tureen.

The door to the adjoining galley opened. They spied a cane before a lean, hard-muscled male emerged. He was dressed in jeans and a gray pullover with the sleeves shoved above the elbows.

When he lifted his head of short-cropped black hair, Greer looked into the face of an olive-skinned Mediterranean man who possessed the kind of dark, dashing looks that caused women to make utter fools of themselves! No one knew about that better than she did.

If he weren't leaning so heavily on his cane, he would probably be as tall as the two men on deck.

"Bonsoir, mesdemoiselles." His deep-set gray eyes assessed Greer and Piper before traveling to Olivia.

There was no attempt on his part to apologize for studying her. His intimate perusal of her face and figure was guaranteed to wring a blush from the most hardened female. Greer had to give her sister points for holding it back.

"You must be the one named after the *olivier.*"

"Then whoever told you that was misinformed," Olivia threw out with gratifying sangfroid.

She'd sensed this gorgeous hunk of male was no chef. Not for this boat or a royal family. If any member of this crew was legitimate, then Greer and her sisters were the three good fairies!

His mouth curved into a wicked smile, verifying Greer's suspicions. "I'm never wrong, *mademoiselle.*"

"Really," Olivia mocked. "Well unless you required a cane from birth, it appears you made a wrong move at least once in your life."

Whoa, Olivia!

His handsome face turned dark as a thunderhead, revealing a man who had a dangerous look now that Olivia had struck him where it hurt.

It was patently clear that not only had the spoils been equally divided ahead of time, she and her sisters were about to be served up for their captors' delectation.

Not if Greer could help it!

"Monsieur *Luc,* is it?" she addressed him in her best bad French. "I'm afraid there was a slight oversight on our part. We forgot to tell Signore Moretti we're allergic to fish."

"It's a shame," Piper played along. "How sad that the beautiful dinner you labored over so long with your bad leg has to go to waste."

On their way out of the saloon Olivia turned to him.

"What was it Marie Antoinette once said, 'If the passengers can't eat fish, let the crew eat it'?"

Bravo, Olivia!

They walked with great dignity to their stateroom. Once they'd locked the door behind them, Greer turned to her sisters. This time she was the one to put a finger to her lips. "We've been *had*, guys."

"Tell me about it!" Piper whispered furiously.

Olivia's angry brows knit together. "It all started when we were detained by the police at the Genoa airport. Three hours for what? In a matter of a minute we told them all we knew which was absolutely nothing!"

"And when I met the *first mate* at the Splendido it certainly wasn't by accident!" Greer muttered through gritted teeth. "When he called for a robe, the waiter obeyed him instantly. How come?

"And why did he empty my suitcase? We didn't pay the kind of money that entitles us to the services of a personal valet. I'm thinking our crew has a friend on the police force."

"Of course," Piper cried. "You can always count on a small percentage of the law being corrupt. Signore Moretti is probably in on it with them. Scamming wealthy tourists is a great way to make extra money on the side."

"Absolutely," Olivia exclaimed. "When we told him the Duchess of Kingston was making the reservation, he probably alerted the others who told that pompous security guard to check us out when we went through customs at the airport."

Piper nodded. "The moment he saw we were wearing the Duchesse pendants, he informed his cohorts. They figured there was a lot more where that came from and scrambled to get the boat ready."

"A chef who looks like him cooking for royalty—I don't believe that for a minute!" Olivia raged.

Greer moaned. "When I think I told you to ask if we could have the boat exclusively if we paid them another $1,000 apiece!"

Olivia shook her head. "They must have rubbed their hands with glee."

"Well they're not going to get away with it!" Piper declared. "When we reach Genoa we'll go straight to the American Consulate and tell them what's happened."

"You mean *if* we reach Genoa." Greer had been looking out the porthole. "Take a look, guys. We're still going east, not west."

"Why aren't we surprised?"

The three of them stared at each other before Olivia said, "We'll swim for it as soon as we get close enough to land or the nearest passing boat. Which ever comes first."

Piper's eyes rounded. "You know we could?"

"Of course we could. There's no current here as strong as the one in the Hudson. If we wear some casual skirts and tops instead of bathing suits when we go up on deck, they won't suspect anything," Olivia reasoned. "Especially if we keep on our sandals."

"Good idea," Greer said. "And we should all keep together so it looks like I'll have to use clothes from one of your cases."

"That's fine. What about our passports and tickets?"

Greer had been thinking about that. "Leave them. We'll line our bras with the twenty-dollar bills we brought with us. When we reach shore and tell the police what happened, our abductors will be hauled in and we'll recover our stuff.

"But just in case something happens and we don't get our belongings or pendants back, I'll tuck mine inside my bra so we'll have at least one heirloom left for posterity."

"Good thinking, Greer." Olivia walked over to the baskets. "Better eat some more fruit and chocolate to give us energy, guys. We're going to need it."

In twenty minutes they were fed, dressed and had worked out their strategy.

"Everybody ready with a life jacket?" Greer whispered. They didn't plan to use them, but would take them topside so it looked like they were following the rules.

Her sisters nodded.

"Then let's go. Play it cool."

They couldn't have asked for a more calm, blue sea. Enough of a breeze filled the sails for the boat to move without the help of the engines. Conditions were perfect to escape.

Once they dived overboard, the crew would have to take down the sails before starting up the engines to catch them. The girls planned to grab that window of opportunity to swim beyond their reach.

All three of their captors were on deck. The first mate stood next to the man named Luc who lounged against the cockpit's exterior where his cane rested. No doubt they were both talking to the captain, relishing thoughts of the night ahead.

Greer turned her head in the other direction to smirk. Relish away all you want. It won't do you any good.

Following Olivia's lead, she and Piper purposely worked their way to the bow. To her joy the boat appeared to be making for a headland. Another fifteen minutes in the same direction and the girls would have no problem swimming the rest of the distance.

Using their life jackets for pillows, they stretched out to enjoy the sun. Though it was after seven o'clock, the rays still felt warm against their skin.

No sooner had Greer closed her eyes than she sensed the shark's presence. A shark that could hunker down next to her. A shark that smelled of the soap's tang he'd used in the shower.

"What a tragedy you didn't stay in the dining room long enough to enjoy the rack of lamb entré Luc prepared."

She sucked in her breath. "We can't eat fish, and didn't realize he'd prepared anything else. I'm sure it made a tasty meal for you," Greer murmured without opening her eyes.

"His cooking is always a treat. You disappointed him by not eating it. At the moment he's very fragile."

What tripe was the first mate feeding her now? "Why is that?"

"He was in a terrible accident and is lucky to still have both legs. In spite of his pain, he prepared a culinary masterpiece for you. The least you could do tonight before going to bed is ask one of your sisters to thank him for his trouble."

You mean you want Piper or Olivia to join him in his bed and give him comfort. Good grief! The man was transparent. Talk about a ship of fools!

"Are you saying he's one of those chefs who's known to get volatile when he thinks he's been slighted?"

"That's the wrong choice of word, Greer. You and your sisters hurt him with their comments just now. Do you want that on your conscience, too?"

"Too—" she blurted.

"*Si, bellissima.* Your lips are to die for, but you stab me repeatedly in the heart with your rapier tongue."

Greer didn't know whether to laugh or cry. One minute he frightened her with his overpowering male charisma...the next minute he turned on an irresistible charm that reduced her bones to jelly.

She couldn't keep up with him, and would probably have forgiven him anything if she hadn't found out he was a thief.

"If that's all you came over here to tell me, then I'd prefer to sunbathe alone."

"We're hardly alone, Greer, and with all those clothes on, there's little of you exposed. Fortunately for me I have memories of last night when I saw much more of the flawless skin you're wise to keep covered. Those images will keep the fire burning hot until tomorrow."

An involuntary tremor rocked her body. "Tomorrow?"

"Um. The secret blue grotto I was telling you about is just outside San Remo, the next stop on your itinerary."

"But you're not following our itinerary."

She peeped at him to see his reaction. For a split second she thought she glimpsed the blaze of raw desire in his eyes before his lids lowered like a shutter against a window.

"Until the Grand Prix is over, you will have difficulty avoiding the wall-to-wall bodies as you try to wade ashore at Monterosso. In fact with so many tourists, it will be impossible to see the Riviera di Levante and do it justice.

"Since you seem to have a particular liking for Dumas, I thought tonight you might like to visit the Villa dei Mulini, Napoleon's retreat while he was in exile on the island of Elba."

Elba.

Just the word conjured up a bygone age of history and enchantment she'd only read about in books.

Was he hoping the mention of Napoleon would cause her to divulge more information about her royal Italian heritage so he could find out if there were other pieces of jewelry for the taking?

"If you like, we'll snorkel at nearby Isola Pianosa in the morning. Its sea bed lies in a preserved park no one can enter without advance permission. In my opinion it is one of the most beautiful underwater sights in the world."

Which underwater sight was he really talking about?

The one where he coaxed her into swimming au naturel with him? And afterward they would make wild, primitive love on some deserted beach beneath a hot sun?

Yes, she could imagine it all, in full Technicolor. If he weren't a scoundrel, she had a feeling he could talk her into doing just about anything...

"After you've enjoyed brunch," he went on chatting her up, "we'll stop at Monte Cristo Island and look for buried treasure. Who knows what we'll find?" he drawled in that seductive way that could only mean one thing to a predator like him. It sent a voluptuous shiver though her body.

"I know exactly what we'll find, *signore*. I did my homework before we came to Italy. It's nothing but a pile of desolate rocks that I have no desire to see. I prefer the humanity at Monterosso."

"Inebriated humanity," he came back quietly. "Tourists who have no idea they're lying on a battlefield where an ancient Roman family fought against the invaders from Pisa. But if that is your wish..."

"It is." On that note she turned on her side away from him.

Greer couldn't believe it when she felt his lips against the smooth stem of her neck. She swallowed hard and stared anywhere except at him. He didn't know the meaning of the word fair. The man had refined the art of going for the jugular.

If she continued to resist him, she wouldn't put it past him or his lusty band of thieves to haul them off the boat to the castle and lock them inside while they made their getaway with the loot.

Not only would it be a much needed balm to their dented male egos, it would satisfy their idea of poetic justice for three upstart Americans who'd given them such a hard time.

Except for one brief moment of insanity when Greer had known rapture in his arms.

I have news for you, Max or whatever your real name is. You haven't seen anything yet!

After a minute she lifted her head to meet her sisters' glances. By the expression on their faces, they'd decided the town of Lerici, or whatever, was close enough to reach. Max had started to make his way back to his cousins; now was the time to carry out their plan.

Olivia gave the thumbs-up signal.

"All for one, one for all," Piper whispered.

In a great lunge they bounded over the railing into the warm, blue water. Together they cleaved the gentle waves with swim-meet speed toward the shore.

Max entered the cockpit with a grimace. Nic flashed him a questioning glance. "What's wrong now?"

"Contact the harbor police and tell them to have a cruiser waiting at the dock. Since nothing I've said or done has broken Greer down enough to give me information, perhaps the threat of the law will put the fear in her. I'm through playing games with the *signorine*. I want to know how they got those pendants," he bit out moodily.

Nic had already started phoning when Max turned to Luc. "Keep a close eye on our precious cargo while I go below to find Greer's pendant. Left unattended, I wouldn't put it past our resourceful guests to grab the kayaks and take off."

Luc frowned. "You think they'd go that far in order to get back to Monterosso?"

"Further." Max chewed on the underside of his lip for a minute. "When was the last time you saw a stone cold sober female wearing the Duchesse pendant plunge head-first into the pool of the Splendido with all her clothes on?"

A gruntlike sound came out of Luc. "Point taken."

After Signorina Greer's surprising display of passion in his arms a little while ago, Max had assumed he had her exactly where he wanted her. But it appeared he was mistaken. The enticing little vamp with the amethyst eyes had been playacting the whole time.

Filled with a negative surge of adrenaline because her performance was one he would never forget, Max left the cockpit first. His gaze flitted automatically to the bow before he stopped dead in his tracks. All he could see were three life jackets lying exactly where the women had left them.

Luc saw what Max saw and moved fast for a man with a cane. "The kayaks are still there. The women must have gone below for something. I'll check."

Perhaps Luc was right, but Max had already learned that the enigmatic Duchess triplets played the game of life by a totally different set of rules.

Following his gut instinct which was telling him something didn't feel right, he retraced his steps to the cockpit where Nic was still on the phone. He grabbed the binoculars, stepped back outside and lifted them to his eyes.

Sure enough about a third of the distance from the boat to the shore he saw three heads of gold bobbing up and down in the water. They swam like a school of well trained dolphins. Surprise grabbed him by the throat to witness such a stunning sight.

He moved inside the cockpit once more. "Our guests have jumped overboard without their life jackets."

"Madre de Dios!"

"Your concern is wasted on them. They can swim like fish and will reach the shore before long. Tell the police to draw alongside and pull them out pronto!"

Another minute and Luc appeared with three passports and airline tickets in hand. "You were right, Max. I should never have underestimated them. Take a look at this!'' He opened Greer's jewelry case. It was empty.

As pure revelation poured through Max, his mouth thinned to a white line of anger.

"No one leaves a passport behind. Not unless they have an 'in' with someone high up in diplomatic circles who can help them."

Nic's gaze locked with his. "That would have to be our jewel thief. Someone operating in our family's inner circle as a friend who happens to own a police commissioner or two?"

"Fausto Galli."

"Why not? He was the one who called you in London to tell you three women had been detained at the airport wearing identical pendants."

"Such irresistible bait in more ways than one," Luc murmured.

Max sucked in his breath. There was little point in responding to Luc's comment when it was a fact that needed no embellishment.

"That was their purpose, of course," Nic concluded. "The whole thing has been a setup from the moment they made a reservation with Fabio."

"You're right. Their escape from the bow was no accident, either. Those women are powerful swimmers. I have no doubt they left the boat to meet a prearranged contact at Monterosso in order to hand over the pendant. Most likely someone handpicked by Galli."

Luc nodded. "It makes perfect sense. The jewel thief plants the original and two fake pendants on the women to confuse everyone. Then he puts you on their trail so *you* will eventually catch them and put them behind bars.

"Everyone will be happy and think the case is closed. You'll have your pendant back, Signore Galli will find a way to get the Americans' sentences reduced for good behavior, and in the meantime—''

''And in the meantime the real culprit keeps the rest of the family's collection and is free to go on stealing more jewels without fear of suspicion,'' Max finished for him. ''Your reasoning makes an incredible amount of sense.

''Luc? Help me with the sails while Nic starts up the engines. On our way to the dock, I'll make a call to Signore Galli and tell him that since the theft took place in Colorno, the situation is longer in his jurisdiction.''

''He's not going to like that,'' Nic warned.

''But there won't be a thing in hell he can do about it. Especially when I inform him I've instructed the police commissioner in Emilia-Romagna to make arrangements for the Americans *and* the pendant to be transferred from the police boat to the jail in Colorno.''

''Better tell the commissioner to split up the triplets so they can't plan another escape. Their minds think alike which makes them particularly dangerous.''

''I'm way ahead of you, Luc.''

Max's eyes glittered as he studied his two cousins. ''Let the Duchesses of Kingston get a taste of life in an Italian prison. It will give them an education they've been needing. Then we'll deal with them in our own time, on our turf and in our own way. *Capisce?*''

Several deep chuckles ensued.

''Sooner...or later,'' he drawled, ''I'll come up with a plea bargain they'll have to accept. We'll be able to flush out the thief masquerading as our family friend, and that will be the end of it.''

CHAPTER SIX

GREER looked through the bars of the cell at the overweight prison guard. The commissioner in the main office had put him in charge of her.

"Is everyone around here crazy? The police were supposed to arrest those wretched jewel thieves out on that catamaran. Instead they arrested my sisters and *me*."

"That is not my problem, *signorina*."

Her hands formed fists. "In the United States every person arrested is allowed to make a phone call to their attorney. If you won't let me use a phone, then *you* phone him for me. I left Mr. Carlson's number with the commissioner. I'll pay for it."

Her four, twenty-dollar bills were sopping wet along with her clothes, but they were still considered legal tender.

"Everything in time, *signorina*. It's midnight and no business can be conducted before morning."

"I want to see my sisters."

"That is not possible. Perhaps tomorrow."

"I'd like to know where we are."

"All in good time."

"I demand to know why you're keeping us here!"

"You women are always demanding something, as if this is a luxury hotel instead of a jail. The Duchesse pendant missing since last year was found around your neck. That should answer your question."

Last year? "You mean there's another one?"

"As if you didn't know, *signorina*."

"But I didn't! *We* didn't!" No wonder they were in trouble... "Listen—the one I was wearing was *mine!*"

"How did it come to be in your possession? Can you answer me that? Did it walk out of the museum at the Ducal palace on its own?"

"I'm trying to explain, and you're being very rude, *signore.*"

"You were very rude to steal it."

"How could I steal it when it was given to me by my parents?"

"And the Vatican City was given to me by mine."

"Go ahead and be as nasty as you want. I've told you the truth."

"So your *parents* stole it, is that what you're saying? The House of Parma-Bourbon will be very interested to learn that piece of information."

"That's *not* what I'm saying. It was handed down in the Duchesse family from generation to generation until it was given to my father by his father!"

He threw back his balding head and laughed. "There is no Duchesse family, *signorina.*"

"If you'll look at my passport, you'll see my last name is Duchess, spelled the American way."

"What passport? When the police pulled you out of the sea you did not have one on you."

"We left them on the boat with our airline tickets because we expected to have them returned when the police caught the real jewel thieves!"

"You Americans love a joke." He seemed to find everything she said hilarious and started down the dimly lit hallway.

"Wait! Come back! Please!"

"Buona notte, signorina."

She heard a clank.

It was going to be a long night, and a damp one. The

police had supplied them a blanket which she still had wrapped around her. There was another one plus a sheet on the cot against the wall of the miniscule cell. No pillow. In the corner stood an old chamber pot.

Greer couldn't believe it. If all the people arrested had to spend a night in a place like this, they'd probably think twice about ever committing a crime again.

The stuffy cell wasn't cold or hot. Still, she felt so uncomfortable in her damp things, she decided to take everything off and wrap the sheet around her. Hopefully by morning her clothes would be dry.

Her poor leather sandals were ruined, but she wouldn't complain. Not after the sign she once saw at the shoe repair which said, "I felt sorry for the man who had no shoes, until I saw a man who had no feet."

She had to be losing her mind to think about that at a time like this.

There was no place to hang anything, so she spread everything out on the cement floor including the damp blanket. After separating the money so it would dry out too, she lay down on the cot.

The lumpy mattress had to be made out of straw, but she was so exhausted it didn't matter. She stretched out on her side using her arm for a pillow. Catching hold of the other blanket, she drew it over her head. No telling what crawly creatures she'd be spending the night with.

Missing her sisters horribly, she knocked on the wall the way she knocked on the front door at home to let them know she was there.

If one of them was lying on a cot on the other side of it, maybe they would hear her and answer back. But after five minutes of bruising her knuckles against the rough plaster, she gave up and closed her eyes.

Their plan to escape had gone without a flaw. It had seemed like destiny when the police cruiser came alongside them and the authorities offered to help them aboard. But then fate played a cruel joke. What happened next she didn't want to think about.

After handing them a blanket, the police took them to the dock, then hauled them into a van without any windows and no explanation. They must have been on the road several hours, only to be dumped here, her pendant confiscated.

What a laugh Max must have had as he and his cohorts sailed away scot-free, possessors of two pendants, one of which might be the authentic piece.

Sorry, Daddy. You and Mother should never have left us money to "try" to find a husband. We're no good in that department.

The men who want to marry us, we don't want.

And the men we shouldn't want...

The memory of a certain male mouth closing over hers took her breath. She pressed her sore knuckles against her lips, wishing she could drive away the ache that had never left her body since he'd first kissed her.

"Signore di Varano! This is a great pleasure."

"Commissioner? Allow me to introduce my cousins, Lucien de Falcon and Nicolas de Pastrana. We're here to interrogate the prisoners."

"What a tragedy that sisters so beautiful have found themselves on the wrong side of the law."

Max didn't want to hear it. "Did you arrange their cells the way I instructed?"

"Yes. Of course."

"How long have they been here?"

"Approximately two hours."

"Good. Have they caused any problems?"

"Problems? No. The one with the violet eyes was dismayed to be shut up without knowing her crime. I must admit I was moved."

Despite his frustration over their incredible disappearing act, Max had to struggle not to laugh. "Did you enlighten her?"

"*Si.*"

"How did she respond?"

"She protested her innocence. At that point they *all* protested their innocence and demanded to phone their attorney long distance. The one with the aqua eyes put a damp twenty dollar bill across my palm for a bribe."

A sound bordering on a chuckle broke from Nic.

"The one with the flame-blue eyes informed me every prisoner in the United States is given a square meal their first night in jail and she was in need of one. It was very amusing as she clearly expected me to comply with her wishes. She, too, handed me a damp twenty-dollar bill."

"Mademoiselle Olivier had her chance to eat earlier," Luc declared in a cold tone, but Max noticed his cousin's lips twitching.

The commissioner glanced at the three of them. "All in all, the *signorine* were well behaved. I have to admit I was surprised. They didn't complain about not having a change of clothes or any makeup."

Women that beautiful didn't need makeup, but Max said something quite different to the commissioner. "That's because these sisters happen to be professional thieves."

"They must be to have carried off the jewelry collection without being detected. Per your instructions I ordered the guards to take them to different floors for the night where they've been put in isolation."

"Excellent. May I have the pendant please."

"Of course." The commissioner opened the drawer of his desk. The police had put it in a bag they used for forensic evidence. He handed it to Max who put it in the pocket of his jeans.

Now that he possessed all three, he would have them examined by Signore Rossi who would know immediately which one was the genuine article.

"If you'll inform the guards we're ready to begin our questioning of the prisoners." Three foreign beauties, alike in some ways, different in others. Intelligent, unpredictable. And all of them...criminals.

The commissioner nodded and picked up his phone to summon them. No longer smiling, Max told his cousins he'd meet up with them in an hour before they returned to the villa. The balding guard beckoned him down a hallway and through a door that had to be unlocked.

"She's in the middle cell of that corridor where there aren't any other prisoners."

"Did she tell you anything you felt could be important?"

"Only that her parents gave her the pendant she was wearing, thereby admitting that they must have stolen it. Of course she said it had been passed down from generation to generation in the Duchesse family. I told her there was no such family."

"I see. Thank you for the information. I'll knock when I'm ready to leave."

"*Bene.*"

In the shadowy light, the first thing Max noticed were her sandals set out to dry. Next to them lay her skirt, her top, then her underwear. His eyes traveled over each item neatly placed in a row down to the individual twenty-dollar bills. Four of them to be exact.

He was intrigued by the way her mind worked. How orderly she was. There was something essentially feminine about the arrangement. Very prim and proper, yet oddly forlorn because it represented all her worldly possessions.

When his gaze discovered her body cocooned in a

prison blanket and huddled against the cell wall on the narrow, insubstantial cot, he experienced a strange tightness in his chest.

But the possibility that she'd heard voices when the guard opened the outer door and she was only pretending to sleep, hardened his resolve to vet her.

"*Signorina?* Come! Wake up!" He rapped on the bars.

She stirred and rolled toward him, still covered in the blanket. "Are you going to let me make my phone call now?" By the sound of her voice, she was still half-asleep.

"To whom?"

"Walter Carlson."

"Who is he?"

"My father's attorney."

"Why not phone your father?"

"I can't, he's dead."

Max blinked. His experience in the courtroom questioning hostile witnesses led him to believe she was telling the truth.

"Where does this attorney live?"

"In Kingston, New York. He'll vouch for my sisters and me."

"He'll have to do a lot more than that, *signorina.* You've passed yourself off as a relative of the House of Parma-Bourbon, and you're in possession of the stolen Duchesse pendant. All of which constitutes a major crime against the Duchy of Parma. I'm afraid you're facing a stiff prison term."

Greer had heard that distinctive male voice before. Her eyelids fluttered open. She sat up so fast, the blanket slipped to the floor.

In the semidarkness she could see the first mate's powerful physique standing in the hall outside her cell. More, she could feel those eyes of black flame scrutinizing her, scorching whatever part of her skin the sheet didn't cover.

With her heart tripping all over the place, she clutched the scratchy material to her neck. "You have your nerve coming here when *you're* the one who should be behind bars, *signore*."

"I'm afraid I wasn't the one caught wearing the pendant around my neck when the police plucked you and your sisters from the sea."

"But you stole the other two pendants, so don't bother denying it!"

"I had no intention of doing so."

The man was amoral.

"How did you get in here? No—don't bother to answer that question. You're all so corrupt there's no point."

"All?" His demand came out sounding like ripping silk.

"What part of that word don't you understand? *All*," she repeated. "Every last one of you down to the captain, the chef, the owner of the boat, the commissioner, the guard, the waiter at the Splendido. Need I go on?

"You're all members of that good old boy network. You scratch my back. I'll scratch yours. It's sickening."

His fingers curled around the bars as if he'd like to get them around her neck. "Since I saw pretty good evidence of the good old girl network in operation today when you executed your escape from the *Piccione*, that's a lot like the pot calling the kettle black, wouldn't you say?"

Her chin lifted a little higher. "I'd say your knowledge of American sayings makes you out to be an even more worldly con artist thief than I'd first supposed.

"But the last laugh's going to be on you when you try to sell off those pendants and discover they're not worth more than a couple of hundred American dollars a piece."

"And what about the one you were wearing when you swam for it?" he reminded her. "Are you going to tell me it's only worth two hundred American dollars, too?"

"What if I am?"

"No jury on earth will believe it. Not when you chose to leave your passport behind, something not even silver and gold can buy if you should happen to end up in the wrong country."

"This is the wrong country all right. Nevertheless, a passport *can* be replaced, *signore*. A family heirloom can't..." Her voice trailed off.

"Ah—now we're getting somewhere."

"Getting somewhere? You're sounding more and more like a slick-tongued lawyer with every word. Why don't you pick on a real criminal, like the one the guard said stole a pendant from the museum?"

"Don't think we haven't tried," he admitted with breathtaking honesty.

"You know something? Though you'll probably continue to get away with your perfidy in this life, you won't in the next!"

"Then I guess we'll burn together, *signorina*. If you recall we were already halfway consumed by the flames in your stateroom today."

She swallowed hard. "Only a real playboy would remind me."

"There speaks a woman who instead of slapping my face enjoyed every breathtaking moment of it. If your sisters hadn't chosen that moment to interrupt us..."

"Yes?" Greer prodded. "Would you have made an honest woman of me and asked me to *marry* you?"

After a pregnant silence, she heard a sharp intake of breath. "Is *that* what this has been all about? *Marriage?*"

A smile of satisfaction broke out on her face. "For such a clever jewel thief, I'm surprised it has taken you this long to figure it out."

*   *   *

Max was surprised, too. Stunned was more like it. He'd wanted a confession, so why all of a sudden didn't it sit well with him?

He and his cousins had been forced to deal with fortune hunters all their adult lives. So far they'd been able to spot them and take the necessary steps to elude them. It was the unpleasant if not ugly part that went with the territory of belonging to the House of Parma-Bourbon.

"So...the whole pendant business was a ruse to win an introduction that could result in a marriage proposal?"

"Exactly. But I suppose it's poetic justice that the men we targeted turned out to be several degrees more unscrupulous than ourselves."

Just when he thought he had things figured out, she said something that shot his theories all to hell. "Then you admit the pendants are copies of the original."

"Except for one of them."

"The one your family inherited."

"Yes."

Max cursed softly. This woman had the ability to twist him in knots. "Which one of you was the mastermind behind that plot?" He might as well hear the rest. In truth he'd never in his life been this frustrated and entertained all at the same time.

"Our parents. But only indirectly," she amended.

"*How* indirectly?"

"We could only use the money from the Husband Fund our father willed to us to go spouse hunting."

Husband Fund? Spouse hunting? A bark of laughter escaped his throat. "How much money?"

"Oh, $15,000. $5,000 apiece."

"I thought the pendants were only worth $200."

"They are, except for the real one and I have no idea how much it's worth. Since we're triplets, and there was only one pendant, our parents had two more made up just like it. They gave them to us on our sixteenth birthday for us to pass on to our future children.

"That was the whole point of the Husband Fund, of course. Mom and Dad wanted to ensure there would be another generation of Duchesses. That's something none of us is interested in yet."

Max's eyes closed tightly for a minute. Was this one of those cases where her story had to be true because no one could manufacture such a fantastic tale?

"Anyway, we used the fund for this trip and to charter the *Piccione*."

"Why did you pick the *Piccione*?" This ought to be good.

"Because Daddy always called us his pigeons. You know, in honor of our ancestor the Duchess of Parma who had a pigeon named after her. It's on our business logo."

Just as he'd suspected, whoever had coached these triplets was intimately associated with his family and its history.

"*What*, exactly, is on your logo?"

"The white Duchesse pigeon!"

More and more Max felt he was in the middle of some amazing dream. She seemed to delight in weaving lies. "And this business...what kind did you say it was again?"

"I didn't. We own a company called Duchesse Designs."

Max rubbed bridge of his nose. "What is it you design?"

"Calendars. Actually Piper does the drawings and Olivia does the marketing."

"And what do *you* do?" This was getting better and better.

"I do everything else."

"Like what for instance?"

"Provide the research and keep the books."

"I see."

"I'm surprised you're asking all these questions. If you and your cohorts weren't so obsessed with taking advantage of rich women, you would have noticed our samples in the bottom of Piper's suitcase while you were rummaging through our personal belongings."

He blinked.

"We passed out some to a few distributors in Genoa yesterday hoping to expand our company to an international business."

So much information had been thrown his way, Max could scarcely digest it, let alone decide what part if any of it was true. But he did seem to recall Signore Galli telling him the *signorine* had come to Europe for a little business, as well as pleasure.

The notes made by the police officers assigned to tail the women after they'd left the airport would clear that up in a hurry.

"You still haven't answered my question about why you chose the *Piccione*."

"I've been leading up to that. When we got on the internet and were looking at a list of catamarans to charter because they were cheaper than a yacht, we saw that one of them was called the *Piccione*. It seemed like fate, so we clicked on to it. As it turns out, it was the biggest mistake we ever made!"

"Do not worry, *signorina*. If you cooperate, we might be able to arrive at a bargain which will be mutually advantageous for all."

There was a prolonged silence. "I knew it!" Her voice came out sounding more like a growl. "Admit that one of your cronies on the police force tipped you off that three women wearing the Duchesse pendant would be staying at the Splendido!

"Admit you were up to no good following me and my sisters around! Explain why the waiter obeyed you like a servant!

"Oh yes, and please explain if you can without lightning striking you, how you could suddenly show up on the *Piccione* as the first mate if you hadn't been orchestrating lucrative conspiracies like these for years! Answer me *that!*"

Her challenge brought an effective end to a conversation that had held him spellbound. There were a few dozen matters he needed to research before he spoke to her again.

"All in good time, *signorina.*"

"That's what the guard said. Typical male rhetoric. You don't fool me. You came to the jail to find out if my sisters and I have more jewels hidden away somewhere.

"Well you won't get that information out of me, not even if the commissioner gave you a key to this cell. I'm warning you now, your powers of seduction leave a lot to be desired.

"Any coward can manhandle a woman confined to a life jacket or behind bars. I have to tell you I would have been a lot more impressed and possibly more forthcoming if you'd tried your best technique while you were escorting me back to my room at the Splendido.

"For a Riviera playboy, I have to tell you that on a scale of one to ten, ten being the ultimate male, you came in a four. Unfortunately a four still isn't passing. Even Don rated a five. Sorry."

"Don? As in Don Juan?" he scathed.

"No. Don as in Don Jardine, an American. I should have given him more credit the first time.

"*Arrivederci, Signore Mysterioso.* Oh—before I forget. On your way out to plot your next heist with your henchmen, turn off the hall light, will you? I'd like to get some sleep."

His body stiffened. "I guess you can try to rest, but for a woman who has as much on her conscience as you do, I don't hold out great hope for you. *Ciao, bellissima.*"

His mood foul, Max went in search of his cousins. He found both of them outside the door to the commissioner's office. When they saw him, they stopped pacing.

"You look like the survivor of an explosion," Nic observed.

"I was going to say the same thing about both of you."

A nerve pulsed at the side of Luc's mouth where a tiny scar from the crash was still healing. "You won't believe what I have to tell you. It has to do with that old wives' tale concerning one of Marie-Louise's granddaughters who supposedly had a liaison with a monk.

"Mademoiselle Olivia claims she and her sisters are the descendants of their love child."

Max's jaw went slack. "That rumor was proven false years ago and few people outside the immediate family ever even heard of it. Can there be any doubt our jewel thief is someone operating from the inside? When we wring a full confession from the *signorine,* we won't have to look far to find the culprit."

"The story goes from one *absurdité* to another," Luc declared. "According to our lovely jailbird, the granddaughter was purported to have suffered a miscarriage. In reality she delivered a son whom the monk, her lover, secretly christened with the last name Duchesse to protect his identity.

"He then arranged to have the baby taken to Corsica where it was raised by a childless woman loyal to the Bonapartes. Inside the infant's blankets he'd wrapped the pendant.

"Several generations later that pendant traveled to America where the Duchesse name was changed to

Duchess. It ended up in New York in the hands of the father of the *belles mesdemoiselles.*

"Not wanting to slight his offspring, he had two more pendants made identical to the original so they would each have one to hand down to their posterity."

The sheer scope of the lie left all of them dumbfounded.

Max eventually glanced at Nic. "Did Signorina Piper tell you the same fiction?"

"No—she fed me another lie," Nic said with asperity. "Something crazy about these pigeon drawings she has done for their family calendar business.

"Get this—" he said in a burst of laughter. "They call the female Violetta, after the Duchess. Since this fictitious monk who remained a mystery for over a century had no first name, she and her sisters decided to call him Luigio, a subtle distortion of the second half of Maria-Luigia's name."

A flashback of a certain moment in the pool of the Splendido hit Max squarely in the gut.

Greer—Your name is as unique as you are. Why don't you guess mine?

Luigio?

The whole time Max had been toying with her, she'd been playing him for a complete fool!

"She says that one of her great-grandfathers, Alberto Duchess, served in World War I in the Signal Corps. Are you ready for this?" Nic's eyes appeared dazed as they traveled from Luc to Max. "He raised Duchesse pigeons for a hobby.

"One of them carried a message that saved the lives of several hundred men and received a medal of honor from Great Britain. Señorita Piper says the medal is at home among their family mementos."

Max's dark head reared back. "Signorina Greer told me

to look in her sister's suitcase and I would find samples of this calendar.''

''Their luggage is in the car,'' Nic declared. ''Do you think the samples are really there?''

No one said anything or made a move to walk outside. Max suspected his cousins were holding back for the same reason he was. But they couldn't stand there forever smoldering with curiosity. It was four in the morning and they were dead on their feet.

Letting out a curse he finally said, ''Come on. Let's find out and get this over with.''

They made their way to the restricted parking area. Luc trailed because at this point he was favoring his cane. They were the only people moving about in the dark.

Max opened the trunk of the estate car they'd driven over from the villa. The inside light made it possible to see enough without needing a flashlight. Nic found the case with the initials PD on it and opened the locks.

After feeling around her clothes, he produced a large square manila envelope. As his cousin proceeded to empty the contents, Max found himself holding his breath.

Out came six calendars.

Luc reached for one of them. ''Men's Most Notable Quotes About Women,'' he read aloud.

''For Women Only,'' Nic mouthed the title of another sample. Max grabbed for a similar calendar and opened the cover to January's quote for the month.

So Many Men... So Few Who Can Afford Me.

Sure enough, *there* was the female pigeon Violetta, dressed in a gown and jewels. The male, Luigio, looking weary and dejected, tagged behind.

Max's eyes widened to realize they'd entered an exclusive designer shop on one of the fashionable boulevards in *Parma.* Next to a pair of shoes, a handbag and dress she'd drawn placards showing astronomical prices both in lire and dollars.

Astonished, he turned to February's quote.

Coffee, Chocolate… Men. Some Things Are Just Better Rich.

This time the two pigeons sat in an elegant pastry shop near the Teatro Farnese in Parma drinking espresso and munching on their world famous chocolate biscotti. While Luigio looked longingly at her, Violetta played footsie beneath the table with a well-dressed Italian pigeon wearing the ducale corona emblem. *Incredible.*

March's quote.

Don't Treat Me Any Differently Than You Would The Queen.

It was yet another drawing of poor, helpless, love-smitten Luigio throwing down his cloak for the treacherous yet delectable Violetta who was visiting Langhirano where you could see the very long, narrow windows, shuttered and open—designated to ventilate the aging hams.

April's quote.

Behind Every Successful Woman Is A Woman.

His curiosity insatiable by now, Max studied each rendition with total absorption. He came to November.

Ginger Rogers Did Everything Fred Astaire Did, But She Did It Backward And In High Heels.

There was Luigio in a tux and top hat. Violetta wore a gown and high heels while she danced backward on the staircase of the Palazzo della Pilotta in Parma.

Like being mesmerized at the scene of a fire where you couldn't look away, he turned to December.

A Man's Gotta Do What A Man's Gotta Do. A Woman's Got To Do What He Can't.

The irony of the quote twisted something unpleasant in his gut. Finally he took in the sketch of the enormously pregnant Violetta lying on a gurney in the Torrile Bird Hospital in Parma while Luigio lay passed out on the floor.

Not that many of his own countrymen knew about the bird refuge his family helped fund. Max was convinced Signorina Greer's research had to be aided and abetted by someone on the inside.

He also had to admit the two pigeons exuded so much individual human charm and personality, one could only marvel. This clever, stunning creation based on bits of myth and reality would have universal appeal for women, even for those ignorant of Parma or its history.

But the acerbic quotes he could imagine coming out of Greer's succulent mouth, served with a contemporary sting, which he as a man felt like the lash of a whip, had wiped the smile off his face.

"Look on the back." Luc's grating voice broke the unnatural stillness. No doubt he and Nic were still smarting from the quotes, too.

Max turned his calendar over. At the bottom center was an oval with a stylized Duchesse Pigeon and the words Duchesse Designs printed inside the rim.

"The existence of the calendars doesn't mean they're innocent of the crime," Luc proclaimed in a wooden voice. "A good liar always mixes in enough truth to be convincing."

Nic exhaled sharply. "You're right."

By tacit agreement they put the calendars back in the suitcase. Max shut the trunk before getting in the car to head for the villa. "As soon as Signore Rossi arrives at his office later on this morning, we'll show him the pendants. When we learn the truth about them, then we'll know what to do with the *signorine*."

CHAPTER SEVEN

ITALY'S top jewelry authenticator of their national treasures barely glanced at the first two pendants front and back before declaring them fakes. But the moment he picked up the third one, he got excited.

Max exchanged speculative glances with Nic and Luc before they followed Signore Rossi to his worktable where he placed the pendant under a special light. With his loupe he wore like a pair of glasses, he performed a meticulous examination.

His finger tapped on it. "Yes," he said after several minutes, nodding his gray head. "This piece has Tocelli's mark in the space between the intertwining D and P on the back. *Momento*—" He reached for his workbook containing photocopies and drawings of the Maria-Luigia collection.

Max's body grew more rigid as he watched Signore Rossi turn to the section on the Duchesse pendant for final verification.

The news that the original had indeed surfaced again meant the theory he and his cousins had come up with still held; Signorina Greer and her sisters were part of a bigger conspiracy.

Which also meant that except for the calendars, everything else Max had heard pour forth from her provocative lips in that jail cell was pure spin!

For some reason he couldn't fathom, he had to admit he was disappointed. When he stole a glance at his cousins, their sobriety revealed a startling bleakness that probably mirrored his own dark thoughts.

The ticking of an antique clock added a dirgelike quality to the unearthly quiet. Then Max heard a strange cry come out of Signore Rossi who started to grow animated. He removed his glasses and rose to his feet, staring at them as if he'd just seen a vision.

"How did you say you came by this pendant?"

"We recovered it from some Americans who were each wearing one when they flew into Genoa-Sestri airport two days ago."

"Then this means the court artisan who was commissioned to fashion the first pendant, secretly made a second one."

Max's thoughts reeled. He exchanged shocked glances with his cousins before addressing Signore Rossi. "With all due respect, you must be mistaken."

"No!" The old man shook his head emphatically. "This is the original pendant. There can be no mistake. But it's not the same original that was stolen with the collection from the museum. The Tocelli mark is there, but more elongated. Come. See for yourselves."

In a matter of minutes Max and his cousins had witnessed irrefutable proof that two authentic pendants *did* exist. As they eyed each other in wonder, all sorts of new possibilities flooded his mind.

If the *signorine* had nothing to do with the theft, then it stood to reason they'd been telling the truth about everything else. Furthermore, with the possession of another original pendant, it could be used to flush out the real thief.

"This is great cause for celebration," Signore Rossi exclaimed, oblivious to their reaction.

"It's fantastic news, *signore,* but you must say nothing about it," Nic cautioned in a grave tone before Max could. "Not until the person who stole the collection is apprehended and the other pendant returned. Then both can be displayed to the public."

"We're certain someone with close ties to our family was behind the theft," Max explained. "With this pendant, we might be able to lay a trap for them, I'm sure they would want this one, too, but we'll need your full cooperation."

Signore Rossi nodded. "Of course. Of course. What can I do to help?"

Luc's eyes had grown hooded. "No one outside this room must know what we've discovered until we're ready to have it announced. That means you can't say anything to anyone. Is that clear?"

"*Si.*"

Max looked around. "Do you have something I can put the pendants in for safe keeping?"

"Right here." He pulled several velvet pouches out of one of the drawers.

In an economy of movement Max put the original in one, the other two in the second little bag. Once he'd closed the drawstrings and the pouches were put safely away in his pockets, he took hold of the old man's hands and shook them.

"One day soon we'll put the real jewel thief behind bars. When that happens, you'll know the extent of our gratitude for your help and cooperation."

After saying goodbye, no one spoke again until they'd gone out to the car where Max eyed his cousins. "Before either of you says a word, let me tell you about the Husband Fund."

"The *what?*" Luc's expression was comical.

"To quote Signorina Greer, it's a fund for husband hunting."

Nic shook his head. "Husband hunting?"

Judging by their reactions, the subject hadn't come up during their interrogation of the prisoners.

"Of course it might be one of her colossal lies, but after

looking at those calendars, I'm not so sure.'' His brows lifted. ''Do you two want to have a little fun before we get back to more serious family business?''

While Greer was playing a game in her head to keep herself from going crazy, a different guard came down the hall.

''*Buon giorno, signorina.* Did you enjoy your lunch?''

''It was the best toothbreaking roll I ever tried to bite into. I can't wait to see what you're serving for dinner.''

''That won't be for a long time.'' He opened her cell. ''The commissioner will see you now.''

''How lovely of him.''

She followed the guard through the door at the end of the hall and around the corner to the commissioner's office. He stood up as soon as he saw her.

''Sit down, *signorina.* Make yourself comfortable.''

''I've been sitting on my cot for over—'' She glanced at the clock. ''Sixteen hours now, and would rather stand, thank you.''

''As you wish.'' He made that typical Italian gesture with his hands, palms up. It reminded her of someone else she knew. Someone she never wanted to see or think about again.

''I demand to be able to make one phone call to my attorney.''

''That won't be necessary. It turns out the pendant your sister was wearing was a copy of the missing Duchesse pendant. I'm sorry you were incarcerated by mistake.

''The first mate of the *Piccione* has been very worried about you and has stayed in constant contact. As soon as I told him you'd been cleared of all charges, your sisters were released into the hands of the crew.''

Noooooooooo. For all she knew Olivia and Piper had been kidnapped. She was still entirely convinced the crew were jewelry thieves who didn't believe the girls had no money. They needed help fast.

"He is waiting outside, ready to drive you to the dock at Lerici so you can continue on with your holiday."

Her body froze. No way.

"I would like to use your phone please. I have money."

"As long as it's a local call, be my guest."

So *that* was how he was going to play it. "May I see your phone directory then."

"If you need a taxi, allow me to take you wherever it is you wish to go, Signorina Greer." The deep, familiar male voice speaking in heavily accented English came from behind her.

Her back stiffened in response. "No, thanks." She was still facing the commissioner. "The phone directory please, *signore.*"

"But I insist," her enemy taunted her.

After no sleep, a crust of week old bread, a thimble of water and no shower or change of clothes, Greer had run out of patience.

She wheeled around, noticing inconsequently that the black-haired god was fresh shaven and wore a cream shirt with tan pants. The fact that his clothes accentuated his well-defined chest and rock-hard legs only increased her rage.

"I'd rather stay in here, thank you." So saying she marched out of the office and down around the corner of the jail where she spied the guard sitting at his post.

"Will you please open the door so I can go back to my cell?"

He flashed her a patronizing smile. "You've been released, *signorina.*"

"I'll pay you to lock me in again." She reached down the neck of her top and pulled out two twenty dollars bills to hand him.

"You Americans—" He threw his head back and laughed.

So far every Italian man she'd met was in cahoots against her. This grinning idiot was as awful as the balding guard from last night.

"If you'll appeal to me nicely," came Max's low, velvety voice over her shoulder, "I'll give you something to prove you can trust me."

How did he do that? How did he make her traitorous body respond like a kitten to cream when she knew one lick would be fatal?

Greer nodded her head in disgust before facing him once more. "Nothing but the return of our pendants, our passports and airline tickets would convince me there's the slightest shred of decency in you. Even then—"

"Yes?" he whispered huskily before pulling things out of the pockets of his pants like passports and airline tickets. Last of all came a little velvet pouch. He handed everything to her. When she looked inside, she counted three pendants.

How clever he was! Give her back their possessions knowing she would never abandon her sisters, knowing they were still helpless. And only *he* knew where they'd been taken by his two cohorts.

"You were saying, *signorina*?"

"I was *saying* that *even then,* it would be an empty gesture because it would mean you'd had the pendants appraised and found out you probably couldn't get more than fifty euros a piece for them."

"Seventy-five on the black market."

The temperature in her cheeks had shot up well over a hundred degrees. "I rest my case."

He cocked his dark head. "I hope that was an olive branch of sorts. Let's agree to agree we all got off to a bad start. You came spouse hunting and were sadly disappointed. My co-workers and I went treasure hunting and came up empty-handed.

"But since Signore Moretti has already paid us our wages from the Husband Fund your parents left you, why don't we start over again. I see no reason why we can't all get along for the next nine days before you have to fly home to Ron, was it?"

It gave her some satisfaction to know she'd dented his ego. Otherwise he wouldn't have deliberately pretended he hadn't heard her say "Don."

"You mean there'll be no hidden agenda," she drawled with heavy sarcasm. "We'll just do whatever comes naturally."

He put a hand over his heart. "You still don't trust me. I'm wounded, *signorina*. At the risk of offending you, if you recall when I asked you to swim with me at the Splendido, you didn't exactly turn me down."

"That's true," she admitted honestly. "However if I had, you wouldn't have taken no for an answer. I saw where your eyes were looking. They erupted like black fires when they recognized the pendant."

"If you'd seen the purple flames in yours while you were watching me walk across the tiles toward you…" His voice throbbed. "I felt like I was being consumed alive. There's nothing more flattering to a man."

"Too bad I had to open the cover of the book and find out you rated a four. I'd thought an eight at least."

"And I'd thought the pendant worth a million. What do you say we bury our disappointments and just be friends for the duration of your trip."

It was a trick.

No women could just be friends with men like the crew of the *Piccione*. But it looked like she would have to go along with him a little longer if she hoped to be reunited with her sisters. Once they were together, they would work out a way to lose the crew and disappear.

"Why not?" She threw out her bluff. "As I've learned in business, you win a few, lose a few."

She started walking back toward the main entrance of the jail. In a long stride he'd caught up to her.

"I don't imagine too many men clamor for your calendars."

Good. He'd rifled through her sister's suitcase. She smiled in spite of her issues with him. "You'd be surprised how many of them buy one to get their revenge on the women who rejected them. Kind of a 'look at yourself in the mirror' dark humor."

He reciprocated with a toe-curling smile of his own. "Has Don sent you one lately?"

Don again. "He doesn't need to. It's his company that prints our products."

"The poor devil gets it on all sides. I'd rate him an eight for hanging in there despite the odds."

"Don't feel too sorry for him. He manages to get his perks," she said as she stepped outside into the hot afternoon sun. It was glorious, liberating, after her windowless prison. "Where's your car?"

He put on his sunglasses. "In the alley around the side of the jail."

There were dozens of funny looking little Italian cars lined up like sardines along both sides of centuries old buildings. He walked over to a well-used blue Fiat with a bike rack. She noticed most of the cars had bike racks. To her surprise he opened the trunk first and pulled out her purse.

"Thank you," she murmured before putting the passports and other things inside. To her relief her wallet, comb and lipstick were still there.

"You're welcome. One thing I've learned about a woman. She doesn't feel dressed without one."

There probably wasn't a man alive who knew more about things like that than he did, but she wisely refrained from commenting.

He helped her into the front seat, then went around to the driver's side. While she combed her seaweed washed hair and put on lipstick to moisten her lips, he somehow, but she didn't know how, managed to get them out of there in one deft maneuver without hitting anything.

They'd only gone two blocks when she saw a gleaming white palace standing out from among the other architectural wonders. Her heart started to pound with excitement.

She may not have been to Italy before, but she'd done enough research to recognize it at once. Piper had drawn two of the calendar pages using the palace and gardens for a backdrop.

"After last night's ordeal, most women would not be smiling. What is going on in your mind, *signorina?*"

"The Colorno ducal palace. It was my ancestor's favorite summer residence. To think I spent the night locked up in a jail within walking distance of it. That'll be a story I'll tell to my children someday."

"You plan to have children, *signorina?*"

"Of course. Don't you? Someday I mean?"

"Not my own. No."

Not his own? Ask a silly question—

"The last thing I would wish to do is destroy a belief you've had since childhood, *signorina.* But when your sister told Luc you were related to the Duchesse of Parma through a granddaughter who had a liaison with a monk, I thought it best you know the truth."

She turned a frowning face toward him. "What truth?"

"There was a rumor many years ago about a granddaughter of Maria-Luigia who fell in love with a monk and bore his child. As it turns out, it was a political lie, spun to discredit her so the arranged marriage to her betrothed in France would not take place.''

''How would you know something like that?''

''Luc is the one who can give you more details. He learns many secrets while he prepares meals for his royal employers. I'm sorry.''

She stared at her hands in her lap. ''It doesn't matter. None of us quite believed it, and Daddy wasn't entirely sure about it. Still, it made for an exciting story.''

''And now you have another reason to dislike me.''

''I don't like or dislike you. You mean nothing to me, *signore*.''

''Can I make this up to you by taking you on a tour through the palace before we return to the *Piccione*? It's quite magnificent.''

''I'm sure it is, but no thank you. I prefer to keep my fairy-tale dreams in tact.''

''So you intend to continue the legacy and hand down your pendant to a daughter someday?''

''Yes. Why not. Only maybe I'll start a new rumor of my own.''

He turned to her. ''What rumor would that be?''

''Maybe the artisan who fashioned the pendant was secretly in love with Marie-Louise. Maybe he fathered a son and gave him the last name Duchesse in honor of the woman he could never have.''

''That's a very romantic story, *signorina*. Of the two, I don't know which I like better.''

His mocking voice was the last straw. She'd been right all along. A shark felt no emotion.

''Here. This will help to sustain you until we arrive at the dock.'' He reached in the back behind Greer's seat and produced a bottle of soda.

Warm orange soda. Ugh. But she'd be a fool to refuse it.

"Thank you."

"I know you Americans prefer ice. I'm sorry. Try one of these with it."

Like magic he'd produced a package of cookies. Chocolate biscotti, just like the kind Piper had drawn in that one calendar picture.

After a swig of pop, she took a bite. "Um. They're good. Better than potato chips. I can't stop with just one."

"Potato chips are one of the two things I like best about your country."

"You've been there?"

"Several times."

Funny to think of him in her part of the world and she never knew it. The trail of broken hearts had to be legion. "What's the other?"

"The long legs on American women. I once saw a movie with Betty Grable. Yours remind me of hers."

Her drink sprayed all over her cotton top.

"Are you all right, *signorina?*"

"Yes, of course. I just swallowed the wrong way."

"Soon we will reach the *Piccione*. There's a washer and dryer on board."

"All the comforts of home."

"That is true. It's my favorite home away from home."

"Where *is* your home?"

"Colorno. My family lives in nearby Parma."

No wonder he'd been able to bribe the commissioner! "Will we be passing through there?"

"Only the outskirts I'm afraid. I must congratulate you on the research you've done on Parma for your calendar business. I recognized every backdrop immediately."

"Piper's a genius."

"I agree, but the drawings would not have come to life

without all the details you unearthed. Genius appears to run in the Duchess family.''

''Thank you,'' she whispered. His compliment warmed her clear through. It shouldn't have, not when he was a thief of jewels...and hearts.

''So does beauty,'' he filled in the silence. ''I've seen you in every condition, yet soaking wet, starving, in prison and exhausted, you are even more appealing, if that is possible.''

What was he after now? All this flattery was so unnecessary now, but she had to admit the things he was saying made it difficult for her to breathe normally.

When he reached down to take a cookie for himself, his hand brushed against her thigh. Greer didn't know if it was intentional or not, but her body reacted as if she'd come in contact with a live wire.

''Luc is preparing a welcome home feast for you and your sisters. I must admit I'm looking forward to it, too. In all the excitement with the police and the hours of waiting for you to be released, none of us took the time to eat.''

Of course not. They were too busy trying to find a buyer for the pendants.

She wouldn't believe any of his malarky until she saw her sister's dear faces back on board the catamaran. Only when she'd discovered for herself they'd survived their hideous night in that ghastly jail, would she be able to take a normal breath.

As one kilometer after another unraveled around hills and bends, a delightful smorgasbord of tiny hamlets, ancient villages and farms filled her vision. If she weren't so worried about her sisters, she could enjoy the fabulous landscape.

''Since dinner is quite a few hours away yet, I thought we'd stop here and satisfy our hunger.''

After coming round a bend in the road, she was surprised to see what looked like an open-air festival of some kind being held in a field. There were all kinds of colorful booths and hundreds of people milling around, talking and eating.

"What's going on?"

"We're at the Fiera de Parma."

"Fiera?"

"*Si*—fairground." He parked the car before trapping her gaze. "You're not only lucky enough to be in the capital of Italy's famous 'food valley' where Prosciutto di Parma ham and Parmigian-Reggiano cheese are celebrated— you've been freed from jail in time to enjoy the International Food Exhibition which is only held every two years. Come with me."

When she remarked on the pungent aroma in the air he told her it was white truffles, a local delicacy. Greer had reached the point of starvation some time ago and didn't need to be urged to join him as they moved about among the crowd sampling the delicious displays.

He fed her everything from emerald green olive oil on chunks of chewy Italian bread sprinkled with cheese, to pale, paper-thin slices of tender parma ham that melted in your mouth.

Every so often he popped a fragrant, fleshy black or green olive in her mouth. As if that weren't enough, he stuffed her with ice cream and more biscotti, giving her the true taste of exquisite Italian cuisine.

Yet more than the food was the excitement of feeling his arm around her waist, his fingers brushing against her mouth, the play of his dark eyes traveling over her face while he waited for her approval of something she'd eaten.

This enigmatic stranger who seduced her with a soft caress, a quick smile, a deep laugh, had created a dangerous state of enchantment for Greer. She rebelled at the injustice of having to return to the car...to painful reality.

Silence reigned as they made their descent to the coast where the shimmering water reflected a cloudless sky. The distinctive multihull of the *Piccione* stood out from the few fishing and rowboats still docked in Lerici's small harbor.

He drove the car into a public area where other cars were parked and got out. Greer grabbed her purse and ran ahead of the man she still didn't trust and never would.

"Piper? Olivia?" Until they answered, she wouldn't put one foot on board.

All she got for her shouting was the captain. He stepped out of the cockpit wearing sunglasses and a broad smile that ought to be fined for being too captivating.

"*Buenos tardes, señorita.* Welcome back. Luc and I brought your sisters home from the jail a few hours ago." Hours? "Señorita Olivo had a headache. They both announced they were going straight to bed and didn't want to be disturbed."

Olivia didn't get headaches.

"Prove it!"

"*Momento,*" the man behind her whispered. "I'll ask them to come up on deck so you'll know they're safe."

"Greer!"

Two blond heads suddenly appeared at the top of the stairs.

CHAPTER EIGHT

THANK heaven!

Greer leaped on board and hurried toward them. They scuttled below to the stateroom they'd used before. Piper locked the door, then they all hugged.

Olivia took one look at her and said, "You've got stains all over you. What happened in your jail cell?"

"Never mind that. We'll talk later." She held up her purse. "The pendants are in here. Max gave them back along with our passports and tickets. He also fed me royally."

"Luc served us a fabulous lunch after they brought us back to the boat."

"They've been exceptionally nice."

"Yeah...well we all know why don't we. They found out our jewels weren't worth enough to bother with, so now they're ready to enjoy *us* for the rest of the trip."

"I'm sure you're right," Piper muttered.

Olivia nodded. "They figure if they feed us and take care of us, we'll be ripe for the picking after the sun goes down."

Greer stared at both of them. "I say we leave for Genoa right now."

"Amen. Everybody grab a suitcase. Let's get out of here before they cast off!"

Greer was first out the door. She almost bumped into Max who grasped her upper arms in a firm grip.

"Where's the fire?" His black eyes scrutinized her. "I thought you would want to shower and rest after your ordeal in Colorno."

Her proud Duchesse nose lifted in the air. It brought their eyes and lips too close for comfort. "I don't need to rest."

He studied her mouth as if he were considering devouring it. What made it so much worse was that she wanted him to.

"I was just coming to ask your sisters if they're ready for their dessert yet. Luc told me to tell them he has made a special *framboise* tart that will satisfy their sweet tooth."

"What sweet tooth?"

"The one you all share," he said in a husky tone. "There is chocolate on your mouth from your last biscotti as we speak, *bellissima*." He brushed at it with his finger before tasting it. The intimate gesture was a reminder of everything they'd shared at the fair.

Crimson flags spotted her cheeks. "We've indulged ourselves long enough, don't you think?" she said before realizing how that must have sounded to him. "Now we're leaving."

Lines marred his handsome features. "To do what?"

"That's our business. Please move out of our way."

"Not until you tell me where you think are you going."

"Oh, I *know* where we're going."

A condescending smile broke out on his enticing male mouth. Prepared for a knock down drag out, Greer was taken off guard when he unexpectedly took a step back so she could proceed.

The girls followed her down the hall and up the stairs to the top deck, all of them carrying their suitcases.

At a glance she could see Luc untying the ropes. Vibrations ran through her feet and legs, alerting her that the captain had started the engine. Without hesitation she raced up the steps with her luggage and stepped onto the dock. Piper and Olivia joined her with their cases.

The first mate walked toward them with his hands on

his hips. His male beauty combined with his sheer audacity burrowed deeply beneath her skin.

Unable to hold back her anger any longer she cried, "So…you were just going to sail off with us after what you've done? No questions asked?"

His dark gaze pierced through to her insides, making her feel quivery and out of control. She hated that feeling.

"We were going to follow your itinerary to the letter. Our first stop for tonight is Monterosso."

"We were supposed to go there last night, but things turned out differently, so we've changed our minds about continuing with this trip."

"I can see that. May I say one thing. Wherever you wish to go, there won't be another train through Lerici for at least two hours. Even then you probably won't be able to get on. It's possible you could end up having to wait till four in the morning."

"Max is right," Luc spoke up. He and the captain had come to stand on the dock next to their partner in crime. "That would be very dangerous for three beautiful, unattached women. With the Grand Prix on tomorrow, transportation is so bad it will be impossible to find a taxi."

"Every hotel room along the coast has been booked for months, *señoritas*," Nic chimed in. "Tell us your destination and we'll take you there in comfort on the *Piccione* without the waiting and the hassle."

The stranger's gaze was riveted on Greer. "I would like to try to make up for the disappointment I gave you during our talk in the car."

"Which disappointment was that?" she fired. "There have been so many."

"When I told you that you have no Italian blood in you. I realize it destroyed a dream for you."

"Max is right," the captain spoke up. "Your Duchesse name came from the French 'Duchesne.'"

"Really?" Greer broke in heatedly. "So our captain-cum resident etymologist is now a professional genealogist, too?"

His white smile was an affront. "*Si, señorita.* They dropped the 'n' and the final 'e' when they arrived in America."

Luc nodded. "I'm afraid the story about an Italian monk who made love to the granddaughter of Maria-Luigia and gave her a son is pure fabrication. We know the news hurts, *mesdemoiselles.*"

The first mate's eyes never left Greer's. "Do not shoot the messenger, instead tell me how I can take away a little of the sting, *bellissima.*"

Oh, brother.

"Admittedly all six of us are liars," she began without preamble, "but if you're being sincere this time, then give us the keys to your car so we can leave for the airport."

"You're planning to return to the States without enjoying the rest of your trip?" he inserted in a silky voice.

"That's not anyone's concern but ours," she declared. "We'll leave the car in the short-term parking at the Genoa airport. You can pick up your keys at the airline ticket counter."

"Why would you fly away now when we've only just started to get to know each other?"

"I know all I want to know!" By now Greer's eyes were spitting purple sparks at him. "With your good old boy network flourishing in this neck of Italy, *signore,* I've no doubt you'll be able to manage perfectly well without your car for three or four hours."

He tossed off one of those careless masculine shrugs that drew her gaze to his remarkable physique. "Be my guest, Greer. We'll help you to the car."

Before she could countenance it, the three men took

hold of their luggage and started walking toward the parking area beyond the dock.

Her sisters flashed her a private message that said they didn't trust the crew as far as they could throw them. Greer flashed them the same message. This was way too easy. There was definitely something wrong here. She could feel it in her bones.

"They could have pulled the distributor cap while we were in our stateroom," Olivia whispered.

Piper nodded. "I guess we'll find out soon enough if it doesn't start."

"It's probably running on fumes by now," Greer theorized. "I wouldn't put it past him to have tampered with the gauge so we'd never be able to tell until it was too late."

"Or—" Olivia rolled her eyes "—the tires will all go flat the minute we try to reach the highway."

"Then we'll drive on the rims as far as we can," Piper stated firmly. "Olivia, you're the designated driver. I'll help navigate."

"I'll sit in the back and be quiet," Greer volunteered.

By the time they reached the Fiat, the men had put their bags in the trunk. Refusing their offers for help, the girls got into the car. Max handed Olivia the key. *"Buon Viaggio, signorine."*

"Goodbye!" the girls called out in unison.

Low and behold the engine actually started up.

As Olivia drove the car out of the parking area past the three smiling men, Greer's gaze was trapped by a pair of burning black eyes.

"Ciao, bella." He mouthed the words.

That place at her throat started throbbing again.

"Okay guys," she said once they'd reached the highway. "So far so good, but something tells me we'll have problems when we reach Genoa airport."

Piper's head swung around. "You're right. It's another setup to get us in their beds. The crew will alert their buddies to be waiting for us. They'll say we've stolen the pendant and the whole rigmarole will start all over again. I wouldn't be surprised if they've got a friend tailing us right now."

"Neither would I," Greer muttered. "One way or the other, they're planning on a little fun in the sun with us. Did you see those Cheshire cat grins they gave us as we were driving away?"

"Deep down they're furious the pendants turned out to be worthless."

"They're not going to leave us alone."

"It's time to call in the troops, guys."

"Tom told me they can get a flight on a military transport whenever they want," Piper informed them. "He was hinting like mad at the time."

"There's just one problem with that," Greer cautioned. "If we send for the guys, it'll be like telling them we're really interested in them."

"Maybe we *should* take our parents' advice and try to fall in love for a change," Olivia muttered wistfully.

After a minute Piper said, "We could look at this as a final test. If the boys can get here by tomorrow, we'll spend the rest of our vacation on the *Piccione* with them. By the end we'll—"

"Be dead of boredom," Greer finished for her.

"That's true," Olivia agreed, "but the crew doesn't have to know that."

Greer started to smile and sat up straighter in the seat. "You're right. Max isn't sure if there's a Don in my life or not. It would really frost him if one of the men answering to that name showed up tomorrow tossing a Frisbee around on the deck."

Piper grinned. "Especially in their military haircuts and

fatigues. They have the kind of obnoxious attitude that'll drive our crew right up a wall.''

"I love it," Olivia exclaimed, "but I guess you guys realize that if they can come, we'll have to pay Signore Moretti more money.''

"If we don't make a decision one way or the other, then we're stuck alone for nine more days with three playboys who intend to play no matter what!" Greer cried.

"Guys? Let's get serious here. I say we just get back home and back to normal. We could ring Walter Carlson and use him to run interference for us at the airport.''

"Good idea," Olivia murmured. "I see a trattoria up ahead. We can pull in there and make a credit card call.''

When they reached the parking area Greer said, "You guys stay put because we don't dare leave the car unattended. I'll talk to Mr. Carlson. It's seven-thirty in the morning in Kingston. I doubt he'll have left his house yet.''

"Let's hope your right.''

To Greer's relief it wasn't long before the wife of the owner of the busy restaurant signaled her to come behind the counter to use the phone.

Greer's fortune seemed to be holding when Mrs. Carlson said her husband was still home.

"Greer?''

"Hi, Mr. Carlson. Sorry to bother you, but this is very important.''

"I heard you girls were detained at the jail in Colorno by mistake," he said right off. "I'm so sorry, my dear.''

She blinked. "How did you know?''

"When you gave the police commissioner my name, he got in touch with the attorney for the House of Parma-Bourbon who rang me to verify who you were.

"We had a long talk about your background and the pendants your parents gave you. After he explained about the confusion over the stolen pendant from the ducal museum, he assured me he would arrange for your immediate release.''

Greer gripped the receiver tighter. ''I wish the commissioner had told *me* he was in contact with you.''

''Though I'm sure it didn't seem that way to you at the time, the Italians have a very efficient system.''

The good old boy network you mean. Greer almost laughed in his ear.

''Are you girls all right now?''

''Actually we're not.'' Without wasting any more time, she told him about their problems with the crew of the *Piccione*. ''We're pretty sure they're in league with one of the policemen at the airport. I'm afraid we might be prevented from boarding the plane for our flight home.''

''Don't worry, Greer. All you have to do is tell the head of security you wish to call me if there's a problem. Just mentioning my name will produce results.''

Yeah. Sure.

''Thanks, Mr. Carlson.''

''You're welcome, my dear. As I told you in my office, women weren't meant to be on their own. The attorney for the House of Parma-Bourbon agreed with me.''

Greer was counting to twenty.

''Perhaps now after this unfortunate experience, you will believe me. As I said, if you have any more trouble at all, give me a ring.''

She was about to tell him the police wouldn't allow her to call anyone, but it would be a wasted effort on her part. At this point she was so furious, she couldn't think, let alone talk. ''I will. Goodbye.''

After hanging up the receiver, she marched straight out of the restaurant to the car.

''How did it go with Mr. Carlson?''

She shot Olivia a speaking glance. ''Remember my

quote, *Don't upset me. I'm running out of places to hide the bodies?*"

"Uh-oh."

"What did he say?"

"I'm afraid we're on our own, guys."

"You mean he was no help at all?" Olivia cried.

"He said all we had to do was tell the head of security to call him if there was any trouble."

"Sure." Piper let out a defeated sigh.

Greer sat back in the seat. "Like I said, we're on our own. But I'll give you the long version of our conversation on the way to the airport."

"Your presence does us great honor, Signore di Varano."

"*Grazie,* Signore Galli."

"What can I do for you?"

Except for an obsequiousness that was irritating, there was no sign the other man seemed nervous or caught off guard by Max's unexpected appearance at the custom's area of the airport.

"The three American *signorine* you detained two days ago have just arrived at the short-term parking area of the airport in a blue Fiat."

Signore Galli's brows lifted in surprise. "I thought they were in the custody of the commissioner at Colorno."

"I'm afraid he was prevailed upon to let them go."

The other man's eyes narrowed. "It would not have happened if I had been in charge."

"I'm sure of that," Max said in an ironical tone. "Therefore I'm enlisting your help."

"Whatever I can do."

"I have reason to believe one of the Americans is attempting to take the original pendant out of the country."

His eyes screwed up. "You mean it is a different one from the three they were wearing when they arrived?"

"Confidentially, I believe they are acting as messengers for the person who stole the whole Maria-Luigia collection."

"You mean—" Max could hear the officer's mind working. "They wore the fake pendants here, then got hold of the real one to wear back?"

"Si."

"That is very clever."

"So are you, Signore Galli. You have a nose for your profession."

The other man's face warmed with pleasure.

"However I must have proof," Max added.

"Of course, signore. As soon as they reach the outer doors, my men will pick them up and escort them here. My office across the hall is at your disposal."

If Signore Galli was acting, he gave a convincing performance of total innocence.

"Grazie. Send the one with the lavender eyes to me first."

Without wasting another moment, Max entered the empty office. Once he'd closed the door, he pulled out his cell phone and rang Nic.

"Where are they now?" he asked when his cousin acknowledged.

"Lugging their suitcases through the upper level to the doors. I never saw three females so determined."

The Duchess sisters were headstrong all right. A breed of women all their own. "You'll be happy to know Galli's men are ready and waiting."

"What's your gut impression of him by now?"

Max pursed his lips. "I could be wrong, but I don't think he's involved. There was a kind of earnestness in his desire to help that didn't seem feigned, but you can never be sure."

"That is true. I'll swing the car around in front of the terminal and wait for you."

"Good. Expect us in about twenty minutes. Ciao."

While he waited, he lounged against the desk and phoned Luc who was standing by on the *Piccione*.

"How's the leg?"

"I picked up another prescription of pain killers. The pills should be working any minute now. How are the *belles mesdemoiselles?*"

"According to Nic, *obstinées comme d'habitude.*"

As both men were chuckling, he heard footsteps outside the door. "Sorry to cut this short, but our lovely jailbirds have just flown in. *A tout a l'heure, cousin.*"

"Oui."

He hung up and waited with growing excitement to see the shocked look on Signorina Greer's face when she discovered him inside the room. But instead of the door opening, he heard a familiar female voice say, "Knock, knock, Signore Max. Come out, come out, wherever you are."

He opened it and glimpsed a pair of eyes that glittered like amethysts in the sunlight. But the mocking smile on that luscious mouth of hers was all he needed to see black.

"Sorry to spoil your surprise. I'm afraid the man of mystery revealed his true colors a long time ago."

"Basta, signorina—" Signore Galli warned in a forbidding voice. "Enough! You do not know to whom you are speaking."

The man came to Max's defense so quickly, he was convinced Fausto Galli was simply a dedicated agent doing his job.

"Of course I do! I may not have been told his real name, *signore,* but I know him very, very well. He is the shark who has been biting at my heels since I made the unfortunate mistake of swimming in these waters.

"He's the one who took me for a little roll beneath the

waves to soften me up. There's nothing he enjoys more than playing with his victim for a while first. A little nip here, a little tuck there.''

A surge of adrenaline exploded inside Max's body. ''Touché, Signorina Greer— Acid-tongued and predictable as ever.'' He looked at Signore Galli. ''Grazie. I'll handle this from here.''

''Handle what?'' she lashed out. ''You've got us where you want us. No more games. Do your worst so we can go home.''

Pleased to see she'd lost some of her cool, he smiled. ''I'm glad you recognize there's no escape. Signore Galli? If you will please instruct some of your men to accompany the other *signorine* to the front of the terminal with their bags, I'll escort Signorina Greer myself.''

''Of course.''

Without waiting for a response from her, he picked up her suitcase, then cupped her elbow to guide her down the hall. She shook off his hand as if it had scalded her and walked ahead of him. It gave him the opportunity to watch her long, beautiful bare legs move faster and faster.

Even without a shower or fresh makeup, and still wearing the same pink skirt and top she was dressed in when she dived overboard last evening, she moved with a feminine grace that was stunning to watch.

Her sisters arrived at the Fiat first. While Nic helped them into the back seat, the security men loaded the bags in the trunk. Max opened the front door for his proud Duchesse pigeon as he'd started to think of her, then he went around and got behind the wheel.

The silence was palpable throughout the drive from the terminal to Genoa's harbor. From time to time he caught Nic's grin through the rearview mirror.

Just for the fun of it he turned on the radio to a music station that played a lot of songs in Italian and English.

As soon as he heard an old Dean Martin classic, he turned up the volume and sang along.

"When the moon heats your eye like a beg pizza pie, that's amore. When the moon starts to shine like you've had too much wine, you'll know you're in love…"

"Oh please—" the woman sitting next to him moaned before bursting into uninhibited laughter.

It was totally unexpected and it enchanted him.

She enchanted him.

By the time they could see Luc waving to them from the boat, her sisters' uncontrollable laughter had joined in. But his senses were only attuned to her.

"I would do more tricks for you if it would make you laugh like that again, Greer."

"A bilingual shark who *seengs* off-key. I underestimated you, *signore*. Better to hear a woman laugh than cry, eh?"

"I would never wish to make you cry."

"What *do* you wish, *signore?*"

"To help you and your sisters enjoy the rest of your vacation."

"No. You want us to help *you* enjoy *your* vacation. Admit it!"

He and Nic got out of the car and assisted their guests to that part of the pier where the boat was moored.

"I admit there is nothing we would enjoy more than to spend nine more uninterrupted days and nights in your delightful company. But you're wrong in assuming that we're on vacation."

She stood there with her arms tightly folded at her waist, not willing to step one foot on the *Piccione*. "That's right. The security guard works hard at spotting rich women for you. You work hard at relieving them of their unnecessary jewels. When you've exhausted that avenue, you work hard at seducing them. I forgot."

"You wound me again, *bellissima.*"

Her head reared back, giving him an even better view of her provocative mouth. "That's another lie. I don't see a mark on you."

"The deepest ones are hidden, but we're digressing from the point."

"So there is one?" she derided.

"On the surface, Luc, Nic and I are guilty of everything you've said."

"Tell us something else we don't already know."

"Gladly, Greer. We're working undercover to find the person or persons who stole the Maria-Luigia jewelry collection from the ducal palace in Colorno. It's one of Italy's greatest treasures and the object of an intensive search that has involved the CIA, Scotland Yard, Interpol and Italy's top investigators.

"Perhaps now you can imagine that your arrival in Genoa wearing three identical Duchesse pendants, drew a collective gasp from not only Signore Galli, but the hundreds of other security people who've been involved in this case for over a year.

"If the American agents had done their part before you left Kennedy Airport, you would never have been allowed to board your plane. Needless to say, their intervention would have spared you all the unpleasantness you've been forced to suffer in the last forty-eight hours.

"From our point of view however, the Americans' lapse in security did us an inestimable favor. Though you've been cleared of any wrongdoing and are free to go—as you found out when you spoke to your attorney from the trattoria—you've unwittingly provided us with a valuable piece of information the jewel thief doesn't know about yet.

"Here is the point you were so charmingly urging me to make, Greer. We would like you to stay in Italy long enough to help us lay a trap for him, or her, or them. Whoever it is...

"You don't have to cooperate, of course. It might even be dangerous to do so, though we'll do everything in our power to protect you.

"If your answer is no, I will drive you to the airport right now and send you back to New York first class on the next plane leaving Genoa.

"If your answer is yes, we will go below for a meal and discuss our strategy in detail." His gaze took in all three of them. "The decision is yours, *signorine*."

Greer eyed her sisters, not knowing what to believe. She eventually flicked the first mate another suspicious glance. He stood there with his long powerful legs slightly apart, his hands clasped in front of him.

"If you're on the level, why didn't you just say all this at the airport in front of the head of the security?"

"Signore Galli may be one of several security people operating on the wrong side of the law. We're not certain who we can trust, perhaps not even the commissioner at the jail in Colorno. That is why we pretended to be members of the crew of the *Piccione*."

"I knew none of you were who you claimed to be," her voice grated.

"You're no captain!" Piper blurted.

"Nevertheless I have done a lot of sailing in my life, *señorita*."

"And you're no chef!" Olivia accused the man named Luc.

"*Non, mademoiselle*. But I like to cook now and then."

"If you showed us identification, we'd never know if it was fake," Greer practically hissed the words. "Are you going to tell us Signore Moretti is your superior?"

The first mate's eyes had narrowed to slits. "No. A personal friend. He lent us the car."

"*And* the boat?"

"Yes."

"Of course he did. Everybody has a friend who owns a catamaran worth close to a million dollars who just lets you take it when you want."

"You watch too many American movies, Greer."

"No—that was our mother," she snapped.

"We'd still like to see your ID," Piper insisted.

Without hesitation the men pulled out their wallets and passed them around. Greer was still staring the shark down when Olivia handed her the first one.

Nicolas de Pastrana, Marbella, Spain: six-three. Brown hair, brown eyes. Age thirty-four. Gorgeous photo.

The next one came around. Lucien de Falcon, Monacoville, Monaco. Whoa: six-two. Black hair, gray eyes. Age thirty-three. Another gorgeous photo.

Greer's hand trembled when Olivia handed her the third wallet. Maximilliano di Varona, Colorno, Italy. Maximilliano— Hah! He's six-three. Black hair, black eyes. Age thirty-four. No photo of him could be as breathtaking as the real thing.

The way European names were put together could be misleading. All of the men had a "de" or a "di" following their first names, which could mean nothing more than the fact that they were the son of so and so. Or it could be a sign they were part of an important family. Take your pick.

No doubt these exceptional male hunks had handpicked their fake names for a reason. One she and her sisters would never know about. She lifted her head and handed him back his wallet.

"I still don't believe a single word you say."

He chewed on his lower lip. "Would it help if I told you I'm chief counsel for the House of Parma-Bourbon?"

"You mean *you're* the one who had a long talk with my father's attorney? The one who affected our release from the prison?" Greer let out an angry laugh. "And would it help if I told you Piper is really the Duchess of Guasfalla, Olivia is really the Duchess of Piacenza, and I'm really the Duchess of Parma?"

"Come on, Greer," he said in a thick toned voice. "Let us put the jokes aside."

CHAPTER NINE

"You know who I am."

She blinked her eyes with great exaggeration. "I do?"

"You as much as admitted it in your jail cell."

"I did?"

"You did, *mademoiselle*," Luc asserted. "Max told me and Nic all about the Husband Fund, so there's no use denying it."

Nic nodded. "The calendars are the proof, *señorita*. To be more specific, the scene in the pastry shop in Parma?"

"You mean where Violetta didn't give Luigio any of her chocolate biscotti? What does that have to do with anything?"

"They weren't the only two characters in that picture," the first mate inserted. "There was a third character recognizable due to the ducal corona emblem."

"Oh that— He was just the local pompous peacock strutting about town in his fancy duds trying to impress everyone with his family title. You know...the symbolic, typical, flamboyant Italian male, all puffed up with self-importance.

"If you took careful notice, Violetta was only toying with him to make Luigio jealous. She really adores Luigio who suffers from a private tragedy he keeps to himself. She's determined to find out what it is. Deep inside she really admires his humility. But we've gotten off the subject again."

"That's another touching story, Greer," Max said, sounding oddly violent. "I'm surprised you're not a writer."

He moved closer to her, invading that circle of space she needed to think clearly. "But you're right. We've strayed from the main line of questioning. Are you going to tell me you didn't admit to using the Husband Fund to go spouse hunting?"

"I admit it, but I still don't have a clue who *you* are."

"You mean you just picked me out of a group of candidates?"

"I might have done if you'd been lined up on the stage at a bachelor auction. For a guy who's been over the hill for thirteen years, you're still not half bad."

His hands were no longer clasped in front of him. They'd formed fists at his side. "Over the hill?"

"Yeah. After twenty-one *all* men go downhill, but as I said, you're still pretty well preserved even if you have some gray hairs at the temple. However getting back to the point *I* was trying to make before you interrupted me, I thought I saw a shark in the pool of the Splendido.

"No one could have been more surprised when I discovered it had legs and had started walking toward *moi*. If you recall, I waited until I was asked before joining you for a swim."

His features took on a chiseled cast. "So what you're saying is, you were so desperate to find a husband, you were willing to go after the first male who approached you, not knowing one thing about him? Not his name? Not his background?"

"Wow!" Her eyebrows lifted. "You sound just like Daddy. I wouldn't be surprised if you faked your age along with your name on your driver's license. Are you sure you don't have a daughter tucked away somewhere? You know—do as I say, not as I do?"

There was an uncomfortable moment of quiet before he said, "Positive."

Puzzled by his brief, quiet answer she said the next thing

that came into her head. "I knew you were a good swimmer. Does that help"

"That's important to Greer," Piper interjected. "That's how Don got her to go out with him in the first place."

"Larry had a phobic reaction to water. That's why he could never get to first base with her," Olivia explained.

"Guys— Signore Maximilliano doesn't want to hear about my love life any more than I want to hear about his."

"Then you admit that a man over the hill can still have one," he insinuated. It was a borderline sneer.

"Of course. And you've already told me about yours. It's the one thing to come out of your mouth I believe with all my heart."

His lips suddenly twitched. "When did I tell you about it?"

"You said, and I quote, 'If there's one thing I know about women, they don't feel dressed without their purse.' You certainly couldn't have made a statement like that unless you'd had prior knowledge.

"But if we could possibly tear ourselves from the riveting subject of your frantic love life, I'd like to know how you thought up such an amazing name for yourself. Obviously it was coined from the bloody days of the Circus Maximus.

"But it truly is fantastic. I mean, if there is an honest to goodness Maximilliano who's a duc or something equally pretentious running around Parma, does everyone really have to call him by his whole name?"

To her surprise, all three men exploded with laughter. The full-bodied kind that brought tears to their eyes.

"Very well, Greer," he said as soon as quiet reigned once more. "It's clear we've reached a stalemate, a term you as an American will recognize from your own courts of law. In the case of Duchess v Varano, trust is lacking on both sides of the Atlantic.''

"That was brilliant, signore. I couldn't have said it better myself.''

He gave an almost imperceptible aristocratic bow that to her surprise seemed instinctive. "Knowing and accepting that fact, I'd like to offer a plea bargain.''

"Plea away, *signore*.''

The corner of his compelling male mouth lifted. "We really are trying to catch a jewel thief.''

She squinted up at him. "I can believe that. A collection of jewels falling into your hands might not make you as rich as the Count of Monte Cristo with Nic and Luc here impersonating the Count of Cabalconti and company. But you'd at least have enough to cover taxes on all the money you make under the table so to speak.''

His smile broadened. "Good. We're making progress.''

"*Are* we. How nice.''

"Come to Monaco with us on the *Piccione*,'' he urged, his eyes focused on her mouth. "A handful of people we've considered prime suspects will be there for the Grand Prix. With your help we might be able to flush them out.''

"We need your help,'' the captain spoke up.

"No way, Jose,'' Piper responded. "The next thing we know we'll end up at the mercy of some potentate from outer Mongolia! Greer's right. You'd sell us to the highest bidder for profit.''

"Then I have another suggestion,'' Luc interjected. His gaze had traveled to Olivia. "Since you are such an excellent driver, you take your sisters to Monaco in the Fiat.

"We'll sail the *Piccione* to the Port d'Hercules and join you at my apartment. That way you won't have to fear we've pirated you away to some distant shore, never to be seen or heard of again. I have to admit that would be a great tragedie.''

One look at Olivia's eyes and Greer could tell her sister was tempted. She'd dreamed of seeing the Grand Prix for years.

''It's a good plan, *signorine*.'' The so-called Max had spoken again. ''Give us tonight and tomorrow. Then we'll put you on the plane home from Nice.''

''What exactly do we have to do?'' Greer demanded.

''Just be the people you were when you came to the Riviera. We'll introduce you as the Duchesses of Kingston. There is no such English title anymore, but most people wouldn't know that, so don't change one iota of your story.'' His eyes flamed like black fires, reminding her of the first time she'd seen him at the pool. ''Wear one of those filmy, floaty concoctions I hung up in your closet.''

Her legs almost buckled from the sensuality in his tone and look. ''And the Duchesse pendants of course,'' she added.

''Of course.''

''And when we're not being used for bait, what *other* plans do you have for us?''

His elegant shrug fascinated her. ''Whatever your heart desires. A private dinner and dancing on a palace patio dripping with bougainvillea, followed by a swim in a secluded lagoon.''

Goose bumps broke out on Greer's skin. As for Olivia, her eyes were glowing a hot blue.

''Instead of swimming, I'd rather go on to a club where some of the Formula I drivers are partying and get their autographs.''

''That could be arranged Mademoiselle Olivier.''

''What about you, *señorita?*'' Nic asked Piper.

''I'd rather go to bed early, then get up at dawn and

walk around making sketches of everything for a new line of calendars I have in mind.''

''I'll prepare a picnic for us. While you draw, I'll feed you.''

''Just no olives, Spanish or otherwise.''

He threw his head back and laughed. ''I promise. Only chocolate truffles and pastries. I happen to be a chocoholic myself.''

For once Greer's sisters wouldn't look at her.

They were *caving*. But who could blame them? Whoever these men really were, Greer and her sisters had no business being around them.

''Where exactly *is* this supposed apartment of yours, Monsieur Luc?''

He flashed Greer a silvery glance. ''I will draw you and your sisters a map.'' For a man needing a cane, he got around with amazing speed and returned from the cockpit with paper and pencil in hand.

Greer could just imagine where his diabolical map would lead. Probably straight to the island castle where poor Edmond Dantes had been imprisoned.

''Don't worry, Greer,'' the dark stranger interjected. ''You won't have to drive as far as Marseilles. In any case, the Château D'If is now a museum.''

Flame scorched her cheeks. He was doing it again. Reading her mind.

Luc handed Olivia the paper.

Greer smirked at Max. ''X marks the spot.''

His heart-stopping smile was in evidence once more. ''You may even find your ultimate treasure there.''

Her eyelids narrowed. ''It's always about the treasure, isn't it, *signore*.'' She wheeled around. ''Come on, guys. Let's go.''

She picked up her suitcase and started walking toward the parking area. By the time she'd reached the car, her sisters had caught up to her. Olivia opened the trunk and they stashed their bags.

"Are you mad at us?" Piper asked after they'd driven off.

"No."

"Yes, you are," Olivia gainsayed her.

"Maybe a little. But after you caught me kissing Maximus the Great in the stateroom, I have no right to point a finger."

"Even if they are a bunch of liars, we weren't exactly telling the truth ourselves when we pretended to be real duchesses. It won't hurt us to try to find Luc's house and enjoy ourselves a little before we go home."

"Come on, Olivia," Greer complained. "Do you honestly think they're going to let us near an airport before the nine days are over? Because if you do, I have a pendant in my jewelry box worth a million dollars I could sell for double that depending on the right buyer."

"Greer! What's happened to you?" Piper cried.

"Not a thing."

Olivia gave an emphatic nod of her blond head. "Yes, it has. You're different. You've been different since the night you jumped into the Splendido pool with the splendid Maximilliano. Let's face it. You finally met a man who caused you to lose your inhibitions," she reasoned.

"Now you're angry because he's the one man on earth you don't know if you can trust. Worse, after we go home, you know no other man is ever going to make you feel the same way again."

Her sisters stared at her in that pitying way she couldn't abide.

"I'm not feeling *that* bad!"

"Yes, you are."

"For someone who gets your directions confused when

you drive, it was very clever of you to notice we were sailing in the wrong direction yesterday.''

''We know how much you'd love to visit Elba and Monte Cristo.''

''Your sacrifice was heroic.''

Greer took a steadying breath. ''So was yours. I know how much you were looking forward to telling Fred and Tom you skied on the Italian and Spanish Riviera.''

''So we'll water ski some more with the guys when we get back home.''

''Yeah.''

''Yeah.''

''It'll be fun.''

''Sure it will. The Hudson Riviera.''

''At least it's safe.''

''Yeah.''

''The guys never pull any surprises. They just ski.''

''Yup.''

''They don't try to be something they're not.''

''Nope.''

''They wouldn't know how.''

''Nope.''

''They speak one language.''

''Football.''

''Yup.''

''I bet Tom doesn't know Pope Gregory was Greek.''

''He isn't Catholic.''

''Nope.''

''Fred hates Italian food. He says olive oil makes him sick.''

''Yup.''

''I bet Don's never heard of Spanish olive oil.''

''Nope.''

''It's for sure he doesn't have a clue Venus rose from the sea. He thinks it's a planet.''

"Yup."

"They're sweet."

"Yup."

"They're boring."

"Yup."

"They're looking for a wife."

"And the crew of *Piccione* are looking for a one-night stand," Greer reminded them. "I for one don't plan to give in when I don't know one thing about Maximilliano, even if that is his real name, which it probably isn't."

"But you know the chemistry's there," Olivia stated. "That's something neither of you can fake."

"So now I'm supposed to let desire take over?"

"Not completely. Just enough to wangle a marriage proposal out of him. That was the whole purpose of the Husband Fund. If you hang in there, then you won't have to pay back the $5,000 after we get home."

"Is that what you're going to do with Luc?"

"I'm thinking about it. I could always grab his cane and beat him over the head if he tries to force himself on me."

"They don't need to force themselves on women," Piper muttered. "If anything, I would imagine it's the other way around. We're probably such an anomaly, it has made them chase after us.

"But I know this momentary thrill they're feeling won't last. The second we *let* them catch us long enough to wangle a proposal out of them, they'll run so fast we won't have to dump them."

"Piper has a point," Olivia said over her shoulder. "Before we left Kingston, you were the one who reminded us we had to try hard to find a husband, Greer.

"To be honest, at this point I'd rather be wined and dined for the next twenty-four hours than have to go home and work my head off for another $5,000 only to have to give it back to Mr. Carlson."

Greer stared blindly out the back window. "Mr. Carlson's an idiot. Can you believe he actually bought all that gobbledygook about some attorney for the House of Parma-Bourbon clearing us?"

"Still, he was Daddy's attorney," Piper reminded her. "And Daddy did stipulate what the money was to be used for."

Yup. There was no way getting around that salient fact. Greer frowned to see that her sisters were ninety-nine percent won over to the idea of carrying out their original plan.

"Has it occurred to you the crew might sail off into the sunset and never be seen again?"

"No—" they both said at once.

It was a dumb question since it would never occur to Greer either. "Okay, but don't cry foul to me if we discover them waiting for us at some disreputable bar on the waterfront where they hang out with the handiest female upstairs."

"Greer!"

"Don't be so touchy, Olivia. I'm only thinking of the movies I've seen about undercover agents and their sleazy apartments."

"I think we all recognize these playboys aren't secret agents," Piper declared. "So where do we go from here?"

Olivia smiled. "Let's leave the car and the keys at the rental place. Since the crew enjoys undercover work, let them figure out where to find it."

"Yeah."

"Yeah."

Once again they found themselves driving on the outskirts of Genoa. After making several inquiries they spotted the sporting goods store pointed out to them. However there wasn't a rental bike to be had at any price.

"So we'll buy the cheapest ones they have and take them home on the plane with us."

By the time they'd purchased helmets, gloves, and water bottles they had to fill with bottled mineral water, they'd each spent $900, which they put on their company credit card. The salesguy was so happy to make an easy sale, he let them use the store bathroom to change into clean jeans, cotton sweaters and sneakers.

They helped each other put on their pendants. After stuffing their pockets with passports, tickets and wallets, they were ready. Olivia left the car parked around the side of the building in an alley with the key under the front floor mat.

Greer didn't shed any tears over their clothes and luggage sitting in the trunk. It had all been a huge mistake.

After looking at the brochure map, they estimated that if they went ten miles an hour, they could reach the town of Alessandria by nightfall. It lay in a northwesterly direction toward Switzerland where they would fly home from Geneva.

There were a dozen little stops they made to rest and snack, but on the whole they weren't unhappy with their progress. The locals waved to them from their fields and farms.

Hardly a man drove by in a car or a truck who didn't try to carry on a conversation with them and throw them kisses. They must have heard the word *"bellissima"* a thousand times if they heard it once.

Obviously Maximilliano came by his amorous ways from the same gene pool as his countrymen. So why couldn't she smile and laugh off his attention the way she did all the strangers along the road?

Halfway to their destination Piper's rear tire went flat. They took it off, then got out her patch kit to repair the tube. That's when trouble started. Every male or group of males who drove by in either direction decided to stop and help.

There must have been ten to fifteen guys young and old standing around creating a bottleneck. One truckful of guys was really pushing it. Talk about being chatted up!

Various offers were thrown out to drive them into town. Most of it was said in Italian of course, but Greer didn't need a translator to get the gist. More guys kept stopping. They were gathering like an army of ants attacking a grain field.

Then suddenly Greer saw Max's tall, powerful body striding toward her with Nic and Luc not far behind.

Like Moses parting the Red Sea, he rapped out Italian in such a forbidding fashion, the crowd of aggressive males dived for the nearest car or truck and drove off. In that instant, her heart thudded against her rib cage.

He picked up her bike with one hand like it was a tooth-pick. "Luc must not have drawn you an accurate map."

"On the contrary. It was marvelously detailed. A child could have found its way. However we decided the Grand Prix was overrated and thought why not see Switzerland instead to avoid the crowds."

"Since this is your first time in Europe, you had no way of knowing you can't go anywhere in summer without bumping into a crowd. Or creating one..." he added in his low, velvety voice.

"I'd like my bike back."

He'd started walking toward the Fiat with it. "All in good time, *signorina*," he announced after he'd put it in the rack on top of the car.

"You have no right to follow us and commandeer our transportation."

When his black eyes flashed right then, she felt the same authority emanating from him that had intimidated the crowd and sent his poor countrymen running for cover.

"Not only is your safety our top priority, we have a responsibility to Fabio Moretti who lent us his boat and his car for our undercover work. Though you didn't realize your Husband Fund escapade would involve you in the center of an international criminal investigation, you no longer have the luxury of throwing caution to the wind.

"If you were to meet up with some unscrupulous men who wouldn't let anything stand in the way of taking what they want, or worse..." He paused for emphasis. "Fabio could ultimately be the one held liable for something that wasn't his fault. And all because you entered into a contract with him."

He was speaking like a lawyer again.

"Since the death of his parents, Fabio has run a respectable business. He has two brothers, a wife, a child and another child on the way who depend on him for their survival."

She didn't flinch. "Don't you dare lay that guilt trip on us. How do we know you're not as unscrupulous as the men you're talking about?"

"You don't. But I can assure you that if we *had* been the kind of men you're describing, you would have been taken directly from the airport to the magistrate of the Genoese court and incarcerated in a prison for months while you awaited trial."

Who was this man?

"To think a female with such skin and eyes, such a beautiful body and intelligent mind as yours, has no softness in her." His gaze pierced hers. "I once suffered a great surprise and disappointment, Signorina Greer. Until now, nothing else has ever come close to it..."

Greer had to admit she was surprised at how deep the wound he'd just inflicted had penetrated. Possibly to the core of her soul.

"Where are you taking us?" she asked in a dull voice.

"To Vernazza, *signorina*, where you will sign a legal form in front of witnesses that releases Fabio Moretti from any and all obligations to you. At that time, your $12,000 will be refunded in cash, never mind that he lives hand to mouth to make ends meet and will suffer for the loss.

"But that won't be your problem will it. You'll be free to ride your bikes all over Europe and reap the whirlwind if that is your desire."

Before long the six of them were on their way back to Genoa and the *Piccione*. With Luc at the wheel, Olivia at his side, the forty miles the girls had covered in four hours only took twenty-five minutes to retrace.

Nic had pulled Piper onto his lap, which left Greer sandwiched in back between him and Max.

While the other two men tried to get her sisters to talk and acted for all the world as if nothing was out of the ordinary, Max treated Greer to a debilitating silence. It enflamed her that he'd placed the blame for the unbreachable wall of anger and mistrust between them solely at *her* feet.

But by the time they were back on the boat, the fear that he'd spoken the truth about Signore Moretti had been eating at her conscience.

"Guys? We've got to talk!" Once they'd assembled in the same stateroom, which was beginning to feel like home away from home, she unloaded on them.

After relating the thrust of her bitter conversation with Max, Piper said, "I'm not sure what's true and what isn't, but I do know one thing. None of those men who stopped to help us fix our bikes did it out of altruism. In fact that one truck load was so aggressive, I was really beginning to get nervous, you know?"

"We all were," Olivia murmured. "Let's be honest and admit we were relieved the crew showed up when they did. There's fright, and then there's fright."

Piper nodded. "With the crew, you're scared you might actually start believing all the words that come out of their mouths in half a dozen languages."

"*Liking* it you mean," Olivia amended. "With those men in the truck, you're just plain scared."

Greer's sisters had put their finger on the dilemma plaguing her since the night Max had asked her to swim with him. He *could* have behaved exactly like those men in the truck. Because of her instant and overwhelming attraction to him, she would have been helpless to deny him anything for long.

But he'd let her go. Not once, but three times. The last being in the jail cell. He'd known how vulnerable she was last night, both physically and emotionally, yet he hadn't taken advantage of her or the situation.

Like a revelation it came to her that his actions weren't those of a despicable brute who preyed on defenseless women. But they *were* the actions of a man searching for answers, determined to find them.

Though Greer didn't know who he was, or what he did for a living, the close call on the road this evening showed her the situation for what it was.

Whether he was a jewel thief or not, seduction was the last thing on his mind. The pendant had been the catalyst to bring them together.

If there really was another pendant like the one their dad had given them, and it had been stolen along with a priceless jewelry collection, no wonder alarm bells had sounded when she and her siblings had waltzed through customs wearing "hot" merchandise.

At this juncture Greer was prepared to believe that once the crew had accomplished their business in Monaco, they would put her and her sisters on a plane home.

Familiar vibrations caused her feet and legs to tingle, alerting her they'd cast off. "Guys? I'll be right back!"

To her sisters' astonishment, she dashed out of the state-room and through the hall to the upper deck.

Genoa, the bejeweled lady of the Mediterranean, was receding in the darkness which had enveloped the coast without her being aware of it. Greer could still make out Luc's physique as he coiled rope.

She turned her head to discover Max securing the bikes next to the kayaks. If he felt her presence, he didn't ac-knowledge it until she'd come within touching distance of him. Then he lifted his dark head and their gazes collided.

His anger had dissipated, but in its place she sensed a new aloofness emanating from him. It was the kind he might show any stranger rather the woman he'd kissed with unbridled passion two days ago.

If anything she should be relieved by this seemingly professional detachment. It was what she wanted. Yet her mouth had gone strangely dry and her heart was behaving like a single engine plane spiraling out of control as it hurtled toward the ground coming up to meet it.

"Whatever you wish to say, tell it to the captain, *signo-rina*. He pilots this boat, not me."

Her awareness of him made it difficult to breathe.

"But he listens to his first mate. Please inform him that we're going to spend the next few hours transforming our-selves into the Duchesses of Kingston.

"After we've reached Monaco, we plan to make such a stunning entrance, even *you* will blink and wonder if you've been wrong about our not having a drop of royal blood in us whether it be Austrian, Italian or something else."

CHAPTER TEN

"OH...YOU guys..." Olivia's voice shook with emotion. "Just look at that sight..."

It was a Monagasque fairyland all right, with the Grimaldi royal palace glowing like the crowning star on the Christmas tree.

From the balcony of the gorgeous villa overlooking the street where the Formula I cars would race tomorrow, Greer and her sisters feasted their eyes on elegant old palaces and buildings with wrought-iron railings, wonderful roofs with thousands of orange tiles laid at all angles in multifaceted splendor. There was a veritable panoply of painted walls, architectural detail, friezes, scrollwork everywhere one gazed.

Farther below lay Monaco's fabulous harbor twinkling with lights from the myriad of small white boats including the *Piccione* and stately yachts the size of soccer fields. Possessions of the world's wealthiest princes and sheiks.

Piper sucked in her breath. "I'm looking and I still don't believe it. Smell the flowers. They're everywhere. Jasmine and rose. Lavender."

It was the stuff dreams were made of all right, Greer mused in awe. Yet this nineteenth-century provencal villa named Le Clos des Falcons was breathtakingly real.

So was the black limo with its royal falcon crest which had whisked them and the crew from the port. Where others couldn't go, they were allowed entrance past barricades, guard rails, fences and gates erected for the world's most famous car race.

153

Olivia nudged Greer in the ribs. "What do you think of Luc's sleazy waterfront pad now?"

"Obviously he has friends in very high places."

"It feels like we're in a beautiful dream."

Greer smiled at her sisters. No doubt she was walking around the sumptuously furnished room wearing their same, starry-eyed expressions.

"If mother could see us in our knee-length white chiffon and pendants, that's exactly what she'd say."

Piper stared at Greer. "We look like identical triplets tonight. It really shows since we're wearing the same hairdos for a change. Wouldn't she love it? Mom always begged us to dress alike on special family occasions."

"I can hear Daddy now," Greer murmured. "Are these my three darling duchesses all grown up?"

Olivia's eyes went teary. That started Piper and Greer. Everything was still blurry when she heard a distinct rap on the outer door of their private suite.

Assuming it was the maid who'd been waiting on them since their arrival, Greer went to answer it, unprepared for the sight that awaited her.

There stood the heartthrob of the century. No doubt about it. Max would win the prize hands down.

He probably heard the moan that escaped her throat, but she couldn't help it. In black and white formal evening wear, this tall, black-haired Italian with his striking aquiline features left her speechless and trembling.

His black eyes roved over her in male admiration. Yet the fire she'd always seen burning in their depths when he looked at her was missing. Extinguished if you like.

Greer didn't like, which was absurd. This man didn't mean anything to her. He was an experience. A phenomenon of nature like the planet Mars coming close to Earth for the first time in sixty thousand years, then continuing its orbit to the far reaches of space.

Tomorrow night Greer's plane would follow its own orbit to another part of the universe. The chance of their ever coming together again, even for an instant, wasn't astronomically possible.

"Buona sera, signorina. In five minutes we'd like you and your sisters to come down the staircase at the end of the hall. There's a drawing room off to the right where you'll be introduced to a group of people. Just play along with the conversation wherever it leads."

She got a sinking feeling in the pit of her stomach. "What if we make a mistake?"

"You won't if you just play at being your unique self which you do superbly."

The acid comment was meant to wound. It found its mark.

"When the time comes for the guests to withdraw to the dining room for a midnight supper, I'll make our apologies and we'll both leave. At which time I will say goodnight."

Greer shivered because beneath his civility she sensed he was still furiously angry with her.

"As for *you, signorina*, you look exceptionally beautiful tonight. Since you will have served your purpose for us with the grace of Violetta herself, you'll be left alone to do whatever you want. The limo's at your disposal. Just tell the maid and she'll arrange it."

"We heard that," Olivia whispered after the door closed in front of Greer's face. "I take back what I said. He's scarier than any man I ever met."

"We shouldn't have bought those bikes," Piper murmured. "I think it insulted him. Maybe it's an Italian thing. You know what they say about travel in a foreign country. In some places it's polite to burp after you eat, in other places it isn't."

"Baloney!" Greer spun around. "It's a *male* thing. He

didn't get his way the minute he snapped his fingers, so now he's having an Italian temper tantrum."

"I think you're having one, too. Your face is all splotchy. It proves we do have some Italian blood in us despite the mean things they said to try to discredit us."

"Thanks, Olivia."

"Don't bite my head off. We know you're disappointed."

"About what?"

"About his intention to leave you strictly alone after we've done our part downstairs," Piper murmured.

"I couldn't care less."

"That's not what your eyes are saying. But don't worry. I'm going up to bed right after, too."

"So am I."

Greer's gaze shot to Olivia's. "I thought Luc had arranged for you to visit a club to meet some Formula I drivers."

"That's out of the question now."

"Why?"

"When I told him Cesar Villon was the only driver I was interested in meeting, he demanded to know why. I asked why he cared. He didn't answer, but his whole mood darkened after that."

"Sounds like he's as jealous as Fred," Piper reasoned.

"No. He's just an egocentric French male who thinks the world begins and ends with him. You know how the French are. His eyelids go all hooded." She imitated him, laying on the French accent. "He becomes the melancholy philosopher's philosopher. He's seen it all, done it all, and he knows it better and has suffered it longer than anyone else."

Whoa, Olivia!

"The captain's the one who *knows* it all," Piper insisted. "He's got what I call the Castilian superiority complex. You can't say one thing that he doesn't know more about it, and he's *the* authority. There is no other above him. In his spare time he makes up Spanish crossword puzzles of the highest difficulty.''

"Did he tell you that?'' Olivia questioned with a chuckle.

"Not yet. I'm waiting. It has to be on his resume somewhere.''

"Piper!'' Greer was laughing, too.

"Do you know he thinks I'm a chocoholic? So of course that's what I am, right?''

"All three of us are,'' Olivia muttered.

"Never mind that. It's what *he* thinks and says I am, I can't abide. You can't win an argument with him. It's impossible. He's always one step ahead of you. That Spanish brain is like a steel trap, stored with obscure trivia he pulls out at a moment's notice.

"He thinks he's spending tomorrow morning with me so he can impress me with more of his vast knowledge.'' Her cheeks glowed a hot red. "Get this— He says I'm the only American woman he ever met who can converse with him on a halfway intelligent level.

"Well guess what? This dimwit American has gathered enough of her scattered brain not to go anywhere with him in the morning or any other time.''

"You won't say that after you've spent five minutes with him again,'' Greer reminded her, "but let's not worry about that right now. It's time to go downstairs and do what it is we're supposed to do.''

"I still don't know what that is,'' Olivia complained.

"You heard Maximilliano.'' She loved to say the name, wondering if it really was his. "Just play ourselves.''

"I think that was meant to be an insult.''

Greer glared at Piper. "You only *think?*''

They made their way through the villa, which felt more

like a palace. There was a striking man in elegant evening clothes waiting at the bottom of the curving staircase. When he smiled up at them, Greer realized it was the owner of the *Piccione*!

What was going on? The girls recognized him immediately and rolled their eyes at Greer.

"*Buona sera, signorine.* You were lovely before. Tonight you take my breath away."

Anger over this whole charade emboldened Greer to say, "You look pretty smashing yourself, Signore Moretti."

He flashed her a smile that could have meant anything.

Sure he was just a poor catamaran owner... One furthermore living hand to mouth who would be held liable if anything happened to the lovely *signorine.*

The man had a great thing going here. If there really was a Signora Moretti and child, Greer felt sorry for them.

"When the other party had to cancel their reservation for the *Piccione* at the time of the Grand Prix, it became your lucky day, did it not?"

"The experience of a lifetime," Piper said through gritted teeth.

Olivia's hand went to her throat in a dramatic gesture. "We still haven't recovered. It's like we're moving through an amazing dream."

Nightmare you mean.

He chuckled. "I'm very happy to hear it. Shall we go in? I'll introduce you to a few guests." He opened one of the ornate floor to ceiling doors.

Greer blinked. A few people? She'd been aware of chamber music, but not voices. There had to be at least seventy beautifully dressed guests congregated in groups around the elaborate appointments of the drawing room! If the crew was there, she couldn't tell.

"Fabio!"

An attractive dark blond woman wearing a stunning oyster toned designer dress, left the people she'd been talking to and hurried across the parquet floor with her handsome escort to kiss Signore Moretti on either cheek.

The other man, evidently her husband, stood a few inches taller than Fabio with enough gray in his black hair to make him distinguished. Both looked to be in their early sixties.

A spate of Italian broke from all three of them, giving Greer the impression they were close friends who hadn't met for a while. But then nothing about this trip had been as it seemed. What was the line, "We are all actors and the world is our stage"?

"Rina? Umberto?" Fabio spoke up. "There are three sisters I want you to meet," he explained in English. "They chartered the *Piccione* for this time slot. When I found out who they were, I decided to keep it a surprise until tonight."

"So much alike, yet the eyes are so different." The woman smiled warmly as she and the other man studied each of them. Then her dark flashing gaze that put Greer in mind of the great black's, suddenly locked on the pendants. She let out a cry that brought her husband's arm around her shoulders. All conversation in the room ceased.

With a chuckle Fabio said, "No, Rina. You and Umberto are not hallucinating. May I present Greer, Piper and Olivia. They are the Duchesses of Kingston of the royal House of Parma-Bourbon, anxious to meet their long lost family."

His announcement created a shock wave of interest throughout the crowd.

"Because of the theft of the Maria-Luigia jewelry collection, there was some unpleasantness when the *signorine* came through customs a few days ago wearing the Duchesse pendants.

"You will be happy to know it is all cleared up now.

Signore Rossi has determined that one of the pendants they're wearing is the other original made by Tocelli for Maria-Luigia.''

"Other?" The word echoed throughout the room as everyone looked at them in astonishment.

"For some reason yet to be uncovered, the artisan fashioned two identical pendants. Therefore it appears that the myth about an ancestral line making its way to America is not a myth after all.''

What? But the crew said—

"*Signorine?* May I present your many distant relatives. First of all, Rina and Umberto, the Duc di Varano of the House of Parma-Bourbon.''

Greer and her sisters let out a collective gasp that was even louder than the cry of the other woman, the woman they'd just been introduced to who could be none other than Max's *mother!* The resemblance to both parents was unmistakable.

But that meant the first mate was the son of a d—

"Come, *signorine.*" Fabio started ushering them around the room. "Meet your hosts for this evening, Violetta di Varano, Umberto's sister who is the wife of Jean-Louis, the Duc de Falcon of the House of Bourbon.''

Another duc? Luc's mother was named Violetta?

Noooooo.

Olivia's groan coincided with hers. Luc's parents smiled broadly. "An exquisite surprise," his father murmured before kissing their hands with the kind of dashing charm bequeathed to their injured son.

Greer was still reeling with shock and rage, unable to take it all in.

"Standing next to them is Maria di Varano, the second sister of Umberto who is married to Juan-Carlos, the Duc de Pastrana of the House of Bourbon.''

"What a thrilling moment for the Varano family," Nic's

mother responded with genuine pleasure. "Niccolo will have to sort all of this out for us. He's the expert in the family."

A hysterical laugh emerged from Piper's throat. Thankfully Fabio continued to sweep them along, making the introductions of the rest of the guests, one of whom could possibly be the person responsible for the theft of the ducal palace jewelry collection. Undoubtedly Signore Moretti was watching everyone's reactions, which he would report to the crew.

There was no sign of *them* yet.

It was a blessing, particularly since she suspected her sisters were on the verge of strangling someone with their bare hands. Greer would be the first in line, and she knew which neck she wanted to start with.

The three of them drew close together for a second.

Olivia drew in a noisy breath. "Luc de Falcon is going to wish he didn't need a cane because when I get hold of i—"

"*Signorine?*" came Fabio's voice. "Last but not least, may I present Isabella di Varano, wife of Giovanni di Luccesi—"

"*And my only sister.*"

Of course.

The grand entrance of Maximilliano the Magnificent himself!

"This is very exciting," the dark-haired beauty exclaimed.

Isabella was as gorgeous as her brother, but Greer refused to look at him.

She couldn't fathom any of what was going on. In truth she was only barely functioning.

"If all of you will excuse our bellissima Duchesse cousins," Max spoke in a vibrant voice that would have penetrated the farthest corners of the room. "They need their rest after spending a miserable night in the Colorno jail while I worked out the legalities with the police."

The crowd's sympathetic reaction couldn't possibly have been orchestrated.

"Following their release they chose to take a grueling four-hour bike ride in the hot sun to see the countryside of their ancestors. Unfortunately they ran into some trouble that required my help again."

Greer stole a look to see if he'd been struck by lightning yet. What a horrible mistake that turned out to be. His black eyes were *laughing* at her.

"I'm quite sure they're at the point of exhaustion, but as the chief commissioner confided to me, they charmed the guards and handled their harrowing ordeal with all the dignity and spirit of the former Duchesse of Parma herself. *Signorine?* May I be the first to say, welcome to the family."

His mockery in front of God and all these witnesses who were clapping after such an amazing speech was too much.

"Thank you," Greer said to everyone with a smile. "It's been a pleasure to meet everyone." Her sisters said virtually the same thing before they all murmured their good-nights.

She made her exit out the door with the kind of poise her parents would have been proud of. The girls weren't far behind. After reaching the foyer, they flew up the staircase to their suite like a bunch of homing pigeons.

Once the door was locked Greer turned to her sisters hot-faced. "We know we're not related, so how *dare* he mock us like that. Now that we finally know which way the wind is blowing, we'll see who has the last laugh.

"No way are they going to get the satisfaction of bundling us up in the royal limo and shipping us back to America like so much unwanted baggage. Obviously that was their plan as soon as they were through using us."

Olivia wore a set jaw. "We came to see the Grand Prix and that's what we're going to do."

"We can escape off the balcony," Piper muttered. "It'll be a cinch. I saw a little portico just below it. From there we can jump to the ground and merge into the crowd before they discover we're gone."

Greer marched over to her suitcase. "This operation calls for jeans and T-shirts, but we'll have to be wearing our travel suits when we ring for maid service."

Within a few minutes several of them appeared at the door to carry the luggage to the limo.

"Thank you. We'll be right down."

The second the door was closed, they peeled off their suits, hung them in the closet, then put on their casual clothes and sneakers.

They met at the balcony. "One for all, and all for one," Piper whispered before going over the railing first. It was like déjà vu, except that instead of water, they landed on pavement.

Piper was off like a shot between two villas across the street. Olivia followed close behind. Greer brought up the tail as they discovered a narrow alley farther on and started running like crazy in the direction of the harbor below.

The crowds of spectators waiting all night to see the race roamed the streets and alleyways, impeding their progress. But it no longer mattered because she and her siblings blended with the crowd.

Farther down when they came out on the main street again, they passed a set of bleachers with a huge "Villon" banner fastened across the top. Olivia stopped in her tracks. "You guys—"

"We know. We saw it, too."

"Let's find out if there's room for three more."

Whether it was because they were triplets, or because the gods were smiling on them, a group of exuberant

French guys probably in their late teens and early twenties seemed only too happy to let them squeeze in next to them.

They spoke little English which made it amusing. In every other way they communicated like mad. Olivia's knowledge of Cesar Villon's racing statistics enamored her to them. Greer and Piper just smiled and pretended they were hard-core fans, too.

For the first time since the girls' arrival in Europe, they were treated like royalty. The one named Simon fed them ham filled brioches. The other ones named Gerard, Jules and Philippe, supplied drinks and treats. They carried pocket transistors that picked up all the information about the drivers and the cars. Excitement ran high.

Then came the first rays of the sun and with it the roar of the race. Screaming engines permeated all of Monaco, loud, close, far and soft. Between the unintelligible reporting of the announcer over the loudspeakers plus the echo of the cars bouncing off the buildings and hills, the thrill of the sport was like a fever in the blood.

Fans dotted the scene before them like bits of pepper in a pasta dish. Some were draped over balconies, others hung out of windows, still others looked through the holes in fences all along the route. When Cesar Villon roared by, there was an explosion of noise that probably broke a few eardrums.

Greer looked over at Olivia who was being hugged by one of the guys in the excitement of the moment. She nudged Piper who put her lips to her ear so she could hear her. "Seeing Villon whiz by has made this trip for our sister."

"I'm glad one of us can go home with a good memory." Greer's temper was still as hot as a firecracker.

"When do you want to head for that youth hostel Simon told us about. I'm ready to pass out from lack of sleep."

"You're not the only one. Let's go."

They called to Olivia who nodded and started making her way toward them. The guys tried to talk the three of them into staying. The only way Olivia could persuade Gerard to let her go was to tell him to come by the hostel that evening. By then they'd be ready to party.

"He drew me a map, guys," she said as soon as she reached the aisle of the bleachers. "With this crowd it's about an hour's walk from here."

"After yesterday's bike ride, it'll be a piece of cake."

Max instructed the helicopter pilot to fly over the *Piccione* again. Since it had been determined that their prize pigeons had flown off the villa balcony while he and his cousins had been picking Fabio's brains for information about the guests' reactions to the news, there'd been no trace of them. Not at the Nice airport, not at the train station.

"Every police officer had been given a description and was told to call in at the first sign of them. Where in the hell could they have gotten to so fast without being detected?"

His cell phone rang. It was Nic who'd been working with the police on the ground. "Did you find them?"

"No. We've checked with the concierge of every hotel. There's been no report of seeing them at the reception counters. They haven't asked for a room. What about the boat?"

"Fabio says they haven't stepped foot on it," Max muttered.

"*Dios!*" Nic thundered.

None of them wanted to entertain the thought that the women had been so desperate to get away from them, they'd asked a lift from some predators who had no interest in racing and only came to Monaco for just such an opp—

"Hang on, Nic. Luc's calling." He put him on hold and clicked to Luc. "Any news?"

"They're seven blocks from the villa!"

"What?" His heart practically leaped out of his chest.

"I just saw them on the TV screen while a cameraman was panning the lower portion of the route chatting with fans. They're being very cozy with a bunch of enamored college guys sitting on some bleachers bearing a Villon banner.

"Mon Dieu— I don't know where my mind has been not to think of that first! The stand is next to the corner of the Rue de Cypres. If I didn't have this damn leg holding me back—"

"You *have* your leg! That's the most important thing, and it's going to get better. Because of you, we now know where our pigeons have come to roost. Nic'll round them up. In the meantime I'll instruct the pilot to fly over the area so I can keep an eye on them. I'll call you back as soon as I know anything more."

He hung up, gave the pilot new instructions, then clicked on to Nic and told him the situation.

"I'm on my way now with the police," his cousin responded with a noise in his throat that sounded oddly emotional to Max. Was it possible Nic was coming back to life after all these months?

Max waited till the helicopter had reached the desired vicinity. Using his binoculars, he zeroed in on the stand in question, but he didn't see the face he was looking for. No hair of spun gold. The knowledge that the women had already fled the scene hit him like a kick in the gut.

"Keep circling," he rapped out to the pilot while he waited for Nic to arrive. In a few more minutes his cousin approached in a police car, followed by two more patrol vans. He and half a dozen officers got out and started interrogating everyone on the bleachers. It seemed to go on a long time.

Eventually he noticed four of the spectators being escorted to the vans. Good. They knew something!

Before long Max received the call he'd been waiting for. "Nic?"

"The women have gone to a local youth hostel on the Avenue Prince Pierre."

Unbelievable.

"Our witnesses refused to cooperate until we threatened them with a night in jail for obstruction of justice. No doubt they were planning to meet them there later for a few nights on the road together," his voice grated.

Max ground his teeth so hard, pain shot through his jaw. "How much lead time do we have on them?"

"Probably forty minutes."

"It's enough for Luc to set things up the way we want. I'll meet you back at the villa."

After clicking off, he phoned Luc and let him know what was happening.

"Leave it all to me, Max. By the time you both get here, we'll be able to relax and catch some sleep before tonight."

Sleep? What was that?

Since the moment he'd followed Signorina Greer inside the San Giorgio church in Portofino where he'd first glimpsed her face in the candlelight, he'd felt an unprecedented stirring in his blood.

The sight of her distinctive profile, the texture of her skin giving off a glow of natural pearls, those violet orbs— all had kept his legs planted in the shadows where he could feast his eyes on her without detection.

She had a lovely body. In the flattering sundress, she was the essence of classic femininity. The kind that would grow more beautiful when she became a mother.

Haunted by that image, he'd left the church ahead of her, hungry and restless for the one thing in life that would always elude him.

"Max?"

"Yes?"

"Are you all right?"

"Of course."

"If you say so, *mon ami*." There was a click as he replaced the receiver.

CHAPTER ELEVEN

"WE DON'T have individual rooms, *mesdemoiselles*. Our dorms have four bunk beds each, eight people to a room. Right now we only have four beds left in the whole center."

"Is it an all women's dorm?"

The receptionist at the Centre de Jeunesse Pierre shook her head. "We don't make distinctions here."

Of course not.

Greer turned to her sisters. "I don't think I can go on without some sleep."

"I can't, either," Piper murmured. "You can bet these are the only four beds available in Monaco."

"I don't see we have a choice, guys," Olivia declared.

"Agreed." Greer pulled out her wallet and handed the receptionist the credit card. At the rate they were spending money, there would be no profit to bank at the end of the year.

So far they were out their designer luggage, their wardrobes, their bikes and $15,000 they would have to give back to Mr. Carlson. If it hadn't been for the generosity of Simon and the boys, they would have been forced to buy breakfast, too.

The woman handed them three sets of clean sheets, blankets and pillows. "You're in dorms four, five and six upstairs."

They wouldn't even be in the same room. "Thank you."

At the top of the stairs they paid a visit to the rest room before moving on to the dorms. To their relief, each one was empty. Naturally no backpackers would be hanging around here. Not while the most exciting event in the world's most romantic spot was happening right outside the building.

All the bottom bunks had already been claimed by other guests. Olivia looked around her dorm. "If our luck holds, no one will show up until tonight. By then we'll have had our sleep and can head for the train station."

"Let's set our watch alarms for 7:00 p.m. That'll give us a good few hours to recuperate."

They hugged Olivia goodnight, then went to their separate dorms. Somehow Greer found the strength to climb up the ladder and fix her bed before collapsing on top of it. Yet five minutes later she was still awake.

Max's last words to the guests in the drawing room kept running through her mind. *Welcome to the family.*

His mockery, meant as the final affront before he put her on the plane home from Nice had been particularly hurtful.

Greer knew why… She was in love for the first and only time in her life.

Hot tears gushed from her eyes. She buried her face in the pillow. It was a good thing her sisters weren't in the room. They'd never seen her cry over a man before. And they never would!

When next she became cognizant of her alarm going off, she was so out of it she rolled off the mattress to get up like she usually did, then screamed to feel herself falling.

"Oh!" she cried out again when a pair of strong masculine arms caught her before she went splat on the floor.

"Easy, *signorina*."

"*Max!*"

She blinked several times while she tried to figure out

if she was awake or dreaming. Right now the black eyes staring into hers at such close range were alive with flame.

"How did you find me? What are you doing here?" She was so in love with him and so cross with him at the same time she couldn't see straight. "Where are all the other people?"

"What other people? Don't I even merit a 'grazie' for saving your life?" he whispered against her lips, nibbling them as if they were delicious morsels he couldn't resist.

She groaned because he was kindling the ache that had never gone away since he'd first kissed her. Rivulets of desire coursed through her body which yearned toward his. She was trembling with needs he'd brought to life, needs that would never go away.

"Put me down first and we'll talk about it," she begged in a breathless voice. This close to him she couldn't think.

His mouth roamed over her face, her nose, her eyes, her hair. "I can't do that, *bellissima*. I've learned that the only way to get anywhere with you is to keep you in my arms. I want you, Greer. I want you with a hunger you couldn't possibly comprehend."

His mouth was doing the most incredible things to her. In his arms she was learning the meaning of rapture. When they got tangled up with each other on the narrow lower bunk, she couldn't tell where one kiss ended and the next one began.

Ecstasy. That's what it was like being kissed by Maximilliano di Varano. Ecstasy.

Her fingers twined in his raven-black hair and she found herself covering his face and throat with her mouth, savoring everything male about him while she worshipped the differences between them.

"You were right to call me a shark," he whispered huskily as he caressed her throat with his lips. "I'd like to take bites out of you in order to make you a part of me.

"But if I did that, then you would be consumed, and I would go mad with hunger because there wasn't any more of you, anywhere. Let me take you back to the *Piccione* where we can be alone and I can love all of you," he begged with primitive longing.

Back to the *Piccione*? For only one night?

In that moment her heart dried up like winter's last prune.

Deliberately misunderstanding him, she leaned over him, pressing his cheeks with her palms. Pain like she'd never known before intensified the purple glow of her eyes.

"You've made me so happy, I'm frightened. Do you think you could talk Fabio into letting us take the *Piccione* on a long, long honeymoon? I want to go to Elba, Monte Cristo and a hundred other islands with you. I want to experience everything with you.

"You've set me on fire, and now I'm the one bursting from the love I want to shower on you. I want to be all things to you. I want to live with you night and day.

"I want to have your babies," she cried against the male mouth that had transformed her. "Beautiful, brilliant, wonderful babies just like their father.

"You won't be doomed to swim forever alone, searching for me but never finding me. Once we're married, you can make love to me whenever you want. Whenever I want. Whenever we both want, for the rest of our lives if we want. How does that sound to you, my darling?

"You are my darling you know," she kissed the corner of his mouth, the lashes of his eyes, the lobes of his ears. "Don't you know a hundred lifetimes from now I will love you even more than I love you right now?

"Yet I can't imagine it being any stronger than it is at this very instant. There's no man who comes close to you,

Max. I love you. I love you to the depth of my soul." Her voice throbbed.

"I honestly didn't know love could make me feel like this. I didn't realize," she whispered, her breathing shallow. "Kiss me again so I'll know this is real."

She sought his mouth once more with soaring passion. "I can't wait to be your wife. I realize we haven't known each other very long, but it doesn't matter. Not when you've found your soul mate."

Staring into the black depths of his eyes she said, "We *are* soul mates. I knew it when you asked me to guess your name, knowing such a task would have been impossible. It was the most thrilling moment for me because I knew you wanted the experience to go on and on and never be over.

"I wanted it to go on and on, too. More than anything in my life I wanted to swim in the moonlight with you. But my feelings were too intense that night, too raw. I felt like one of those white-hot stars out in space ready to implode. Oh Max, I—"

"Greer—" he spoke her name in a gravelly voice, shifting her aside so he could get to his feet.

His breathing sounded ragged. The broad chest beneath the cream knit shirt he was wearing rose and fell visibly, like he'd just run a marathon. She'd terrified him.

That was the prophecy she'd made to her sisters months ago. It had come true. She knew he would run once he thought marriage was on the cards. But it hurt with a pain from which she would never, ever recover.

She slid off the bottom bunk. "What's wrong, darling?"

He rubbed the back of his neck with his hand. His face was a study in agony. She had no idea he could look that way.

"I forgot I was dealing with a woman who has obviously never been to bed with a man before."

Really. Her inexperience stuck out that badly? She'd thought her wild response to him was probably more un-inhibited and reckless than any initiated woman he'd ever made love to before.

"No," she answered in a bright tone. "I haven't. I've never had the slightest inclination until I saw you get out of that pool and come walking toward me as if you wanted to devour me. Since then I haven't been able to think about anything else but marrying you and making love with you for the rest of our lives."

After a long, palpable silence, "Greer—" he said her name again. The ultimate playboy of the Riviera seemed to be choking on monosyllables. It had to be a first for him, so why wasn't she jumping up and down with glee?

He raked a hand through his hair. "I'm afraid taking you out to the *Piccione* isn't going to work after all."

He'd finally been able to spit out the words, but they emerged sounding like a tormented whisper. How weird!

With the entire female population throwing themselves at him from every direction, why was it causing him such upheaval? Why such suffering to deny himself the pleasure of a one-night stand with a virginal American from the wrong side of the tracks?

"What do you mean?" she cried out in spurious alarm.

When he didn't say anything else, she decided it was time to help him out.

"Why don't you just admit you would love to make love to me, but not if it means getting hitched first!"

"Greer—"

She laughed. If her sisters had been present, they would have called it her cruel laugh.

"Take it easy, Max. It's not the end of the world. You're off the hook. You always have been."

His dark head reared back, exposing his hard jaw. "Ex-plain that remark."

Putting her hands in her back pockets, she smiled up at him. "I'll be happy to. At the jail when I was telling you about the Husband Fund, I'm afraid so many other matters were discussed at the same time, I left out the most important part."

"Which part?" he demanded in a chilly tone.

Greer cocked her head to the side. "This'll take a few minutes. Would you like to sit down first?"

Like a magnificent colossus, he remained standing there. "Fine. Have it your way." She flashed him another sunny smile. "My sisters and I never worried about getting married, but our parents did."

His scowl was quite frightening. "We've been over this ground before."

"True, but there's more. Unfortunately you have to be patient because I'm a woman, and you know how women are. They have to lay everything out and build up to it, analyze it, discuss it, and dissect it to death before they get to the point.

"It's just one of the great differences between the sexes men have so much problem with. Especially a man like you."

His mouth thinned. It delighted her, even if the withered prune which had been her heart was dissolving fast.

"As I was saying, our parents were concerned enough about the situation that during Mr. Carlson's reading of a letter our father had written to us, Daddy asked us to watch a movie about these ladies who try to find millionaires to marry."

"I've seen it," he interjected in a low voice.

"Of course you have. Anyway, the whole idea was to put ideas in our head to find a rich man and settle down.

"The film was a complete turnoff."

She paused. "You're pacing. Why don't you sit down? I told you this would take a while."

If looks could kill. "Go on."

"The loss of both our parents who needed constant nursing care over a couple of years was harder on us than we thought. After Daddy died, we moved across the street to a basement apartment so the house could be sold to pay the bills. I guess we didn't see that we needed a break until our landlady suggested to Piper we could use a vacation.

"But you know how it is when you're a workaholic, because that's what we are. We loved college, love our work and find it much more stimulating than anything else we do.

"So…until Mrs. Weyland brought up the idea of a vacation, we really hadn't entertained the thought. But with $15,000 suddenly in hand, it sounded kind of fun to go somewhere exciting. If only the money didn't have to be used to find a husband which none of us wanted.

"That's when Olivia reminded us we were the Duchesses of Kingston, so why not pretend *we* were the millionaires and see how many men we could get to propose?

"Piper picked up from there and said why not wear the Duchesse pendants to bring the really hard-core playboys out of the woodwork?

"Both their ideas were brilliant. At that point I merely suggested that we vacation on the Riviera if we wanted to hit the jackpot. When any of those phony playboys actually did propose, they would disappear back into the woodwork as soon as we told them we were the poor Duchesses from Kingston, New York, with no titles, no money, no lands.

"Then we could go home as free as the air to breathe having had a fabulous time visiting the home of our ancestor and maybe picking up new markets for our calendar business."

By now Max's eyes resembled shards of black ice. He

shifted his weight, making her aware of his intimidating height. "So if I had proposed—"

"If you *had* proposed fair and square, I would have told you the truth about myself knowing you would bail."

"Which was exactly what you wanted to happen."

Ah hah. His Italian ego had been dented again.

"I thought I'd already made that clear. But to reiterate, yes! That's exactly what we wanted to happen. Don't you see? We would have obeyed Daddy's stipulation to try and find a husband.

"Could we help it if in the end our eager suitors took back their proposals when they realized there was no gold at the end of the rainbow?"

She flashed him her diabolical smile. "I certainly didn't have to worry about you though, did I. Maximilliano di Varano baled ahead of time because you don't need to force a woman to have her, and you're not stupid. Otherwise you wouldn't be chief counsel for the House of Parma-Bourbon even if you are the son of a duc."

"Grazie, *signorina*," came his brittle reply. She could envision him making that slight little aristocratic bow.

"You're welcome." Her brows lifted. "You want to know something really ironic? We even planned our scheme so that on the last night of our trip when we unmasked ourselves, we would arrange to do it at a youth hostel just to prove our point.

"I had no idea it would be this one, though. Our original plan was to end up on the Spanish Riviera where we would lure our opportunistic playboys to a hostel, the last place they would think where we were staying.

"Unfortunately nothing went the way we expected and I was denied the fun of telling one of those losers, 'Sorry. No money. No tiara. What? You mean you're taking back your proposal? Well don't go away mad. Just go away.'"

His expression had darkened as if there'd been a total

eclipse of the sun. "What if one of those…losers hadn't bailed?"

She laughed. "The kind of men we planned to target were safe bets. But wearing the pendants threw a monkey wrench in the works. Are you familiar with that expression?

"I can see that you are," she said when there was no answer. "The point is, we never did have a chance to meet a real playboy. All we've met up with so far is the good old boy network. Its members don't count."

"So there's an age?"

"Absolutely."

"How old's Don?"

Don. Again?

"He's the right age, but he's not a playboy. He's a fine man who wants to marry me and have a family. Six little boys who will all grow up to be football players."

"What's wrong with that?"

"Not a thing if you love football, which I don't mind. Sometimes it can be pretty exciting. But I'd prefer not to be looked at as a breeder."

"Breeder?"

"So—there *is* one vagary about American English you haven't run into yet. You have no idea how pleased I am to hear that. Piper complains that Nic claims to know everything about everything."

"You were saying?" he reminded her in a gruff tone.

"I was *saying* that I would prefer to be looked upon as a woman first. Complete. Total, in and of myself! I mean, what if I couldn't have children? Would that suddenly make me less desirable in his eyes? And even if I could turn out a football team for Don, what if they were girls instead of boys? Heaven forbid! Who would watch the football games with him in his old age?"

One of Max's black brows dipped. "A minute ago you

told me you wanted to give me wonderful, brilliant babies like their father.''

"That was different. You were kissing me and telling me you wanted me with a hunger beyond comprehension. You had no expectations except to enjoy me like a piece of chocolate. I liked that. You weren't looking at me as the mother of creation.''

His eyes narrowed on her face. "But you admit you'd like to be a mother one day.''

"Well, yes. One day. Of course by the time I'm ready to get married, I'll probably end up with someone who's been divorced and has children of his own.''

"I thought you wanted to marry *me*.''

"I do,'' she said honestly, "but I also have brains in my head, and eyes that can see you're not for sale at any price. Otherwise you would have married a woman of your own station and breeding years ago.''

"You're right. There's a reason why I didn't.''

"I'm sure it was good one,'' Greer asserted. "Tragedy is no respecter of persons.''

"Tragedy?''

"Yes. You're the one who said some wounds weren't visible. I got the impression you were trying to tell me something. You truly are Signore Mysterioso.

"However there are things about you I *do* know. For one thing you're not a man who plays around with other women while your wife is home trying desperately hard to pretend it doesn't bother her.

"For another, you don't take advantage of foolish virgins. On the contrary, you rush about saving them from a fate worse than death while they're trying to make an escape on their bicycles.

"Furthermore, I don't think you're the type to carry on with married women behind their husbands' backs. You don't need to when every eligible maiden in Parma would sell her soul to be *the* woman in your life.

"All in all I think you're quite a rarity, Signore di Varano. For a man that is. And now it's time for me to go find my sisters. We have a plane to catch."

He shook his handsome hand. "Not quite yet. By now they're aboard the *Piccione* waiting for you."

"For such an honorable man I must say it was very cruel of you to welcome us to the family in front of your parents and relatives after Signore Moretti told that lie about our pendants. For that I will never forgive you." But really she just couldn't forgive him for not loving her.

"Careful, *signorina*—sometimes all is not as it seems."

"Meaning what?" she grumbled.

"I'll let Nic tell you this evening while we enjoy our meal on deck."

"And then will you give us our freedom?"

"I will do better than that. When the celebration is over, I swear an oath on the graves of your beloved parents I'll take you wherever you wish to go."

She didn't think the mention of her mother and father was a subject Max would bring up if he weren't being sincere.

"Very well then. I'm ready."

He opened the door of the dorm and escorted her down the hall to the stairs. "Do you know one of the many things I find fascinating about you is your ability to travel light?"

"Normally I don't," she said as they left the hostel. He helped her into his car parked around the side.

After they'd driven off he turned to her. "The point is, you're adaptable."

"I am when I'm running for my life."

His deep chuckle resonated to the tips of her toes. "That was some disappearing act you did off the balcony."

"Did the three of you tape our escape and then watch reruns until you'd decided we'd had enough sleep?"

"No, *signorina*. We waited in the limousine to spirit you back to the boat for a midnight supper."

She couldn't help laughing at that admission. "Which Luc prepared of course."

"Actually it was Marcel, one of their chefs who wasn't very happy no one showed up to eat his masterpiece."

Uh-oh. "How did you find us?"

"Luc saw you on TV enjoying yourselves with a bunch of hormone-riddled fans. They were so taken with you, Nic had to get the police to threaten them with jail time before they would admit where you'd gone."

"You're kidding! They were very nice to us."

"That's only natural since they expected to join up with you tonight for more fun and excitement."

She bit her lip. "They fed us breakfast."

He gave her that wounded look again. "All along, my cousins and I have been prepared to see to your needs."

"Unfortunately we didn't know until a little while ago that we weren't going to be served up as the main course to fill *your* needs."

His rich male laughter filled the interior.

"Whose idea was it to serve us petrified bread in the Colorno jail? Remember you are under oath, counselor."

"That was different."

If all traces of Greer's heart hadn't disappeared, his grin would have made it flip-flop as they wound their way to the port. Everywhere she looked, the rich and famous were dancing the night away to music coming from the dozens of nearby yachts and boats.

Monaco was in full party gala. So was the festive deck of the *Piccione*. The boat sat sheltered beneath one of the many blue canopies. She discovered her sisters and Max's cousins sat eating with an unexpected dark-haired guest who bore a superficial resemblance to Luc.

When Max introduced her, the man who appeared to be in his midtwenties got up to shake her hand.

"Greer Duchess, meet my younger cousin, Cesar. You will know him as Cesar Villon."

Villon? Her gaze flitted to Olivia's in confusion.

"He's Luc's younger brother," her sister murmured, looking completely dazed.

"The race car driver—" Greer cried softly. That meant—

"*Oui, mademoiselle.*"

"But if your last name's Falcon?"

"It is, but Villon is another family name I use on the track." He exuded the same devilish charm of all the Falcon men.

"I see. My sister is a great fan of yours. It's a thrill to meet you. We saw you whiz by the stand early this morning. How did you fare in the race over all?"

"I came in second."

"That's fantastic. Congratulations."

"*Merci.* At first I was not happy about it, but since Luc introduced me to your sister, I have discovered all is not lost. She wanted to wait until you arrived, but now that you are here, we're going to move on to a club where a party is being held in my honor. I would like it very much if you joined us."

"Perhaps later, Cesar," Max answered for her. "Right now Signorina Greer and I have a little celebrating of our own to do."

"Ah oui?"

Everyone's gaze swerved to Max. Greer couldn't imagine what he was talking about, but when she turned to him, he was staring pointedly at Nic. "Did you tell them yet?"

"No. As Cesar said, we were waiting for you."

"We're here now." Max helped Greer to a place next to Piper, then he sat down next to her, keeping his arm around the back of her deck chair. She could feel his heat through the material of her T-shirt. It melted her insides till they ran like butter.

Nic's Castilian white smile gleamed in the candlelight. Luc's dashing features on the other hand were as somber and remote as she'd ever seen them.

"Señoritas, when Fabio Moretti announced that one of you was wearing an original pendant like the one in the Maria-Luigia collection that is missing, it wasn't a lie to smoke out the thief."

Her sisters gasped, but Greer jerked her head around to stare at her host for verification.

"It's true," Max claimed. "Therefore, it's entirely possible that you *are* our distant cousins. In time Nic will solve that particular mystery. For the present we intend to catch the people responsible for the theft. That's one of the reasons why I said welcome to the family. But there *is* one more."

Suddenly he grasped her hand so that everyone could see. His actions caused a pounding in her chest that almost knocked her off the chair.

"As I told Greer the other day, life plays strange tricks. Once a long time ago it played a bad one on me. Then very recently, while I was defending a court case in the House of Lords, life played a good trick when I received a phone call from Signore Galli at Genoa airport.

"To make a long story short, it brought Greer Duchess into my life. I knew I loved her the moment I first laid eyes on her in the San Giorgio church."

He was *there?*

"But I wasn't sure she would have me if she knew I couldn't give her children. An old soccer injury put my spleen out of commission and that was that."

Greer's breath caught, but she couldn't stop the tears that welled in her eyes for the disappointment he'd had to suffer knowing he couldn't father children.

"Tonight she took away my fear and asked me to be her husband."

"Greer!" Her sisters sounded ecstatic.

"I hope that's a sign of approval," he kept talking, "because I'd like everyone here to know I've accepted her proposal."

Max—

"No details have been worked out yet. No date has been set. We need the rest of the vacation on board the *Piccione* to get to know each other. To my knowledge we haven't even shared a meal together."

His gaze swerved to her sisters. "Since your parents aren't here, do I have your permission to marry her? I know this must come as an enormous shock."

Olivia shook her head. "No, it doesn't."

"Not at all," Piper concurred. "We knew it was a fait accompli when we caught her kissing you in the stateroom."

"She just doesn't do things like that," Olivia confided.

"The minute we heard she dived into the Splendido pool to join you, we realized our plan had worked and it was only a matter of time."

Greer froze in place. "What do you mean *your* plan worked?"

"Who do you think gave Daddy the idea for the Husband Fund?" Olivia said.

"Until you caved first, there was never any hope for us. Since you've always been the cautious one, we decided something drastic had to be done."

"You're kidding! You mean from the very beginning, you let me believ—"

"If everyone will excuse us," Max interrupted, pulling

her straight out of the chair into his arms. "I'd like to take my fiancée below and make this official."

When they reached the stairs he crushed her against him, kissing her passionately. "You know I love you," he whispered against her lips. "I wanted you for my wife when I first saw you in the church. My life would be nothing without you, Greer."

"Now you tell me," she teased. "But since you've demanded so nicely…"

WEDDING DATE WITH THE BEST MAN

BY

MELISSA McCLONE

To Virginia Kantra for her wonderful writing insights, support and friendship.

Special thanks to Amy Danicic, Terri Reed and *Girls' Weekend in Vegas* authors

Myrna Mackenzie, Shirley Jump and Jackie Braun, and editor Meg Lewis.

CHAPTER ONE

CONVERSATION and laughter surrounded Jayne Cavendish. Sitting at a small table tucked away in a corner of the Victorian Tea House, she glanced around the room.

Pairs of women sat at tables nestled among potted plants and curio cabinets filled with an eclectic collection of teacups and saucers. Everyone seemed to be having a great time at one of San Diego's favorite Old Town establishments. Everyone but her.

She stared at her steaming cup of Earl Gray, wishing she could conjure up one of her three best friends. She missed Alex, Molly and Serena so much.

Sure, they kept in touch via phone calls, texting and Facebook. Twitter came in handy, too. Alex jetted back from Las Vegas when she could, and Molly would be returning once her and Linc's dream house was built and his business moved here, but it wasn't the same as all four of them living in San Diego, dishing face-to-face, getting pedicures and going to tea.

Jayne sank in her chair, feeling as buoyant as a deflated hot air balloon.

Maybe coming to the teahouse this Saturday afternoon hadn't been such a good idea. She remembered her first visit, when her then-fiancé's sisters had thrown Jayne a bridal shower. That 'welcome to the family' party seemed like years ago, even though it had been only months.

So much had changed since then. She touched the bare ring finger on her left hand. So much still hadn't changed.

At least not for her.

Jayne looked down at the silver-rimmed plate containing two golden-brown scones and a dollop of honey butter.

Too bad she wasn't hungry.

Uh-oh. If she weren't careful she'd soon be hosting a pity party for herself. Jayne sipped her tea to clear her head.

No sense wallowing in the past.

Her teacup clinked against the saucer as she placed it on the table.

So what if memories of her bridal shower with the Strickland sisters were bittersweet? Jayne had other memories, good memories, of subsequent visits here with Alex, Molly and Serena. Her three friends might not be related to Jayne by blood, but she considered them the sisters of her heart. Nothing, not distance or their marriages, would ever change that.

Determined to make peace with the present and enjoy herself, Jayne removed a library book—the latest offering from a top personal finance guru—from her purse. She opened it to her bookmark: a picturesque postcard with a palm tree arcing over a crescent of sugar-white sand and turquoise water stretching all the way to the horizon.

A perfect place for a honeymoon, she thought with a twinge of regret.

No regrets.

She straightened.

So what if things hadn't turned out with Rich Strickland as she'd planned? Because of what had happened—er, hadn't happened—her three best friends had found the loves of their lives. Jayne could never regret the end of her engagement and the wild weekend with her friends in Las Vegas afterward that had brought romance and so much happiness to the three people who mattered most in her life.

She flipped over the postcard she'd received two months ago and reread Serena's loopy, almost whimsical handwriting.

Jayne
Having a great time! This trip was the perfect way to celebrate Jonas' election victory and recoup from campaigning! As soon as we're home you must come to Las Vegas! I want to see you! Alex and Molly want to see you, too! Hope all is well! Miss you!
Love,
Serena and Jonas

The number of exclamation points brought a smile to Jayne's lips. Serena lived life as if an exclamation point belonged after everything she did, whether at work or play, but she'd found her center with Jonas Benjamin, the newly elected mayor of Las Vegas. He absolutely adored his wife.

As soon as we're home you must come to Las Vegas!

Jayne wanted to see her friends, but she'd been putting off their invitations to visit. Venturing back to the neon-lit city, with its monstrous resorts and hundred-degree-plus temperatures, held little appeal and way too many memories of the time right after the breakup. Hmmm, maybe she could talk them into coming to San Diego instead. Her friends could bring their husbands and show the three men what their lives here had used to be like.

A life Jayne was still living.

She placed the postcard next to the plate of scones on the table and adjusted the book in her hands. Happily living, she reminded herself, even if her dreams had been put on hold and she was alone. Again.

She focused on the page, mentally taking notes on fresh ideas that might help the clients she counseled at the debt management center where she worked. No wonder the book had hit the bestsellers' list. The author had some great ideas for getting one's finances under control.

Several minutes later, the noise level in the teahouse increased exponentially, as if a crowd had entered all at once.

She looked up from the book, glanced behind her and saw a large group of women standing around and holding presents.

Her gaze collided with someone she recognized—Savannah Strickland, her ex-fiancé's youngest sister. A look of disbelief filled Savannah's hazel eyes before she turned away.

Was this a birthday party? Perhaps a baby shower for Grace, the oldest sister? Her third child must be due soon.

Curious, Jayne peeked at the colorfully wrapped presents. No bunnies. No duckies. No baby carriages. A few umbrellas, though.

Rich's other sister, Betsy, noticed Jayne, gasped and elbowed her twin, Becca. Both turned bright pink.

Jayne didn't understand their embarrassment. Sure this was a little awkward, considering what their brother had done to her, but his sisters weren't to blame for his...

Oh, no.

There she was.

Every single one of Jayne's nerve-endings stood at attention with a combination of shock and horror.

The other woman.

The reason Jayne was still single and her three friends were now married.

She forced her gaping mouth closed.

Jayne had only seen the woman once. At Rich's apartment. Days before their wedding. A living, breathing Barbie doll in lingerie.

Today, the woman's modest Wedgwood-blue dress and smart cap-sleeved white jacket were one hundred and eighty degrees from the black push-up bra with a bow at the center and the lace-trimmed leggings she'd worn at Rich's place. The pristine white headband securing long, straightened blonde locks was a far cry from the bed-tousled hair that had left no room for misinterpreting what had been going on between two consenting adults.

But it was *her*.

The woman's flushed cheeks were exactly the same.

And so were Jayne's feelings of betrayal.

Not a baby shower, she realized, stricken to the heart. A wedding shower.

Rich was getting married, and his sisters were throwing a bridal shower for the woman their brother had cheated on *her* with.

Jayne struggled to breathe.

Look away, she told herself. But, like a moth drawn to a flame, Jayne couldn't.

The scene was surreal and eerily familiar. A lot like her own bridal shower.

Tears stung her eyes. A lump formed in her throat.

How could his sisters bring *her* here? It was as if Jayne had never existed in their lives. As if she hadn't spent every Sunday having brunch at their parents' house or helped paint Grace's kids' bedrooms or a hundred other things Jayne had done with them.

For them.

For Rich.

Having him betray her was one thing—but his entire family, too?

Her stomach roiled. Jayne thought she might be sick.

Self-preservation instincts kicked in. Get out. Now.

She shoved her book into her purse, ripped out a twenty-dollar bill from her wallet and tossed the money on the table. The amount was double the cost of her tea and scones, but for once she didn't care about wasting a few dollars.

Jayne stood.

Someone called her name.

She cringed.

Not someone, but Grace, Rich's oldest sister—the one person in his family who'd called after the breakup to see how Jayne was faring.

Torn between what she wanted to do and what she should do, she looked over to see a very pregnant Grace. The concern in her eyes—eyes the same color and shape as Rich's—pricked Jayne's heart. She gave her almost-sister-in-law a pained, hesitant smile. That was all she could manage at the moment.

Grace moved awkwardly through the crowded room toward her.

No!

The air rushed from Jayne's lungs.

She had no idea what Grace wanted, but only one thing, one horrible thought, sprang to mind. No way could Jayne allow herself to be introduced to that woman. The other woman. The future Mrs. Rich Strickland.

A potent dose of anxiety fueled Jayne's already desperate panic. She mouthed *I'm sorry* to the fast approaching Grace, turned and fled.

The next day, Grace Strickland Cooper stood at the sink in her parents' kitchen after her family's weekly get-together for Sunday brunch. "I need a favor."

Must be his turn to wash. Tristan MacGregor stopped drying a saucepan and stared into the familiar brown eyes of his best friend's oldest sister. "If you leave your husband and two and three-quarter kids and run away with me, I'll do anything you ask."

Grace motioned with wet hands to her bulging baby-filled stomach. "Oh, yes. I'm exactly what an adventurous photo-journalist wants to wake up next to every morning."

"You're a beautiful woman. Any man would want to wake up next to you."

Her eyes narrowed. "I bet you say that to all the girls, pregnant or not."

"I will neither confirm nor deny." He hung the saucepan on one of the pot rack's hooks. "Though I usually try to stay away from the pregnant ones."

She shook her head. "You never change, MacGregor."

He flashed her his most charming grin. "But you still love me."

"In your dreams."

Tristan winked. "I'll take what I can get."

Laughing, she rinsed out a soapy pot. "I'm sure you have no problem getting whatever you want. You never did."

That had been true. At least until recently.

He avoided serious relationships, but he liked having fun. Lately he'd found himself comparing the women he met to an unattainable ideal. That was severely limiting his fun.

He picked up the towel and dried a frying pan. "So what do you need? Want me to take over washing?"

"No." She glanced around, as if to make sure they were still alone. "I saw Jayne Cavendish yesterday."

Hearing the name of Rich's ex-fiancée jolted Tristan from the inside out. He nearly dropped the pan. A big no-no, considering Mrs. Strickland's year-old marble countertops.

Jayne. His ideal woman...

A million questions sprang to mind. Not one could he ask. "Where?"

"She was at the teahouse where we had Deidre's shower. It was the same place we took Jayne, which must have made her feel even worse."

For Rich's sake Tristan had tried not to think about Jayne Cavendish, but she'd invaded his thoughts and taken over his dreams. She'd become the woman he measured all others against. He even carried her picture in his wallet.

"We were so embarrassed. I'd forgotten how much she liked the place," Grace continued. "Anyway, Jayne made a beeline for the exit before I could reach her."

"Do you blame her?" His words came out too harshly, given his role in the breakup.

"Not at all." Grace frowned. "I love my brother, but he acted like a complete jerk with Jayne. Rich should have broken off the engagement, not led her on the way he did after he met Deidre."

"I agree."

"But he didn't, and Jayne's the one who's suffered."

"Suffered?" Tristan hung the frying pan on a hook. "She should be relieved she didn't get married. Rich might be my best friend, but Jayne's better off without him."

"I call it as I see it." Grace dried her hands with a dishtowel, rummaged through her purse and handed him a postcard. "Jayne was in such a hurry to leave she forgot this at her table. I thought you could return it and check if she's doing okay."

See Jayne?

Tristan's heart pounded as if he'd stumbled across the perfect shot. No lighting or camera adjustment needed. Just point and click.

He'd wanted to see Jayne for months now, but two reasons kept him away: his travel schedule, and Rich. Speaking of which...

"Just call her," Tristan said.

"I can't," Grace admitted. "Deidre's feeling very insecure right now."

Not his problem. Rich had been so mad at Tristan for breaking his engagement. He didn't want to go through that again.

He returned the postcard to Grace. "Sorry, but I'm not sneaking behind Rich's back to do this."

"You wouldn't be sneaking behind his back." Grace shoved the postcard into Tristan's hand. "I figured there must be some kind of guy code you two follow, so I asked him about it when he arrived this morning."

"He's okay if I see Jayne?"

"Better you than me."

"Because I'm not family?"

Grace flushed. "You've been friends with my brother since you were toddlers. You're family. But Deidre really freaked out yesterday, so I told her I wouldn't have any contact with Jayne. There's no harm in you returning the postcard. Deidre won't feel as threatened if she finds out *you* saw Jayne. Everyone knows you didn't like her."

No one had a clue how Tristan felt about Jayne. "She and Rich weren't right for each other."

Staring at the soapy water in the sink, Grace shrugged. "Rich may have put Jayne behind him, but I can't forget about her and stop caring that easily."

"You didn't know her long."

"Length of time doesn't matter. She was going to be my sister-in-law and the baby's godmother. She even painted the kids' rooms for me. I can't help but think about her every time I'm in there." Grace placed her hands on her belly. Worry filled her eyes. "And when I saw Jayne yesterday, she seemed…"

Tristan's shoulder muscles knotted. "What?"

"Different," Grace said. "Jayne's lost weight. She's cut her hair short. But most of all she looked so sad. I guess that's normal under the circumstances. It's only been a few months since the breakup."

Seven months, one week and four days, Tristan thought.

"She probably shouldn't look like her cheerful self after everything that happened, but I can't help but worry about her." Grace drew her brows together. "Her parents are dead. She has no siblings. Jayne has no one to look out for her except her three best friends, and they weren't with her yesterday. She needs somebody, but it can't be me."

Rich's oldest sister had been Tristan's first crush years ago, but at this moment he loved Grace more than he ever had back when he'd been a kid. Her thoughtfulness had provided him with a valid reason to see Jayne Cavendish again. Not only a reason, but also permission from Rich.

Tristan could see if his attraction for Jayne was real or if he'd built her up in his mind because she was off-limits. He clutched the postcard as if it were a ticket to Shangri-la, even though his visit would probably be nothing more than a reality check for him.

"Stop worrying." He squeezed Grace's shoulder. "I'll head over there this afternoon, return the postcard and find out exactly how Jayne's doing."

"Thank you." Grace hugged him. Well, as much as she could hug given her beachball-sized belly. "And if you happen to know any nice single guys you could introduce her to..."

Tristan stiffened at the thought of Jayne with any of his friends. "One thing at a time, Grace."

Two hours later, Tristan noticed a California State Patrol car parked on the side of the 405 freeway and a radar gun pointed his way. He lifted his foot from the accelerator and tapped the brake pedal. Getting pulled over for speeding would only slow him down.

He gripped the leather-wrapped steering wheel as he passed the black and white police car. The officer didn't glance his way.

Good.

Tristan pressed down on the gas, making sure this time the speedometer didn't ease into get-a-ticket territory. He wanted to get to Jayne's.

She needs somebody, Grace had said, *but it can't be me.*

It shouldn't be him, either, but here he was, speeding—within safe limits, of course—to see Jayne.

Jayne Cavendish.

He remembered so much about her—the strawberry scent of her hair, the bubbly sound of her laughter and the warmth of her touch. Okay, one touch—a handshake—the very first time they'd met...

* * *

"Just because your marriage didn't work out—" Rich Strickland maneuvered his four-wheel drive pick-up truck into a spot at one of Balboa Park's parking lots "—doesn't mean mine won't."

"True." Still, Rich's fast approaching wedding date bothered Tristan—bothered him enough that he'd almost said no when his friend had asked him to be the best man. "But you weren't dating anyone when I left on assignment. I'm back a few months later, and now you're getting married in a couple of weeks. I don't understand the big rush."

"No rush." Rich removed the key from the ignition. "Jayne says when it's right it's right."

Tristan's concern ratcheted up three more notches. "Jayne says a lot."

Rich sighed. "Look, you're going to like her."

Maybe. Probably not.

But Tristan would refrain from saying more until he got to know her. That was one reason he'd given the couple a photoshoot around town as a wedding gift—to spend time with the woman who'd made his friend want to take the leap into domesticated hell, aka marriage.

"Give me some time to get used to the idea." Tristan stared at his blond-haired best friend. "I hate the idea of hitting the town without my wingman. That firefighter shtick you've got going is a real babe magnet."

"If it's any consolation, Jayne's friends are really hot," Rich said. "You might get lucky after the wedding."

Tristan wanted Rich to be the lucky one. He hoped his best friend's marriage turned out better than his had. Love, the forever kind at least, was as rare as a photograph of a rainbow's end. Rich's parents had found it, but few others. Tristan forced a smile. "That would be good."

"You mean great." Rich's cellphone rang. He glanced at the number. "I need to take this. I'll meet you by the fountain in the Rose Garden."

With a nod, Tristan grabbed his camera pack, exited the truck and entered Balboa Park along with a busload of German-speaking tourists. The park was home to museums, several gardens, and the San Diego Zoo.

He crossed the footbridge to the popular Rose Garden.

A breeze blew. The sweet scent of roses wafted in the air.

Tristan preferred taking pictures of people, not scenery. Faces, and especially eyes, told a story in a way landscape couldn't. A photographer took pictures of nouns—persons, places or things. A photojournalist captured verbs—action verbs—in a single image.

But the bursts of color coming from the circular tiered flowerbeds had him reaching for his camera anyway. His mother loved roses. He couldn't pass up this opportunity to take pictures for her, especially with her birthday next month.

As he moved toward the fountain, Tristan zoomed in on a nearby blossom—a lush orange rose that reminded him of the sky at sunset.

Satisfied he'd captured the image, Tristan looked around. An arbor covered with white roses. A gray-haired couple holding hands next to a yellow rosebush. And...

Pink.

Tristan did a double-take.

A tall, graceful figure stood among the full round blossoms. Her shirt was the same pale pink as the petals. She should have faded into the background, but she didn't. If anything, she seemed to be an extension of the flowers.

The play of light and shadow had him composing a long shot.

And what a shot.

Waist-length chestnut hair gleamed beneath the sun's rays like oiled teak, a complete contrast to the soft, warm shapes and pastel colors surrounding her.

Captivated by the scene, he took picture after picture.

She seemed oblivious to him, so he moved to shoot her from different angles. He drew closer for a medium shot, but that wasn't enough.

Tristan zoomed in on her face.

Large blue eyes framed by lush lashes focused on the delicate petals of a single rose. His pulse kicked up. He snapped a picture.

Full, pink-as-a-rosebud lips curved into a wide smile. His mouth wanted a taste of hers. He pressed the shutter button.

She bent to smell the rose. The scooped neckline of her shirt fell away, giving him a tantalizing view of ivory flesh and a white lace bra.

Nice—very nice.

And hot.

She straightened and smoothed her above the knee skirt.

Great long legs, too.

He widened the shot, squeezed off more photos and moved to intercept her. No way would he let this opportunity escape him.

Forget about asking for a model release. He wanted her.

"Hello," Tristan said.

Not exactly the most memorable of lines, but she'd rendered him speechless and short-circuited his brain. Rare feats. Ones he hadn't experienced in over a decade.

"Hi." Her sparkling blue eyes nearly knocked him off his feet. "I've been waiting for you."

Great line. Tristan didn't believe in love at first sight, but lust at first sight was another story. He curved his lips into a devastating grin—one that usually got him whatever he wanted. "I'm Tristan MacGregor."

"It's so nice to meet you." She stepped toward him, extended her arm and clasped his hand with hers. A burst of heat shot through his veins. "I'm Jayne Cavendish. Rich's fiancée."

CHAPTER TWO

Please pick up, please pick up, please pick up, please...

Sunday afternoon. Jayne tightened her grip on the phone receiver. She wanted to talk to someone about what had happened at the teahouse yesterday, but hadn't been able to reach any of her friends yet.

She paced across the living room.

How could she have not seen Rich for who he was?

But Jayne knew the answer. She'd let her desire for a happily-ever-after cloud her judgment. Never again.

Still, the familiar feeling of being a crumpled aluminum can tossed in the recycle bin was back. She'd been discarded, replaced by something else—someone better. If only she hadn't been so trusting, so naïve

The line clicked. Thank goodness.

"Hi. This is Molly. I can't get to the phone right now..."

Jayne's heart dropped to the tips of her bare feet.

No, no, no, no, no.

She didn't want to hear Molly's recorded voice. Jayne had already listened to Alex's cellphone message two hours ago. And she knew Serena was busy today.

A beep blared.

"Hey, Molly, it's me. Jayne," she added, as if one of her best friends and former roommate could have forgotten her name.

She winced. What a loser.

"Um. Call me when you get this. If…you know…you have time."

Jayne hit the "off" button and slammed the receiver in its charger.

Okay, that was totally pathetic. Nothing new, but pathetic just the same.

What was wrong with her?

Too bad Jayne knew the answer.

She needed to get out more. She needed to make new friends. She needed to get a life.

A twenty-eight-year-old woman needed more to fill her days than checking off items on her "To Do" list. Not that there was anything wrong with being home, but too much time alone wasn't good for her. Today was a prime example. She'd already organized her sock drawer, clipped the Sunday coupons and played enough games of Spider Solitaire to make her eyes cross. If she weren't careful, she'd wind up like her next-door neighbor, grandmotherly Mrs. Whitcomb, who loved to eavesdrop as she sat on her porch, and offered cookies to passersby in order to learn the latest gossip.

Jayne bit her lip.

Maybe she needed a hobby or a pet. She missed being welcomed home by Rocky, Molly's dog. A puppy would be too much work with Jayne's job, but a rescue dog—a housebroken one—might be a better choice. The yard was fenced. She'd have to talk with Molly, since this was her house, and see what she thought.

A knock at the door sounded.

Jayne's heart leaped.

She had no idea who it could be, but even a kid selling magazines to go to band camp would be a respite from the lonely quiet. She hurried across the gleaming hardwood floor, unlocked the deadbolt and whipped open the door. A tall, attractive man, dressed in a black T-shirt and faded blue jeans, stood on the "Welcome" mat.

Her mouth dropped open.

He was hot. Really hot. And vaguely familiar.

She pressed her lips together. In fact, he looked a little like... Just like... "Tristan?"

"Hello, Jayne."

His easy smile caught her like a softball under her ribs. She'd never expected to see Rich's best friend—his best man—again. In fact, she'd pretty much forgotten about Tristan MacGregor during the aftermath of the breakup. But now...

He seemed taller, his shoulders wider. Had he always had such intense green eyes?

Unwelcome awareness trickled through her. *Oh, my.*

His sun-streaked hair had grown longer. Whisker stubble covered his face. He should have looked scruffy, but Tristan didn't. With his long lashes, full, kissable lips and high cheekbones, he looked ruggedly handsome and dangerously sexy.

Jayne swallowed.

Not sexy. Bad-boy types didn't appeal to her. She preferred clean-cut, fresh-shaven, all-American types. Men like...

Rich.

He'd seemed so perfect—a handsome, stable firefighter, with a big family who all lived here in San Diego. But he hadn't been perfect. Far from it.

He'd let her down in every way possible, making her feel so stupid for rushing into the relationship and marriage. She hadn't spoken to her ex-fiancé since that night at his apartment. His last words to her had been, "Guess the wedding's off." He hadn't even given her the chance to break up with him. She'd received no explanation, no apology, nothing.

Now Rich's best friend was standing here. Alarms sounded in her head. "Why are you...?"

Tristan pulled something from a back pocket. Serena's postcard, Jayne saw with surprise. He handed it to her. "Grace asked me to return this to you."

"I must have forgotten it at the teahouse," Jayne said, thinking aloud. She rubbed her thumb along the edge of the postcard, remembering how quickly she had fled yesterday. "But why didn't Grace…?"

An image of Rich's oldest sister making her way across the tearoom flashed in Jayne's mind. Others, including his new fiancée, would have noticed.

"Grace couldn't come herself," Jayne said.

"She didn't want to upset Deidre."

Deidre. So that was *her* name.

Jayne couldn't believe Rich was already getting married when she hadn't even started dating again. Granted, he'd had a head start. Still, it seemed…wrong.

She took a deep breath and exhaled slowly. "I understand Grace has to put her family first. I wouldn't expect any less of her. She's always done the right thing for as long as I've known her."

Which hadn't been all that long, Jayne realized.

"Doing the right thing isn't always easy," Tristan said, as nosy, white-haired Mrs. Whitcomb exited the house next door and sat on her porch rocking chair. Her little dog Duke, a black and white Papillion, hopped on her lap.

Jayne waved at her elderly neighbor, who raised her cup of coffee in acknowledgement.

"Would you mind if we talked inside?" Tristan asked.

She took a quick, sharp breath. "You want to come in?"

He nodded.

"Um, sure."

But she wasn't sure about anything except for Mrs. Whitcomb's pastime of spying on neighbors. Jayne could only imagine what her neighbor would think of her inviting a strange, attractive man into the house, but she'd rather do that than talk within range of eager ears.

Tristan showing up out of blue left Jayne feeling off-balance. The guy had never been friendly or sought conversation with her. She didn't know why he wanted to start now. "If you really want to come in, okay, but please don't feel obligated. I mean, you returned the postcard. Mission accomplished."

"Actually, I wanted to talk to you," he said.

Apprehension coursed through her. She knew better than to trust a friend of Rich's. "Why?"

"Grace is worried about you."

Grace, huh? The tension knotting Jayne's shoulders eased slightly.

"Come in." She opened the door wider. "But you should know there's no reason for Grace to worry about me. I'm fine."

"Glad to hear it." His voice was low and smooth. "Then I won't have to waste a lot of your time."

"How is Grace doing?" Jayne asked. "It must almost be time for the baby to be born."

"Past time, but she's enjoying being with her other two kids, so she's happy."

"That sounds like Grace."

As Tristan walked past Jayne, the scents of earthy male and salt filled her nostrils. Quite a difference from the hyacinth potpourri she was used to smelling in the bungalow. She preferred the floral scent. "I appreciate you going out of your way to do this, but I'm sure you have somewhere else to be."

He stood in her living room, making the area feel cramped. "No, I'm free the rest of the day."

As she closed the door, Jayne hoped he didn't plan on staying long. Sure, she might have the company she'd been longing for, but Tristan wasn't who she had in mind. All she wanted was to get this visit over with. "Sorry you got roped into this by Grace."

"I'm not."

Jayne didn't know what to say to Tristan. She found herself glancing around the living room to avoid making eye contact with him. At least the house was clean—dusted, mopped and clutter-free. She'd done nothing but chores most of the weekend. That was what she did every weekend to keep busy.

Still, she couldn't be rude.

"Would you, um, like something to drink?" she asked. "A glass of iced tea, maybe?"

"That would be great," he said. "Thanks."

Jayne headed into the kitchen. She'd expected Tristan to wait in the living room, but he followed her instead.

No problem. He could see for himself that she was doing well and relay the information to Grace.

Except his six-foot plus frame took up a lot of space in the galley-style kitchen, making it hard for Jayne to maneuver without bumping into him. She noticed she'd left a bag of coffee on the counter—Kenyan roast: her favorite—and put it away.

"Need help?" he asked.

His offer surprised her. The guy looked as domesticated as a rampaging hippo. "Thanks, but I have it under control."

She wanted him to tell Grace that Jayne Cavendish had everything under control. No need to worry.

Tristan leaned against the counter and crossed his booted feet at the ankles. He might look out of place, but he sure acted comfortable—as if he were used to hanging out in women's kitchens.

He looked around. "I smell cookies."

His sense of smell was spot on. "I baked chocolate chip cookies this morning. Would you like one?"

"Please."

She reached for the plastic container full of cookies and placed a few on a plate. These homemade treats would give Tristan one more reason to tell Grace that Jayne Cavendish was fine and dandy.

Oh, no. She dropped a cookie onto the plate.

Forget fine. She wasn't dandy, either. She cringed.

She'd asked about Grace. Given the chance, Jayne would have asked about the other Stricklands, too. Maybe even Rich. She stared at the cookies with a sinking feeling in her stomach. She was turning into Mrs. Whitcomb.

Too late to renege on the offer of refreshments, but Jayne would not ask Tristan about another one of the Stricklands.

She would be polite. She would be gracious. But that was it.

With her resolve firmly in place, Jayne added ice to the two glasses, filled them with tea and handed one to Tristan.

He took a sip. "Sweet."

"Oops. I should have warned you," she said. "In the South, that's the only way they make it."

He considered her over his glass. "I don't hear an accent."

"I lived in North Carolina for a couple of years when I was younger." She remembered the humid summers, the enormous flying bugs, and missing her dad. "My father was in the military, so he was stationed all over the place."

"Lucky you." Tristan took another sip of his tea. "I was born in San Diego. My parents still live here."

"I'd say you're the lucky one." Jayne grabbed a few napkins. "I never want to move away from San Diego."

"It's a nice place to call home."

Too bad this place didn't feel like home at the moment. The kitchen was feeling a little too…crowded.

Jayne picked up the plate of cookies and her tea. "Let's go into the living room."

"After you."

In the living room, she placed the cookies on the scarred maple coffee table Molly had left when she moved to Las Vegas and pulled out two coasters for their glasses. Jayne sat on one end of the yellow plaid couch. "Tell me what you need to know to appease Grace."

And what it will take to get you out of here.

Tristan lowered himself onto the couch, making the full-sized sofa seem suddenly way too small. He set his glass on a coaster, adjusted a floral print pillow behind his back and stretched out—a mass of arms and legs. "Just a few things."

"Like what?"

As he placed his hand on the back of the sofa, his hand brushed Jayne's bare shoulder. Accidentally, of course.

Still, heat rushed down her arm like a lit fuse on a stick of dynamite.

She guzzled her tea, but the cold drink didn't cool her down at all. Even her fingertips seemed to sizzle.

Her reaction disturbed Jayne. It must be because she'd sworn off men. For the past seven months she'd barely seen a man outside of work, but the one sitting next to her on the overstuffed sofa was too warm, too solid, too…male. No wonder her body was so confused.

But being even the slightest bit attracted to Rich's best friend was a huge no-no.

She scooted away from Tristan until her hip collided with the sofa-arm. Darn. That wasn't far enough for her peace of mind.

He picked up a cookie. "Grace will want to know how you've been."

Add Rich's oldest sister to the list. Alex, Molly and Serena all kept asking how Jayne had been doing, so she wasn't surprised Tristan—make that Grace—would want to know, too.

"Please don't answer *fine*," he added. "You've already used that one."

Jayne usually answered *fine*. The word fit her most days—good or bad. She didn't want people worrying about her.

"I've been busy trying to make this house a home—my home, that is—when I'm not at the office," she said. "Everything is going…okay."

Okay seemed like the best, the safest answer. Because, face it, things might be fine, but they hadn't been great for a while now. Months, actually. She kept second-guessing herself. Something she had never done before. That had made things…harder.

He held his cookie in mid-air. "Okay, okay? Or okay, but I'd rather not talk about it?"

Her gaze met his. She hadn't expected him to delve further or to read so much into her simple answer. "A little of both."

"An honest answer."

She raised her chin. "I'm an honest person."

"Honesty is a rare quality these days."

"No kidding." Jayne wasn't about to disagree with him, especially after her experience with Rich. The cheating jerk.

And what did that say about Tristan? He and Rich were best friends.

She watched a bead of condensation drip down her glass.

"You cut your hair," Tristan said.

Her gaze met his. "I'm surprised you noticed."

"I'm a photographer, remember?" he said, as if that explained anything. "An eye for detail."

She'd forgotten. Her cheeks burned. How could she have forgotten what he did for a living? He'd spent two days trailing her and Rich around town, taking their picture. But then again, she'd pushed as much of that painful time out of her memory as possible. That included her groom's best man.

Still, she wanted to cover her embarrassment.

"My friends treated me to a makeover at a fancy salon in Las Vegas." She fingered the short ends. "Rich told me never to cut my long hair, so I told the stylist to chop it all off. I had a moment of sheer panic when she did, but decided I actually liked the shorter length and have kept it this way even though there are times I look in the mirror and don't recognize myself."

Tristan drew his brows together.

Uh-oh. Deep in thought? Or disgusted by her rambling? Not that his opinion mattered to her. "Too much information?"

"Not at all," he said. "I was just looking at your hair. The longer length was nice, but this style flatters your features better. You should get your picture taken."

Thinking about the deposit she'd lost canceling the wedding photographer sent a shiver down her spine. Of course she'd lost a lot more than money with the breakup. Pride. Respect. Confidence. "I don't like having my picture taken."

"I remember." His lips formed a wry grin. "But I managed to get some good shots anyway."

"I never saw any of them."

"I'll get you copies."

Jayne crossed her arms over her chest. "Um, I..."

"Bad memories?" Tristan guessed.

"Yeah, sorry, but thanks for the offer." She picked up a cookie. "I know Rich is your best friend, but he wasn't the man I thought he was. I wouldn't want to spend the rest of my life with someone like him."

Even if she'd thought he could give her everything she'd wanted. Everything, that was, except his love and fidelity.

Dredging up the past made her uncomfortable. This called for chocolate. She bit into her cookie.

"Then everything worked out for the best," Tristan said.

Still chewing, she nodded.

"You'll find someone else," he said. "Someone better."

Jayne choked, coughed, and reached for her tea. Plunging back into the dating scene was about as appealing as a case of food poisoning. Taking a year off from dating seemed a reasonable amount of time after a broken engagement. She needed time to regain the self-confidence to make the right decisions and trust her judgment again.

Besides, her three friends had found the loves of their lives when they hadn't been trying to find "the one." Maybe Jayne had been going about this happily-ever-after business the wrong way. Maybe she'd been trying too hard to get what she wanted. "I'm not really looking."

"You don't have to look. Someone will find you."

Her breath caught in her throat. Tristan sounded so…romantic—a way she'd never heard him sound in the short time she'd known him. He'd always seemed so unfriendly, almost arrogant, back then.

"You won't have to do anything," he added.

Her heart melted a little. That sure would be nice.

Thanks to what had happened to her best friends in Las Vegas, Jayne knew Mr. Right finding her could happen. And she really did want it to happen one of these days.

Ever since she was a little girl Jayne had wanted the fairytale to come true. She was over the heartbreak Rich had caused, but she wanted to focus on work and getting her life back in order first. Her heart had fooled her. She didn't want to be duped again.

"I hope that happens *someday*." She emphasized the final word. "Just because things with Rich didn't work out doesn't mean I can't live happily ever after here in San Diego with my one true love."

"If that's what you want, go for it."

She thought about her and her mother's dream. "Isn't that what everybody wants?"

Tristan set his iced tea on the table. "Not me."

Okay, so maybe the guy wasn't so romantic after all. She shouldn't be surprised, given his long-time friendship with Rich. A true romantic wouldn't condone a cheater's behavior. "That sounds a little…bitter."

"Not bitter, just experienced." He stared at his glass. "I gave marriage a try. It didn't work out."

She leaned toward him. "You were married?"

He nodded. "You sound surprised."

"I am," she blurted. He was attractive enough to have his pick of female companionship, yet had chosen to settle down. She wondered what kind of woman had made him want to say *I do*. No doubt a gorgeous model or actress-type, with a killer body. "I mean, you don't seem like the marrying kind."

"I realized I'm not, but I tried to make it work."

Yeah, right. That was what all men said, but actions spoke louder than words. If only she'd realized that with the first man in her life…her father.

Her dad had done nothing to make things work with her mother. Jayne still remembered hearing her parents' yelling late at night when she'd be in bed. Still, she'd never thought he'd leave one day and never contact her again. "Let me guess—you were misunderstood?"

Tristan laughed. "No, she understood me quite well. I take full responsibility for the failure of my marriage."

His words touched Jayne. Her father had never admitted failure. He'd blamed all their problems on her mother. God rest her soul. "That must be a hard thing to admit."

"I'm just being honest."

"I appreciate that," she said. "As you said, honesty is a rare quality these days."

One she hadn't expected from Tristan MacGregor.

"Have you been married before?" he asked.

"No, my parents were divorced, so I told myself to make sure it was right first and not rush into anything."

"Until Rich."

She nodded. "I didn't follow my own advice with him, and rushed in with my eyes full of stars, but I won't do that again."

Jayne looked at the table. Only crumbs remained on the cookie plate. Her glass was empty. Tristan's was only a quarter full. By now he should see she was fine and be able to reassure Grace. Nothing left to do but say goodbye. Except…

He didn't seem in any hurry to finish his iced tea and leave.

"Anything else you want to know so you can tell Grace?" Jayne asked, trying to move him along. "I hate keeping you here."

"You're not keeping me." His gaze took in the knickknacks on the bookcase and the framed photographs on the fireplace mantel. "It's nice be in a house. I just got back from two months in Malaysia and Bali."

Two months? That would have included last month... December. "You were overseas for Christmas?"

He nodded. "You can celebrate Christmas anywhere."

But it wasn't the same as being home. Not that Christmas alone here had been all that great. Still, she'd had a small tree and presents sent by her friends—including a filled stocking.

"I can't imagine being on the go so much." Just the thought gave Jayne the heebie-jeebies. She rubbed her arms. "Away for weeks or months at a time. I get tired thinking about it."

"I get more tired when I'm *not* traveling," he admitted. "If I'm in one place too long I get antsy."

She'd heard that so many times. "My father was like that."

"What about you?"

"I take after my mother," Jayne said with pride. "I traveled so much when I was younger there's no place I want to go now. I'm pretty much a homebody."

Tristan's eyes narrowed. "You don't seem like a homebody."

"You just don't know me that well. Growing up, I was always bugging my parents for a house with a yard and a puppy."

"You want a dog?"

"Maybe." She shrugged. "My former roommate had a dog. I walk my neighbor's dog most evenings. But I'm still debating whether this place needs a pet or not."

"It's a nice place."

"Thanks," she said. "I lucked out getting to live here."

"How's that?" Tristan asked.

"Well, I'd given notice on my studio apartment to move in with Rich after the wedding, so I found myself homeless after he—I mean we—broke up. My friend Molly had a spare bedroom and told me to move in with her. It was only supposed to be a temporary arrangement, but she fell in love with a man she met during a girls' weekend in Las Vegas, married him a few months later, and relocated to Sin City. And that's how I ended up with this charming bungalow to call home."

"You did luck out."

Jayne nodded. "Though I liked having Molly for a roommie. I miss talking to her late at night over a pint of Ben & Jerry's."

"So find a new roommate. Preferably one who likes ice cream."

A new roommate. Jayne thought about his suggestion. Someone to talk to. Someone to split the rent and utilities with. "You know, Tristan, getting a roommate is a really good idea."

"Unless you prefer living alone."

"I don't like being alone," she answered quickly. "I mean, Molly and my other two best friends have moved away. With the three of them gone it's been a little…"

Loser, Jayne thought. When would she learn to keep her mouth shut and not say so much?

"Lonely?" he finished for her.

"Yes," she admitted, wishing she'd put more cookies out.

"You lost your fiancé and your three best friends."

She nodded. "The only two things that haven't changed in the last seven months are my job and my car."

"That's tough."

"It's been…challenging."

He scooted closer. "I guess it has."

Oh, no, she thought. He was Rich's friend. And here she was babbling about her life and sounding really pathetic. What if Tristan told Rich?

Her insides clenched. She couldn't bear the thought of that happening.

"Not that I'm unhappy with the way things turned out," she added hastily.

"Glad to hear it."

Tristan shifted position. His leg touched hers. No skin-on-skin contact was made, but warmth emanated from the spot. Worse, his jean-clad leg remained pressed against hers.

Maybe he didn't notice, but she sure did.

Unfortunately she couldn't move. The sofa-arm blocked her in one direction, Tristan in the other. She was…trapped.

The only thing she could do was ignore it. Him. "I wonder how hard finding a roommate would be."

"You can't beat this location." As he looked around the living room, she prayed he would notice his leg was still touching her. "And you keep the place nice. Neat. It'll all depend on the room."

Companionship and only paying half her current living expenses sounded like an ideal combination. Why hadn't she thought of getting a roommate herself?

"Oh, the room is lovely. It's not that large, but has lots of windows."

"Show me," Tristan said.

"Sure." Jayne jumped up, eager to get away from the intimacy of the couch. She led him past her room into the other bedroom. "This used to be Molly's room."

"Great room." He checked the closet. "Why didn't you take this one for yourself?"

"The two bedrooms are almost the same size, and I didn't want to move."

"Across the hall?"

"My room is decorated the way I like it."

He looked out one of the large windows facing the backyard garden. "Nice view."

His position gave her a view of his backside. His faded jeans fit well. "Very nice."

What was she *doing*? With cheeks burning, she looked away.

"You'll have no trouble renting this room out," he said.

The thought of not being alone all the time made Jayne wiggle her toes. Maybe something good would come from Tristan's impromptu visit. "I better put together an ad."

Tristan turned toward her with his brows drawn together. "You're serious about this?"

She heard the surprise in his voice. She was a little surprised herself, but loneliness could drive a person to do some crazy things. "Yes, and it'll give me something to do this afternoon." Jayne winced when she realized how her words must have sounded. "I mean —"

"Forget the ad," Tristan interrupted. "Spending the rest of this beautiful afternoon inside would be a crime."

Yes, but she didn't have anything else to do, and the last thing she wanted was his pity. She didn't want anything to do with him.

She raised her chin. "I happen to like staying home."

"That's okay, but you should get out more."

Going out alone had gotten old fast. She shrugged.

"Let's go on a hike," he said.

Her heart picked up speed. "A hike?"

"Yes." Mischief gleamed in his eyes. "The fresh air will be good for a homebody."

"Why would you want to go on a hike with me?" She felt as if she'd entered an alternative universe. One where everything had flipped upside down and inside out. "You don't like me."

Tristan jerked as if she'd slapped him. "I like you."

"No, you don't."

"Yes, I do."

"The only reason you're here is for Grace."

"Grace asked me to stop by, but that doesn't mean I don't want to be here."

Jayne didn't—couldn't—believe him. Her assessing gaze raked over him.

No way was he telling her the truth.

"Have you forgotten the way you acted toward me before the breakup?" His unfriendly behavior had gotten worse each time she saw him. "It was pretty obvious to everyone—including Rich," she added, as if that was the clincher. As if Rich's judgment could be trusted. As if *Rich* could be trusted, the lying rat.

Tristan's dark eyes locked with hers. "Everyone, including Rich, is wrong."

The words hung in the air, as if suspended in a floating bubble.

Wrong.

Emotion tightened Jayne's throat.

She'd never understood why Tristan had behaved the way he had. *Could* she be wrong? She wanted to believe him. Which made her mistrust her own judgment even more. She wasn't a good judge of character when it came to men. Taking a man at his word, even when he said he loved you, was a huge mistake. One she'd made with her father and with Rich. Trust had to be earned, not given.

Tristan rocked back on his heels. "Come on. It'll be fun."

Fun. When had that word become an alien concept? Maybe...

No.

Tristan MacGregor wasn't some attractive stranger inviting her for a walk. He was Rich Strickland's best friend. His best man. She'd have to be out of her mind to go anywhere with Tristan. Out of her mind or very, very lonely.

Her own thought ricocheted through her brain.

Loneliness could drive a person to do some crazy things.

She swallowed a sigh.

"What do you have to lose?" Tristan asked.

Nothing. Jayne's shoulders had started to sag, but she squared them instead. She'd already lost everything.

Her fiancé, her trust, her hope, her three best friends.

Life had become one lonely hour followed by another. She rarely left the house, and when she did she couldn't wait to get home.

Just like her mother.

The unsettling realization made Jayne straighten.

Her mother had stuck close to home after her father had left. She'd gone to work, the store, and occasionally to church. She hadn't even wanted to go to the doctor's office when she'd started feeling poorly, and because of that she'd ended up dying way too soon.

Jayne didn't want that to happen to her.

Something had to change. *She* had to change. Now.

Maybe one small step—one short hike—would start her on a new road…a path toward the life she wanted to live, not the one she was living. Even if the hike *was* with the last person, next to Rich, she wanted to spend time with.

"You're right," she said finally. "A hike will do me good."

CHAPTER THREE

"HIKING has been good for me—" Jayne puffed behind Tristan "—but I don't know how much further I can go."

He turned on the trail, happy to be finally spending time with her. She might not be exactly the woman he remembered, but the woman he was getting to know intrigued him.

She closed the distance between them. Her feet dragged—something they hadn't done at the start of the hike. But even tired, flushed and sweaty, with her hair sticking out of that old San Diego Padres baseball cap she wore, she was still the best thing he'd seen in weeks…maybe months.

"We're almost to the beach," he said.

She adjusted the brim of her hat. "Okay, then. I guess I can make it."

"Sure you can." But Tristan didn't want to wear her out before they reached their destination. He opened his water bottle. "I need a drink first."

Relief filled her pretty eyes. "That sounds good to me, too."

Talk about a good sport. Tristan took a swig of water. He liked that about her.

Despite an extended and thoughtful moment of hesitation back at her apartment, she'd gamely accepted his invitation to go hiking at Torrey Pines State Park. She hadn't once complained about the hot afternoon sun blazing down on them even though it was only January.

Jayne drank from her water bottle. Her pink tongue darted out to lick the liquid off her lips.

He took another gulp from his bottle.

She sure was a nice addition to the already beautiful scenery surrounding them. Her legs, exposed between the hem of her khaki shorts and hiking books, looked long and slim and smooth. The sky intensified the blue of her eyes. A hint of a smile tugged at the corners of her glossed lips.

Tristan put away his water bottle and focused his camera on her.

Jayne pretended to scowl. "Again?"

He preferred her mock exasperation to the loneliness he'd glimpsed earlier at her apartment. "Just capturing memories."

Lines creased her forehead. "Memories of a day spent with a stranger?"

Her suspicious tone bothered him. "We're not strangers."

"We aren't friends."

"We could be friends," he countered.

She pursed her lips. "Why are you being so nice to me?"

Because he liked her. He wanted her to like him. But she wasn't ready to hear that.

In her wary eyes he was still only Rich's best man. Rich's best friend. And Rich had let her down big time.

"You're a nice person," Tristan answered.

"Nice, huh?"

He nodded.

"The last time we were together you didn't even look me in the eye."

Tristan remembered. He wasn't as nice as Jayne was. But even a jerk would have had trouble looking a bride straight in the eye when he knew her fiancé was two-timing her with another woman.

Tristan aimed at the basket. Swoosh. Two points.

"Lucky shot," Rich said, taking away the ball.

The two had been co-captains of their high school basketball team and won two district titles. Whenever Tristan was in town they would shoot hoops at the gym.

"Next time it'll be for three," he said.

Rich dribbled the ball and scored with a lay-up. "You'd better hope so."

A cellphone rang. Rich's. For the third time in the past hour. For the third time he ignored it.

"You want to get that?" Tristan asked.

"Nah. Probably just Jayne."

Tristan held the ball. "I'll wait."

"No. She keeps bugging me about the wedding." Rich rolled his eyes. "Everything's about the wedding with her."

"Your wedding, too, buddy."

"You're sticking up for her?" Rich asked.

"No, but remember how Grace and Becca turned into Bridezillas before they got married?"

No answer. Something was up.

"Tell me what's going on," Tristan said.

Rich started, then stopped himself.

"Come on." Tristan passed the ball hard at Rich's chest. "It's me."

Rich looked around, as if to make sure no one else was there. "I met someone."

Tristan got a sinking feeling in his gut. "A female someone?"

Rich nodded and tossed the ball back. "She's a dental hygienist and totally hot. Smokin'."

"So is Jayne." Okay, maybe Tristan shouldn't have said that about his best friend's bride to be, but Rich didn't appear to notice. He was still going on about this other girl. Deidre Something.

Annoyance flared.

Cold feet or not, Rich was being an idiot. Time to call him on it.

"You can't drill your dentist, bud." Tristan dribbled the basketball. The sound echoed through empty gymnasium. "What did she do? Put the moves on you in the chair?"

"She was in a car accident we responded to." Rich glanced around the empty court again like a man being watched. Or one who didn't want to get caught. "A few days later she brought brownies to the station and invited me to dinner. I couldn't say no."

Rich could have said no, but he hadn't wanted to. Not good.

Tristan spun the ball in his hands. "So you screwed up one time? You're engaged. Just tell her."

"It was more than once," Rich admitted. "And I'm not telling her about Jayne. Deidre wouldn't see me anymore."

"She's not going to see you anymore anyway, bonehead. You're getting married in a week."

"I know, but... Hell, I think I'm in love with her. Deidre," Rich clarified.

Tristan dropped the ball. "What? Are you kidding? What about the wedding?"

"I'm sick of thinking about the wedding. That's all Jayne can talk about. All she sees. Deidre treats me like I'm the best thing that ever happened to her. The most important thing in her life."

"Probably because you saved her life," Tristan countered, wanting, needing to say something. Anything. An image of Jayne, bright-eyed and smiling, flashed in his mind. He couldn't believe Rich was doing this to her. "It's a crush. Deidre will get over it."

"Maybe I don't want her to get over it. Maybe I like being somebody's hero."

Damn. Tristan thought for a minute. "How long has this been going on?"

"Not long," Rich admitted. "A couple of weeks, maybe."

"You've got to talk to Jayne."

Rich stared at Tristan as if he'd grown antennae and a third eye. "Why?"

"You can't get married if you're in love with someone else."

"I'm not canceling the wedding." Rich set his jaw. "I asked Jayne to marry me, and I will marry her."

Uh-oh. Tristan knew that mulish tone of Rich's all too well. "What about Deidre?"

"I'm trying to figure that out."

"Better figure it out fast, because you can't have both."

"I know." Rich looked miserable. "Look, just don't… Don't say anything to Jayne. Promise me you won't."

Tristan had kept his mouth shut. But his guilt over knowing the truth had made it difficult for him to face Jayne the next time he saw her, and each time after that. He'd thought by ignoring her he would buy Rich the time he needed to make the right decision.

Wrong.

Rich had ignored the matter, forcing Tristan to keep his best friend and Jayne from getting married. He didn't regret his actions one bit. But dragging up the past and telling Jayne what he'd done to engineer her discovering Rich's cheating now wouldn't help anyone. She'd admitted she wouldn't have wanted to marry Rich. She was moving on. Rich was getting married. Tristan was finally getting to spend time with Jayne. It was better to bury the past.

"It wasn't you," Tristan said finally.

The doubt in her big blue eyes hit him right in the gut.

You don't like me.

The problem was he did like her.

He'd always liked her.

Too much.

And for that reason he'd kept his distance from her and limited his contact with her. Even after the breakup. For all their sakes.

Yet he was here now, and he wouldn't want to be anywhere else.

"It was me," he finished.

She smiled crookedly. "Yeah, that's what the guy always says."

He winced. "I'm...sorry."

"Hey," she said. "I'm sorry for putting you on the spot like this."

"No worries."

Her closed-mouth smile turned into a wide grin. His pulse kicked up.

Man, she really had a great smile. He took another picture of her.

"Knock it off," she said, but her eyes gleamed with laughter.

"Professional photographer, remember?" A gull flew overhead, its sharp white wings contrasting with the cloudless blue sky. He turned his camera from her to the bird. "It's an occupational hazard."

"I'd say it's more a hazard for anyone who happens to be around you."

"Having your photograph taken isn't a hazard."

"Some cultures believe being photographed steals a part of your soul."

"I'm not a soul-stealer," he said. "I'm only after the image. The best photographs tell a story, and can often be described by a single verb."

She took another slug from her water bottle. "Well, as long as you aren't stealing souls, I suppose it's okay, but please don't go overboard."

He gave a mock bow. "Your understanding is much appreciated, since my camera follows me everywhere. No questions asked."

"Sounds like a perfect relationship for you."

"It is," he admitted. "My camera packs light, doesn't hog the bed, and never gets upset when I don't remember its birthday."

"Men."

"We are what we are."

A breeze caught the ends of her hair. He snapped her picture again.

She sighed.

"I'm not going overboard," he said.

"Just make sure you delete the bad ones."

Tristan feigned innocence. "You mean I can't post them on the internet?"

She grimaced.

He laughed. "I'll delete the bad ones. Scouts' Honor."

"A Boy Scout, huh?" Jayne studied him. "I'm not seeing it."

"My Scout days were brief," he said. "I was more interested in spying on girls than lighting a fire with flint and learning first aid techniques. Though the orienteering I learned saved my neck in Afghanistan, so it wasn't a total waste."

"You were over there?"

He nodded. "Iraq, too. Gotta be where the action is to get the good shots."

Biting her lower lip, she stared off in the distance.

Tristan looked through his viewfinder in the same direction. He focused his camera on the weathered and wrinkled hills full of caverns, caves and creases. Beyond them, a sea of blue stretched to the horizon.

"Interesting geography," she said softly. "I didn't realize the coast had badlands."

He snapped a picture of the scenery. "I thought everyone who lived in San Diego had been here before."

"Not me," she said. "This is the second time I've lived in San Diego, but the first time I was only six, so the Zoo and Sea World were on the top of my must-see list."

Tristan glanced her way. "Sounds like you need to play tourist as an adult."

"Maybe I do," she said.

"Homebodies aren't us."

"Even homebodies need breaks."

Now that was more like it. Her eyes were brighter. Her color was better. "Well, Ms. Homebody, ready to head to the beach?"

She nodded.

"Lead the way."

Jayne glanced down the trail and then up uncertainly at his face. "I suppose with the beach as our final destination it would be hard to get lost."

"Nearly impossible."

"Okay, let's go." She headed down the trail.

As he followed her, the sound of waves crashing against the shore became more distinct.

"The view is incredible," she said.

Tristan agreed. He really appreciated the view of Jayne's swaying hips in front of him.

A family of five going in the opposite direction passed them on the trail. A harried, sweat-soaked dad wore a backpack with a wiggling kid inside. A sunburned mom trudged uphill, holding the hands of two little girls, dressed in matching pink outfits and sunhats, each of whom wanted to go their own way.

Jayne glanced up the trail as the family continued on toward the top of the bluff. "Cute kids. I bet they had fun out here."

"The parents didn't look like they were having fun. More like they were in need of alcohol and lots of it."

"I'm sure they have their hands full with those three."

"Better them than me."

"Don't you like kids?" she asked.

He shrugged. "I'm an only child. I don't have a lot of experience with kids except for Grace's brood."

"I'm an only, too." Jayne got a wistful look on her face. "I would like to have a big family."

Tristan imagined her leading a child with one hand and holding a baby in the other. She would be a good mom.

"You coming?" Jayne called from a few feet ahead of him.

He shook the disturbing image of her from his head. A wife and kids were not in his future. No way, no how. He'd never had any desire to take family portraits for a living; he sure as hell didn't want to be in one. "I'm right behind you."

Continuing down the trail, she made her way through the sandstone-lined entrance to the wet sand beach where waves crashed against the shore.

She stared up at the walls of eroded sandstone. "Wow."

Wow was right. The look of awe on her face tightened his chest. She seemed so young and vulnerable next to the weathered old rock. He took her picture.

She gave him a look.

He didn't care. "Some day you'll thank me for capturing these moments."

"You think?"

He shrugged. "Time will tell."

Jayne stared up at him with a puzzled expression on her face.

His answer seemed to catch her off-guard, but she looked damn adorable right now. He wanted to kiss her soft, moist lips and watch the confusion in her eyes turn to passion.

He'd wanted to kiss her from the first moment he'd seen her, but doing so now would be a bad move.

She was sending out no signs that she wanted to be kissed.

If she did he would be all over it. Over her.

Tristan smiled at the thought. "Ready to explore the beach?"

* * *

Exploring the beach with Tristan showed Jayne a different side of him. With his camera in hand and a smile on his face he seemed as carefree as one of the gulls flying over the water. So different from when he'd photographed her and Rich.

But, however relaxed, Tristan was still Rich's best friend. No way could she let her guard down. Not even for a minute.

She followed Tristan back to his car. Her thighs burned. She tugged on the straps of her daypack.

"Need help?" he asked.

"I've got it, thanks."

Jayne removed her pack, unlaced her boots and took off her socks. She placed everything on the floor of the backseat, as Tristan had done. She slid into the front seat, where her sandals were waiting for her, fastened her seatbelt and relaxed against the car's leather seat.

It felt so good to sit. She almost sighed.

Tristan placed the key in the ignition. "How about a bite to eat?"

The idea appealed to her. She didn't relish the thought of returning to an empty apartment, but she'd spent enough time with him today. "No, thanks."

He started the engine. "Aren't you hungry?"

Surprisingly, she was. She'd wondered if her appetite would ever return or not. Maybe she should take up hiking as her hobby. "Yes, but I'm sweaty, dirty, and not dressed to go out."

His gaze lingered on her shirt that stuck to her skin. "You look fine to me."

She couldn't imagine he was flirting with her, but still she crossed her arms over her chest. "Thanks, but—"

"What sounds good?" he interrupted. "Thai? Mexican? Italian?"

"Mexican, but—"

"I know just the place."

Half an hour later Jayne found herself seated across from Tristan at a small table for two while a Mariachi band played outside on the tiled courtyard. She stretched her tired legs. Her feet bumped Tristan's. The material of his jeans brushed her calf for the second time in less than five minutes.

"Sorry," she mumbled.

"No worries," he said.

Maybe not for him, but the quickening of her pulse had nothing to do with the hiking they'd done earlier. She curled her feet beneath her chair so she wouldn't end up touching him again. "The table's a little crowded."

"Cozy," he corrected.

Cozy was the last thing she wanted. Jayne downed her glass of ice water. Cozy implied romantic. No way did she want this dinner to be romantic at all.

That begged a question.

What was she doing having dinner with a guy who happened to be her ex-fiancé's best friend?

Jayne eyed the full basket of corn tortilla chips and the small bowl of *pico de gallo* salsa. Better to look at the food than at Tristan. He had enough appreciative stares from the other females in the restaurant. Surely he had better things to do on a Sunday than spend time with her?

"You're quiet," he said.

Because she was thinking about him. No way could she admit that aloud. Serena probably would have, but not Jayne. "Just taking it all in after the long hike."

A busboy, wearing all white and carrying a silver pitcher, refilled her water glass.

She thanked him as he walked away. "I have no doubt I'll be sore tomorrow. A good sore."

Tristan reached for a chip. "Fresh air and exercise are good for the soul."

"Well, I definitely needed both."

"And company."

It wasn't a question. Jayne met his gaze. She cleared her dry throat. "That, too."

He smiled at her.

Easy, charming.

She didn't trust charm.

She didn't trust him.

She couldn't trust him.

He was Rich's friend, after all.

Still, Jayne couldn't deny there was something pleasant about sitting across a restaurant table from a handsome man who looked at her with appreciation in his eyes and a smile on his lips. Much better than, say, heating a frozen entrée in her microwave and eating in an empty house alone. That was where she'd be if Tristan hadn't taken matters into his own hands.

"Do you always get your way?" she asked.

"Usually, but in this case it was for your own good."

"How do you figure that?"

"You looked hungry."

"Well, I am now," she admitted. "So thanks."

"You're welcome." He raised his water. "That's what friends are for."

"Is that what we are? Friends?"

"We could be."

Jayne couldn't imagine her and Tristan ever being friends. Not the kind of friend you called late at night when your car wouldn't start or some guy had broken your heart. He looked more like a heartbreaker than a best bud or best friend forever.

He scooted back in his chair. The movement caused strands of his hair to fall forward across the right side of his face. He really was attractive. Okay, gorgeous.

She fought the urge to push the locks away so she'd have a better view of his eyes. She liked how his green irises seemed to change shade with his emotions. A vibrant jewel-like color when excited. A lighter, more subdued one when thoughtful. She wondered what the color looked like when he kissed.

Uh-oh. That wasn't a very friend-like thought. Not that they *were* friends. Jayne shoved a chip into her mouth.

A waiter, wearing a long-sleeved white shirt, black pants and a colorful sash around his waist, placed dinner plates in front of them and walked away. The scents of cilantro, tomatoes and chili peppers brought a sigh to her lips.

"Good call on Mexican food tonight," Tristan said.

"It's one of my favorites." Though she couldn't remember ever having such a strong reaction to food before. Her mouth practically watered as she stared at her plate of Chile Rellenos, refried beans and rice.

"Mine, too." Tristan picked up his fork. "It's the first thing I want to eat when I get back into town. Good Mexican food is hard to find."

"My dad used to say the same thing, but my mom never had any luck using that argument to convince him to make San Diego their home base when they were married," she said. "That was her dream. To live here again. But she never got the chance."

"You're living the dream for her?"

Jayne straightened. "I am."

And one of these days she'd fulfill the rest of the dream they'd talked about over the years.

Tristan dug into his Chile Colorado. "Eat up."

She did.

As they ate, they quizzed each other on favorites—television shows, movies, sporting teams. Their tastes converged, diverged, and found common ground with the San Diego Padres and Chargers.

Jayne scooped up the last forkful of rice. "I can't believe I ate everything. I haven't had this much of an appetite in months."

"Seven months?"

She nodded. "In case you're wondering, I'm over Rich. It just takes time for things to get back to normal. At least that's what Molly told me. She said you can't rush it."

"She's right."

"Molly is usually right," Jayne said. "She was divorced a couple of years ago, but she's remarried and expecting her first baby. All because of our weekend in Las Vegas."

"Sounds like a wild time."

Jayne blew out a puff of air. "You have no idea."

"Tell me about it."

"I wouldn't know where to start," she admitted. "I mean, my three best friends ended up with husbands because of that one weekend. Alex received a job offer and never came back to San Diego. She ended up falling in love with her boss, Wyatt. Molly met Linc while having a glass of wine in a hotel lounge, and that led to—well, a baby and marriage. Then there's Serena, who met Jonas at a bar and ended up marrying him that night."

"And you?"

"Well, I was in my hating-men phase then. I wanted nothing to do with any of the pondscum-sucking species. No offense."

"None taken."

Jayne fluffed the ends of her hair. "So I came home with a new 'do instead."

"A lot less of a commitment than a husband or a baby."

"Most definitely."

"You made the right choice."

The relief in his voice surprised her. Jayne studied him. "You really don't want to get married again?"

"I don't."

"Even after everything I went through with Rich I can't imagine growing old on my own. Celebrating a fifty-year anniversary just sounds so right."

"To you, maybe," he said. "I'd consider that a life sentence."

"It's one I'd happily serve." When she found the right man—a trustworthy man. The last thing she wanted to do was be swept off her feet by another Mr. Wrong.

The waiter placed the bill on the table.

Tristan reached for the black vinyl folder.

She grabbed hold at the same time. "No."

"Guy rules." He pulled the check toward him. "The guy pays for the date. Especially the first date."

Jayne tugged on the bill. "But this isn't a date."

He started to speak, then stopped.

"You're right. It's not a date." Tristan let go. "Let's split the check."

"Thanks." Jayne opened the folder, added a twenty percent tip and divided the total in half. With her purse open, she removed the envelope with "Eating out" written in black marker and counted out in cash the exact amount she owed. She tucked the money inside the folder. "Here's my half."

"What's with the envelope?" Tristan asked.

"It's a way to keep track of your spending money when using cash."

Tristan tossed a platinum-colored credit card into the folder. "I prefer using plastic for everything and earning frequent flier miles."

"Don't you earn enough miles with your job travels?" she asked.

"I use the mileage for my personal travels," he said.

Jayne didn't understand why a person would want to be away from home that much, or use a credit card that way, but she bit her tongue. Tristan wasn't one of those clients who needed to hear her spiel about the dangers of relying and living off credit. Or how much interest people ended up paying to get a "free" plane ticket or a minuscule cashback reward.

"Besides, credit cards are more convenient than cash," he added.

"Convenient?" Oops. She hadn't meant to say that aloud. She pressed her lips together and counted to ten, the way Alex always did. It didn't help. "You may think credit cards are convenient, but only until you find yourself in debt with collection agencies stalking you."

"Huh?"

"I'm a debt management counselor," she said. "Everyday I help people get their finances under control. The first thing I tell my clients is to stop using their credit cards. A person can't get out of debt while racking up higher credit card balances."

"As long as you pay the balance every month you'll be fine," Tristan countered.

"Fine until one month something happens and you can't pay the balance," she said. "Millions of people are struggling because they lost their jobs or had a pay cut or spent more than they bring in, and now find themselves under a mountain of debt. It's the worst feeling in the world, and if I can help someone escape from that living nightmare I will."

He studied her. "You're passionate about this."

"It's my job."

"Sounds more like a crusade."

"Possibly," she admitted. "After my parents divorced, my mom relied heavily on credit cards to survive. I can't help but think the stress of having so much debt and no way to pay it off contributed to her death."

Tristan reached across the table and touched Jayne's hand. "No wonder you feel the way you do."

She stared at his hand covering hers. His warmth comforted and soothed. "I'm sorry if I got carried away."

"No worries. I get it."

She jerked her gaze up to search his eyes. "Get what?"

"You," he said, as if they were talking about her favorite flavor of milkshake. "What you do is a calling, not just a job."

Alex, Molly and Serena knew that, but Rich had never really understood. Yet Tristan...

Jayne glanced down at his hand still covering hers.

He got it.

Got her.

That's what friends are for.

Surprise rippled through her, followed by an unfamiliar sense of contentment.

But he wasn't a friend. After tonight they would probably never see each other again, so his understanding her so well didn't matter. Truth was, he'd simply made a lucky guess.

Not so, her heart countered.

Jayne didn't listen. She couldn't.

She'd learned how dangerous, how risky, following her heart could be. It wasn't worth the gamble. She knew how easily feelings could lead you astray and affect your judgment.

She pulled her hand from under Tristan's, ignoring how cold she felt without the warmth of his touch.

The smart thing to do—the only thing she could do—was follow her head.

Jayne ignored the gorgeous pair of friendly green eyes staring down at her.

Better that way.

Safer that way.

Especially when a part of her wished the evening with Tristan didn't have to end. The best thing she could do was say goodbye to him. Forever.

CHAPTER FOUR

GRACE would be proud of him, Tristan thought as he drove Jayne home from the Mexican restaurant. The sparkle he remembered hadn't returned to her eyes, but they'd brightened more than once. Her lips had curved into a smile more easily as the day went on. And if she continued eating like she had tonight her weight loss would be a thing of the past and all her curves would return.

Yeah, Grace would be pleased.

Rich, not so much.

Tristan lifted a hand from the steering wheel to rub the sudden tension at the back of his neck.

His friend might have given him the okay to see Jayne and return the postcard, but he doubted Rich would be pleased with Tristan spending the afternoon and evening with her. Still, he had no regrets.

He'd liked getting to know Jayne the woman, not Jayne Rich's fiancée. She wasn't the typical kind of woman Tristan dated, but that made things more interesting.

He signaled, exited the freeway, and headed west from the off-ramp.

She was wary of him. Her eyes, body gestures and words made that clear. Tristan would have to show her he was more than Rich's best friend. But how?

Jayne yawned.

Tristan glanced her way. "Tired?"

"A little, but nothing a cup of coffee won't fix. Caffeine will wake me right up."

"Do you have plans tonight?" he asked, curious as to what she would do after he dropped her off.

"Not really plans," she admitted. "But I want to write my roommate ad."

She liked his idea. Tristan smiled. "Where do you plan on looking for a roommate?"

"I was thinking the internet—one of those networking sites, maybe?"

Uh-oh. The idea of her meeting strangers who responded to her ad didn't sound like such a good idea after all. "Be careful with the wording. You don't want to attract any crazies. Take a peek at the personals so you know what not to say."

"I'm looking for a roommate, not romance."

"A lot of those personal ads aren't interested in romance either."

"I appreciate the concern." She smiled at him. "I promise I'll be careful."

That didn't make him feel any better.

"The house is the third on the right," she said, in case he'd forgotten. He hadn't.

Tristan parked at the curve in front, set the emergency brake and turned off the ignition.

Her eyes widened. "You don't have to walk me to the door."

So much for her being careful. He pulled the keys out. "Yes, I do."

"But it's not a date."

"Walking someone to the door when it's dark outside is not only polite, it's also common sense," he cautioned. "You shouldn't take unnecessary risks."

"Oh—okay, then."

Tristan met her on the sidewalk. A light illuminated the front door of the bungalow. It was a nice little house with charming architectural details in a quiet neighborhood.

Hipsters, artsy types and surfers weren't going to want to live here. Maybe she could find a librarian to share the rent. Or a schoolteacher.

Maybe he was overreacting about this roommate search.

Jayne dug in her purse for her keys.

Not the safest action if she had been alone.

His concern over her safety rose.

What did a sheltered homebody know about scoping out roommates over the internet?

Probably nothing. That could lead to all kinds of trouble for her.

"So, what kind of roommate do you want?" he asked.

She climbed the first step of the porch. "Someone who is friendly, respectful, gainfully employed."

"What about sex?"

Her head swung toward him. "Sex?"

"Female or male."

"I…" She hesitated. "I've never lived with a guy, but I guess it would be okay as long as it was platonic. Of course it would depend on the person."

Open-minded. Good. But unsavory sorts still might apply. "Are there any other qualities you're looking for?"

"Why are you so interested in my future roommate?" she asked. "It's none of your business."

No, but Tristan didn't want someone taking advantage of her the way Rich had. "It could be."

"Come on," she said. "Getting a roommate might have been your idea, but it's not like you're applying for the position."

He hadn't been planning to do that at all, but if it kept her from taking in some predatory loser and gave him a reason to keep seeing her…

"I could."

No, he couldn't. Rich would kill him. Hell, Tristan would kill *himself*. Living with all that temptation sleeping in the next room and doing nothing about it.

But maybe he could play along, keep her considering him long enough to get to know him, see he wasn't Rich and weed out the really bad apples.

Then, when the right person presented herself, he could bow out. She would have her roommate, and he'd have gotten to enjoy her company and, by then, her kiss.

A perfect solution.

He hooked his thumb through a belt loop. "I know it might sound off the wall, considering how long we've known each other, but what would you think about me for a roommate?"

Tristan her new roommate?

Jayne stared up at him, baffled and unable to speak.

That wasn't an off-the-wall suggestion. It was total insanity.

She could think of a hundred better roommates, including Dr. Hannibal Lector or Norman Bates. Okay, a psychopathic killer might not be a better roommate, but at least she'd know where she stood with them.

With Tristan, she hadn't a clue. And the thought of seeing him every morning in the kitchen, or bumping into him in the hallway before bedtime, or imagining him in the shower...

Jayne balled her fingers around her keys until the metal edges dug into her skin.

Why was she even thinking about this? Jayne flexed her fingers.

"I don't think us being roommates would work," she said, not wanting to be rude or hurt his feelings.

"Why not?"

Darn him. He wasn't supposed to ask questions. All she wanted was for him to agree with her and say goodnight. Goodbye would be even better.

"Because..." She noticed the swarm of insects flying around the porch light. "You're Rich's best friend, and that would be too..."

Incestuous? Her cheeks warmed. No, that wasn't the right word.

"Awkward," she finally settled on. "Could you imagine what it would be like if you ever invited him over to the house?"

"I wouldn't. I'm hardly ever home, because of my job, and Rich has too much other stuff going on right now."

Like his wedding.

Jayne grimaced.

Tristan didn't seem to notice. "I wouldn't do anything to make you uncomfortable in your own home."

She appreciated his words, but his showing up today had done just that. Right now she was awfully uncomfortable. "That's my point. If you were paying rent it wouldn't be my home anymore. It would be…"

She couldn't bring herself to say *our home.*

Jayne continued. "I appreciate the offer…suggestion…but we don't know each other well enough to say we'd be compatible roommates."

"True, but you could say that about any potential roommate you'd find on the internet, too."

He had a point. Still…

"It's not a bad idea," he said. "I'm friendly, respectful and gainfully employed. I'm neat enough. And I have the single most important qualification you're looking for in a roommate."

Jayne had no idea what that might be. She couldn't imagine he'd have figured it out on his own after spending one day— half a day—with her. "What qualification is that?"

He smiled at her. "I love ice cream."

Reluctantly, she smiled back. Okay, she'd give him points for that one. But sharing a pint of Ben & Jerry's Chunky Monkey with him wouldn't be quite the same as it had with Molly.

"Just think about it," he said.

"I don't have to think about it," Jayne countered. "You'd probably eat all the ice cream."

"I know how to share, if that's what you're afraid of."

"I'm not afraid," she said, a little too quickly. "But a male roommate would be one more change. I've had enough of those in the last few months. Nothing personal, but it might be nice to have a roommate who would want to go with me to the nail salon."

Wicked laughter lit his eyes. "They do call it a *man*icure."

She glared at him.

He grinned. "You got me there. I've never stepped foot in a nail salon before. But there are a few advantages to having a male roommate you might not have considered."

Jayne should thank him for today and be done with it. With him. Except curiosity got the better of her. Again. "Such as?"

"Opening jars."

"I have a tool that can open anything."

"Changing lightbulbs."

He was going to have to come up with something a lot better than that. "I have a step ladder."

"Killing bugs."

She glanced up at the porch light, at the buzzing winged creatures. "Okay, you got me there."

"The one downside I see is my travel schedule," Tristan admitted. "I wouldn't be around much."

If he were her roommate his not being around would actually be a plus in his favor. Of course that would defeat one of her main purposes for getting a roommate as a cure for loneliness. "Yeah, I would rather live with someone who—"

"You weren't even considering a roommate until today," he interrupted. "Take some time to make an informed decision."

"You're right," she admitted. "But..."

"You're lonely," he said perceptively.

Her cheeks flushed.

"So let's use the time to get to know each other better," he suggested.

"I don't think—"

"How else will you know whether I'd be a good roommate or not?"

She was tempted. Appalled.

A mix of emotion churned inside her: relief at the thought of having someone to hang out with, and anxiety at realizing that the person was Rich's best friend. She had no idea about Tristan's motivation behind his roommate suggestion, but it didn't really matter. "I still know what my answer will be."

"You can always change your mind."

She'd had enough change in her life. She wasn't going to change for anyone—especially Tristan. "I won't."

A beat passed, then another.

"Then let me help you find a roommate," he offered. "I can be your guinea pig applicant."

"My guinea pig?"

"Yeah," he said. "You can learn my bad habits and figure out what your roommate deal-breakers are."

He was her ex-fiancé's best friend.

That was a pretty significant deal-breaker right there.

And yet…

Tristan had brought up a good point. She'd had roommates in college, and most recently Molly, but Jayne didn't know the first thing about what questions to ask. She'd entangled herself with the wrong fiancé. She didn't want to saddle herself with the wrong roommate.

And that could happen. Her judgment was obviously off. She didn't want to make another mistake, but she didn't know if trusting Tristan was the right move, either.

What you do is a calling, not just a job.

Yet he seemed to understand her and connect with her in a way only those closest to her had. But Alex, Molly and

Serena weren't here to help. Maybe Tristan's perception could help Jayne overcome her poor judgment and find the perfect roommate.

"Okay." She hoped this wasn't a mistake. "You can be my guinea pig as long as you're clear you won't be my roommate."

"I understand." A satisfied grin settled over Tristan's lips. "So I'll see you tomorrow night."

"Tomorrow?" she croaked.

He nodded. "You need practice getting to know me so you're ready when people answer your ad."

"I thought you said not to rush."

"This isn't rushing," he said. "It's preparation."

For what? she wondered. He seemed a little too slick and charming.

The porch light cast intriguing shadows on his handsome face. Jayne gazed up into Tristan's green eyes. Long, thick lashes like his really should be illegal on a man.

"I'll pick you up tomorrow night at seven."

"That sounds a lot like a date," she said.

"Not a date," Tristan countered. "We'll stay here and get to know each other."

"But what will we do?"

"Hang out."

She couldn't imagine her and Tristan sitting around and doing nothing. "We need something to do."

"You're the self-proclaimed homebody," he said. "What do you usually do?"

Jayne didn't want to confess to watching TV and organizing her socks or spice cabinet. "I…like to play Sudoku."

"We could play together."

He was easygoing, enthusiastic…and nearly impossible to resist. A lot like Rich when she'd met him. "I don't—"

"I should warn you, though, I'm going to win."

"I haven't even agreed to play with you yet."

"You have other plans?"

"I…" Of course not. "I'll have to check."

He pulled out a business card and handed it to her. "This has my cell number on it. Let me know if tomorrow works for you."

Tomorrow sounded so…soon. But the alternative was another night alone.

You're lonely, he'd said. Yes.

But not stupid.

She held the card tight between her fingers. "I'll think about it."

Inside the house, Jayne watched the taillights of Tristan's car grow smaller, until the two red dots disappeared down the street. She'd had fun today, but was happy he was gone. Maybe he'd decide he had better things to do than help her find a roommate.

She glimpsed Mrs. Whitcomb peeking through her lace curtains. Jayne smiled.

Nothing got past her neighbor. It had become more endearing than annoying. Especially once Molly had told Jayne how the woman had lost her husband of fifty-five years and all her children and grandchildren lived out of state. Most of the other neighbors felt the same way, and made sure to keep Mrs. Whitcomb in the know and even entertained.

Jayne placed the business card on the desk in the corner of the living room. She would decide later when—make that *if*—she wanted to see him again.

She noticed she had voicemail. Three messages, in fact. Only three people ever called. Well, sometimes four, when Cynthia, Molly's mom, dialed the number out of habit, but Jayne knew whose voices she'd hear on the other end.

Smiling, she picked up the phone and listened to the messages.

"Hi, it's Molly," a familiar voice said. "Sorry I missed your call. We were out looking at flooring, fixtures and furniture for the new house. Are you okay? I'm around. Call back."

"I got your message," Alex said. "Wyatt and I spent the day planning a much needed vacation to Tuscany. I'm home. I'll be up late. Call me."

"Hey, Jayne," Serena said. "I spoke with Molly and Alex. How are you doing? We want to have a chat tonight. Nine o'clock in the usual chatroom. It's time for us to catch up, so see you there."

Jayne glanced at the clock. Almost nine. She couldn't believe she'd spent that much time with Tristan. It hadn't seemed that long.

Without enough time to brew a cup of hot tea, she settled for a glass of iced tea instead. She skipped the cookies because she was full from dinner and all those tortilla chips.

She returned to the desk, sat, and logged into the chatroom. Too bad her webcam had broken or they could have done a video chat. Jayne wanted to see Molly now that she was seven months pregnant.

The chat window popped open on the monitor. Alex with her efficient blue font, Molly with her easy-to-read green font and Serena with her whimsical magenta font were chatting away.

Seeing their names and the words on the screen filled Jayne with warmth. Her three friends could see each other face-to-face any time in Las Vegas, but Jayne appreciated them taking the time so the four of them could still be together, albeit virtually.

Jayne: Hi.
Molly: You didn't sound like yourself on your message. Are you okay?
Alex: What's going on?
Serena: We're all yours tonight.

So many things were running through Jayne's head at the moment. Most of them having to do with Tristan, not Rich.

She wanted to tell her friends about yesterday, so typed everything that had happened at the teahouse, in order. Going there on her own. Seeing the Strickland sisters. Recognizing the woman—Deidre. Realizing Rich was getting married. Running away.

The words spilled out in a practical black font. It might have been the default font for the chat. Jayne didn't care. She knew her friends would offer an endless supply of support and love. The way they always had with each other.

But as she finished typing her experience at the teahouse, the hurt and betrayal she'd felt yesterday and this morning were all but gone. No sting remained. No tears welled in her eyes.

That pleased her.

"I'm not as bothered by it tonight," she wrote.

Jayne hit the "enter" key and stared at her blinking cursor.

Molly: Oh, Jayne. I'm happy you're feeling better, but I'm so sorry you had to go through that alone. How horrible.
Alex: I wish I had been there.
Molly: Me, too.
Serena: Me, three.
Alex: Jayne, I hate that you had to be hurt all over again. But Deidre's going to be the unhappy one in the end. Especially if she thinks that jerk will be faithful. Once a cheater, always a cheater.
Molly: That's for sure.
Serena: You're way too good for him.
Jayne: Thanks :) xoxox I'm over him, and he's the last person I'd ever want to be with, yet finding out he was getting married to her pretty much floored me.

Molly: You would have been shocked even if you two had had an amiable breakup. It hurt a lot more than I expected when I found out Doug was remarrying. And I was happy we'd divorced.

Alex: Is there anything you need, Jayne? Something we can do from here.

Jayne: You're doing it now. Thanks!

Molly: She's serious, Jayne.

Jayne: So am I.

Serena: Where were you when I called? I was worried when you didn't answer. I tried your cell, too.

Jayne: I was hiking at Torrey Pines. Or we might have been having dinner by then. I didn't hear my phone ring, sorry.

Alex: We?

Jayne: Me and Tristan.

Words flew across her monitor. Line after line of questions. Jayne had never known her friends could type so fast, and with such accurate spelling.

She laughed at the number of exclamation points and capital letters being used. And not just from Serena.

This was more entertaining than watching television. Jayne smiled.

The questions continued. One after another. No way could she answer them in real time, so she would wait until they'd finished. She sipped her tea as the words scrolled by.

Finally the typing stopped.

Serena: Hello, out there. We're waiting!!!!!

Jayne: Just wanted to make sure the three of you were finished with your questions first. Or maybe I should say inquisition.

Serena: :P

Molly: Spill. Now. Or face the consequences.

Alex: You won't like the consequences.

Jayne: LOL! But there's not much to tell.

Serena: We'll be the judges of that.

Jayne: His name is Tristan MacGregor. He's Rich's best friend and was going to be the best man at our wedding.

Alex: The photojournalist?

Jayne: Yes.

Molly: You said he was a hottie, if I remember correctly.

Jayne: I did?

Alex: You did.

Serena: Yes. I remember because you were hoping one of us might like him.

Molly: You thought having one of your bridesmaids fall in love with the best man would be romantic.

Jayne: I don't remember.

Alex: So tell us more about your date.

Jayne: It wasn't a date!

Anxiety rocketed through her, making each muscle tense. She didn't want to date Tristan. She didn't want to date period.

Jayne: Tristan just showed up on my doorstep because Rich's sister, Grace, was worried about me after yesterday at the teahouse.

Molly: So he shows up, the two of you go hiking, and then out to dinner?

Jayne: Yes. Well, we had iced tea and cookies here first.

Alex: That sounds like a date.

Jayne: We split the check.

She remembered how he'd wanted to pay until she reminded him they weren't on a date. Had she been wrong? No, he'd agreed it wasn't a date.

Serena: Did he kiss you goodnight?

Why would he kiss her? They hadn't been on a date.

But she'd been a tad disappointed he hadn't done...something. A handshake. A hug.

Jayne stiffened.

No, she hadn't been disappointed. She'd been relieved. Really, truly relieved. Rich's friend, his best man, remember?

Jayne: NO! No kiss!!!!
Molly: Are you going to see him again?
Jayne: He gave me his card and told me to call him so we could get together this week.
Serena: He wants to date you.
Alex: Definitely.
Jayne: He doesn't want to date me. He wants

A knock sounded at the door. Twice in one day? What was going on?

Serena: Wants what?
Jayne: Someone is at the door.
Molly: It's late. Ask who it is before you open the door.

"Who is it?" Jayne yelled.

"Tristan."

Every nerve-ending stood at attention. Her stomach did a cartwheel.

What was he doing back? She was about to stand up and find out when she remembered the chat. Her fingers flew across the keyboard.

Jayne: It's just Tristan. BRB

She rose from her chair and made her way to the front door. Curiosity clashed with apprehension. She unlocked and opened the door.

Tristan stood in her doorway the way he had earlier.

Okay, he was a hottie. Many women would agree. But Jayne wondered why she'd thought one of her friends might fit with him. Free-spirited, commitment-phobe Serena might have connected with Tristan on some level, but he wouldn't have been as good for her as steady and stable Jonas Benjamin.

"Hi," Tristan said, as if dropping by her apartment at this hour was normal.

"Hello." No doubt Mrs. Whitcomb would be happy she'd set her TiVo tonight. "Did you forget something?"

"No, but you did." He raised her boots and daypack in the air. "I thought you might need them if you caught the hiking bug today."

"Thanks." Jayne didn't want to be impressed, but she was. She took the items from him. "That was very thoughtful of you."

His mouth quirked. "We all have our moments."

She didn't trust him, but the guy had done her two favors today. Three if she counted his offer to help her with the roommate search. The least she could do was repay his kindness.

"If you're free Tuesday night, swing by after six," she said. "We can have a bite to eat, talk about my getting a roommate and see who is the Sudoku master."

His gaze held hers. "Sounds great."

She narrowed her eyes, ignoring the fluttering of her heart. "Just don't forget your wallet."

"Excuse me?"

She'd finally managed to surprise him. She grinned. "Loser buys the ice cream."

He laughed. "You're on."

Jayne stood at the doorway as he walked to his car. Once again she watched the taillights disappear down the street only this time knew exactly when she'd see him again. She sure hoped she hadn't made another mistake.

She returned to the desk and scanned her computer screen.

Serena: It's taking her a long time.
Alex: Too long. I hope she's okay.
Molly: If she's not back soon I'll call our neighbor, Mrs. Whitcomb. She's probably watching Jayne from her window now.
Alex: Unless they're inside.
Serena: I wonder if this is how my mother felt when I started dating?
Alex: If so, you owe her an apology.

Jayne frowned.

She was *not* dating. She was…

She typed. "Back! Sorry it took so long."

Alex: Is he gone?
Jayne: Yes, I forgot my hiking boots and daypack in his car so he was returning them.
Serena: That was nice of him.

He seemed nice. Very nice, in fact. But appearances could be deceiving.

Jayne: So, where were we?
Molly: You said Tristan didn't want to date you, but you never told us what he does want.

Jayne didn't want her friends' pity because Tristan didn't want to date her. The truth was he did want to spend time with her, and that made her feel good—even if he was Rich's best friend.

Jayne: Tristan just wants to move in with me. But don't worry. I said no.

CHAPTER FIVE

MONDAY dragged. Tuesday, too.

Tristan had a story due, but seeing Jayne was the only thing on his mind. A phone conversation with Grace had appeased her concerns, but talking about the lovely Jayne and thinking about they day they'd spent together only added to his impatience.

When their date on Tuesday finally arrived, he sat across from her at the patio table in her backyard. She looked hot in her lime-green T-shirt. The stretchy fabric accentuated her breasts. A great view, but if he didn't stop admiring her he would lose. Again.

Tristan focused on his Sudoku puzzle. Numbers from one to nine filled many of the boxes. Only a few more to go. Jayne was smart and fast, but he would not lose this time.

"Finished," she said.

No way. He glanced at his watch. Six and a half minutes. He set his pen on the table. "You *are* the Sudoku Master."

She bit her lip. "Do you want to play again?"

"You won three out five games."

"We can make it even," she suggested.

"Or you could beat me again," he countered.

"But I wouldn't."

"What do you mean?"

She stared down at her puzzle.

"You would *let* me win?" he guessed, unable to keep the disbelief from his voice.

A charming pink colored her cheeks. "It's just a game."

"Exactly."

"Well, sometimes it's easier if the other person doesn't like to lose."

"You mean Rich."

Her cheeks turned even redder. "He liked winning."

"So do I. But I can still be a good sport if I lose."

The doubt in Jayne's eyes told Tristan she didn't believe him. No matter what he said or did, when she looked at him she must see Rich. Changing that opinion might take time. Time he really didn't have with a new assignment coming up.

The setting sun provided the perfect backdrop to her dark shiny hair. A golden aura, almost like a halo, surrounded her. She reminded him of an angel—one who needed to learn to use her wings. He might not have the time, but he wasn't ready to give up on her yet.

"I'm sorry," she muttered.

"You don't have to apologize for being good at something, especially after that amazing dinner."

"I made the lasagna. The bread came from the bakery and the salad from the garden." She narrowed her eyes, but couldn't keep the corners of her mouth from curving upward. "But if you think flattery will get you out of buying the ice cream tonight, think again."

He grinned, more at ease than he could remember being in a long time. Maybe being her roommate wasn't such a crazy idea.

What was he? Nuts? Even if she had a change of heart, he could never live with her. The separate bedrooms clause was a total deal-breaker for him. "Hey, a guy's gotta try."

That was his problem. Even though he knew Jayne was his best friend's ex-fiancée, he couldn't stop himself from wanting to be with her himself.

She laughed.

The warm sound flowed through him, as if his blood were as thick as honey, and filled up all sorts of empty places he hadn't known he had. Tristan had never felt anything like it, and he wasn't sure he liked the feeling. He shifted in his seat. "Seriously, though, I'm only giving compliments where they're due."

She blushed again. "Thank you."

"You're welcome."

With her pink-tinged cheeks and bright blue eyes she was more than another pretty face. Not many people put other's feelings before their own the way Jayne did. Her sharp intellect kept him intrigued and entertained. And her honesty made him feel he could trust her even though they were still getting to know each other.

Rich had really screwed up letting Jayne get away.

His loss, Tristan's gain?

Except he was looking for fun, a good time, not something serious. His job didn't allow for that. Even if it did, he wasn't looking to make a commitment. Now or in the future.

A dog yipped. The high-pitched sound made him think of the small, ankle-biter type.

"Quiet, Duke," Jayne called to the fence.

The barking stopped.

"Sorry," she said. "I usually take him for a walk after dinner. We're starting a dog agility class on Thursday, so we've been practicing a little, too."

He glanced toward the spot where the sound came from. Across the freshly mowed grass, next to the fence, was a small garden. "Is that where you got the salad from?"

She nodded. "I've been trying to make sure Molly's hard work doesn't go to waste. She used to spend so much time working out here."

Little signs marked each of the neat, straight rows of what he assumed were vegetables. He didn't know anything about gardening himself, but he liked eating what came from them. "So how's it going?"

"Well, I did some yardwork when I was a kid, but never gardening, so I've been learning as I dig in the dirt, plant and prune. There's been a bit of trial and error," Jayne admitted, "but I haven't killed anything yet. Molly will be happy when she sees it."

"What about you? Does working in the garden make you happy, Jayne?"

Looking at the garden, she crinkled her nose until a satisfied smile settled on her lips. "Actually, I'm enjoying myself more than I thought I would."

"I'm not surprised."

"Why do you say that?"

"It's all about putting down roots," he said. "That's what you want, and you're good at it."

Girlfriend material, sure. Wife material, most definitely.

Tristan didn't want either. So what in the hell was he doing here?

He picked up his glass of lemonade and drank. The tart sweetness matched his mood.

Jayne didn't need a roommate. She needed a husband. Best to cut his losses and say goodbye.

"You know, I never thought about it like that," she said.

Her features looked more animated. Too bad he didn't have his camera out here. Though he probably had enough pictures of her to last a lifetime.

She continued. "I think you're right."

He'd bet a million dollars he was correct. He wished he were wrong.

She sipped her lemonade. He did the same, listening to the sounds of the neighborhood. A child's squeal could be heard over a lawnmower. A woman called her family inside for dinner.

The noises were more foreign to him than gunfire, thanks to his being embedded with a unit in Afghanistan. He'd avoided this kind of life in the suburbs before. The life his ex-wife wanted. The life Jayne wanted.

I hope that happens someday.

Someday, she'd said. Not now.

Maybe he didn't have to bolt out of here. She'd told him she wasn't looking for a relationship at the moment. That could mean she would be up for something more…casual.

She set her glass on the table. "Do you garden?"

He rarely noticed landscaping unless it caught his eye for a possible photograph or food. "Digging in dirt doesn't appeal to me."

"Do you live in an apartment?"

"Hotel."

Her mouth formed an o. "A hotel?"

Tristan thought of the mega-story steel and glass building—one of San Diego's most luxurious hotels—he currently called home. At least until his next assignment came up. "Yes."

"Why?"

"Staying at hotels is easier than renting an apartment," he said. "It gives me the flexibility I need with my travel schedule. Plus I can always move if I don't like it or get bored."

"So you don't even want to commit to a six month lease?"

"I don't like leaving a place empty for so long."

"What about your stuff?" she asked.

"Stuff?" he asked.

"Books, CDs, computer, clothing, old report cards. You know…stuff," she explained. "When I moved from my apartment into here I had so many boxes. Mementoes from when I was a kid. Things I never want to let go of."

"Everything I own fits into a couple of plastic bins, so it's easy to move from place to place."

"I could never fit all my kitchen stuff in a couple of bins." She sounded grateful for that. "I grew up moving around a lot. 'Live light, move light,' my father used to say. But a person needs to have some things that have meaning or hold memories for them."

"I have those things," Tristan said. "It just all fits into the bins."

"So living out of a suitcase really works for you?"

"Yes."

"But how do you know if you're traveling or not?" she asked. "You're never home if you live in a hotel."

"The hotel is my home."

"So you always go back to the same hotel? The same room?"

"Well, no…" Her reaction didn't surprise him, but it did make him vaguely defensive. "My life makes sense for me. I travel too much to take care of a place. I'd just be wasting money paying for an empty apartment. This way I check in and out as need be."

"If you had a roommate, your place wouldn't be empty."

He raised a brow. "Are you offering?"

"Just offering up the great suggestion you gave me," she said. "Living at a hotel has to be really expensive."

"I can afford it."

"If you can afford the nightly rate at a hotel, then you can afford to buy a place."

His ex-wife, Emma, had wanted to buy a house and have a baby before their first anniversary. Finally an adult and free from college at twenty-two, Tristan had wanted her to travel with him around the world while he took photographs. Hell, at *thirty*-two that still sounded like a good way to spend a year or two. "I'm not looking to make a thirty-year commitment to a mortgage anytime in the near future."

"I'd hope not." Jayne sounded aghast. "That would be a huge mistake."

That didn't sound like the domestically inclined, angelic homebody he'd come to know tonight. Intrigued, Tristan leaned toward her. "I'm surprised you agree with me."

"Of course I agree with you. Who wouldn't?" Lines creased her forehead, the way they did anytime she got serious about something. "You should never take out a thirty-year mortgage. Fifteen-year mortgages are the only ones that make financial sense these days."

Tristan would have laughed except for the sincerity in her voice. The last thing he wanted to do was hurt her feelings when she was trying to be helpful.

Surprisingly, he found this financially astute side of her utterly charming and totally appealing. He respected her dedication to her job and what she believed even, if it were the exact opposite of his thinking. "I'll have to remember that if I ever buy a house."

"Not if, when," she said. "Seriously, Tristan, buying a condo or a townhouse and finding a roommate would be such a smart move right now with the current market conditions. You'll build equity fast as the market rises again rather than throw your dollars away living at a hotel."

She sure was tenacious when it came to money. He leaned back in his chair. "Home ownership just isn't for me."

"There are tax benefits." She said the words as if she were dangling a cookie in front of him.

"Why aren't *you* taking advantage of the tax benefits?" he asked.

"Excuse me?"

"You rent," he pointed out.

"Well, yes. I like living in Molly's bungalow," Jayne said. "But I can't wait to buy a house of my own."

He thought about the house he'd grown up in, on the same street where Rich's parents still lived, and the bigger one his parents lived in now. "Saving up for a big, splashy house with an ocean view?"

"No, a fixer-upper would be best." Her eyes sparkled. "For as long as I can remember, through all the countries and different bases where I lived as a kid, I've dreamed about owning my own house. Putting down roots, as you said."

The passion in her voice appealed to him on a gut level. Tristan didn't want a house for himself, but he wanted Jayne to have one. "What's stopping you?"

"There are a few things I need to do first."

"Like what?"

"I need to save enough for a down payment and get married."

Tristan did a double take. The down payment he understood. The marriage part, not so much.

He thought Jayne might be joking, but one look at the determined set of her jaw told him she wasn't. Still, he needed to state the obvious. "You don't have to be married to buy a house."

"I know, but it just seems…I guess it seems like the easiest way."

"Easier if you need two salaries to qualify for a mortgage," he conceded. "But marital status shouldn't stop anyone from buying a house. Lots of single women and men buy houses. Look at your friend who owns this place. She's single. Or was single."

"Molly and her ex-husband purchased this house when they were married. She bought Doug out when they divorced."

"Bad example. But there are lots of other good ones out there," Tristan said. "Maybe in our parents' generation women waited. But you shouldn't wait to buy a house if that's what you want to do."

"I'm not really that old-fashioned." She sounded defensive. "But I guess I've always imagined things happening in a certain order in my life. Marriage comes before a house."

"So this thing with Rich really messed with your plans, huh?"

She swallowed. Nodded.

Just because things with Rich didn't work out doesn't mean I can't live happily ever after here in San Diego with my one true love.

Tristan felt like a real heel.

He wasn't a big fan of plans. Emma had been full of them. But at least sweet Jayne was up-front about hers. She wasn't hiding who she was or what she wanted. Or demanding he change what he was and what he wanted.

"Imagine and plan all you want," he said. "But if you dream of owning a house you should go for it. Now, if you're able."

"That would be like asking me to jump out of a fully operational airplane. I couldn't do it."

"Jumping out of an airplane isn't so scary," Tristan said. "It gets easier each time."

"How many times have you jumped out of an airplane?"

He shrugged. "More than fifty. Less than a hundred."

Her eyes widened. "That's…insane."

"Insane fun," he agreed. "I'll have to show you the photographs."

Her mouth dropped. "You take your camera with you?"

"Never leave home without it."

"And I just never leave home." She laughed. "We're quite the odd couple."

"Not so odd."

"And not a couple."

Too bad.

Although…

Maybe they did want different things in the long term. That didn't mean a short-term relationship couldn't work between them.

He could help her loosen up and have fun. He could show her she could pursue her dream of putting down roots without a husband by her side.

Jayne could help him, too. She had brought up a good point. Maybe it was time he stopped living out of a suitcase. Some mornings he'd wake up and forget where he was.

Not to mention if Jayne got what she wanted—her own house—maybe he could get what he wanted—her.

"I have an idea," he said.

"Not roommates again."

"No, houses."

She straightened.

Good, he had her attention. "Maybe I was a little quick to shoot down the idea of buying a place. If the market's that good—"

"It is."

"I suppose I could see what's out there," he conceded. "Having a home base might make sense, and it sounds like it could be a better move financially."

"A much better move."

"I'd need someone to look with me." He would make sure they looked at condominiums for him and houses for Jayne. "You interested?"

"I love looking at real estate, but I'm not the right person to do this with you."

"I trust your judgment."

"You shouldn't," she said, without any hesitation. "We're looking for completely different things."

He could see her point, but still..."Are you sure I can't change your mind?"

"No." The determined set of her jaw told him she meant it. "I'm sure you can find someone else to go with you."

"Sure, but I know at least you'd be honest with."

"That's the problem, Tristan," she admitted. "You wouldn't like what I had to say."

Thursday night, Jayne slipped out of her shoes. Her feet ached. She'd had a long day at work, followed by a dog agility class with Mrs. Whitcomb's Duke.

Ice cream sounded really good. Jayne thought about Tuesday night and the ice cream cone Tristan had purchased for her...with his credit card. She shook her head.

Tristan MacGregor needed help. The guy used his credit card for everything and lived in a hotel. He'd deluded himself into living a life based on credit and borrowing, but she wasn't the one to help him. They'd said goodnight. She'd considered it goodbye.

Jayne padded her way into the kitchen. Before she reached the freezer, the telephone rang.

Alex, Molly or Serena?

Smiling, Jayne picked up the telephone receiver from the charger on the counter. "So, what was the high temperature in Vegas today?"

"I have no idea," Tristan said. "But if you give me a minute I can check *weather.com*."

"Tristan. I'm so sorry. I thought you were one of my friends." Jayne cringed, realizing how that must have sounded. Like she didn't have many friends. Like she didn't think of him as a friend. "Other friends, I mean."

Shut up, Jayne.

Mercifully, he changed the subject. "How was the class with your neighbor's dog tonight?"

She couldn't believe he'd remembered. "We both got a workout and met some nice people."

"Good." He paused. "And the roommate search? I never asked. Have you posted an ad yet?"

"No." She leaned against the counter, realizing how empty the house suddenly felt. Eating a bowl of ice cream alone was no longer so appealing. "My friends wanted to look over my ad first."

"Good friends."

"The best." Thinking about Alex, Molly and Serena brought another smile to Jayne's face. "I realized it would be nice to have someone living here, but there's no real hurry. I want to make sure I do this roommate thing right and not rush into anything."

"Smart thinking," he said. "Never rush into making any big decisions."

She tightened her fingers around the receiver. "I learned that lesson the hard way."

"With Rich."

Jayne swallowed. "Yes."

"Tough," Tristan said sympathetically.

"You have no idea," she said, a trace of bitterness creeping into her voice.

"Actually, I do." His words surprised her. Could he actually be trying to alleviate her discomfort?

"Your ex-wife?" she guessed.

Silence filled the line. It must be his turn to feel uncomfortable.

"Yeah," he said finally.

She thought about her own experience. "Because you got engaged too soon?"

"Because we got engaged at all," he said frankly. "I met Emma during freshman orientation in college. By senior year everyone, including both our families, expected us to get married. It was what she wanted. So I proposed."

"Is that what you wanted?" Jayne asked.

"It was what I thought I was supposed to want. So we had a big wedding after we graduated."

"You were young."

"Too young," he admitted. "I didn't think I'd rushed into the decision at the time, but college is its own bubble world. If I'd just put a little more thought into it I would have waited until after graduation and we were supporting ourselves to propose. Turns out Emma didn't like being the wife of a struggling photojournalist. She wanted me to go work for my father instead."

"Didn't she know that you wanted to be a photographer?"

"We talked about it, sure, but I guess not nearly enough. She thought I'd change my mind. I tried."

"Changing your mind?"

"Being a desk jockey. I hated it. Even my dad said I wasn't cut out for the office and told me to give photojournalism a shot."

"You could have tried counseling."

"We did," he said, surprising Jayne yet again. "I just couldn't make myself into the man she wanted me to be. She didn't want the kind of life my job required. We gave it two years, but after we'd exhausted every other option divorce seemed to be the only alternative."

She appreciated Tristan opening up the way he had. Most guys she knew wouldn't have.

"When my father finally wanted out of marriage he just left," she confided. "No compromising. No counseling. Nothing. At least you tried to save your marriage. That says a lot."

Maybe Tristan MacGregor wasn't an identical cookie cutter image of Rich after all.

"Tried, but didn't succeed. Emma found what she was looking for. She married a doctor, lives in Laguna Beach and has kids now."

"What about you?" Jayne asked. "Have you found what you wanted?"

"I have everything I want." Tristan said. "But getting to this point hurt someone I loved. I never want that to happen again."

"I wish learning the big lessons didn't have to hurt so much."

"If they didn't hurt, we wouldn't learn."

"Good point," she said.

He cleared his throat. "Speaking of learning, I'm planning to look at condominiums on Sunday. I'd still like you to go with me. I know I could learn a lot from you."

Jayne nearly dropped the phone.

Say no. That was all she had to do. They were looking for different things in homes and from life. Yet she felt closer to Tristan after the conversation they'd just shared.

He was still Rich's best friend.

But Tristan wasn't exactly like Rich or…her father. Oh, Tristan still had problems. He knew nothing about finances. He lived in the now without regard to tomorrow. And he couldn't even commit to a six-month lease let alone a relationship.

But, like her, he'd made mistakes and learned hard lessons. She didn't want that to happen to him with his real estate search.

She could help him.

She wanted to help him.

"I might have some free time on Sunday," Jayne said.

Of course she had the time.

But did she have the courage?

CHAPTER SIX

LOOKING at condominiums with Jayne was more fun than Tristan had thought it would be. He was happy she'd decided to change her mind and come with him today. He tapped his thumb against the steering wheel to the uplifting beat of the song on the radio.

Maybe by the time they were finished with their open house tour he could change her mind about a few other things, too.

As he flicked on his blinker to move to the right lane of the freeway, he glanced toward the passenger seat. Jayne sat with a three-inch binder full of real estate information on her lap.

Leave it to Jayne to come so prepared.

He'd brought the real estate section from the paper, but he had no plan of attack. His best shots were often as much a result of luck as of planning, so he was comfortable winging it.

Tristan should have known Jayne would think otherwise. She'd charted their entire day, printing out directions, maps and information on each listing.

Organized and orderly.

Not such a bad thing, Tristan realized.

He and Jayne might be different in the way they approached things, but they had more in common than he'd realized. Similar tastes in architecture and interiors and food. They made a good team. A very good team.

Now all he had to do was convince her to play with him. Maybe after their next stop. He smiled.

"What's so funny?" she asked.

"Just thinking about the day so far." And how he would like it to end with a little one-on-one contact.

"We've seen so much." Excitement laced her words.

He wondered whether she was excited about the real estate or him.

"I really can see you living in the beachfront condo," she added.

Real estate. Damn. But he wasn't giving up.

"So can I." Her observation didn't surprise him. They were getting to know each other better every time they walked through a property. "The location is perfect. I really like the layout of the place."

She nodded. "Don't forget the kitchen. It's to die for."

"It is nice as far as kitchens go," Tristan admitted. "But, face it, any kitchen would be an improvement over what I have now."

"You don't have a kitchen."

"Exactly," he said. "But I do get nightly turndown service and a chocolate on my pillow."

Jayne dimpled. "True, but think of all the chocolate you can store in those gorgeous maple cupboards. One piece versus many pieces. Seems a no-brainer to me."

Tristan slowed to allow a truck to merge onto the freeway. "You may be right."

He exited the freeway.

"Wait a minute," she said with surprise. "Where are we going?"

A smug smile settled on his lips. She was going to love this. "It's a surprise."

She leaned back against the seat. "I don't like surprises."

Her tone and reaction bothered him.

No, Tristan assured himself, Jayne needed this whether she thought so or not.

He stopped at the red light at the bottom of the ramp. "Why don't you like surprises?"

Her full lips pressed together.

"Come on," he urged.

She shook her head.

He turned west when the light changed to green. "Talk to me, Jayne."

She stared straight ahead out the windshield, her expression carefully blank. "Three days before our wedding Rich sent me a text saying he had a surprise waiting for me at his apartment. Only I'm guessing he must have sent the message to me by mistake. When I got to his apartment—"

"Okay." Tristan gripped the steering wheel until his knuckles turned white. "I get the picture."

"So did I," she said bitterly. "He was with Deidre when I arrived."

Tristan knew that. Oh, man, he knew. He'd just never faced the emotional impact it must have had on Jayne. His insides twisted. "Jayne—"

"Sorry," she said quickly. "I shouldn't have told you."

"That's okay." But it wasn't. A lump of guilt the size of a basketball lodged in his throat. "I asked."

He wished he hadn't.

Because Rich hadn't sent the text message to Jayne. Tristan had...

Tristan stood in the dressing area of the tuxedo rental shop. He'd already tried on his tux while waiting for Rich, who was running late.

Rich strutted out of his dressing room wearing a black tux. "This will work."

"Not bad," Tristan said.

"Jayne will like it."

Tristan nodded. Jayne would love it. "So, you must be breathing easier with Deidre out of the way."

Rich stared at his reflection in a three-panel mirror. He smoothed the lapels, turned and checked out his backside. "I haven't broken up with her."

Tristan's mouth gaped. "You're getting married this weekend."

Rich shrugged. "She's coming over to my apartment tonight."

"Cutting it a little close, bud."

"I'm not breaking up with Deidre," he said. "I'm in love with her."

Tristan couldn't believe what he was hearing. Rich had never acted like this before. "What about Jayne?"

"Jayne thinks I'm working a shift for someone tonight so I can have more time off for the wedding and honeymoon. She'll never know."

"You idiot." Tristan's temper flared. "You can't promise to love her, to cherish her, when you're seeing another woman."

Rich turned red. "I promised to marry her. I'm keeping my promise. It's the only honorable thing to do."

"You're cheating on her." Tristan lowered his voice so no one in the other part of the shop would hear them. "That's not honorable."

"So you'd rather I broke Jayne's heart?" Rich shook his head. "I'm a man of my word. I'm the only one she's got. Maybe once the wedding's over things will get better."

"What about Deidre?"

"Things are already great with her," Rich said.

The guy didn't have a clue, but Tristan would be shirking his best man and best friend duty if he didn't say something. "You're the closet thing I have to a brother, but I have to tell you, dude, you're screwing up big-time. Forget Jayne. Forget Deidre. You're not ready to get married."

Rich's nostrils flared. "Says the divorced guy?"

A beat passed. And another.

This wasn't a game of one-on-one or one-upmanship. This was real life. Rich's life.

"Yeah, I'm divorced." Tristan rocked back on his heels. "And you of all people should remember what that was like for me. Hell on earth. My worst nightmare. I don't want you to experience that, but if you marry Jayne this weekend you will. I guarantee it."

"Hey, I know you mean well, but Jayne's parents were divorced. It was messy and really affected her," Rich said. "She won't divorce me."

Tristan stared at his buddy in disbelief. "So you'll spend the rest of your life being married and miserable?"

Rich stuck out his jaw—a sure sign he wasn't going to listen to reason. "I'll be fine."

What about Jayne? Tristan didn't think she'd be fine. "You have to tell her."

"I don't have to do anything except show up at the church on Saturday."

"Maybe if you talked to her—"

"I'm not talking. And you better not say anything, either."

"Rich—"

His best friend's gaze held his. "You promised me."

"Dude—"

"You always said you had my back," Rich reminded him. "You can't let me down now."

Tristan swore savagely.

Rich smiled in satisfaction, recognizing his capitulation. "These shoes are a little tight. I'm going to see if they have a larger size."

He walked out of the dressing room area and into the main shop.

Unbelievable. Tristan dragged his hand through his hair. Rich needed to listen to him and call the wedding off.

A cellphone rang. The sound came from Rich's dressing room.

Tristan glanced inside. A cellphone sat on top of a pair of board shorts.

You always said you had my back.

Maybe if he had more time he could talk some sense into Rich, but with only three days until the wedding…Tristan couldn't let Rich ruin his life and Jayne's, too.

Promise me you won't.

Tristan couldn't say anything. But maybe he could *do* something.

He looked again at the cellphone. Jayne was calling.

Maybe it was a sign.

Maybe…

Damn, he didn't have much time. Rich could return any minute.

Tristan urgently typed a text message: *Be @ my apt 8 pm for big surprise.*

This was for Rich's own good, Tristan told himself. For his future happiness. And Jayne's, too.

Not wanting to waste another second, he hit "send."

Seven months later, Tristan still believed he'd done the right thing to keep both Rich and Jayne from making the mistake of their lives. But maybe he could have accomplished the same thing in a less cruel way.

He'd hurt Jayne. More than he realized.

Tristan took a left hand turn.

Maybe he could make it up to her.

He'd been less than honest then. He couldn't be less than honest now. "About that surprise—"

"I don't know why I brought it up now." She looked at him with regret.

His stomach clenched. He had to tell her the truth. "There's something—"

"Stop. Please." Her gaze implored his. "What happened with Rich is in the past. That's where I want to leave it. I only want to look forward now. Okay?"

Tristan wanted to tell her the truth, but he also wanted to do what she asked. He sure as hell didn't want to cause her any more pain. The truth would hurt her. He had no doubt about that.

He weighed his options.

Jayne had admitted she was relieved she hadn't married Rich. Maybe how she'd found out the truth about the cheating wasn't that big a deal. Not telling her sure would make things easier for Tristan.

"Okay," he agreed.

She gazed out the passenger window. "This is such a cute neighborhood."

He appreciated her comment—a distraction to bridge the awkwardness. "Yes."

Bungalows and cottages lined the street. A twenty-something woman pushed a baby stroller on the sidewalk while a chocolate Lab trotted next to her. "It's a great location—walking distance to shops and the library."

At least that was what the listing agent had told him when he'd called her yesterday for more information.

"But I don't see any condominiums or townhouses," Jayne said.

He parked in front of an open house sign.

She gasped.

The cottage with a "For Sale" stuck in the overgrown front yard defined the term fixer-upper. The white picket fence had seen better days. The exterior needed paint. The porch railing was splintered and broken.

Uh-oh, Tristan thought. Maybe this hadn't been such a good idea.

Except the price was right, and Jayne was staring at the little house as if it were a big, beautiful castle straight from the pages of a fairytale.

"I don't understand." Her gaze remained fixed on the house. "You want don't want to buy a house."

"No," he admitted. "But you do."

She turned to look at him. With her eyes wide and her nose crinkled she looked oh-so-adorable. "Me?"

All his doubts vanished in that instant. He'd made the right choice bringing her here.

"We're here to look at a house for you, Jayne." Tristan grinned. "Not me."

Standing in the dream-come-true cottage, Jayne ran her fingers along the built-in buffet in the dining room. She would never have expected Tristan MacGregor to take something she associated as bad—a surprise—and turn it into something so good.

"What do you think?" he asked.

"A fresh coat of paint would spruce this right up." Jayne wondered what kind of wood lay underneath the chipped and battered green paint. Going natural might work, too.

"You like the house?"

"Yes." She spoke calmly, considering inside she felt like a kid on a shopping spree in a toy store. She loved everything she'd seen so far, and even knew where the Christmas tree should go, but something kept her from showing her excitement. "The house has lots of potential."

Someone, she realized, not something.

Jayne couldn't fathom how Tristan, of all people, had found this nice little neighborhood in a great location and this quaint fixer-upper—a house that was everything she could have ever hoped to own. It was if he'd peeked inside her heart somehow and turned what he'd seen into reality.

That bothered her. Okay, scared her.

Because Jayne didn't know whether to hit him or hug him.

"Check in here," he said.

She peeked around the corner. "A clawfoot tub."

"Look at the hand-held shower head." He pointed to the tub. "That could make showering interesting."

The last thing Jayne wanted to think about was Tristan in the shower. She glanced around the bathroom. "If I took out the vanity and put in a pedestal sink there would be room for a stall shower."

"That would be a lot of work and expense."

Jayne shrugged. "Not that much, considering everything else that needs to be fixed is cosmetic. Paint, flooring, some trim."

"The house seems priced right."

She nodded.

"So you could afford it."

It wasn't a question. "I..."

She could afford the foreclosed, bank-owned property on her own. No husband required to purchase the charming house.

Imagine and plan all you want. But if you dream of owning a house you should go for it. Now, if you're able.

Her heart bumped. She felt a flutter in her stomach.

But she couldn't. Not really.

Still, the possibility, the temptation, left her conflicted and confused.

Jayne liked everything to go according to plan. She resented Tristan for creating uncertainty. She didn't want—didn't need—that right now.

"I could afford it if I wanted to buy a house on my own. Which I don't," she said. For his sake or hers, she wasn't certain.

"But you could," he stressed.

She wished he would be quiet.

A young married couple glanced into the bathroom and continued to the bedrooms. The pair held hands as they walked, reminding her of everything she'd dreamed of having.

Jayne's chest tightened. "You don't get it. I wanted... I want to be like them."

"Who?" Tristan asked.

"That couple," she whispered. "I want to look and pick out a house with my husband."

"Just see the possibilities, Jayne."

His smile sent an unwelcome burst of heat rushing through her veins. She gritted her teeth.

The platinum blonde realtor hosting the open house ran after the young couple like a hawk looking for prey.

"What possibilities?" Jayne asked.

"Whatever ones you can imagine," he said. "Just because we're looking at a house and you like one doesn't mean I expect you to buy it."

"I know that."

Except she wanted to buy it.

Jayne bit her lip. No, she didn't.

"Lighten up," he encouraged. "You don't always have to be so serious about everything."

She raised her chin. "Says the man who can't commit to an apartment lease."

He laughed.

"Anyway, I'm not always that serious," she added.

He eyed the thick, heavy binder she held.

"You wanted help," Jayne said, in her defense. "I like being prepared, but that doesn't mean I'm not trying to have fun."

"Stop trying." His tone softened. "Let the fun happen."

His words sank in, like rain against dry soil after a long, hot summer.

Hadn't she been telling herself the same thing about relationships? Love would find her when she wasn't looking. The same way it had found Alex, Molly and Serena.

Jayne wet her dry lips.

"I'll help you," he offered.

She eyed him warily. "How?"

"Having fun is my specialty," he said. "You're young, Jayne."

"I'm twenty-eight."

"Young," he reiterated. "I know you want that happily-ever-after, but even you said not now. Someday."

She nodded.

"So stop being so serious and have fun. Explore, look at houses you might want to own, experience, date."

The air whooshed from her lungs. She struggled for a breath. "I'm really not looking—"

"For a relationship," he finished. "Casual dating is different. What's holding you back?"

Nothing. Except Jayne wasn't an explorer. She didn't like new experiences and she'd never casually dated in her life. "I…"

But what she'd done in the past hadn't worked.

She stepped out into the hallway and looked around. Finding this place had shown her what was possible. Not today or tomorrow, but someday.

Maybe if she adopted a more casual attitude toward dating and embraced fun the way Tristan did she would finally find what her friends had found in Las Vegas. She would find love.

Or rather, love would find her.

She straightened. "Nothing is holding me back."

Tristan smiled at her. "Then let me show you how."

Anticipation flew through her like a boomerang. "But you're Rich's—"

"Casual and fun, Jayne," Tristan countered. "Emphasis on the fun."

Fun? With Rich's best man?

With Rich's best friend?

With a man who didn't believe in marriage or happy endings?

That would make him…

Perfect, she realized.

Tristan was actually the perfect person to show her how to have fun. Even date casually. He was the last person she would ever fall for—the last man she could ever have a future with. Her heart would be safe, reserved for the real thing when it found her.

"Casual and fun," she repeated.

"What do you say?" he asked.

Jayne grinned. "Sounds good to me."

CHAPTER SEVEN

TONIGHT was the night. Tristan glanced at Jayne, sitting beside him in the front seat.

This first date would give her a glimpse of the good times ahead. One taste and she would embrace the concept of casual and fun. Embrace him, too.

He'd never had to work this hard for a woman. He was no believer in delayed gratification. But Jayne, with her bright eyes and caring heart and sexy body, was worth the wait and the effort.

Everything tonight would be perfect. He'd made sure by taking a page out of Jayne's playbook and planning ahead. He couldn't wait to see her reaction.

Tristan parked his car at the Loews Coronado Bay Resort, grabbed his camera bag from the back seat and made his way around to the passenger side. He opened Jayne's door. "Don't forget your jacket."

She tossed her jacket over her left forearm and slid out of the car. "I just love Coronado. I lived here when I was six."

Her wide smile that reached all the way to her baby blues hit him right in the solar plexus. He nearly stumbled back. Somehow he managed to close the car door.

He'd wanted her to be pleased with tonight, but his reaction to her caught him off-guard. Then again, an attractive woman could take any man by surprise. He cleared his throat. "You'll have to show me around."

Her eyes gleamed with excitement. "Tonight?"

Seeing her so happy filled him with warmth. Jayne needed this. She needed him.

"Another time." He swung the strap of his camera pack over his shoulder. "I have plans for tonight."

"Plans?" Jayne's nose crinkled. "I thought fun was just supposed to happen."

"Fun can be spontaneous," he explained. "But extra-special fun takes a little planning."

Her mouth quirked. "Extra-special fun, huh?"

"You'll see."

Tristan placed one hand at the small of her back. The palm of his hand fit nicely, comfortably, against her. He led her inside the resort hotel.

A group of men and women in track outfits and with camera cases stood at the front desk. Two men in tuxedos spoke with the concierge. Uniformed bellhops rolled luggage carts.

"Have you been here before?" he asked.

Jayne looked around. "No, this place was a little out of our budget back then. It probably still is."

A grand split staircase with brass railings stood out in the lobby. Chandeliers added an air of elegance. Large windows provided ocean views. But Jayne was the only thing he wanted to look at.

"It's absolutely lovely." She eyed him mischievously. "I think I might like having extra-special fun with you."

Tristan knew without a doubt he'd enjoy it. The thought of the evening ending with more than a goodnight kiss was looking better and better. "You might even find it addictive."

She pursed her glossed lips. "You think?"

Her gaze held his for a long minute. Some connection flowed between them.

Definitely addictive. He couldn't wait to see how it all played out and how those lips of hers tasted. Tristan grinned.

Jayne looked away, almost shyly. "Well, you've definitely got me intrigued."

"Intrigued is good. Not as good as naked."

She stared at a potted palm. "What about nervous?"

Not so good. He raised her chin with his fingertip. "You have nothing to be nervous about. I'm not trying to get you upstairs into a room." Not exactly. Not yet. "Tonight's about having fun. Nothing to worry about, okay?"

She nodded. "You must think I'm—"

"You're you, Jayne," he said softly. "I like being with you."

Gratitude filled her eyes.

Tristan felt an unfamiliar tug on his heart. He straightened. "Remember on the beach hike, when we talked about you playing tourist?" At her nod, he motioned to the marina office. "Tonight we're going to see a different view of San Diego."

"I haven't been on a boat in ages."

She sounded pleased. Good. "What about a gondola?"

"Seriously?"

"I told you fun was my specialty."

"Remind me never to doubt you again."

"I'll them we're here."

In the office, he gave the bottle of champagne in his pack to the desk person. She handed him a receipt for his payment and told him where they could wait.

"We have about fifteen minutes to wait," he told Jayne. "There's an area outside where we can sit."

A clear night sky greeted them. The temperature had dropped. Jayne put on her jacket.

They walked to a patio area by the marina. Italian music played from the sound system. Strands of lights provided a festive glow. A man and woman sat at one of the bistro tables holding hands. They stared into each other's eyes. Tristan didn't blame them. The setting oozed romance.

Romance could be casual and fun. Granted, a gondola ride under the stars was a little over the top, but Jayne deserved it.

He pulled out a chair for her.

She sat. "If I look past all the boats with American flags moored at the dock, we could almost be in Italy."

The couple at the other table kissed. Tristan looked at Jayne.

"A homebody who's been to Italy?" he joked. "Is that possible?"

"Well, it was eighteen years ago," she said. "I was ten."

"Vacation? Or did you live there?"

"Vacation. My dad was stationed in Crete. Or maybe it was Spain. I sometimes mix up all the different places we lived, but I remember our vacation in Italy."

"I would have done anything to been able to travel like you did when I was a kid," he said. "Aspen and St. Martens got old fast."

"No matter where else we lived, my mother always referred to San Diego as home."

"I don't really think of home as a place," Tristan admitted. "It's more a state of mind."

"Too bad we couldn't have traded places when we were kids." She glanced at the other couple, who were still making out. With pink cheeks, she focused on the table's centerpiece, an empty Chianti bottle with a candle stuck in the top. "You must have gone to a lot of trouble to arrange tonight."

She sounded too much like cautious, serious Jayne. Tristan didn't like that. "One telephone call. That's all."

"But the champagne and the boat ride and parking—"

"Before you tell me you want to split the bill, this is my treat." He leaned forward. "You cooked me dinner last week."

"You bought the ice cream."

"If I'd won, you would have bought the ice cream," he countered.

"That's true." She still sounded unconvinced.

"But...?" he prompted.

"But I'm really uncomfortable with you using a credit card to pay for all this," Jayne said in a rush. She looked up miserably. "Any of this, really. I don't want to be a wet blanket, but that takes some of the fun right out of it for me."

"You see financial irresponsibility every day at your job. I get that. I know your mom had it rough, too." Tristan fought the urge to reach across the table and take her hand. "You have to understand, Jayne, I'm not like that. Whether I use credit cards or cash, I am financially responsible. I pay my debts, okay?

She nodded gamely. "Okay."

"I'll have you know I used my debit card to pay for tonight."

She leaned forward. "Really?"

"I swear."

A dazzling smile lit up her entire face. "I'm impressed."

Tristan wondered what she'd look like if he actually paid cash. He would try that next time, because it would make her happy.

"You think you're impressed now—wait until you see the boat."

The gondolier, wearing a traditional striped shirt, dark pants, red sash at his waist and a straw hat adorned with a red ribbon, arrived. He carried an ice bucket with the bottle of champagne chilling and a tray of plump chocolate covered strawberries.

"Ready to depart on your cruise?" the gondolier asked.

"Yes." Jayne rose. "Fun's the name of the game tonight."

Tristan grinned at her enthusiasm. "You're a fast learner."

She winked. "You're a good teacher."

They followed the gondolier to a black gondola tied to a dock on the marina.

Jayne gasped. "It looks like one from Venice."

"They are imported," the gondolier said.

She smiled at Tristan. "You're right. I am impressed."

He bowed. "The evening is only beginning."

The gondolier assisted Jayne from the dock and into the gondola. The man continued holding onto her hand once she was aboard. Maybe he was just being safe, but Tristan didn't like it.

Jayne sat. The gondolier let go. Finally.

Tristan boarded and sat next to Jayne on the padded black bench. The dessert tray, champagne and glasses were set out. Italian music played.

"Help yourself to refreshments." The gondolier handed them each a blanket. "It can get chilly out on the bay."

"Thanks," Tristan said. Cozying up with Jayne sounded like a better way to keep warm.

The overhead lights from the dock shone down. The boat rocked against the deck.

Tristan dealt with the bottle of champagne while Jayne sampled a strawberry.

She sighed in satisfaction. "This is wonderful."

"Enjoy every minute," he said.

"I plan to."

The gondolier pushed off and headed to the canals of Coronado Cays.

"Simply amazing," Jayne said with a hint of wonderment. "And fun. Can't forget the fun."

"I thought you'd enjoy this."

"I love it."

Tristan smiled smugly.

"Let me guess." She studied him with an assessing gaze. "You were the kind of kid who always said 'Told ya so.'"

"Yes," he admitted.

"Then it's a good thing you were an only child."

The calmness and quiet made it seem as if they were the only ones out one the water. Even the gondolier faded into the background.

"Why is that?" he asked.

"Well, if you were the oldest child and always said 'I told you so' your younger siblings would have hated you. If you were the youngest and said it, you would have gotten beaten up by your older brothers and sisters."

"I'm happy I'm an only, then. But you're an only, too," he said. "How do you know what siblings would do?"

"I know because I used to hang out with big families every chance I got."

I would like a big family. Someday.

A family like the Stricklands, Tristan realized. Where kids, grandkids, parents, grandparents, aunts, uncles and cousins all lived within a thirty-mile radius of each other.

Guilt coated his mouth. No, he shouldn't feel guilty. Big family or not, Rich wouldn't have been good for Jayne. "I bet it was nice when you got home to your own room, where it was quiet."

"Yes, but I wouldn't have minded sharing a bedroom, and noise has never really bothered me."

Tristan wouldn't mind sharing her bedroom, either. Until he had to leave town and she found someone who could give her what she really wanted.

Way too serious. Time to lighten the mood. He poured champagne into the glasses and handed one to Jayne.

As bubbles streamed to the top, she raised her glass. "To a wonderful journey."

Tristan raised his glass. "And seeing things from a different view."

He sure was.

The first time he'd seen Jayne she'd blown him away with her natural beauty and smile. Then, when he'd learned who she was, he'd tried to view her strictly as Rich's fiancée. When she'd opened the door to her apartment he'd been shocked by her short haircut and pale face. But now he saw a beautiful woman who'd changed on the inside as much as on the outside.

Tristan tapped his glass against hers. The chime of glass on glass held on the air.

She took a sip. So did he.

The sway of the boat brought the two of them closer on the bench. Her hip pressed against him. Soft and warm. A perfect combination. Tristan liked how that felt—how she felt.

He took a bite from one of the chocolate-covered strawberries. "Delicious."

With an even wider smile on her face, Jayne took another one and bit into it. "Yes, they are."

Her lips parted, then closed around the remaining piece of her strawberry.

Tristan's groin tightened. She was really turning him on, but it was too soon for him to make his move. He didn't want to ruin the evening.

Desperate for a distraction, for distance, he removed his camera from his bag and put on a lens.

He would be an impartial observer. He was better at that than being a participant.

Turning, he took a picture of the gondolier, who stood behind them.

"And so it begins," Jayne said.

He focused on her. "Smile."

She looked over the top of her glass and stuck her tongue out.

"Please."

"Just having a little fun." Jayne smiled. "Cheese."

He hit the shutter button.

One photo opportunity after another appeared, and though taking pictures helped, nothing around him could compete with the beautiful subject seated next to him.

"You know," she said finally, "this really isn't fair."

Confused, he looked at her. "What's not fair?"

"I'm here in this brand-new fun zone," she clarified. "But you're still in your comfort zone."

"My comfort zone?"

"Behind the camera."

He stiffened. "It's my job."

She raised a brow. "Are you working tonight?"

Okay, she had a point. Tristan put the camera away. "Sorry."

She smiled. "You're forgiven."

The gondola floated by multi-million-dollar bayfront homes. Lights illuminated the balconies and patios. A few residents waved from their terraces.

"Look at those houses." Awe filled Jayne's voice. "I wonder what it would be like to live in an expensive home like that."

He knew, because his parents owned a house like that. It had never brought them happiness. "Lonely," he said before he thought.

Her eyes glowed with moonlight or compassion. He wasn't sure which. "Are you speaking from experience?" she asked.

He shrugged, his hands itching to take up his camera again. But under that soft, observant gaze he didn't dare.

"My folks have a big house," he admitted. "Too big, with just the three of us rattling inside."

"If I had a house…" She stared at the house they were passing—a two-story McMansion.

"Tell me."

She got a wistful look in her eyes. "I'd invite friends over all the time. I'd cook big meals. And at Christmas I'd have everyone I know over and the biggest Christmas tree that would fit in the living room."

That sounded pretty good to him. But when was the last time he'd been home for Christmas? He downed the rest of his champagne. "You're not going to tell me you didn't have a Christmas tree."

She flushed. "I always have a tree. But there have been a few times I've ended up on my own for the holidays."

"This year?"

She nodded. "I've always wished I lived in a house where I had enough room to invite people over for dinner or get-togethers."

"You live in a house now."

A thoughtful expression formed on her face. "I do, don't I? Molly's house is bigger than my studio apartment was, so maybe I will do that this year."

"Forget maybe," he encouraged. "Make it this year."

A part of him wanted to buy that little cottage for her as a present, even though he doubted she would accept it.

"Nothing should stop you from making that dream—any dream—a reality," he added.

"Well, first I need to learn how to cook a turkey."

Women didn't usually talk about things like this with him. The images she painted with her words appealed to him on a gut level. Something he would have never expected, given how holidays had been a sore point with Emma. He'd had no clue how to respond to his ex-wife then or to Jayne now.

"If guys can barbecue or deep-fry a turkey, I'm sure you'll have no problem," he said finally. Weak, but what else could he say?

Jayne made a face. "Deep-fried turkey sounds...I don't know...wrong."

"Ever tried a deep-fried Twinkie?"

"Uh, no."

"We'll have to add that to our list."

"List?" she asked.

"Of fun things to do."

She smiled. "Don't forget the tour of Coronado."

He tapped his head. "Already there."

The gondola made its way through the inlets and canals of the cay.

The two sat in comfortable silence, taking in the views. One by one the remaining strawberries disappeared from the tray, as did the champagne in the bottle.

Words weren't necessary. Neither were pictures.

The gondola made its way back to the resort.

Across the water of Coronado Bay, the lights of downtown San Diego glimmered.

He placed his arm around Jayne. She settled closer against him.

As a new song played, the gondolier sang in Italian. A love song, if Tristan's translation skills were correct.

"I've never been serenaded before." Jayne leaned closer against him. "Everything is just…perfect."

He'd planned on perfection. What he couldn't have planned for was the way she made him feel. The smell of her shampoo filled his nostrils. The softness pressing against him heated his blood. He wondered if she'd taste like champagne or chocolate strawberries or a combo of the two.

"I wish this didn't have to end," she said.

He knew exactly how she felt. There was no other place he wanted to be. No person he'd rather be with. "It doesn't have to end."

A part of him wasn't thinking only about tonight.

She looked up at him with a question in her eyes. Her lips parted as if to speak.

Tristan didn't give her the chance. He captured her mouth with his.

Sweet. Soft. Sexy.

She tasted like chocolate and wine and something else. Something warm and feminine. Jayne.

This was what he'd been waiting for since that first day he'd seen her in the Rose Garden. He increased the pressure of his mouth against hers.

She returned his kiss with the same hunger he felt, the same need. Her eagerness let him know she was into this as much as he was, and he wanted more.

He knew the gondolier was behind them, but Tristan didn't care.

He pulled her even closer to him. She went willingly, her breasts crushed against his chest. She buried her fingers in his hair.

Heat exploded, pulsing through his veins.

His tongue explored, tasted, and tangled with hers.

Her kiss consumed him, overloading his senses with sensation.

His heart jolted.

A sense of urgency drove him. Desire intensified. Need built within him.

He didn't just want her. He needed her. In a way he'd never needed anyone or anything before.

Warning bells sounded in his brain. Red lights flashed before his closed eyes.

The gondolier. They weren't alone.

Tristan dragged his lips from hers.

He stared at her flushed cheeks and her swollen lips. Her ragged breathing matched his own. He'd bet the fire in her eyes did, too.

A good thing they *hadn't* been alone.

Tristan was supposed to keep things light. He raked his hand through his hair. Fun and casual, remember?

But he was ready to take Jayne to bed and never let her go.

Not so casual. Not by a long shot.

Tristan reached for his camera and took more pictures. A lot more pictures.

She gave him a *what-are-you-doing?* look, but didn't say anything.

What could she say with the gondolier right there?

Tristan couldn't believe he'd gotten so caught up in kissing Jayne with an audience. He couldn't believe he'd lost control of his own feelings like that.

The gondola returned to the marina.

After tipping the gondolier, Tristan stood on the dock. No way would he allow the other guy to help Jayne off the boat. He extended his arm. Her hand clasped with his.

Her touch sent a burst of heat shooting up his arm.

Chemistry he understood, but that kiss had gone deeper than physical attraction. He didn't do deeper. He didn't even do deep.

He knew he could have fun with Jayne, but he didn't know if being casual with her was possible. He wanted it to be, but after that rock-his-world kiss he had doubts. Serious doubts.

When he'd married he hadn't had a clue what Emma had wanted from him.

But he knew exactly what Jayne wanted. What she needed. And she deserved more than he was willing to offer. Especially after what Rich had done to her.

Jayne moved carefully, with purposeful footing, until she stood on the dock. She needed to feel safe, secure. He knew that. Yet.

She looked up at Tristan. Her face was mere inches from his.

The urge to kiss her again was strong. If things had been different, if *they* had been different, he would have made his move now. But his need to protect her, to preserve his own life, made him shove his hands in his pockets and rock back on his heels. "What did you think?"

"I enjoyed the gondola ride. I liked…everything."

The kiss. The closeness.

"So did I," he said honestly.

She pulled her hand from his. "But—"

He stiffened. He hadn't been expecting her not to like any of this.

"I think I may have enjoyed myself too much. I don't want to overdose on fun my first time out."

Strange, but he actually agreed with her. "Wise girl."

Too smart for him. Too kind and genuine and open.

She bit her lip. "Maybe we should postpone our next outing."

Tristan felt an odd mix of relief and disappointment. The whole atmosphere had changed with that kiss. He didn't like it, but he didn't know how to make things go back to the way they'd been. Truth was, he needed some distance himself. "The timing couldn't be any better for postponing."

"Why is that?" she asked.

He thought about the calls he hadn't returned. All because he hadn't felt like leaving town so soon. Okay, leaving Jayne. "I've got a new assignment."

Her gaze jerked up to meet his. Lincs creased her forehead. Her eyes clouded. Tristan hated how the serious Jayne could take over so quickly and completely.

"Where?" she asked.

"Central America."

CHAPTER EIGHT

Two weeks later, Jayne sat on a log at the dog park, with a silent cellphone at her ear, waiting for Molly to get back on the line. Jayne whistled to Duke and Sadie, a blue-eyed Australian Shepherd from the dog agility class, who were exploring the opposite side of the grassy fenced field. The two dogs sprinted back to her.

Jayne wished she felt as carefree and playful as the dogs, but ever since Tristan had left she'd been feeling a little...off. Oh, she hadn't retreated into the house like her mother had used to do when her father went away, and the way Jayne had done after the breakup with Rich. This time she had gone out—and even made new friends. But she couldn't stop thinking about Tristan and his kiss, a kiss that had stolen her breath and made her rethink...well, everything.

That ride on the gondola with him had opened her up to so many different possibilities—ones she'd never imagined. She felt as if her world had been turned upside down, but she had no idea how to turn it right side up again.

Truth was, Jayne wasn't sure she wanted to.

"I'm back," Molly announced.

Jayne adjusted the cellphone at her ear.

"Sorry for keeping you waiting like that." Molly's voice came across so clear, as if she were only across town instead of in another state. "Linc had a question from the contractor about the new house that needed answering right away."

"You'll be back in San Diego before you know it."

"I can't wait," her former roommate said. "Though you won't recognize me. I'm huge. I'm sure people think I'm having twins."

Molly sounded as if she was smiling. That made Jayne happy. "I saw your picture on Facebook. You look beautiful."

"Thanks." Molly laughed. "But I swear I've grown out another foot since Linc took that photo. You need to come here and see my gigantic stomach for yourself. I miss you, Jayne. Serena and Alex would love to see you, too."

The invitation hung in the air. Jayne swallowed.

"I miss you, too." She watched the dogs chase a bird. "I'll come soon."

"Before the baby arrives?"

The hope in Molly's voice pulled at Jayne's heart. "Yes. I'm sorry I haven't come sooner. I got stuck in at rut and didn't feel like doing much. But not any longer."

"What's changed?" Molly asked.

"Tristan." Jayne hoped he was well. Safe. Happy. "Though he's gone now."

"Gone? Where?"

She pressed her lips together to keep from sighing. "Central America."

"You miss him?"

Her friend knew her too well. "I do, which is really silly."

"Why silly?"

"One date and one kiss don't mean anything."

"Not usually. But this was one very romantic date and one totally toe-curling kiss," Molly reassured her. "Besides, you've spent more time than that together."

"We're just having fun," Jayne protested weakly. Tristan's kiss had made her lips throb, her heart go pitter-pat and her mind think way too serious thoughts. She'd felt herself falling hard and fast. She'd wanted—no—needed to pull back. She had to remind herself what spending time with Tristan was all about. And what it *wasn't* about—a potential long-term relationship.

"Tristan says…" She stopped.

"What?"

"He thinks I need to get out more. Let go more. Have more fun."

"Mmm. Sounds exciting."

It was.

"Maybe too exciting," Jayne admitted. "I've never been a risk taker."

"True, but is Tristan changing your mind?"

"No, I told you—we're just… I stopped looking for love after Rich."

"Be careful," Molly cautioned. "In my experience, that's when love finds you."

"I thought about that," Jayne said. "The way you and Linc got together. Alex and Wyatt. Serena and Jonas, too."

"And now you and Tristan?" The concern in Molly's voice was unmistakable. "Are things more serious than you're letting on?"

"Definitely not serious." Jayne hastened to reassure her. "Okay, I admit I imagined the two of us living in that cute fixer-upper cottage he took me to, even though he'd prefer living in a beachfront condo. But daydreaming is a long way from reality. I can fantasize with the best of them, but there's no way I can delude myself into thinking a relationship with him could ever work."

"Just remember," Molly said gently, "even if you think it couldn't be him you don't always get a lot of choice when Cupid shoots his arrow."

"Cupid better aim elsewhere, because I know it's not Tristan."

"You sound so certain."

"I am." Jayne kept an eye on the dogs. "Look at Tristan's job. He travels all over the world to take photographs. When he's not working he still likes to globetrot. I hate traveling."

"You hated living in so many different places," Molly countered. "You haven't really traveled in years."

"He'd still be gone all the time. It would be just like my parents. I could never be happy in a marriage like that."

"No, you couldn't," Molly agreed.

"Besides, even mentioning marriage is a moot point. Tristan docsn't want to gct marricd again."

"You've put some thought into this." Molly sounded amused.

"A little. And I keep coming to the same conclusion. A relationship is out of the question."

"Does Rich have anything to do with this?"

"No," Jayne said certainly. "I'm so over Rich."

"I meant because Tristan is Rich's friend."

"Oh. Maybe at first."

"Because, as much as I hate to see you rush into anything, being Rich's friend doesn't mean Tristan's anything like him."

"I know," Jayne admitted. "But I'm still me."

"Are you sure about that?" Molly asked. "I haven't seen you in a while. For all I know this could be a rebound or a transition relationship after Rich. You and Tristan do sound very different, but he seems to make you happy—happier than you've sounded in months. That's not a bad thing, Jayne."

"Being with him does make me happy." She'd had so much fun and excitement. Except everything he made her feel was the polar opposite of what she'd been craving all these years. She'd believed stability and commitment would make her happy. Yet she couldn't deny the happiness she felt with Tristan. "I guess I just never expected to feel this way with him."

"You never do," Molly admitted. "But promise me you won't do anything rash where Tristan's concerned. Doing that can have life-altering consequences."

Jayne thought about Molly's decision to spend the night with a total stranger when they were in Las Vegas. "Things worked out great for you."

"That's because Linc and I love each other. Things could have turned out very differently," she cautioned. "You've been through so much already. I don't want you to do something that will end up hurting you."

"I promise, Moll." Jayne appreciated her friend's concern. The two dogs stared at her with expectant gleams in their eyes. "I just need to figure out a few things. That's all"

"Uh-oh. That doesn't sound like the Jayne Cavendish I know." Worry filled Molly's voice. "You've always known exactly what you want."

Jayne tossed each dog a treat. "I know."

That was the problem. The one she'd been dealing with ever since the night of the gondola ride.

Thanks to Tristan MacGregor, she no longer knew what she wanted. The future she'd dreamed about wasn't as clear.

And that scared her more than anything.

Where was Jayne?

As Tristan sat on Mrs. Whitcomb's porch, frustration gnawed at him. Two weeks away from Jayne hadn't given him the distance he'd wanted, but it had clarified his feelings for her.

He and Jayne wanted different things from life, but not every relationship had to end up at the altar. He didn't have to be her Mr. Right. He could be her Mr. Right *Now*.

"Thanks for letting me wait here for Jayne," Tristan said.

"I enjoy the company." Mrs. Whitcomb raised her carafe of coffee. "Would you like more to drink?"

The coffee was strong enough to strip barnacles from the bottom of a boat. One cup would probably keep him awake all night. "Thanks, but I still have some left."

He appreciated the neighborly hospitality and the conversation, but impatience was making it harder for him to sit still. He glanced at his watch. "Jayne's out kind of late for a work night."

"You never know what kind of traffic you'll hit these days. She and Duke will be home soon." Mrs. Whitcomb motioned to the mountainous plate of chocolate chip and oatmeal raisin cookies. "Have more cookies."

"I will." Tristan took three. "I spent the last two weeks eating random meals. A few were non-edible, too."

"Lou would have liked you. He had an adventurous soul, too."

The affection in Mrs. Whitcomb's voice for her late husband made Tristan believe they were one of the rare couples that had found something special. The vast majority wasn't so lucky.

He'd spent his adulthood exploring the unknown. He'd never backed down from a challenge no matter what the risk—sometimes to life and limb. He'd thought he knew what relationships were about, but nothing had prepared him for this. For Jayne. She was both unknown and a risk, but he was ready for both.

He hoped she would accept what he was offering.

A dark four-door sedan with tinted windows pulled to the curb. The non-descript car reminded him of a vehicle from a detective show on television.

The police? Jayne?

His concern quadrupled. Tristan stood.

Mrs. Whitcomb used the porch rail to help her stand. "See—I told you they would be home soon."

They?

A few seconds later Jayne got out of the car, placed a black and white dog with butterfly ears and an ostrich plume tail on the ground and shut the passenger door.

His heart beat faster.

He'd taken the J-peg files of her with him on his assignment, but photos couldn't capture the essence of Jayne. Or the way her jeans cupped her bottom perfectly.

Another car door slammed.

A man, probably about his age, walked around the front of the car to the sidewalk where Jayne waited. Every one of Tristan's muscles tensed. A blue-eyed dog followed at the strange guy's heels. With his casually styled blond hair, wrinkled navy polo shirt and khaki shorts, he looked an awfully lot like Rich. Except for that carefully nondescript car.

Jayne's type?

Tristan set his jaw. "Who's that?"

"Kenny... I can't remember his last name. He attends Duke's dog agility class." Mrs. Whitcomb said. "He had an errand to run, so Jayne offered to take the dogs to the park. I think Duke has a crush on Kenny's dog Sadie."

Jayne laughed at something the guy said.

Tristan thought Sadie's owner had a crush on Jayne. He clenched his hands.

Mrs. Whitcomb sighed. "The two of them look so good together."

The guy touched the small of Jayne's back. The possessive touch had Tristan ready to hurdle the porch rail and tackle Kenny head-on.

"That guy does *not* look good with Jayne."

"I was talking about the dogs."

Tristan charged down the steps. He positioned himself in front of Mrs. Whitcomb's porch. No way could Jayne miss seeing him or Kenny get around him.

Duke scampered ahead of them. The sissy dog barked at Tristan. He had to be careful not to step on the damn thing.

Jayne looked toward the house.

Damn, she was gorgeous. Not just her face and her body, but her heart.

He knew the minute she saw him. Her smile widened and spread all the way to her eyes.

His breath caught in his throat.

"Tristan." Jayne quickened her steps, and he met her halfway down the front walk. "You're back."

"I am." He sized up the blond guy and nodded in acknowledgment. "Tristan MacGregor."

"Kenny Robertson," the other man introduced himself. He looked from Tristan, to Mrs. Whitcomb on the porch, to Jayne, obviously waiting for an explanation.

Let him wonder, Tristan thought.

"Tristan's a friend of mine," Jayne said.

The word "friend" grated like fingernails against chalkboard. Tristan had thought that kiss on the gondola had made it clear he wanted to be more than friends. Guess not.

She continued. "He's a photojournalist and has been out of the country on an assignment."

Kenny's stance relaxed slightly. He offered his hand. "Nice to meet a friend of Jayne's."

Tristan bared his teeth in a smile, feeling like a dog with a bone. He tightened his grip. Kenny did the same.

Jayne's brow creased as she apparently picked up on the unspoken tension. "Tristan is the one who told me to stop being such a homebody and get out of the house more."

"Right before he left the country?" Kenny asked.

"I was only gone two weeks," Tristan said.

"Well, it's been a great two weeks." The guy made puppy eyes at Jayne. "Jayne is an amazing social director."

Tristan raised his eyebrows. "Social director?"

She nodded, her cheeks pink with enthusiasm. Or maybe embarrassment. "For the dog agility class. I've been organizing get-togethers and events for people outside of class."

"You'd be good at that," Tristan said.

"Jayne's great at it," Kenny said.

The color on her cheeks deepened. "It's given me something to do."

"I have something to do. It's past Duke's bedtime," Mrs. Whitcomb announced. "We're going to call it a night."

"I'd better get going, too." Kenny rubbed Sadie's head. "Work tomorrow."

"Me, too," Jayne said.

Tristan stood his ground. He wasn't going anywhere. "Nice to meet you, Kenny."

The guy nodded. "See you at the next agility class, Jayne. Let me know if you want to carpool again."

Carpool? Tristan fought the urge to grimace. Saving gas money would appeal to Jayne. The guy probably knew it and was trying to earn bonus points.

"I will," she said.

After a chorus of goodnights, Tristan was finally alone with Jayne. About time. "Come with me to my car. I have to get something out of the trunk."

She fell into step next to him.

"So you got out of the house?" he said.

"I've decided I'm not quite the homebody I thought I was." Her smile dazzled Tristan. "Tonight Molly invited to me to visit Las Vegas again, and this time I said yes."

"Impressive."

Pride gleamed in her eyes. "It's a step in the right direction."

"I'd say you've taken a few steps forward." He pulled out the bag that contained the present he'd purchased for her on his trip. "Traveling to Vegas. Becoming a social director."

"Yes, you're right." Her confidence appealed to him. "I've enjoyed meeting some new people. Dog people, but they're very nice."

"Like Kenny?"

She nodded. "Making new friends has been good."

That word again. This time applied to Kenny. Tristan didn't mind so much. He opened the trunk.

"So good, in fact," she continued, "I've decided not to get a roommate."

Tristan closed his trunk. He was fine with her decision. It would make it easier for her to move out of the bungalow if she bought a place of her own. "You sound sure about that."

"I am pretty sure," she said. "So when did you get back?"

"Today. I wanted to see you right away." He stared into her warm, clear eyes. "I missed you, Jayne."

"I missed you, too."

"Good."

"I'm not so sure."

Tristan realized she wasn't smiling. He noticed Mrs. Whitcomb peeking out her window. "Why don't we talk about this inside?"

Jayne nodded, and he followed her into the house.

He set the bag on the coffee table. "Tell me what you're not sure about."

She looked up, down, around. Everywhere but at him.

Not a good sign.

He had a pretty good idea what the problem was. "It's me?"

Her startled gaze met his. "It's not you. It's me."

That caught him off guard. "You?"

Jayne nodded, her eyes clouded with unease. She wrung her hands. "After what happened with Rich I don't trust my judgment when it comes to relationships. Men."

Damn. Tristan wanted to go back and make things right. "It's not your fault Rich wasn't ready for marriage."

Lines creased her forehead. "But I thought… He said… I was so sure…"

"This is a completely different situation." Tristan wanted to take away her uncertainty. "Rich didn't know what he wanted. I've been honest with you from the beginning about what I want and don't want."

"You have."

"You know what you need to know about me," Tristan said firmly.

Her anxious face looked up at him. "Do I?"

A tense silence filled the living room.

He thought about his role in her and Rich's breakup. Telling her the truth would only make her mistrust herself more. Yet Tristan had learned from his first marriage the importance of honesty in a relationship if you wanted to share a future.

"Let's talk about what happened with Rich."

"Let's not," Jayne said without any hesitation. "The past is in the past, remember? I don't need to talk about it. I don't want to talk about it."

This wasn't the first time she'd talked about putting the past behind her. "Fine."

What else could he say? Do?

Nothing good would come of the discussion anyway. Honesty was important, but it wouldn't change anything between them. He and Jayne weren't looking to share a future. They didn't want the same future.

Happily-right-now.

That was all Tristan could offer Jayne.

He hoped it would be enough for her.

Tristan picked up the bag from the table and handed it to her. "I brought you something from Honduras."

"The bowl and candlesticks are lovely." Warmth flowed through Jayne as she sat at the kitchen table with Tristan. The black and white handcrafted Lenca Pottery was her new centerpiece. "Thank you."

Tristan placed his spoon in his ice cream bowl. "I thought they might come in handy when you have people over for those big dinners you mentioned."

The gift pleased Jayne, but confused her, too. "You seem to know me pretty well."

He shrugged. "I saw them in a window and thought of you."

His present symbolized hearth and home, gatherings of family and friends. All the things he claimed not to want or care about. "They're perfect."

Tristan's mouth curved into an easy smile. His lips looked soft and welcoming, the kind meant for long, slow, hot kisses. The kind of kisses he gave.

She felt a flutter in her chest. "You'll have to come to one of my dinners."

"Just tell me when."

Jayne reached out and touched one of the matching candlesticks with her fingertips.

"In case you were wondering—" his eyes twinkled with amusement "—I paid cash. You must be rubbing off on me."

His lighthearted tone teased, but his words sparked a connection. Jayne could sense something drawing them together as if they were magnets. Perhaps opposites did attract.

"That makes them even more special," she said. "I wish I had something to give you."

The amusement sharpened. "You gave me ice cream."

"I definitely got the better end of the deal."

Tristan laughed. "You could give me a proper welcome home."

Before she could respond, he'd scooted his chair closer. He wrapped his arms around her in a comfortable embrace.

An intoxicating aroma of soap and male surrounded her.

A sigh threatened to escape.

Her hands splayed over his back. Underneath the fabric of his button-down shirt she felt muscular ridges against her palms and fingers.

Welcome home had never felt so good.

Jayne felt right at home. Safe. Secure. A way she hadn't felt in months. A way she'd never expected to feel with Tristan.

Maybe she did know all she needed to know about him.

She knew Tristan didn't believe in forever, but he made her happy. Molly was right about that. He'd also brought fun back into Jayne's life. Excitement, too. Nothing wrong with that.

He could give her more of that.

She knew better than to expect anything else from him. She wouldn't allow herself to get carried away like she had before.

She couldn't.

Because Tristan wanted fun, not forever.

And that, Jayne realized, was okay with her for now.

His warm breath fanned her neck. "It's good to see you."

Her pulse quickened. "Yes. I mean I'm pleased to see you, not me."

"I know what you mean." Tristan pulled her closer. "It feels even better to hold you."

Her chest pressed against his. So solid and strong. The pounding of his heart matched her own. "Uh-huh."

She glanced up to find him gazing down at her. His eyes so intent. His lips so close.

Her mouth went dry.

He was going to kiss her. Heaven help her, she wanted him to kiss her.

Tristan lowered his mouth to hers until their lips touched. A spark arced through her from the point of contact.

She gasped, but he didn't back away. Nor did she.

She closed her eyes and let sensation take over. The same way she had on the gondola. Only this time they were alone. There was no one serenading them, no one watching them. She liked this much better.

He moved his lips against hers, softly and deliberately, testing and tasting.

Hot ice cream. An oxymoron, yes, but that was what Tristan's kiss tasted like tonight, and it would be her new favorite flavor.

Eager for more, she leaned into him.

His lips moved expertly over hers. She found a sense of belonging, the home she'd always dreamed about. His jean-clad leg pressed into her. His tongue explored and danced with hers. Her insides hummed.

Tristan kissed her so thoroughly, so completely.

She wanted him to keep kissing her. She needed him to keep kissing her.

Slowly he drew the kiss to an end and sat back.

Her lips sizzled.

She wished the kiss hadn't ended.

Jayne didn't know how long they sat at the table staring at each other. He looked the way she felt.

Happy. Turned-on. Hungry for more.

She took a deep breath. "So…"

"So let's go to Vegas."

She stared at him, stunned. Images of the chapel where Serena had eloped and the hotel where Molly had spent the night swirled through Jayne's mind. "Vegas?"

He nodded. "You said you were going. Let's go together. You can see your friends. They can meet me and tell you how great I am for you."

She laughed, relieved to know what he was thinking, but a tad disappointed, too. "You think that's what they'll say?"

"Yep."

His confidence didn't surprise her. She wished some of it would rub off on her. "You're really up for this?"

"I really am," he said, without the slightest hesitation. "Call Molly and see if this weekend works."

That sounded dangerous and wild and so appealing—because Jayne hadn't done anything like that since saying yes to Rich's marriage proposal after only a month of dating. She wanted to know that things could work out better than her ill-fated engagement. "Just like that?"

"Yes, Jayne," Tristan said.

The way he said her name made her feel all tingly. Her tummy felt like a butterfly house.

Promise me you won't do anything rash where Tristan's concerned.

Jayne remembered Molly's words as well as the fun her three friends had had in Vegas.

Uh-oh. A weekend out of town in a place known as Sin City. They would spend a night or two in a hotel. Tristan might assume—would probably assume—that meant staying in the same room and sharing the same...

Her insides quivered. "I—"

"What's wrong?"

She raised her chin. "Why do you think anything's wrong?"

He touched her forehead with his fingertip. "These little lines show up when you're either thinking or getting serious about something."

His perception disturbed her. "I didn't know that."

"So tell me what's on your mind."

Blurting the word "sex" might not be the best move. She needed to figure out a subtle way to broach the subject. "I'm not sure I'm ready for that much fun."

"I'm not following you."

She thought about the queen-sized bed in her bedroom. They didn't have to fly to Vegas to... "I don't believe in casual sex."

The words rushed out like the overspill from a floodgate. *Subtle, Jayne. Real subtle.*

"What I mean is there's no one else I'd rather go to Vegas with, but I'm not... I would prefer it if we had separate beds. Or rooms. I like you. A lot. And I really like kissing you. But I don't want to rush into anything. Or do something we might regret. I understand if you're disappointed and don't want to go now."

Feeling like an old-fashioned maiden, she stared at the centerpiece he'd given to her. Maybe she should forget the entire thing, get a dog, and resign herself to being single the rest of her life.

"Two rooms are fine, Jayne," he said gently. "There are lots of ways for us to have fun that have nothing to do with sex."

Her gaze met his in gratitude. "Thank you."

"So Vegas is a go?"

The anticipation in his voice buzzed through her. Jayne would love to hear what her friends thought of Tristan, too, though she thought they might warn her off him. "It's a go."

His smile crinkled the corners of his eyes, and her breath caught in her throat. "You get in touch with your friends and see if this weekend works for them. If not, find dates that do. Then I'll make all the travel arrangements. This trip is on me."

"That's really generous of you, but Alex's husband Wyatt owns a hotel. I'm sure we can get rooms—"

"Let me take care of it, Jayne."

"But airfare and a hotel," she countered. "It's going to be expensive."

"I can afford it."

She started to speak, then stopped. She nibbled her lip.

Shut up, Jayne. Shut up.

But her training and her conscience wouldn't let her stay quiet. "Are you sure? Because a lot of people feel that using credit—"

"Jayne." He scooted his chair closer. He took her hands in his strong, reassuring clasp. "I can afford it."

"If you were super-rich you could."

He nodded.

Oh, man. She almost slid off her chair.

"My dad has a plane we can use, too."

All the pieces fell together. Paying off his credit card each month. Working for his father. Growing up in a big house. Traveling the globe to take photographs.

He was serious. He *was* rich. Really rich.

Even if he didn't wear designer clothing or drive a flashy car or live...

She sighed. "I'm an idiot."

"No, you're not."

"We're even more different than I thought." Tristan had grown up with a silver spoon. Hers had been plastic. "And here I was, giving you financial advice."

He squeezed her hand reassuringly. "You gave me very good advice that I needed to hear."

Jayne appreciated his words, and the sincerity in his eyes. She smiled. "Well, you're making sure I have the fun I need."

"We're a good team."

She nodded. Team, not couple. She just had to remember that.

CHAPTER NINE

THURSDAY night, Tristan sat in a local sports bar, waiting for Rich. A Los Angeles Lakers basketball game played on the large screen television.

The game couldn't hold his attention.

Face it, not much had held his attention this past week.

Tomorrow he was leaving for Vegas with Jayne.

He took a swig from his pint of beer.

He wanted her friends to give him the thumbs-up. Maybe then Jayne would trust her own judgment. Maybe she would trust *him*. And maybe she would want them to get…closer.

A lot closer.

He'd asked her out tonight, but she had the dog agility class with Duke. Duke and Kenny. So Tristan had accepted Rich's invitation to hang out and watch the game. They hadn't talked in weeks. It was time—past time—to come clean to his oldest friend about seeing Jayne.

"Chicken wings and fries." Rich put the food on the table and sat across from Tristan. "Seems like old times. The only things missing are a couple of beautiful babes checking us out."

Unease inched down Tristan's spine. He reached for a couple of fries. "How's the wedding planning going?"

"Okay, I guess."

A feeling of *déjà vu* washed over him. Not again. "You met someone?"

Rich nodded.

Damn. "I'm not going down this road with you again, bud."

Rich squared his shoulders. "It's different this time. She's different."

Annoyance flared. "I don't care if she's a *Sports Illustrated* swimsuit model. You can't do this again."

"I haven't done anything."

Yet. The unspoken word floated between them.

"But you want to," Tristan said.

"Hell, yeah," Rich admitted. "She's hot."

"You said the same thing about Deidre. Smokin' was your exact word."

Rich shrugged.

"Don't hurt Deidre the way you hurt Jayne."

"You played a part in hurting Jayne, too, dude."

"But I wasn't the one screwing around on my fiancée," Tristan ripped out the words. "You messed with her heart and her confidence."

"I would have never proposed if she would have just slept with me."

"Huh?"

"Jayne doesn't believe in casual sex. I thought if we were engaged she would finally give in and say yes."

Every single one of Tristan's muscles tensed. "You asked Jayne to marry you to get her in the sack?"

Rich shrugged and flashed his *hey-buddy* grin. "It seemed like a good idea at the time."

Tristan shook his head. "For you, maybe."

"Well, it didn't work out like I planned," Rich admitted. "She wanted to wait until our wedding night to do the deed."

That explained the short engagement. "It was still a jerk move."

Rich downed the remainder of his beer while Tristan's gut churned.

Poor Jayne. While she'd been planning her wedding and dreaming of her happily-ever-after, Rich had been thinking only of having sex with her.

Tristan shifted uncomfortably, reminded of his own plans for the weekend. He was hoping for the chance to sweep Jayne off her feet and into bed himself. But at least he wasn't dangling the together-forever carrot in front of her the way Rich had.

Images of Jayne sprang into Tristan's mind. The excitement on her face at the cottage. The wistful yearning in her voice on the gondola ride. The passion in her eyes right before he'd kissed her.

What the hell was he thinking?

"I don't want to see you make another mistake, Rich. Marriage is a serious business." The words sounded hollow to Tristan. He reached for more fries. "My marriage failed because I wasn't ready then. You're not ready now."

Rich pressed his lips together.

"I'm not going to be there to watch your back this time," Tristan said. "Break it off with Deidre the way you should have with Jayne."

"I'll think about it."

The Lakers scored a three-point shot. The crowd in the bar cheered.

"Looks like they could go all the way this year," Rich said. "Wanna try to score tickets to a game this weekend?"

"I'll be in Vegas."

"Without me?"

Tristan shrugged.

"There's gotta be a woman involved," Rich said. "Who is she?"

This was the moment of truth. No woman had ever come before their friendship, let alone threatened it. Tristan inhaled slowly, as if waiting an extra five seconds to answer would make a difference.

"Jayne," he said finally. "We're leaving tomorrow."

Rich's mouth gaped. "*My* Jayne?"

"She hasn't been yours for a while."

"Is this payback for when I dated Julia Sommers after she broke up with you?"

Julia had been the captain of the cheer team, a pretty, ditzy blonde who'd ended up dating the entire basketball team. Tristan had forgotten about her until now. "That was back in high school, bud."

Rich studied him. "But you don't like Jayne."

"I have always liked her, but I knew better than to put the moves on my best friend's fiancée."

"Is it serious?"

Tristan hesitated before answering.

"Who am I kidding?" Rich said before Tristan could answer. "You don't do serious."

The words bristled, but a cold knot formed in the pit of his stomach at the truth behind them.

Tristan didn't do serious.

He knew it. Rich knew it. And so did Jayne.

Inside the suite at McKendrick's, Tristan flipped a ten to the bellman clad in a hunter green uniform with gold trim.

"Thank you, sir. Please let me know if you need anything else." The attendant pocketed the bill with a smile. "Enjoy your stay at McKendrick's."

The bellman left, closing the door behind him.

Tristan looked at the two bags sitting next to each other on the living room floor. Soon the bags would be carried into separate bedrooms. Not ideal, but better than the thought of them in completely different hotel rooms. Or back in San Diego.

"Wow, this place is so huge." Jayne pirouetted like a ballerina across the carpet.

Seeing her so carefree and happy brought a grin to his face. She was definitely embracing the concept of having fun.

As she spun, the hem of her little black dress clung to her thighs and hips, making her curves and already long legs seem almost criminal. Her strappy sandals only added to the alluring picture. His hands itched for his camera, and for her.

He was determined not to take advantage of her the way Rich had. Tristan wasn't hiding behind a careless marriage proposal. Jayne knew exactly where he stood when it came to relationships. He'd been open and honest. If she was game for more fun, then so was he.

She stopped twirling and faced him, her cheeks flushed and her eyes sparkling.

Jayne was—in a word—stunning. Forget about traveling not appealing to her. Tristan had never seen her so radiant, so animated before. He wanted to show her the amazing sights he'd seen all over the world. He wanted to kiss her on all seven continents, across every time zone.

She trailed her fingertips along the back of an elegantly upholstered chair. "I've never stayed in such a luxurious room before."

Tristan glanced around. It was nice as far as hotels went.

"I guess you must be used to nice hotels like this," she added.

He shrugged. "I've stayed in some pretty crappy places on assignment, especially when I was first starting out."

Jayne drew her brows together. "But I thought you had money."

"I didn't gain access to my trust fund until I turned thirty," he explained. "Now that I have, I've continued to support myself. But I remember being married and trying to establish myself as a photojournalist. It was a struggle to make ends meet."

"I didn't think you knew what it meant to struggle."

He laughed. "I do. Well, did."

She started to speak, but stopped herself.

"What?"

"It's just…the more time I spend with you, the more I realize how much I don't know about you."

"By the end of this weekend you should know most everything."

Jayne's smile could have lit up the Las Vegas strip. It sure was lighting up him.

"I hope so," she said.

The anticipation in her voice sent a burst of heat rocketing through his veins. He'd never been so physically attracted to a woman before, yet he wanted all of Jayne—not only her body. "I want to know everything about you, too."

She struck a pose. "What you see is what you get."

He flashed her his most charming grin. "I like what I see. I'm sure I'll enjoy whatever I get."

She swirled into his arms and kissed him firmly, quickly, on the lips. "This is all you're going to get right now."

Before he could embrace her fully and kiss her again she twirled away. A hint of her strawberry and wildflower scent lingered.

The coy look in her eyes told him she knew he wanted more. Okay, he was a guy. Of course he wanted more. But Tristan didn't know whether to be proud of Jayne for taking control of the situation or annoyed at her for getting away from him. Thinking about his conversation with Rich last night, Tristan settled on proud.

"It's enough." He winked. "For now."

Laughter spilled from her lips. "Separate bedrooms, remember?"

"I'm the one who booked the rooms, remember?"

"I haven't forgotten."

His gaze locked on hers. "Neither have I."

The air sizzled with attraction. The desire in her eyes held him captive. He didn't know how long they stood there, staring at each other, but he didn't care. Being with Jayne was all that mattered.

Too soon, she broke the contact.

She walked to the bar where a large fruit basket and a bottle of wine sat. "Look at this."

Tristan hadn't ordered anything. "See if there's a card."

Jayne opened the small envelope, pulled out a card and read.

Jayne and Tristan
Enjoy your weekend at McKendrick's! Let us know if you need anything!
Love
Alex and Wyatt

"Wyatt McKendrick is my friend Alex's husband," Jayne explained. "He offered Alex a job while we were staying here. Her life has never been the same, but she has no regrets."

"Lucky lady," Tristan said. "Not many can say that."

"True, but all three of my friends have no regrets over what happened during that wild weekend."

"Are you ready to have your own wild weekend?" he asked.

She raised her chin. "Well, I'm here. That's a pretty big step for me."

"I know." He strode to her side, raised her hand to his lips and kissed the top of it. Her skin was soft and smooth. "I'm going to make sure you have no regrets."

"So far, so good."

His heart beat faster. He wanted to make sure she never forgot this weekend. Whatever it took, he would do it. Or… not do it.

"We should probably get ready for tonight." She pulled her hand away. "Which bedroom would you like?"

Whichever one you choose. He pushed the thought from his mind. "I don't care."

He didn't. Knowing she was in bed in the same suite was going to make sleep impossible.

"The room on the left can be yours," Jayne said. "The room on the right will be mine."

She was so damn cute. Tristan smiled. "You sound like you're dividing spoils after a war."

Jayne straightened. "Just making sure we each know where we'll be sleeping."

"The living area can be neutral territory. If you don't like sleeping alone, there's a sofabed out here we can share."

With wide eyes she stared at the sofa, then back at him.

Tristan didn't know if she was tempted or upset or nervous. Only one of them appealed to him. The others made him feel like a jerk after he'd told her no regrets.

"Kidding," he joked. "I have no idea if the sofa turns into a bed or not."

She cast him a mischievous glance through her lashes. "Maybe you should find out."

Definitely tempted. His heart skipped a beat. Okay, three.

Humor glinted in her eyes. "I'm kidding too. I know you're a man of your word."

A man of his word.

Just like...

I'm a man of my word. I'm the only one she's got. Maybe once the wedding's over things will get better.

Rich.

A lump the size of a neon lightbulb lodged in Tristan's throat.

Rich prided himself on being a man of his word, even if that meant being a jerk and hurting Jayne.

Tristan didn't want to be lumped into that category. Rich's marriage proposal hadn't been his friend's smartest move, and Tristan knew better than to try and steal home this weekend. He wasn't about to start rounding the bases without a clear signal from Jayne.

He could never be what she wanted, needed, deserved. He couldn't give her the fairytale and forever, but he could make sure she had the time of her life this weekend.

And Tristan would.

A DJ spun a mix of indie rock and eighties songs. A handsome bartender concocted cocktails with improbable names. A manicurist provided demonstrations.

Jayne was as far away from home as she could imagine, but there was nowhere she'd rather be right now than in the fifties-beauty-salon-themed bar in downtown Las Vegas.

Alex sat on an old-style hairdryer seat and raised a martini glass filled with a Blue Rinse. She looked beautiful in a magenta dress and matching heels. Not quite so serious or professional as the practical suits she wore to work at McKendrick's. "To the best friends in the world."

Jayne lifted her drink, a Drop Dead Gorgeous—a delicious combination of vodka, pineapple juice and an energy drink. Molly and Serena joined in the toast, too.

The flash from Tristan's camera lit up their table. He hadn't wanted to join them for drinks, but had paid for theirs. He'd asked if he could take a few pictures before leaving them alone for some much needed girl-time.

He took candid shots of them as they chatted and sipped their drinks. Though she was delighted to finally be with her friends, it was all Jayne could do not to stare at him. His short-sleeved green shirt was tucked into his khaki pants. His leather shoes had been recently polished. He wore a belt.

Comfortable, yet stylish. Smart-casual. And once again he had the look down.

"How did we miss coming here the first time we were all in town?" Molly drank a mocktail—a non-alcoholic version of a Pink Blush martini. The name matched the glow of her cheeks. She rested her left hand on her tunic-covered belly. "It's kitschy, but hip."

"Totally hipster." Serena drank a Platinum Blonde. Wearing a purple cocktail dress, she looked like the same artsy type who'd lived in San Diego, except she seemed a little more… serious and aware of her surroundings. She waved to people she recognized and said hello to those she didn't. "I just love 'Martinis & Manicures' night."

Jayne struggled to take it all in. The change in her friends. The change in her since Tristan had re-entered her life. She sipped her drink.

Tristan stopped circling the table. "I have enough pictures for now."

As he stood next to her, her pulse quickened. She couldn't forget the change in the way she thought of him—Rich's best man to friend to date to boyfriend.

Possible boyfriend, she amended.

Jayne knew better than to get ahead of herself. She had been a little too carefree and flirty at the suite, but the way he'd kept looking at her had made her feel sexy and desirable. She liked how that felt.

"Thank you for being such beautiful subjects," he said.

The four of them thanked him for their cocktails.

"The driver knows what time our dinner reservations are, in case you ladies forget to check the clock." Tristan kissed Jayne on the lips. The brief kiss claimed her attention and nearly made her spill her drink on her lap. "Have fun."

Another kiss would be fun. She took a sip of her drink instead.

He swung his camera pack over his shoulder and walked out. As soon as he was gone she looked to her friends, hoping they would reassure her that seeing Tristan was a good idea. "So, what do you think?"

"Definitely hot," Alex said.

Molly nodded. "Gorgeous."

"Total eye candy. He looks more like a model than a photographer." Serena laughed. "I can't believe you actually thought you could be just friends with a man like that."

Jayne remembered what he'd said about the sofabed in neutral territory. Tempted? Yes. Which was why she would lock her door tonight. Not to keep Tristan out, but to remind herself she needed to stay in her own room. "Our friendship is evolving into something more, but the emphasis is on good clean fun."

At least that was what Jayne kept telling herself. Back at the suite, she hadn't been so sure anymore.

Molly tucked her dark hair behind her ears. "Spending a weekend in Las Vegas with a guy is a little more serious than what you're making it out to be."

"We're spending a weekend with all of you," Jayne clarified.

"And we're so glad you're here," Alex said.

"I feel better having met Tristan." Serena picked up her drink. "It's obvious the guy adores you."

Molly grinned. "I'd say the feeling's mutual."

"I agree." Alex stared over her martini glass. "I've never seen you look this happy before."

Jayne had never felt happier. She should probably be more concerned than she was. Tristan must be rubbing off on her. Or maybe knowing the relationship wouldn't last forever took some of the pressure off. Whatever it was, her affection for him grew every day. So did her respect.

"Tristan's great. Wonderful. Insert any other positive adjective here," Jayne admitted. "But I'm not about to jump into anything like I did with Rich."

"Rich said all the right things," Alex said. "He fooled all of us, Jayne. But it seems like Tristan is *doing* all the right things."

Serena nodded. "Words are easy to say, but actions take a lot more effort and work."

Jayne thought about how fluttery she felt when she was with him, or talking to him on the phone, or..." Tristan has been good for me—getting me out of the house and doing things."

"Clean things?" Alex asked.

Serena winked. "Or dirty ones?"

"Either can be fun," Molly added.

The implication of their words sent excitement rippling through Jayne. Not that she would. Or he... Strike that. Tristan probably would. She sighed. "You guys never used to talk like this. Is it marriage?"

Alex drew her brows together. "I'm not sure if it's marriage per se..."

"It's probably the sex," Serena said with a grin.

Molly nodded. "You and Tristan—?"

"Are sleeping in separate bedrooms," Jayne finished for her. She felt a pang at her heart, remembering the tension in the suite. He'd wanted to kiss her. She'd wanted him to kiss her, too. But she had to be smart about this. About him.

"They're staying in one of McKendrick's two bedroom suites," Alex added. "The guy has excellent taste."

"Of course he does," Molly agreed. "He's dating our Jayne."

"Casually dating." Jayne took a sip of her drink. "Having fun is one thing, but getting serious with a man who wants such a different future than I do would be a huge mistake. I learned my lesson with Rich."

Rich had seemed like the perfect match. Everything she'd ever wanted he could have given her. Tristan, however, was all wrong for her. And yet...

Jayne could imagine herself with him.

She liked the person she was around him, even though the way she'd acted when they'd arrived at the suite had been all heart and no head. Maybe she had loosened up a little too much and put the wrong amount of emphasis on having fun.

"Coming to Las Vegas with Tristan might have been premature. A little caution might be prudent," Jayne decided.

"Nothing wrong with being cautious," Alex said.

"If I had been cautious I wouldn't have married Jonas," Serena countered.

Molly patted her belly. "And I wouldn't be having this baby and be married to Linc."

"I could say the same thing about me and Wyatt," Alex said. "But we're not Jayne."

"And Tristan isn't like your husbands." Jayne didn't have to think hard to remind herself of all the reasons he was wrong for her. "I'd be crazy to fall head over heels with a guy who doesn't believe in commitment."

If only he did believe…

She stared in her drink.

"The fact Tristan travels even more than your father did can't help," Serena, also a military brat, said shrewdly.

Jayne nodded, acknowledging the truth. "Tristan does travel a lot, but when he was in Honduras I knew he would be coming back. I never felt that kind of certainty when my father went away. But I know it would get old fast."

Once that happened, the resentment would start to build. She'd seen it with her parents. Her mother had wanted her father home. He hadn't been able to wait to leave again. The disagreements had become arguments. The arguments had become battles. She wouldn't want Tristan to be unhappy.

"Tristan might have to go away for his work, but I don't think he's going anywhere else," Molly said. "He didn't take his eyes off you. This bar is full of women and he saw only one. You."

"Tristan hasn't given me a reason not to trust him," Jayne admitted. "But Rich didn't, either."

"Be cautious, then," Serena said. "But remember love knows no logic."

Molly laughed. "Just look at the three of us."

"That's true. You should make sure Tristan knows where you're coming from," Alex added. "The guy really does seem to like you, and men aren't known to slow down when they want something. Or someone."

"Thank you, but he knows exactly where I stand." Too bad Jayne felt as if she were standing on shaky ground. "I'm trying to be smarter this time."

At least that was her plan. She wasn't too confident of its execution so far.

Serena smiled at her. "Well, I think you're doing great."

"I agree," Alex said.

"Me, too," Molly chimed in.

The three women sitting at the table with Jayne meant the world to her. They had shared the highs and the lows. She would trust them with her life. But Tristan saw something in her they didn't. He pushed her, challenged her to be more.

She'd taken a gamble coming to Vegas with him. Still, that didn't mean she should bet the farm on their relationship. She knew he wanted more from her. A part of her wanted that, too. Except…

Tristan couldn't give her the future she dreamed about—stability, a home, marriage and a family.

Yet he was one of the sweetest, hottest men she knew. He was also a man of his word. He'd always been honest with her.

The truth was, she'd come to care for him. She cared for him a lot.

But even if she trusted him, could she trust these new feelings of hers?

CHAPTER TEN

At Sparkle, *the rooftop* restaurant at McKendrick's, Jayne sat at a round table with Tristan, her friends and their husbands. The view from the thirtieth floor mesmerized her. A crescent moon shone high in the desert sky. The clear night provided views for miles, from the dazzling neon of the strip to the small twinkling lights of homes farther away.

"What are you looking at?" Tristan asked, sitting next to her.

"All those little homes, far off in the distance."

"A home doesn't have to be so far off," he said.

Her heart beat a little faster.

When she was with Tristan, Jayne felt as if she was already home. No picket fence, leaded-glass built-ins or hardwood floors required.

What had he said?

I don't really think of home as a place. It's more a state of mind.

She was beginning to understand what he meant.

"Make your dream come true, Jayne," he encouraged, his voice low.

His warm breath practically caressed her earlobe. She could hardly breathe.

Her dreams—ones she'd held close to her heart since she was a little girl—were suddenly changing. Maybe emotion was leading her astray again. Jayne only knew that however her dreams evolved she wanted someone like Tristan to share them with.

Those feelings clogged her throat.

Jayne stared at the flickering white votives surrounding a green hydrangea centerpiece. Servers, dressed in black pants and crisp white shirts, circled the linen-covered table, clearing the dishes from the delicious meal.

Linc, Molly's husband, removed his suit jacket and rolled up his sleeves.

"Your friends are great," Tristan whispered. "I'm enjoying myself."

"I'm glad." She was surprised how well he fit in, like the final piece of a jigsaw puzzle. "They like you."

"Told ya so."

A smile tugged on her lips. "Yes, you did."

The tenderness in his gaze brought a sigh to her lips. He hadn't physically touched her, but Jayne could feel his imprint on her heart.

Jayne felt so comfortable with him tonight, as if they were in a relationship with feelings and a future.

But she knew it had to be the situation. Surrounded by three happy, contented couples, it would be easy for her to read more into Tristan's presence, into his words.

She wouldn't allow herself to do that.

Daydreaming was bad enough.

She focused on the people at the table.

Conversation flowed as easily as the wine, though Molly wasn't drinking. Neither was Linc.

Jayne sipped her red wine as Molly entertained them with stories of her efforts to get Linc to help her fill out a baby journal for the baby before they had gotten married.

Molly shook her head. "He actually said the book shouldn't be called *Memories For Your Baby*, but *What Every Hacker Wants To Know About You*."

Everyone laughed, but Tristan looked at Jayne with a question in his eyes. "Linc is the CEO of his own software security company," she explained quietly.

"Got it."

"In my defense." Linc's smile reached all the way to his eyes. "They *do* ask for some very personal information."

"Because it's for a baby book." Molly touched her stomach. "Your baby."

"Our baby," Linc countered.

"Yes, he is." She had changed physically with her pregnancy, but Jayne loved how Molly also appeared to have loosened up, and she laughed more freely than she'd used to.

Tristan raised his wine glass. "Here's to a healthy baby."

Molly beamed. "Thank you."

"It's great you could join us, Tristan," Serena said.

"Thanks for having me," he replied. "It's nice to put faces with names."

"We're glad you could get away," Molly said. "I understand you travel a lot?"

Uh-oh. Jayne wondered if an interrogation was about to begin.

"I'm a photojournalist."

"Wire service or newspaper?" asked Wyatt, with his arm around Alex.

"Freelance," Tristan said.

Linc set his water glass on the table. "Competitive field."

"It is," Tristan agreed. "But that just means I have to be that much better than anyone else."

Jayne exchanged looks with her three friends. Serena winked at the guys being guys, but Jayne found it interesting to watch Tristan holding his own during the testosterone driven exchange.

"Tristan took pictures of us at the bar earlier," Serena said. "I can't wait to see them."

Jonas' brow furrowed at his wife's words. "I thought that was girls'-only time."

Tristan flashed a charming smile, the kind that made Jayne go weak in the knees. "I was simply the photographer."

Wyatt McKendrick refilled Jayne's wine glass. He cut an imposing figure at the table, with his designer suit, black hair, chiseled features and electric green eyes. The staff buzzed around like perfect worker bees. No doubt having the boss there meant extra special service. "Alex tells me this is your first time at Sparkle, Jayne?"

"Yes, we ended up eating at the Bistro Lizette when we stayed here in June."

"We wanted to eat here, though," Serena said.

"But none of us could afford it then," Alex added.

Jayne still couldn't. She looked at Tristan. He had money, just like her friends did now.

Underneath the table, he clasped her hand and gave a reassuring squeeze. She squeezed back.

Wyatt raised a dark brow and stared at his wife. "Are you trying to tell me our prices are too high?"

"Nope," Alex said, without a moment's hesitation. A grin lit up her face. "Just that our bank accounts were too small."

The way Alex no longer felt the need to count to ten before she said anything pleased Jayne. Her friend could be herself and not hold back and worry about the consequences anymore.

Jayne expected Tristan to let go of her hand, but he laced his fingers with hers, as if settling in for the long haul. As if he wouldn't drop her as soon as an interesting assignment beckoned from some faraway land.

If only...

No, that wasn't fair.

Tristan had a job to do, one that had nothing to do with her.

He rubbed her hand with his thumb. Maybe she needed to stop thinking so much and just enjoy the moment.

"I'm glad I finally got the chance to eat here. It's...amazing," Jayne said, distracted by Tristan, who kept playing with her fingers. "Definitely worth the wait."

His thigh pressed against hers.

"Sparkle is just another jewel in the McKendrick's crown." Jonas Benjamin had removed his suit jacket, and finally loosened his tie. "I hope to see Wyatt and Alex's portfolio of properties expand in the not-so-distant future."

"In case you haven't figured it out, Tristan," Serena said, "my husband is the Mayor of Las Vegas, and sometimes forgets he's not at City Hall."

Jonas put his arm around her. "But you love me anyway."

"Yes, I do." She kissed him. "Even if you won't get an 'I Heart Las Vegas' tattoo. You might appeal to another constituency if you did that."

Jonas laughed at her joke. "I'll consider a tattoo when you start wearing pastel jackets with matching skirts and a strand of pearls."

Serena smiled mischievously. "Let's not forget a hat, gloves, and coordinating handbag."

"Those would be excellent touches, my dear," Jonas teased.

Her eyes sparkled. "Except we both know I'll never be a typical politician's wife."

He pulled her close. "And I wouldn't have it any other way."

Serena might not have thought she'd ever fall for a buttoned-down lawyer turned politician, but the two were a perfect match. Jayne had noticed the changes in her friend at the bar earlier.

"Opposites attract," Tristan said.

Linc smoothed Molly's hair. "I'd say they do."

She stared up at her husband with adoring eyes. "Most definitely."

"I'd agree," Alex said.

"Me, too." Wyatt hugged Alex. "There's no way I could let a ten-pound chocolate bar go uneaten for months."

"Now you're just humoring me," Alex teased. "He would never eat it."

"No, but I'd share it with you," Wyatt said.

Jonas laughed. "No question about us being opposites here, but it works."

Everything Jayne had wanted for her three best friends—love, happiness and health—had come to them. Everything she'd gone through—betrayal, heartbreak, pain—had been worth it to see this right now. Jayne wouldn't change anything.

She stared at Tristan.

Everything had worked out for the best.

Serena looked from Tristan to Jayne. "I guess opposites really do attract."

Jayne's cheeks warmed. She would love to be married like her friends, but she knew that wasn't what Tristan wanted.

She waited for him to say something, to voice the distance between them or emphasize the casual fun factor.

"Jayne and I are opposites." He brought their clasped hands up onto the table. "But we're helping each other see different points of view. It's all been good. I'm sure it will continue to be."

Her heart lodged in her throat. A warm feeling of contentment flowed through her. His words gave her hope.

Each of her friends had found the perfect mate, a partner for life. She wanted what Alex, Molly and Serena had found here in Las Vegas. Not the white picket fence and the nine-to-five husband, but someone to cherish who would cherish her. That had always been Jayne's dream.

One true love. A happily-ever-after.

That much was still a part of her dreams.

She looked down at her fingers entwined with his.

It wasn't Tristan's dream.

But maybe, just maybe, it could be.

* * *

Tristan stood with Jayne in the atrium lobby of McKendrick's. Light jazz played from speakers hidden in columns. An elderly couple in matching red, white and blue jackets shuffled across the marble floor. A bride and groom sipped champagne from crystal flutes and accepted congratulations from strangers.

Jayne's friends had called it a night, but Tristan knew heading to the suite this early might not be his smartest move. Not when he couldn't keep his hands off her.

Time to make plans for the rest of the evening. Fast.

"The night's still young," he said.

"I'm game."

Her mischievous smile hinted at a challenge and heated his blood.

A small group of people entered the lobby. Women wearing floor-length gowns, teetering on stilettos and sporting bling, clung to the arms of men in tuxedos. An almost toxic mixture of expensive perfumes hung in the air after they passed.

"Let's go to the Bellagio," he suggested.

"I'm not much of a gambler," Jayne admitted. "I can't understand why anyone would want to throw money away like that."

"We aren't going to gamble," he said, almost desperately. Going up to their suite would be the biggest gamble they could take right now. "The Bellagio is America's playground. There's plenty to do that has nothing to do with gambling."

Three gray-haired women dressed in various shades of purple and red and wearing outrageous hats sashayed and kicked in unison across the lobby, as if they were Rockettes.

"Lead the way," Jayne said with a grin. "I know I'm in good hands tonight."

He wanted her in *his* hands. Tristan swallowed.

"Come on," he said.

A taxi dropped them off at the Bellagio as one of the choreographed water fountain shows in the lake was coming to an end. Tristan led her into the lobby. He noticed men staring at her and brought her closer to him.

Jayne stared up at two thousand colorful blown glass flowers hanging from the ceiling. "Gorgeous."

He glanced her way. "Very."

The heels of her sandals kept her from moving too quickly across the marble and mosaic flooring. Tristan slowed his pace so his steps matched hers. "This way."

"You know your way around." She sounded curious. "Come here often?"

"Actually, yes," he admitted.

Piano music played from a nearby lounge.

"I think that's the piano bar where Molly met Linc." Jayne peered inside. "Serena met Jonas in another lounge here somewhere."

"Sounds like your friends hit the jackpot."

"They sure did." A contented smile settled on Jayne's lips. "Lady Luck was smiling down on them."

"She could be doing the same thing with you."

Jayne's gaze met his. She blushed. "I hope so."

So did Tristan.

"This is the Conservatory and Botanical Gardens," he said as they walked through the entrance into a huge glass dome.

Colorful blossoms, green plants and flowering trees surrounded a large fountain. A sweet floral fragrance hung on the air as they followed the path around.

She looked around. "It's incredible."

He nodded. "I've gained a new appreciation for flowers."

"Any reason?" she asked.

"Meeting you in the Rose Garden at Balboa Park."

Jayne smiled. "That kind of sweet-talk could have consequences."

"I'll take my chances."

Even though he knew the odds of getting burned were high.

"Risk-taker," she teased.

"How about you? Ready to take a chance?" he asked.

"Not completely, but I wouldn't mind dipping my toe in to test the water."

A start. He would take it.

"I want to show you another place." He exited out a door on the left. "Close your eyes."

Jayne did. "I trust you."

Her confident tone made him uneasy. He tugged at his suddenly too tight shirt collar.

"We'll be there in a minute." He led her up to the patisserie and stationed her in front of the chocolate shop's masterpiece. "Okay, open your eyes."

Jayne stared at the twenty-seven-foot, floor-to-ceiling fountain. Behind a wall of glass melted white, milk and dark chocolate cascaded down, pooling and streaming until it reached the bottom.

"Wow," she said.

"Up for some chocolate?"

"I think I must have died and gone to heaven."

"I thought you would like this."

"I do," she admitted. "I love it. Everything. Thank you."

She rose on her tiptoes and brushed her lips across his.

His heart lurched. His pulse raced.

That was when he knew.

He was falling for her. Hell, he'd already fallen.

Tristan gazed into her sparkling eyes and saw stars. White picket fence stars. Two point four children stars. Happily-ever-after stars.

What was he doing? What had he done?

His stomach clenched.

He had fallen in love with her. That was bad.

She was falling for him. That was unforgivable.

He'd already given his best shot at being what someone else needed him to be. He hadn't been able to do it.

He wasn't going to lie to Jayne the way Rich had. She trusted him to be honest with her. Tristan wasn't going to fool himself, either.

No matter how he felt about her, no matter how she might feel about him, he was not what she needed.

The sooner she realized it, the better.

Standing in the elevator on the way up to their suite, Jayne tingled all over. She'd never felt so courted, so cherished, so treasured, so…loved. She clutched the bag of chocolates Tristan had bought for Mrs. Whitcomb.

"Everything has been so perfect tonight. Dessert at the patisserie was the icing on the cake. Thank you."

"You deserve it, Jayne." He looked closely at her with an unreadable expression on his face. "You deserve…"

Her heart pounded in her ears. Maybe he would…

"You have chocolate by your mouth," he said, catching her off-guard.

Self-conscious, Jayne looked at her reflection in the shiny gold-walled elevator. "Where?"

"A tiny smear," he said. "By the edge of your lip."

Jayne licked the side of her mouth with her tongue. "Did I get it?"

"Not yet." Using his thumb, he wiped the corner of her mouth. His thumb pad was rough, his touch slow and intimate, almost a caress.

Jayne's breath caught in her throat.

Sensation surged from her lips through the rest of her. Heat pulsed through her veins.

His gaze met hers. "All gone."

She wanted to grasp the fleeting moment before it disappeared.

The heat in his eyes held her captive. She melted, feeling all liquid and warm, like the chocolate from the fountain.

A single thought, a lone desire, rang through her mind.

Kiss me.

That was what she wanted. A kiss. Kisses.

He continued staring at her. Her eyes. Her mouth.

Her own need shocked Jayne. She'd never felt this way before.

Kiss me. Kiss me. Kiss me.

Tristan took a quick breath. But he didn't kiss her.

Of course not.

He was keeping his word. He might not be the kind of man to get on bended knee, declare his undying love and propose, but he had her best interests at heart. That made her love him even more.

Love him?

Jayne's breath caught in her throat.

She loved him.

Her heart swelled with emotion.

Somehow, somewhere, she'd fallen in love with Tristan MacGregor.

The realization didn't scare her as much as she'd thought it would.

She wanted this.

She wanted him.

And that left her only one choice.

To kiss him herself.

Rising on tiptoe, Jayne balanced herself with her hands flat against his smooth cotton shirt, against his strong, warm chest, above his rapidly thudding heart.

He stiffened in surprise.

Dizzy with her own daring, she pressed her mouth to his.

The touch of Jayne's lips shocked his system like a jolt of caffeine. The taste of her—chocolate, sweet and rich—went to his head faster than the wine he'd drunk with dinner.

Bad move, his brain yelled to him. Bad idea. He should end this now.

He couldn't be what she needed. He couldn't... Oh, hell.

The way her lips moved over his, devouring him as if he were the slice of chocolate cake she'd eaten earlier, ignited a flame inside him. His brain shut off. His body flared to life.

Her kiss made it hard to think, impossible to do the right thing.

Tristan wanted her.

Even if he knew he shouldn't.

A sexy moan escaped her lips. The sound pushed him closer to the edge. He struggled to hang on. "Jayne…"

She leaned into him, pushing him back against the wall of the elevator. Her hips rocked against his.

Her mouth pressed harder against his, taking the kiss deeper. Her lips moved over his with impatience, hunger. Her tongue tasted, explored, plundered.

Jayne's aggressiveness surprised him. She'd seemed more kitten than man-eating tiger. But he had no complaints. He loved her daring.

He loved *her*.

She wove her fingers through his hair.

A hot ache built low in his gut. He needed her closer.

He wrapped his arms around her until her soft breasts pressed against him. She went willingly. That only stoked the fire. He wanted to be inside her. He slipped his thigh between her legs.

He ran his hand along her smooth thigh. The hem of her dress inched upward.

His control slipped another notch. Maybe ten.

Back away, Tristan told himself. Pretty soon he wasn't going to want to stop. He didn't want to stop now.

Ding.

Jayne jerked away from him, her eyes wide and her lips swollen. She smoothed her dress back into place, her fingers trembling. He felt a pang deep in his belly.

The elevator doors opened. A middle-aged couple stepped toward the car.

"Going up?" the man in a Denver Broncos jersey asked.

"Yes," Tristan said.

"Oops." The woman, wearing a navy blue tracksuit, smiled. "I must have pressed the wrong button. Sorry about that."

So was Tristan. But a part of him was thankful. He knew where that kiss had been leading. Where he'd wanted it to go.

The elevator doors closed. He saw Jayne's reflection. Her pink flushed cheeks. The rapid rise and fall of her chest.

She looked so sexy, so vulnerable. He wanted to take her in his arms again and kiss her. The way he felt about her right now, kisses would never be enough.

But he couldn't afford to do anything else. Truth was, he couldn't even afford more kisses.

Tristan touched her shoulder, wanting to reassure her.

The shy invitation in the depths of her eyes nearly bowled him over.

"Want to take this into neutral territory?" she asked.

Tristan could have what he wanted. He could have her.

But there was no thrill of victory. No shot of pride. No fist-pumping.

If Tristan took what he wanted from Jayne he would be no better than Rich.

Strike that. Tristan would be worse, because he actually loved her. He loved her quick smile, her generous nature and her rock-his-world kisses. He loved her.

No matter what Jayne thought she wanted, he knew better. She was awash in a glow of emotion and sensation. Her heart was leading her someplace she'd said she didn't want to go. He had to protect her. He had to protect himself from acting on the way he felt.

No regrets.

For either one of them.

CHAPTER ELEVEN

Keep moving, Jayne thought as she and Tristan entered the suite. If she slowed down to think about what she was doing—what they were about to do—she might stop altogether.

And she didn't want to stop.

She never wanted this night to end. Euphoria bubbled over. She felt giddy, as if her smile was permanently fixed upon her face. Her pulse leaped with excitement.

Jayne floated to the sofa. She could barely feel her feet touch the carpet. The air seemed charged with electricity, with attraction. The anticipation was almost unbearable.

Her heart stuttered with love and nerves and desire.

She reached the sofa.

Neutral territory.

Her insides tingled. She felt breathless.

Tristan stood on the other side of the living room, his eyes, dark and intent, never leaving her for a moment.

He was so handsome, so strong, so caring.

A dizzying shiver of wanting coursed through her. She fought an overwhelming need to be next to him. Soon, very soon.

Holding his gaze, Jayne sat.

He took a step forward, then stopped. "You want something to drink?"

Her heart fluttered wildly.

Had he forgotten his comment about the sofa? How could he forget?

No, she realized. A warm glow settled the wild beating of her heart. He was trying to do the right thing. He was a man of his word. Her feelings for him intensified. How could she not love him for looking out for her?

She gave him a shaky smile. "Not a drink."

Come here. Her eyes implored him. *Don't make me say it.*

"Well, then," he said. "Maybe we should call it a night."

Oh, no. That wasn't how she wanted tonight to end.

Jayne couldn't say what she wanted, but she could show him.

With unfamiliar bravado, she tapped the cushion next to her.

He didn't move, didn't take the hint.

Her heart raced uncomfortably.

She loved him. She wanted this. She wanted him.

What was she doing wrong?

Maybe she should try what had worked in the elevator.

Jayne rose, crossed the room and stood in front of him. He was so tall and his shoulders so wide.

A sense of urgency drove her. Her body ached for his touch.

She placed her palms on his chest.

Heat emanated from him. His heart pounded. She felt his breath hitch.

Good, he was turned on, too. Her pulse-rate skyrocketed.

She ran her hands up his chest until they reached his shoulders, put her arms around his neck and pressed her breasts against his hard chest. She waited for him to pull her into an embrace.

The muscles beneath her palms tensed. "What are you doing, Jayne?"

He still hadn't wrapped his arms around her.

"I'm trying to seduce you," she admitted flirtatiously. "But I don't seem to be getting very far."

"You're doing great, but..." His warm breath fanned her face. "Why are you doing it? I can't give you what you need."

All she needed was him. Him, and the feeling of being loved, valued, cherished that he gave her.

Her confidence spiraled upward. "All I need right now is a little cooperation."

He laughed, and for a moment she thought everything would be all right.

And then he took her arms from around his neck and pressed a tender kiss in each palm. "Jayne...you deserve more than cooperation."

He knew her dreams. She'd told him what she had wanted with Rich. What she hadn't told Tristan was that *what* she felt for him, with him, was so much greater than what she'd ever felt for Rich.

"I'm not expecting any promises," she said sincerely.

"I can't be a suburban husband."

"I'm not asking you to marry me. I'm not asking for anything." She glanced over Tristan's shoulder at her open bedroom door. "Well, except..."

Her cheeks burned at her brazenness, at the implication.

"I can't," he said firmly.

She looked at him confused. "Can't?"

The silence stretched between them.

He stared at her as if he were photographing her with his eyes, but then broke the contact. He kissed each of her fingers—ten perfect, heart-wrenching kisses—and let go of her hands.

He glanced at the door to his bedroom and sucked in a long breath. The unfamiliar vulnerability in his eyes squeezed her heart. "This isn't what you want."

Well, no. She wanted everything. The magic and forever. She wanted him in her life for always. But if she couldn't have always she would gladly take tonight.

Jayne raised her chin. "Yes, it is."

"You don't really know me."

"Yes, I do," she countered. But his words stirred old doubts about her judgment. As much to reassure herself as him, she said, "I know enough. You're kind. You're giving. You've helped me get a life. You've shown me what's possible and how I can make my dreams come true. My friends like you, too."

"Sweetheart, I'm overwhelmed. Flattered. But—"

"You're looking out for me," she said. "That's all I need to know. I trust you."

"You shouldn't. You don't know what I'm capable of."

A chill shivered down her spine. Could she have misread him that badly? The way she'd misjudged Rich when he'd claimed he wanted to marry her? "I thought you wanted this, too?"

"Not now."

His rejection stung, but she refused to let go of her hopes for the evening, her trust in him.

"I don't understand." She was lost in a confusing haze of feelings and desire. His words, his abrupt change of mood, made no sense. Maybe he just needed reassurance. "You were honest about what you want. I'm fine with that. I don't need forever. I'm ready to accept your terms. Here. Now."

A vein throbbed at his jaw. "Jayne…"

Why wasn't he taking her into his arms and kissing her? She couldn't believe she was throwing herself at him and he didn't want her. Doubts swirled, gnawing at her confidence. "What's wrong with you? What wrong with *me*?"

"It's not you. You're perfect," he said gently. "It's me, Jayne."

"It's you I want."

"You deserve more than me."

A beat passed. And another.

She couldn't take it any longer. She didn't want to beg. "Tristan…"

His features tightened. His gaze clouded. "I'm the one who sent the text message telling you to go to Rich's apartment for a surprise."

Her mouth gaped. She felt an instant squeezing hurt. Jayne took a step back. "What?"

She waited for Tristan to say something—anything.

Instead, he strode to the bar and poured her the drink she hadn't needed before. "Rich wouldn't tell you about him and Deidre and he made me promise I wouldn't, either. So I had to find another way to make sure you found out before the wedding."

"No." Jayne's knees quivered. She staggered back until she bumped into a chair. She sat before her legs buckled. "You're just saying that. I don't know why, but…"

Tristan gave her a glass of red wine.

Her hands trembled so badly she had to set the glass on the end table.

"It's true," Tristan said.

True.

The word seared her heart. "How…?"

"I was waiting for Rich in the dressing room of the tuxedo shop when I saw your name flash on the display screen of his cell. I knew he was seeing Deidre later, so I took your call to be a sign and sent you the text message."

Emotion tightened her throat. "I never understood why Rich felt the need to orchestrate me finding out that way. It was so cruel, so heartless. Wondering why he'd planned the breakup that way kept me awake for weeks. Now I realize it wasn't him at all."

"If I had it to do over again—" Tristan shoved his hands in his pockets "—I would do it differently."

The words crashed down on her. Not just the words. The evening. Her hopes.

Tears pricked her eyes, but she kept them in check.

How could this be happening?

Jayne loved Tristan. She had trusted him. She had felt safe with him. She had believed he would be good to her. But she'd been wrong. Dead wrong. "So would I."

"I know you're upset."

Grief ripped through her. She wanted to throw up. "You have no idea how I feel right now."

"You're right. I don't." Red stained his tanned face. "What I did was cruel, but not heartless. I was desperate to stop the wedding. I knew you'd be miserable if you married Rich."

"You're Rich's best friend." She struggled to hold herself together. She felt as if she would lose it any second. She squared her shoulders. "Why did you care about me?"

"Because I liked you."

"You didn't know me."

"We had this same discussion that day I returned your postcard," he reminded her.

Jayne remembered.

You don't like me.

I like you.

No, you don't.

Yes, I do.

The only reason you're here is for Grace.

Grace asked me to stop by, but that doesn't mean I don't want to be here.

Jayne's mind reeled. She tried to force her confused emotions into order so she could understand. "But you were Rich's best man."

"Let me show you." Tristan removed his wallet, pulled out a photograph and handed it to her. "See yourself through my lens. Through my eyes."

The picture was of her. She wore a pink blouse and skirt. Pink rose blooms surrounded her.

"I saw you standing there and that was it. I fell. Hard." The honesty in his voice cut through her pain and confusion. "I took your picture, lots of them. This one is my favorite."

Jayne stared at the photograph. It was as if the camera had worked magic. The lighting and soft focus made her look so pretty.

Not the camera. Tristan had made her look that way.

Something clicked in her mind. Her heart drummed. She looked from the picture to him. "You liked me?"

Tristan nodded. "From that first day. The very first moment, really. But then I found out you were marrying my best friend, and I was his best man, *his* best friend, so I had to keep my distance."

It all made sense now. Tristan's glares had been a disguise. His silence had been his shield. But that knowledge didn't ease the pain in her heart.

A hot tear slipped from the corner of her eye. She wiped it away.

He continued. "When I learned Rich was cheating on you, I couldn't stand to look you in the eye."

But Tristan was looking her in the eye now, with a combination of regret and affection that splintered her broken heart even more.

She blinked back the rest of the tears stinging her eyes and threatening to fall. "All I see is a woman who's been fooled again by a man she trusted—by her own foolish hopes and bad judgment."

"Jayne—"

"I trusted you." Her voice cracked.

"Trust yourself."

No, she couldn't. And that, Jayne realized with sudden clarity, hurt most of all.

Her judgment wasn't simply bad. It was totally off. Totally wrong. Just as it had been with her father. Just as it had been with Rich.

And once more her heart would pay the price.

A lump burned in her throat. "Why didn't you tell me this before?"

The muscle ticked in Tristan's jaw again. "Because you wanted to put the past behind you. And I just wanted you."

He had tried to tell her, she remembered now. She pressed her fingers to her aching forehead. She didn't know what to think, what to say.

The silence intensified the tension between them.

Jayne's chest hurt. She could barely breathe. Emotion and hurt raged inside her.

She let go of the photograph. It floated to the carpet.

And I just wanted you.

"Too late for that," she said in a choked voice. "I could never love someone, trust myself to someone, who could hurt me like that—who could make me question my own judgment again."

"I understand."

And he did, Jayne realized with another tear of her heart. That was why he had stopped things from going too far tonight.

"For what it's worth," Tristan said quietly, "I'm sorry. You'll never know how sorry I am."

His words ripped at her heart. At her soul.

"Me, too," she admitted, her voice as raw as her heart. "But sorry isn't going to change anything."

Tristan sat up all night. Waiting for something. The dawn. A sign. Jayne.

But she'd retreated into her bedroom and locked the door.

He hadn't seen her.

Not that seeing her would have made any difference.

Sorry isn't going to change anything.

He stood at the window of their suite, watching the brilliant desert sunrise take over the lights of the strip, feeling cold and empty. He couldn't justify what he'd done to her or to himself. He wasn't going to be like Rich and make excuses.

Tristan had made his own choices. He would accept the consequences.

But he wanted to know she was okay.

He stared as the new day broke, surrounded by lonely silence, assailed by regret.

As time passed his concern over Jayne increased, until he couldn't stand still any longer. He paced across the living room.

Tristan noticed Jayne's picture lying on the carpet. He picked it up and stared at the image. His chest constricted.

No reason to keep this any longer.

He walked to the trashcan. His hand hovered over it, ready to drop the picture inside. But his fingers wouldn't let go.

Truth was, he didn't want to let go.

He put the picture back in his wallet.

Tristan glanced at the digital clock. Eight o'clock.

He resumed his pacing.

Shouldn't she be up by now? Unless she'd had as restless a night as he had?

Last night he'd heard voices—a phone call to one of her girlfriends, perhaps?—and other sounds, until the room had fallen silent around four in the morning.

Should he check on her? Should he call her friends?

The lock on Jayne's door clicked.

He froze.

As the door opened, Jayne appeared.

She'd been crying. Her red and puffy eyes made his heart hurt even more. The dark circles under her eyes and pale skin told him she hadn't slept much, either.

A heaviness settled in the center of his chest.

He'd done this to her.

Tristan felt like an even bigger jerk.

She held her packed bag in her hand.

"You're leaving?" he said hoarsely.

Jayne nodded.

Don't go, he thought.

But what had he expected her to do? He'd hurt her in the worst possible way. He couldn't offer her any reason to stay. She deserved better.

"When?" he asked.

"After lunch." Her voice sounded strained. "I'm going to spend some time with my friends first."

Tristan hated how she wouldn't look him in the eyes. His already aching heart seemed to split open. He wanted to make things better between them. He wanted her to want him again. He wanted her to love him. Instead, all he could do was help her leave.

"I'll call a cab to take you to the airport when you're ready," he said. "My father's plane will be waiting for you."

Tristan would call the pilot so he could make the necessary preparations.

Her lower lip quivered slightly. "No."

The one word spoke volumes. Disappointment weighed down on him. "Then I'll buy you a plane ticket."

She inhaled deeply. "I'll buy my own plane ticket."

"You can't afford it."

The knuckles of the hand holding onto her bag turned white. "If I can afford a down payment on a house, I can afford a damn plane ticket."

He admired her flash of spirit. He fought the urge to go to her, to take her in his arms and make this all better. But she didn't want that.

She didn't want him.

Tristan stiffened. "I don't want you spending your money. I got you here. I'll get you home."

She met his gaze.

The raw hurt he saw in her eyes made him grab the back of the chair. He loved her. He hadn't wanted it to turn out this way. His fingers dug into the upholstery.

"I'm tired of you telling me what I want and what I need." Her voice never wavered. "I can take care of myself."

"Let me," he offered sincerely. "Let me give you this much."

"You can't give me what I need."

Tristan flinched. She'd tossed his words back at him. Rightly so, he realized.

With her bag in hand, she walked quickly across the living room to the front door.

He wanted to stop her, but he didn't. He couldn't.

She deserved her exit line, at least.

Jayne opened the door.

Wait, Tristan wanted to yell.

She didn't glance back. She didn't even say goodbye.

Instead Jayne Cavendish stepped out of the suite and out of his life.

"Are you sure you want to leave today?" Alex sat on the floor of her penthouse apartment in front of a coffee table covered with dishes: fruit kabobs, pastries, bagels, yogurt and quiche. "We can get you another room to stay in."

"Or you can stay with one of us," Molly suggested.

Serena nodded. "We have plenty of room at our place."

"Thanks, but I want to go home." Jayne forced the words through her raw throat. Her heart ached. The sight of all that food made her churning stomach lurch. Couldn't eat, couldn't sleep. Must be… No. She struggled to keep her voice steady. "I'll be back soon, though. We need to throw Molly a baby shower."

"Don't think of me right now." Molly sat on the couch. Rocky, her Jack Russell terrier, slept at her feet. "I'm not going anywhere. Just getting bigger."

Everyone laughed.

Jayne pasted a smile on her stiff lips.

"Wyatt's made arrangements for you to fly back on the McKendrick's jet," Alex said.

"Thank you so much."

"It needs to be in Los Angeles on Monday anyway, so it's no big deal." Alex held a mug of coffee. "There's a car to take you to the airport whenever you're ready."

Jayne swallowed around the lump in her throat. "I really appreciate all you're doing for me."

"You don't have to put on a front, Jayne," Serena said softly. "It's okay to cry."

"It is, Jayne." Alex handed over the box of unused tissues. "We're well stocked."

She'd told them about what had happened with Tristan after the dinner at Sparkle. Her friends had offered her support, friendship, hugs and chocolate. She loved them so much.

"Thanks, but I cried buckets last night. I'm all cried out today." Right now Jayne clung to a fragile thread of self-control. The endless wallowing and pity parties after her breakup with Rich had taken their toll not only on her emotions but also her health. "I don't want a repeat performance of the hysterics after Rich."

Even though this hurts more.

She hadn't been engaged to Tristan, but she loved him.

Had loved him. Had thought she loved him. She didn't trust her own judgment anymore.

"Rich." Serena groaned. "If it had been him last night, he would have slingshot your panties across the suite before you could blink."

"Rich was a hound," Alex said. "Even if he was your fiancé."

"A hound and a liar," Serena added.

Molly adjusted the pillow behind her back. "I guess the two men aren't that different after all."

"I liked Tristan," Alex admitted. "Well, before he hurt you."

"Jonas thought he was a nice guy," Serena said.

Molly frowned. "Why are we saying nice things about Tristan? He hurt Jayne."

Fairness compelled Jayne to speak. "Tristan was trying not to hurt me last night. Otherwise he would have taken advantage of the situation, of me."

Alex and Serena exchanged glances over the coffee table.

Serena's eyes darkened. "Sounds like you still have feelings for him."

"I do," Jayne admitted. "I thought I'd wake up this morning and feel differently, but I don't. Still, I let my desire cloud my judgment. With Rich I wanted happily-ever-after. With Tristan I wanted love."

Alex leaned forward. "If you love him—"

"We were never going to have a forever kind of relationship. That's not what he's looking for," Jayne interrupted. She wasn't supposed to have been looking for that, either. "Besides, he never told me he loved me."

"Unlike Rich," Molly said. "Didn't he tell you that early on?"

"The third date," Jayne answered. Rich had declared his love over and over again, but besides proposing he never had shown it. Tristan had never mentioned love, but his actions last night proved she meant something to him.

Her breath caught in her throat.

No, Tristan couldn't love her. If he did, he would have said something.

The apartment door opened. Wyatt walked in with an envelope in his hand. "This was left at the front desk for Jayne."

She took the envelope with a tentative hand. Her name was scrawled on the front in sharp, bold letters. She opened the flap with a mix of anticipation and dread.

"What does it say?" Serena asked.

Jayne removed the contents. "It's a plane ticket. A first-class plane ticket to San Diego."

Molly rubbed her lower back. "That's impressive."

"He wants to take care of you, Jayne," Wyatt said.

Even after she'd asked him not to, Tristan was still trying to take care of her. Jayne noticed a yellow Post-It note stuck to the ticket.

You deserve more.

The words stabbed at her broken heart. She fought to control her swirling emotions.

She reread the three words. *You deserve more.*

This time the words didn't bother her as much. She reread the note a third time. *You deserve more.*

She remembered what he had said to her.

You deserve more than cooperation. You deserve more than me. You deserve more.

Maybe Tristan was right. Maybe she did deserve more.

Maybe it was time for her to finally get what she deserved.

Jayne straightened.

She just needed to figure out what that might be.

CHAPTER TWELVE

ON HER knees in the garden, Jayne attacked the new weeds sprouting between the rows of carrot and radish plants. It was only seventy-two degrees, nothing like the hot summer temperatures Southern California was known for, but still the winter sun beat down on her. A trickle of sweat ran between her breasts and soaked her bra.

But she was keeping occupied. Work and gardening and the dog agility class and finding excuses not to go out with Kenny kept her busy.

She didn't think about Tristan at all.

Well, not much.

Only every, oh, minute or so.

She swiped her forearm across her forehead.

When the phone rang it was a relief. Maybe it was Alex or Molly or Serena. Jayne's friends called her every day. Or maybe it was...

Tristan.

She jumped from her knees and bolted to the house.

Stupid. He wouldn't call. It was over. And yet...

No matter how many times Jayne told herself it was over with Tristan, a part of her still wanted him to call or show up at her door. She had no idea what she would say or do, but she just wanted to see him again.

"Hello?" she said, sounding breathless from the sprint inside.

"Hi, Jayne," a familiar male voice said. "It's Rich."

Reality hit with a thud. She clutched the phone receiver. Nine months ago a call from Rich would have made her happy. Even after the wedding fiasco she'd prayed for him to call, to apologize, to explain. Now it was too late. Anticlimactic. A bit of an annoyance, actually. "Why are you calling me?"

Silence filled the line.

"I talked to Tristan," Rich said finally. "He told me I was a real jerk."

"Yes."

"That I hurt you."

She had been hurt. Hurt and furious. Now she was relieved she hadn't married him. "So?"

"Tristan told me I wasn't ready to get married. To you or anybody else. I want you to know I should have listened to him."

Tristan had been looking out for her—then and now. She bit her lip. "Sounds like you're listening now."

"Yeah," Rich admitted. "His friendship matters to me. Whether you believe it or not, what you think about me matters, too. I called to apologize, Jayne. I'm sorry. I really am."

Okay, this was really, really awkward. She didn't need his apology. And yet she was glad to clear the air, close the book. She was glad the man she'd thought she'd loved had finally grown up to acknowledge what he'd done.

"It's okay, Rich." She had let go of the past. It was time to live now and be ready for the future. "I'm over it. I've moved on.

"Yeah, I heard," Rich said. "Good luck with that."

She wasn't sure what he was talking about. "Uh, thanks."

"You know, Tristan is a really good guy."

"I know."

"Loyal," Rich said earnestly. "He stuck by me when I was acting like a complete idiot."

Tristan must have told Rich about them. Not that it mattered now. "Friends do that."

"So...I'll see you around?"

"Probably not."

"When Tristan gets back from his assignment in Africa," Rich clarified.

Her heart beat faster.

Africa. Was that why Tristan hadn't called or stopped by? Because he was out of the country?

Hope sprang to life.

No, she wasn't going to delude herself again. She deserved more than that. She deserved—

"Jayne...?" Rich said.

"I'm here. Sure," she said, distracted by her thoughts. "See you then."

"Bye." Rich hung up.

Jayne set the phone on the counter and returned to the garden, walking as if she were in a dream. She knelt on the pad and picked up the trowel.

She had what she wanted all wrong.

It wasn't the husband. A man like Rich could have offered her the trappings—but not love and fidelity.

It wasn't the house. Oh, she still planned to submit her offer on the fixer-upper cottage tomorrow, but four walls and a roof, no matter how quaint or perfect, didn't make a home.

She dug in the dirt, the desire to plant roots stronger than ever.

A house and husband were the beginning, not the end.

Jayne knew with pulse-pounding certainty what she wanted, what she deserved.

She wanted a man who saw her and loved her for who she was. A man who was not afraid to say he loved her and commit. A man who would work to build a life with her.

That man was out there somewhere.

She wished it could be Tristan. She wanted it to be him. But, she realized with a pang, he had never given her a chance. Never given her the choice.

Jayne remembered what Tristan had said to her that first day he'd shown up on her doorstep.

You don't have to look. Someone will find you.

She hoped he was right.

In Botswana, Tristan aimed his camera at the traditional Tswana village gathering. The men sat apart from the women in the courtyard where the festivities took place. The bright colors of the women's aprons contrasted with brown houses that looked more like thatched huts. He hit the shutter button.

This was the kind of assignment he thrived upon. He'd flown into Johannesburg and had been traveling around Botswana for the past week to take photographs for an article about the impact of tourism on economic development. Not as exciting or dangerous as being embedded with a battalion in the Middle East, but he could take his time framing perfect shots.

The midday sun beat down. Sweat beaded on his forehead and dampened his hat. He'd be drenched by the time he finished today.

The village was in the Kalahari Desert, seemingly left behind by time. Only wildlife in search of food or adventure and tourists on safari visited.

He could imagine Jayne here with him.

With her appreciation of small things she would like this place and these people. She could appreciate the scenery surrounding them, the smells of the food boiling in the courtyard and the sounds of the music—a mix of vocals and stringed instruments. She would also love the animals. Maybe not the Puff Adder which had slithered across his path yesterday, but the mesmerizing zebras and playful meerkats would be right up her alley. She would also have gotten a kick out of the toilet at the luxury camp he'd first stayed in. It had been an actual throne.

Yes, he could picture Jayne enjoying herself here.

But she never wanted to see him again.

The day before he'd left for Africa he'd received her plane ticket in the mail, with a note saying she'd found her own way back to San Diego.

His chest tightened.

He refocused the camera on a group of children dancing barefoot on the dirt. The joy on their faces pulled at his aching heart.

He snapped more pictures.

A young boy stumbled. Hit the ground. Wailed.

A woman with a baby strapped to her back with colorful fabric rose from the group of adults and ran to the sobbing child. She brushed the dirt from the child's knees, wiped the tears from his eyes and kissed him.

He snapped a picture.

Love.

That was what he'd felt as he watched. That was the verb he'd captured.

It made him think of Jayne again.

Damn. He missed her. Each day he seemed to miss her more, not less.

He would be glad to get home. Not to San Diego, he realized, but to wherever Jayne was.

She was home now.

If only she would be waiting to welcome him…

That night in Vegas he'd told her she deserved more than he could give her. He still believed she deserved the best life had to offer and a better man to share it with her.

But the one thing she wanted, needed most, he knew he could provide.

Love.

It was as simple, as complicated, as that.

He loved her.

Tristan wasn't the man she wanted—he would never be the perfect husband of her dreams—but he loved her. He could be a husband who loved her completely.

But he'd never told her how he felt. He'd never given her the chance to decide for herself if love was enough. If he was enough.

I'm tired of you telling me what I want and what I need. I can take care of myself.

Jayne deserved a choice.

Tristan would give her that choice.

He only hoped he could live with her decision.

A big red "SOLD" was plastered over the real estate agent's "For Sale" sign on the lawn. Jayne's heart tripped with pride and excitement. After a week of offers and counter-offers, the cottage was hers. Well, almost hers.

The home inspector had found nothing to make her want to pull her offer. The agent had locked the house and left to contact the sellers.

As soon as the house closed escrow Jayne would own a home in San Diego.

One dream come true she could check off the list.

The corners of her mouth curved upward. She sat on the rickety porch steps, studying her new property.

The amount of work facing her was daunting, but Jayne couldn't wait to get started.

She surveyed the shaggy garden beds and straggling lawn. Weeding was a must, but everything else, including painting and repairing the white picket fence, could wait until the interior was completed. No sense moving items in only to have to move them out to remodel and refinish and paint.

She closed her eyes, imagining what the house would look like after all her hard work. The only thing missing was someone to share it all with.

You don't have to look. Someone will find you.

Jayne bit back a sigh.

"You look right at home."

Tristan. Her eyelids flew open. Her heart slammed against her chest. The air rushed from her lungs. Every single one of her nerve-endings stood at attention.

He stood outside the front gate, his hands shoved in the pockets of his wrinkled navy pants, the sleeves of his rumpled gray shirt pushed up onto his forearms. Stubble covered his face. His hair looked as if it hadn't been brushed in a couple of days.

He looked tired, tanned, great.

Jayne stood.

She wanted to fling herself from the porch steps and into his arms. But there was too much said and unsaid between them. Nothing had changed.

But, oh, was she glad to see him.

She ignored the pounding of her heart and smiled instead.

"I am home." She was about to tell him what the home inspector had told her, but decided not to. This was her dream, not his. "Well, it'll be my house as soon as escrow closes."

His steady gaze locked immediately with hers. "You bought the house?"

She nodded. Would he be glad for her? Or did her decision only underscore the differences between them?

His wide smile reached all the way to his eyes. He opened the gate and stepped inside. "Mrs. Whitcomb told me you were looking at a house today. I guessed it was this one, but I had no idea you were buying it. Congratulations. That's fantastic news."

That explained how he had found her.

But what was he doing here?

"Thanks. I would have never taken the plunge without your encouragement. You made me realize I can make my own dreams come true." Most of them. Not the hot, sweaty ones that plagued her at night, but the rest. Jayne stared at the "SOLD" sign. "And I am."

"I'm really happy for you."

He sounded sincere. His eyes were warm. She swallowed and looked away, down. "When did you get back from… Africa, was it?"

He nodded. "My plane landed about an hour ago."

Her heart thumped as she took in his wrinkled shirt, that movie star stubble. "You came straight here?"

"After a quick stop by your place."

"Where are your things?"

"In the car."

So he hadn't even checked into a new hotel yet. Her heart did a slow roll in her chest.

He took a step forward. "I didn't want to wait to see you."

"Why?" she whispered.

"You deserve everything you've ever wanted." He strode up the walkway until he stood in front of her. "You deserve a better man than me. You can probably find him, too. But I'm the one who loves you. I love you, Jayne."

He loved her.

She'd never expected to hear those words from his lips, but now that he'd said them she couldn't imagine not hearing them again. Joy flowed through her.

"You accused me of telling you what you wanted, what you needed, when we were in Las Vegas," he continued.

The beating of her heart was all she could hear. She wondered if he could hear it, too.

"But I'm offering you my heart, Jayne." He reached for her arm and took hold of her hand. "It's up to you to decide if that's enough."

He was giving her the choice.

Her spirits soared. Tingles burst through her like fireworks. He loved her. He really loved her.

It was all up to her.

Jayne's heart sang.

"Things don't make a family or a home. I have friends who are my family. A home can be anywhere there is love." She stared at the love shining in his eyes, love for her. She entwined her fingers with his. "Your heart is all I need, Tristan. Your heart. Your love."

He let go of her hand and embraced her. "Are you sure this is what you want?"

Jayne thought about her mom and the dreams they'd shared. She thought about what she'd gone through with Rich. She thought about her trip to Vegas with Tristan and the weeks without him since.

She completely trusted her judgment. She completely trusted her heart. She completely trusted Tristan. "I'm positive."

Her heart would be safe in his hands.

Tristan knelt on one knee. He pulled out a black velvet ring box, opened it, and removed a sparkling diamond solitaire. "I love you, Jayne Cavendish. I want to spend the rest of my life with you. Will you marry me?"

Happiness bubbled over. Love had found her. Her one true love. "Yes, I'll marry you."

He slipped the ring onto her finger. A perfect fit. "A good thing you said yes. I bought the ring in Africa. It would have been hard to return."

Jayne laughed. "I'm so happy I said yes, then."

He laughed, too.

"It's beautiful. Thank you." She stared at the breathtaking ring. The large diamond must have cost him a fortune. "Somehow I think you'll be contributing more to our finances, but I like knowing I'm bringing something to the marriage."

His tender gaze was practically a caress. He kissed her hand. "All I need is you."

"You don't mind, do you?"

"Mind what?"

"That I'm buying the cottage?" she said. "Maybe you'd rather live someplace else. Like the beach."

He kissed her hand again. "Anyplace where you are is home to me."

A sense of peace and contentment filled her. "I'll always be here waiting for you to come home."

"And when you come with me the house will be here, waiting for both of us to come home."

A bluebird landed on the gate of the picket fence. A breeze carried the scent of freshly mown grass from the yard next door. Children rode their bikes along the sidewalk, ringing their bells. Rays from the sun cast dancing prisms of light from her diamond ring on the house and yard.

They were home.

She smiled. "Yes, it will."

He swung her around, placed her on her feet and hugged her again.

In his arms she found a sense of belonging and home. She kissed him hard on the lips.

"If being engaged gets me kisses like that," he said, "I can't wait to see what marriage brings."

"I don't want to wait too long to get married," she said. "I know this is right."

"Then we'll have a short engagement."

She kissed him again.

"An even shorter engagement." He brushed the hair from her eyes. "Do you want to have a big wedding here in San Diego?"

She shook her head. Her dreams had changed. She didn't need the trappings of an expensive wedding. Not when she had the security of Tristan's love. "Not unless that's what you want."

"You're all I want."

She grinned. "No more neutral territory?"

"No separate bedrooms, either."

"I know the perfect place we should get married."

The glint in his eyes matched the glow in hers.

"Las Vegas," the two of them said at the same time.

EPILOGUE

STRAINS from the organist's version of Beethoven's "Ode to Joy" filled the wedding chapel at McKendrick's. The hunter green and gold décor provided a luxurious setting for the romantic ceremony. Sunlight streamed through the stained glass windows, as Jayne and Tristan made their way, arms linked, down the aisle after their wedding ceremony.

Tingles flowed all the way to the tips of Jayne's fingers and toes. She clutched the handle of her bouquet, a mix of white and pale pink roses.

The hem of her ballroom-length gown brushed the tops of her feet. The white silk and lace dress was simple, yet elegant, perfect for the afternoon's exchange of wedding vows.

Her friends' wide smiles echoed the joy in Jayne's own heart.

In the foyer outside the chapel Tristan twirled her into his arms. "Mr. and Mrs. Tristan MacGregor. I like the sound of that."

She leaned against him, feeling the beat of his heart. The rhythm matched hers. Opposites, yes, but love made up for all their differences. Love made up for everything. "Me, too."

"Good, because you're going to have to hear it for the next fifty years or so."

"Why don't we shoot for sixty?" she suggested.

"I'm game."

The wedding guests filed out of the chapel as the music spilled out behind them. The reception was being held upstairs on the roof at Sparkle. Alex had taken charge, carefully consulting Jayne and Tristan's preferences and working with the hotel's wedding planner to make sure everything would be perfect.

Knowing Alex, it would be.

"I'm so happy for you." Molly hugged Jayne, then looked at Tristan with a big grin. "I can't wait until we're back in San Diego."

"We're looking forward to it, too," he said, hugging her.

Jayne nodded. "I'm just so glad you're here. I know it can't be easy with a new baby."

"I would have come to see you married straight from my hospital bed," Molly said.

Baby Marcus, named for Linc's late brother, squealed. Molly took the two-week-old from her husband's hands. "He's hungry."

"That's one thing I'm not equipped to handle." Linc hugged Jayne and shook Tristan's hand. "Congrats. Once we're moved into the new house in San Diego we'll have you over for dinner."

"Once we finish remodeling we can do the same thing," Jayne said.

"Sounds great." Linc hurried to catch up to his wife and son.

Tristan leaned in toward Jayne. "Do you know how many people you have invited to dinner?"

She beamed. "Of course I do."

"We'll have to buy a bigger table."

"I was thinking the same thing."

Serena, who had been her matron of honor, practically exploded out of the chapel. The hem of her pink dress swirled about her legs. She looked more like a dancer than the first lady of Las Vegas.

"For the record." Serena's eyes twinkled as brightly as Jayne's engagement ring. "I told Jonas the two of you were meant to be together."

Jonas nodded. "She did."

Jayne hugged her exuberant friend. "Thanks, Serena."

"Thank you for proving me right." Serena hugged Tristan. "Jayne's a special woman. I trust you'll take good care of her."

"Promise," Tristan said.

Jonas shook his hand. "She's going to hold you to that promise."

"I expect her to."

Rich came through the chapel doors, walking with his remembered swagger. But his eyes, when they met Tristan's, were steady and clear.

"Guess you really *are* the best man, dude." He put out his hand. "Congratulations."

The two men embraced in a hard, double-pat hug.

"Thanks for coming, bud," Tristan said.

Jayne heard the emotion in his voice, and her heart swelled.

"I wouldn't have missed this for anything," Rich said sincerely. "Jayne." His gaze met hers. "May I kiss the bride?"

Smiling, she offered her cheek.

He brushed his lips lightly over her cheek and moved on, making a beeline for one of the more attractive wedding guests.

Jayne nudged Tristan and laughed.

Tristan squeezed her hand. "Thank you."

Her ex-fiancé was Tristan's oldest and closest friend. She was the one who had suggested they invite him. "He needed to be here."

"You're the best wife in the world."

She grinned. "That's all it takes?"

He laughed. "It's a good start."

Alex walked out of the chapel arm and arm with Wyatt. "Congrats," she said. "It was a lovely ceremony."

Jayne hugged her friend.

"Thanks for everything," Tristan said, before Jayne got the chance. "There's no place else we'd rather have had this wedding."

Alex beamed. "Wait until we get up to Sparkle."

"You don't want to spoil the surprise," Wyatt cautioned.

"Don't worry. Nothing could spoil today." Jayne stared up at Tristan. "It's a dream come true for me."

He smiled at her. "It's a dream come true for both of us."

MILLS & BOON®

Helen Bianchin v Regency Collection!

40% off both collections!

Discover our Helen Bianchin v Regency Collection, a blend of sexy and regal romances. Don't miss this great offer - buy one collection to get a free book but buy both collections to receive 40% off! This fabulous 10 book collection features stories from some of our talented writers.

Visit **www.millsandboon.co.uk** to order yours!

MILLS & BOON®

Why not subscribe?

Never miss a title and save money too!

Here's what's available to you if you join the exclusive **Mills & Boon® Book Club** today:

✦ *Titles up to a month ahead of the shops*
✦ *Amazing discounts*
✦ *Free P&P*
✦ *Earn Bonus Book points that can be redeemed against other titles and gifts*
✦ *Choose from monthly or pre-paid plans*

Still want more?

Well, if you join today, we'll even give you
50% OFF your first parcel!

So visit **www.millsandboon.co.uk/subs**
to be a part of this exclusive Book Club!

MILLS & BOON®

Why shop at millsandboon.co.uk?

Each year, thousands of romance readers find their perfect read at millsandboon.co.uk. That's because we're passionate about bringing you the very best romantic fiction. Here are some of the advantages of shopping at www.millsandboon.co.uk:

* **Get new books first**—you'll be able to buy your favourite books one month before they hit the shops

* **Get exclusive discounts**—you'll also be able to buy our specially created monthly collections, with up to 50% off the RRP

* **Find your favourite authors**—latest news, interviews and new releases for all your favourite authors and series on our website, plus ideas for what to try next

* **Join in**—once you've bought your favourite books, don't forget to register with us to rate, review and join in the discussions

Visit **www.millsandboon.co.uk**
for all this and more today!